TORN *from* YOU

BOOK 1: TEAR ASUNDER

NASHODA ROSE

Torn from You
Published by Nashoda Rose
Copyright © 2013 by Nashoda Rose
Toronto, Canada

Cover by Kari Ayasha, Cover to Cover Designs
Edited by Kristin Anders, The Romantic Editor
Formatting by Self Publishing Editing Service

Warning: This book contains offensive language, abuse, very disturbing scenes and sexual content.

ISBN: 978-0-9917327-4-6

Dedication

Bloggers, Reviewers, Goodread and Facebook Friends, this book is dedicated to you. Thank you for all your support and kind words. My dream is alive because of you.

Prologue

When I woke it was dark outside, and I was snuggled in Sculpt's arms, sitting between his legs, his lean, hard body draped around me. His fingers slowly stroked my outer thigh while his other hand rested on my abdomen, one finger circling my belly button. I turned to look up at him over my shoulder. He was staring out across the moonlit field, observing the horses in the distance.

"Eme." He leaned into me further and kissed the side of my neck.

"Sorry, I didn't mean to fall asleep. It must have been your sexy, raspy voice." I cuddled closer, and his arm tightened. "Did you finish the song?" His guitar lay in its case next to us.

"Yeah, Mouse. It's good."

I sat up, excited for him. He'd told me last week that he hadn't written anything for the band in a year. I had yet to see them play, and I was excited to hear them, but nervous too. I mean, Sculpt was six foot three and all muscle. He has what I call sexy bedroom hair, always a little messy with the odd lazy curl that falls over his face. And he had ink running down his left arm to his elbow, which made the hot a scary, badass hot. Then put in that fact that he was in a band and did some illegal underground fighting ... Well girls were no doubt all over him, and I wasn't ready to face the reality of what dating Sculpt entailed.

We'd been hanging out ever since I asked him to help me learn how to fight a couple months ago. I was assaulted a week before I sought out Sculpt, coming home from my friend Georgie's coffee shop where I work. I'd been so shocked and terrified that when my assaulter pushed me to the ground I just froze.

When I pulled my head out of deep freeze, I managed to bite his hand and scream my head off, which scared the guy away. After that I was on a mission to learn how to fight back. Sculpt, being an underground fighter was the perfect choice. I'd also heard he needed money to go on tour with his band, and I was willing to pay.

He never let me.

I reached up and ran my finger over the slight indent in his chin. "Can I hear it?"

He shook his head, and despite his lack of smile, because he rarely did smile, I saw the flicker of amusement in his eyes. "No, Eme. You'll hear it with the band on stage and me singing to you." The amusement left his eyes, and I felt him stiffen. "Did you think about what I asked, Emily?"

I knew exactly what he was referring to. I had a perpetual war in my head for the last three days—I wasn't ready to have my heart blasted with porcupine quills when Sculpt left me to go on tour, but I also wasn't ready to go on the road with a group of guys I hadn't even met yet and have Sculpt responsible for me. I planned on starting college in a month. I had a life here with my best friend Kat and her brother Matt who were also my roommates and my only family.

Ever since grade school when Kat and I had started hanging out, Matt had been there for the both of us. He was eighteen and

Kat ten when their parents died in a drinking and driving accident. He'd instantly become Kat's guardian. Since I no longer had a dad, Matt sort of became the male figure in my life. I looked up to him.

I'd snuck in Kat's bedroom window numerous times after running away from my mom's when she brought a new boyfriend home. Matt never kicked me out, never told me to go home, nor did he call my mom. Instead, he bought me a cell phone, programmed his number in it, and told me if I ever needed to leave home that I was to call him, and he'd come get me.

The three of us were close and even though I didn't want Sculpt to leave, I couldn't see myself leaving either.

"Eme." His arms tightened around me. "Tell me." He shifted, easily picking me up under the arms and bringing me around so I sat facing him, my legs bent on either side of him. It was intimate, and Christ, it was hard to resist him and not just say screw it and tell him how I feel and go with him. "Eme, tell me."

"Tell you what?"

He watched me carefully, eyes never once wavering. "You know what I'm asking, but this once I'll indulge you. Tell me you don't want more."

Shit. He knew I was crazy about him. I'd been trying to keep my feelings ... well hidden, somewhat. It obviously wasn't working. I licked my lips and tried to look away, but he was ready for that and held my head between his hands.

"Eme."

I was so not good at this. The last person I expressed my feelings to was my dad while he lay in the hospital dying of lung cancer.

"Mouse." He leaned in, and my hands went to his upper thighs feeling the flex of his muscles beneath my palms. "Look at me." I did. "I want you with me. I'll look after you." His voice lowered. "I'm not happy leaving you here, baby."

And that was the problem; I didn't want to be "looked after." I'd looked after myself all my life. My mom ... I sometimes wondered if she even remembered she had a daughter.

"Emily. I don't play games. I told you what I want, and I know you want me."

I didn't know whether to be pissed or laugh at his arrogance. What I did know was that I was turned on—big time. How could he do that? I mean, he was just looking at me, and yet ... his eyes abducted me. "Sculpt ... I ..."

Sculpt tightened his legs around me. "Eme." He gripped my chin and held me steady. He waited several seconds, and I finally inhaled a shaky breath. "I'll never hurt you. I know you're worried about the women." I opened my mouth to speak, but his eyes narrowed, and I shut it again. "I'm a fighter. I'm in a band. The women will always be there, but I'm with you."

And that was the issue. Why was he with me? I wasn't pretty, had big hips, mousey, brown hair, and my thighs were my best feature. Most guys wouldn't say so, because I was only five foot three, and they liked the tall, skinny fawn-like legs. I liked my thighs, because I rode horses, and they were the most muscular, lean part of my body.

He stiffened, and I recognized the russet in his eyes reflect in the moonlight. I laid my hands flat on his chest feeling his beating heart beneath my touch. "Jesus, Emily, you have to bury that shit your mother tells you. I swear if she wasn't a woman, I'd kick her ass."

I gasped. How did he know about my mother?

"Yeah, Mouse, I know it's swimming around in your head like a shark eating all your confidence. Do you think I don't pay attention? I've asked you about your mother, and I see what it does to you. You spent most of your childhood at Matt and Kat's. A girl doesn't do that if her mother is something special. I'm certain yours is not. She's put toxic shit in your head."

"Sculpt ... I ... my ..." Yeah. I had no words. He was right. My mom was toxic, and that was why I never saw her, not that she'd remember if I did.

He tucked my hair behind my ear. It seemed so natural; I wondered if he even realized he was doing it. "We're exploring this, Eme. I want you on tour with me."

"I need more time, Sculpt. I can't suddenly decide to change my life and go with you. I have school starting and Matt and Kat ..." My voice trailed off.

Silence.

"You want to train horses. Why are you wasting your time going to college taking accounting?"

We'd been through this. "Sculpt, it's a silly dream. I need to focus on what's real, and that is finding a career and making money."

"You're wrong, Eme. You should be chasing your dream." He sighed. "I'm leaving. Next week."

My breath hitched, and my heart felt like it had been pierced with quills, and he hadn't even left yet. "But I thought—"

"Things have changed. We're leaving sooner than we planned."

I couldn't go. God, I wanted to, but he needed to live his dream, and I had to make my own way. I never wanted him to regret being with me. Anything I wanted in life I had to reach for myself. I didn't want someone else supporting me. One good thing I'd learned from my mother was that if I wanted anything, I had to get it myself, because she sure as hell wasn't going to give it to me.

"Sculpt. I can't."

"Emily." He lay back in the grass scowling. "You're overthinking this."

"But Sculpt—"

"No buts, Emily. I can't handle any buts. I'm pissed right now."

"But—"

He sat up again, brows lowered. "No."

"But you'll like my but." I leaned toward him and nipped his chin. That got him to ease up, and his muscles relaxed.

"I already like your butt." His hand slid down the small of my back to my ass and squeezed. It was playful, but I could still see the darkness in his eyes, and his face was hard.

"Sculpt. My but is important."

"Yeah, Eme, it is." I slapped him on the shoulder, and I was glad when he laughed. "Okay, what's your but?"

"I was going to say, *but* ..." His brows rose. "Before you go, I want you to make love to me." I paused, seeing his brows rise with surprise, then I pushed on quickly before I lost my nerve. "Like now, Sculpt. Right now. Here in this spot where we always hang out together. Our place. You with your guitar, and me with the horses."

His hands that were slowly roaming, stopped squeezing my upper thighs, and he stared at me with such intensity that I was getting hot just watching him watch me. "That's your but?"

I nodded.

"I knew I liked your butt." He put his hands on either side of my face and met my eyes. "If you're in my bed ... you're not in anyone else's. You got that, Mouse? Even if I can't convince you in the next week to come with me—no one else's."

"Okay. Same goes for you." Surrounded by women night after night would be a lot harder for him than for me.

Sculpt stroked the side of my face. "Emily. You erase the bad in my life."

I couldn't imagine Sculpt having any bad. He was hot, had an incredible voice, had a body that was no doubt in the dictionary under the definition of muscle, and he had sexy bedroom hair with intense, dark eyes.

He may not laugh often, but when he did it was magical and made up for all the other times he didn't. I sensed the hardness in him, the untouchable part that he refused to let me discover, but we'd only known one another for a couple months.

His thumb caressed my lips, and the ache between my legs intensified. My stomach wasn't just pretty little butterflies; it was a flock of Egrets taking flight.

He picked me up and set me on the grass beside him then got on his knees in front of me. He tilted forward, and I leaned back until I was resting in the grass, and he was hovering above.

My nerves were sparking off in every direction while the twinge between my legs became a spasm of aching need. I was breathing so fast that it was like I'd run a marathon.

"Have you ever been touched, Emily?"

I shook my head too breathless to respond verbally.

"If you're not ready ... tell me now. Be damn sure about this, Eme."

He was dead serious, and it sent a strange thrill through me. I didn't want to wait. I wanted him here and now with the wind against my skin, being in my favorite place in the world with Sculpt. "I don't want to wait."

His hand swept into my hair and weaved through the strands. His fingers tightened, and he pulled back, and my breath hitched. "I'm tasting your pussy. Then Emily, I'm going to fuck you until you scream. Does that make you nervous? Because you're trembling all over."

"Yeah," I whispered.

"Yeah, nervous? Or yeah you're going to scream when I sink inside of you for the first time?"

"Yeah, to all of it." I'd wanted Sculpt since the night I met him. Needed him. It was like I had been living with anticipation for this moment my entire life. It scared the hell out me. What if I sucked at it? What if we were incompatible? What if it was awkward?

"I want you screaming and quivering. And baby, you should be nervous ... because I plan on changing your mind and having you begging me to take you on tour." The corners of his lips twitched, and my insides lit up like a goddamn firecracker. I couldn't help but think about what he could do to me, how I'd say goodbye when it was time for him to leave. "You're Lego building, Emily. Rethinking your decision?"

I jerked and met his eyes. There it was—his eyes dancing with laughter and desire, a sexy combination that had me tightening my grip on his biceps.

He didn't wait for my reply. "Too late, Mouse. You're mine."

He tilted his head like he always did before he kissed me, and claimed my lips. And he did claim, devour, and feed the hunger we both felt between us. Heat flowed over my skin as if the afternoon sun was beaming down on it. Little sparks tap-danced shivers through my body. There was no hesitation in what he was taking, what he wanted, and I fell into his kiss like melted butter.

His hands stroked up my sides then down again. "God, these curves."

He groaned, and the vibration sent my heart rate spiking. My hands found their way into his hair, pulling him closer, harder. God, I needed him. It was like I was breathing for this man. It wasn't normal. Was this normal? Did it matter?

"Sculpt."

He took my hands and placed them above my head, locking them down with his own. "Logan. Call me Logan, Eme."

Oh God. His name. He told me his real name. No one knew his real name. "Logan," I said and heard him groan.

"Again."

"Logan."

His lips trailed succulent kisses down my throat, his teeth nipping, then his tongue licking to take away the bite. "I want you to call me that whenever we're alone, Emily. Call me Logan."

"Okay." It was a whispered moan mixed with a sigh. Eyes closed, head thrown back, I edged my legs out from under him on either side and wrapped them around his hips. He grunted as I clenched, hoping to ease the ache, but all I did was make it more intense. More aware.

"Oh God, Logan, please. I need you." We could savor and taste and discover one another the rest of the week, but right now I wanted Logan inside me. I wanted to feel him naked against me. It was like waiting at the top of a toboggan hill and being rocked back and forth before being pushed over the edge.

"I know, Mouse." He nipped at my ear lobe then suckled, and I fought against his hands that kept me pinned to the grass.

I had to touch him, feel his skin, get rid of the clothes that separated us. "Logan, please. Clothes."

His head came up from him kissing my collar bone. "We're taking this slow. My way. I've waited too long to have you right where you are now, under me, pussy aching, hot and sexy as hell."

I'd never been called sexy in my life, and it sent a shudder straight through me hearing it from Logan.

"I like to play, Emily. It's who I am. And it's in you too. I know you get turned on when I take control." Did I? I wasn't experienced enough to really know what he was talking about. "But if you're scared of anything, I need you to say no. That's all it takes, and we stop. Understand?"

I got what he was saying. I mean, I wasn't oblivious to sex. I knew "play" could mean a few things, and it made me nervous and excited at the same time.

He let go of my wrists, and I put my hands on his abdomen and lifted his shirt inch by inch. Logan hovered over me, watching my eyes. I saw him suck in air and close his eyes for a second when my hands crept up his chest then slowly caressed his nipples.

I kept my eyes on him, loving his reaction. Loving how my touch was driving him crazy. My fingertips traced every muscle on his chest then down to his abdomen. Every contour was a new mountain for me to explore. I was panting, and Logan had his eyes closed and was breathing harder than I was.

"Shirt, Logan." I lifted it upward, and he succumbed to my bribe and threw off his shirt. My hands went to the button on his jeans, and he grabbed my hands and stilled them.

"No. I let you play so you could relax. Now it's me." Within seconds he had my shirt up, over my head, and his fingers were working at my bra. The snaps gave, and my breasts fell from their confines into his hands. *"Emily."*

"Yes," I whispered.

He lowered his body, and then his tongue circled my nipple while his hands caressed my side, down to my hip then back up again to tease my breasts. My body was exploding with sensations, pain as he bit my nipple, then pleasure as he suckled sweetly and licked the sensitive skin with heated moisture.

I gripped his hair, eyes closed and body arching into him as he sent me into a furnace of heat. Getting myself off to him over the last couple months couldn't even begin to compete with the real thing.

He moved lower, soft kisses trailing down my chest to my stomach. "This. And this." He slid his hand to my hip. "I love everything about your body." His kisses went further, and my body was already anticipating him. Ache was no longer a word associated with what he was doing to me; it was much, much more than that.

My hands curled in the grass, and I moaned as his fingers undid my jeans.

The button popped.

The slow descend of my zipper drove me crazy.

The sound was agonizing, because I wanted him to rip them off and plunge deep inside of me, hard and fast. But Logan wanted to do this slowly. Relish every moment, and yet, I was dying for him.

"Logan." My whispered moan was met with a muffled, "Christ" as I felt his fingers reach in my jeans and go lower. And lower until—

I stiffened, sucking in air.

"You're wet."

Well, yeah, I'd been wet for two-and-half months. Logan turned me on just by looking at me. I ran my hands through his hair. "I've been wet since the day I met you, Logan."

His head came up, and his eyes widened. God, he had to have known how much I wanted him.

"Jesus, Emily." He was kissing me again, hands curled into my hair, and his mouth hard against mine. There was no breathing, no thinking, just pure hunger.

He raised his head, both of us breathing hard, his sexy bedroom hair falling in front of his right eye while he looked at me with haunted openness. "I'm not letting you go."

I cupped his cheek with my shaking hand, my thumb stroking across his stubble. "Don't ever hurt me."

"Never." He sat up then moved down me as he grabbed the edges of my jeans and pulled. I lifted my butt, and my panties came with the denim.

He stopped at mid-thigh. "Beautiful. And shaved. That is a ... surprise."

I did have a small, what they call, landing strip, but the rest was waxed clean—Brazilian. I'd never liked hair down there, and Logan liking it—it made me giddy inside.

His fingertip ran down the small patch of hair, and I gasped as he spread the folds then slipped into the wetness.

"Logan, oh God," I arched my back, trying to bend my knees but unable to because of my jeans trapping my legs. "Jeans, Logan. Jeans."

"Wait." He continued to enjoy caressing my clit until I screamed and panted, then when he felt me close to the edge, he backed off and went further down to circle my opening.

I wanted him inside me so bad that I was arching up to meet him until he put his hand on my stomach and forced me to stay down.

He put two fingers on either side of my folds, slid through the wetness then hesitated at my opening.

"Logan. Please."

"Beg me."

"Logan."

11

"Emily."

"Please, Logan. I'm begging you."

He plunged two fingers partly inside, and I inhaled sharply at the sudden assault. It grabbed me. Held me. It didn't let go.

He pulled out, and I cried out with disappointment only to be met with a quick kiss on the top of my clit. Then he tore my jeans off the rest of the way and lay between my legs.

"Bend your knees."

I did.

"Open. Wide."

I did that too. I trusted him implicitly and him taking control felt like it was fulfilling a need in me to surrender to him. I was able to forget everything and bask in whatever pleasure he gave me.

He gently pushed them a little wider still, and I closed my eyes and bit my lip as I felt the first suckle on my clit. Oh God. The sensations inside me were so heightened that I knew I wasn't going to last more than a few minutes with Logan's mouth on me. Never had I imagined it being like this. I moaned, arching my back as Logan's tongue slipped inside me.

Gripping the grass on either side of my head, I groaned as he worked magic with his tongue through the folds, tasting the wetness then suckling my clit again. The pressure in my abdomen ached, built, and was cresting. I tensed. So, so close to the edge, nearly pushed off the hill.

He stopped. "Not yet, baby."

Oh God, how could I do that? "Logan, I can't. I can't hold—"

"You will." His voice was rough and demanding, and it made me even hotter. His fingers pushed inside me, but never all the way. "So tight."

He pumped in and out of me several times then licked me again. "Your pussy is perfect. I knew you'd taste this way. You're made for me, Emily."

"Logan," I panted, every muscle tightening. "Please. I need

12

you inside me now."

He pulled his fingers from me, and then I watched as he licked them off one by one. I nearly came just watching him. The way his eyes glued to mine as if he could see right into me. How the curve of his mouth partially crept up to a smile as he tasted me.

It was him. Everything he did, I adored. How he walked with confidence, not a swagger, but when he came into a room it was with presence. How he was chasing his dream with his band, willing to take all the money he had to try and make it in a business that was saturated with great bands. He took risks because he had faith in himself. How he didn't take shit from anyone. How he put all of himself into whatever he was doing. But most of all, I loved how he looked at me and saw everything I am and could be.

"Are you on something?"

I nodded. "The pill. To control my ovulation pain."

"I'm clean. I was checked two weeks after I met you and have been with no one since."

He'd been with no one. He went and got checked? Was it because he thought ... was he thinking about us?

"Yeah, Emily. I wanted to make sure I was good before I ever touched you, condom or not."

Wow. "I want you inside me, Logan. I want to feel all of you."

He leaned to the side and yanked off his jeans. I glanced down before he moved on top of me and glimpsed his erection— pulsating, huge—and wondered how the hell that was fitting inside me. Before I could start Lego building and scaring myself, I reached between us and touched him.

"Eme," he murmured as my fingers curled around him then stroked every inch of him.

His penis was throbbing and hot, and as I caressed, his eyes closed, and his head tilted back as he groaned.

"Stop. Fuck. I'm going to come before I'm even inside you." He grabbed his cock and rubbed it between my legs, the wetness clinging to him. "I'll go slow, Mouse."

My hand reached up to lock my fingers in his hair. "No, go fast. Just get that part over with."

"No." His voice was hard and firm. "You're going to remember this and not with pain." His mouth descended as he sunk lower, his cock nudging my opening.

Wrapping my legs around his waist and my arms around his back, I pressed upward with my hips, and the tip pressed against my barrier. I couldn't get him in any further, and my body was aching so bad I was going to scream.

He tore his mouth away from mine and grabbed my chin. "Look at me, Emily. I want to see you when I take you. I want to watch you while you scream my name."

"Logan."

He pushed his hips forward and moved in me a little further. I could feel him stretching my hymen, and I was sure he could too. He gripped my chin to make certain I didn't move then rotated his hips and withdrew, and I moaned.

"Slow, Eme."

He moved inside me again, and this time he kept going until I felt a sudden sharp pain as if he'd stabbed me.

Fuck. Shit. It hurt.

And yet ... him erect and full inside me was ... it was so connecting and surreal. As if we'd become one.

He leaned in and kissed me while he was sunk deep inside. A slow languished kiss that had me forgetting about the pain and instead filling me with a new urgency. I wanted him to move.

"Logan." God, I needed him to move. I pushed upward, and he sunk even deeper. Yes, God yes.

"You good?"

The tenderness was overridden by the aching need. I nodded, and he began to move. I clenched my legs around him, ankles crossed on his back, both of us panting, our eyes locked on one another.

"You're mine, Emily." He moved harder, faster, and I tried to close my eyes, but he grabbed my chin. "Look at me."

Each push brought us closer; I was on edge, ready, the ache heightened to a place it could go no further. He pressed his hips in an upward motion so he rubbed against my clit, and a jolt went through me, then another and another. The intense building inside was too much.

He pressed harder.

"Oh God. Logan. Logan." I let go, my eyes squeezing shut. "Logan!" I screamed as everything in my body exploded into tiny bursts.

"Emily." He pumped harder, the smack of flesh on flesh loud. He thrust deeper. Then he took my mouth with an insane hunger as his body stopped pumping, and his muscles tightened while his body shook.

"Mouse." He fell to the side and brought me with him so I was snug to his chest, my legs tangled within his. "Emily. You're a fuckin' trophy. My trophy."

I closed my eyes, head resting on his chest next to my hand.

He leaned upward and kissed my head while his hand stroked up and down my arm. His other hand linked with my fingers on his chest.

"Logan?"

"Yeah, baby."

"Um, someone is watching us."

Logan looked up, and we both started laughing as the appaloosa stared down at us.

2 days later

Day 1

I woke up lying on a damp cement floor.

I sat up and immediately wished I hadn't when my head ignited into throbbing, pressurized chaos. The room spun, and my vision blurred for the first few minutes as I tried to piece together what happened.

Then everything came flooding back like a tsunami. The bar. Logan getting ready to sing with his band. Kat telling me how gorgeous I looked. Going to the washroom and hurrying, because I didn't want to miss Logan on stage for a single second.

Then an arm hooked around my waist just as I placed my palm on the bathroom door. A sweet-smelling rag was shoved over my nose and mouth.

Then nothing.

Oh, God.

Fear catapulted into me. It was like being zipped up tight in a sleeping bag with no escape. I was suffocating, couldn't breathe. I felt pins and needles in my limbs as the fear became the stepping stone to a full-out panic attack. Shivers racked my body, and my breath became quick inhales as I started hyperventilating. Tears streamed down my cheeks then dripped onto my collar bone and slid into the material of my dress.

My dress. The one I picked out for Logan, agonized about for hours at the store with Kat. I wanted to look beautiful for him, and me looking beautiful was a hard task considering I never felt beautiful. It was something I lived with and accepted after years of hearing my mother tell me I was ugly.

But with Logan ... Even if I wasn't pretty, he made me feel that way. He made me feel protected and cared for, and it was because I trusted him. He knew what I needed even if I didn't. There was this natural desire to give up my control to him, not so he could use it against me. No, it was so he could give me what I needed. And what I needed right now was Logan.

Rolling over I crawled to my knees, and my stomach objected to the movement. I slapped my hand over my mouth and made it to the corner of the room where I vomited the two beers I'd had at the bar then dry-heaved several times until my sides cramped.

When I finally stopped, I breathed in the smell of stale urine, and my stomach reeled again, and I gagged. I put my head down, taking several deep breaths through my mouth while I leaned my hands against the wall for support.

I knew I was in a basement, and it was dark outside. I could see a single beam of moonlight streaming in from a small window high up on the far wall. The damp cellar was small and completely empty except for a wooden staircase that had a railing that looked like it would crumble the moment you put your hand on it. The walls were greenish tinged on the bottom half as if the basement had at one time been flooded.

Something crawled across the back of my hand, and I stumbled backward shrieking. My spine hit the opposite wall, and I squelched, turning, wrapping my arms around myself as I backed into the middle of the room.

What was happening? Why was I here? Where was Kat? Was she somewhere here too?

I ran up the stairs and started yanking on the door. When it wouldn't budge, I pounded on it and screamed then threw my body against it until every part of me was bruised.

My white chiffon dress I'd bought especially for watching Logan perform was covered in brown smudges. Two snags ripped the lace right off the front, leaving the silk material beneath exposed. My arms were sore and tender, and my legs had several bruises on them, and I was bleeding from a small cut just above my right knee.

I had no idea who had taken me or why, but everything inside me was screaming to get out.

I staggered back down the stairs, and then, on my hands and knees, began searching the floor for anything to help me escape. I prayed that my purse had been thrown down here with me. Even though I knew whoever was doing this to me wouldn't be stupid enough to leave my purse with my cell phone in it. But panic surpassed sensibility, and I searched every inch of the floor, my hands sweeping the damp cement, occasionally hearing something scurry away from my movements.

I tried to keep my sanity, but the terror was like a red flag on the beach warning you to not go swimming because of the strong undertow. I was in the undertow, and I couldn't get out, and it kept pulling me further out to sea.

I was crying full-out now, my chest heaving with each ragged breath. *No. Please no. Logan.* He'd find me, wouldn't he? He was looking for me right now. The police ... Did they call the police? Would they look for me? How long had I been gone? God, I didn't even know what day it was or how long I'd been passed out.

Finding nothing on the floor, I bolted up the stairs and started pounding on the door again.

"Help! Let me out. Help! Oh God. Please! Please let me go."

I punched the door over and over again until my throat was raw from screaming. When my fists were too sore to hit the wood any longer, I slapped the door with the palms of my hands.

"Please," I sobbed. "Please let me out of here."

I fell to my knees, uncontrollable cries racking my body, my hands up against the door, my cheek pressed to it. Fear coursed through my insides, tearing apart my sanity with each breath.

I had no idea how long I stayed curled in a ball on the landing, but it must have been hours as the sun's rays finally peeked through the window. My throat was so dry that it was as if I'd been sucking on sandpaper all night. My lips stuck together, and when I separated them it tore a thin layer of skin off my bottom lip.

All I wanted was Logan. I needed him to hold me, tell me everything was going to be alright. But hour after hour passed, and he never came. No one did.

I ended up having to pee in the corner of the room, and I never felt so dirty in my life. I felt like an animal, and I sobbed as I did it. It was humiliating, and it made me go crazy again, and I screamed and yanked, pulled, and kicked the door.

Nothing.

Was I going to starve to death? Die forgotten, never to be found?

My fingernails scrapped at the wooden door until splinters stuck in my nail beds. But nothing compared to the torture of the thirst. My mouth tasted like dried vomit, and even trying to swallow was painful.

After hours of scraping at the door I curled into a ball, my fingertips pushed under the thin space beneath the door. The word terrified took on a whole new meaning as I lay there in a whimpering mess. My mind was poisoned with the possibilities of what was going to happen to me. I'd watched *Criminal Minds*; I knew what people were capable of. But I think what was worse than anything was the fear of the unknown. My kidnapper's silence was eating away at my sanity as I lay quivering at the top of the stairs.

I don't know how long it was before the doorknob turned. Maybe a day, could've been two. All I saw was the sun rise and fall, but when I fell asleep I was never sure how long I'd been unconscious.

The door opened, and a large shadow cast over me.

I managed to beg one word from my parched lips, "Please."

The man leaned forward, grabbed me by the arm, and hauled me up.

I couldn't scream. I merely hung like ragdoll, my limbs feeling numb and weak.

He slapped me on the cheek, and I jerked as pain exploded in my head. I tried to speak, but nothing emerged from my mouth except a croak.

He picked me up and threw me over his shoulder like a sack of grain then carried me down a hallway. The light blinded me, and for several minutes I was unable to see anything except a bright yellow blurriness. It burned my eyes, and I had to close them until the pain eased.

"Hang her up there."

I winced as I opened my eyes again, looking up toward where the voice had come from, but it was dark on the other side of the room, and all I saw was the outline of a man standing near the wall. I was placed on my feet, and instantly they gave out, and I crumpled to the cold tiled floor.

I managed a moan while looking up at the man. "Please. Water."

His broad face was like the front of a Mac truck, flattened nose, wide cheeks and forehead, and beady green eyes. He stared at me for a second, and then a cruel grin appeared just before he raised his foot and kicked me in the ribs.

I screamed, trying to crawl away, the pain plunging into my chest over and over again as he continued his assault until I rolled up into a ball and tried to protect my chest and stomach from his foot.

"Enough. We don't need her face accidently bruised."

The kicking stopped. Flat-faced guy picked me up by the hair, and I scrambled to get to my feet as he yanked hard, my scalp burning.

"What do you want? God, please just let me go."

My mind was rolling with fear pouring down over my sanity. Were they going to rape me? Beat me to death? Torture me?

I couldn't let this happen. I wouldn't. I didn't want to die like this.

My survival instinct was still strong, and despite knowing that escape may not be possible, I had to fight. Adrenaline pumped through my veins as Logan's words during self-defense blasted through me, and I reacted.

I swung my elbow backward hard and fast. Jarring pain went through my arm as it made contact with his nose, and I heard the distinct crunch.

"Bitch." He staggered back holding his bleeding nose. I heard a man shouting in another language as I continued my pursuit and went for flat-faced's eyes. My fingers jammed into them; he shoved me back with one arm. I was so weak and off-balance that I fell to my side, and it took me a second to gain my feet again.

I turned to run past him and banged straight into a hard, unmovable body. The man spun me around so my back was to his chest then locked his arm around my throat and squeezed. I moved my hip back behind his pelvis like Logan had taught me and was about to unlock his hold when the cold metal pressed to my head.

I froze.

"A pity I don't have time to sample you myself. I enjoy a good fight." His accented voice sent cold shivers down to my toes. "Alfonzo. Tie her up." His arm loosened, and I tried to get a glimpse of him, but he shoved me forward into flat-face—who I could only assume was Alfonzo—and walked away.

Alfonzo had blood dripping from his nose, and his eyes were bloodshot. He grabbed my wrists, and I felt the heavy, thick manacles clasp around them.

"You'll pay for that, bitch," Alfonzo said beneath his breath as he pulled me in close.

I jerked my knee upward, but he was ready for it and jumped back. I felt the burning pain in my cheek as he slapped me.

"Not the face," the accented man shouted. *"Dios."*

Alfonzo crudely pulled my arms above my head, and I felt pressure on my wrists and heard chains clank. I looked up—the manacles on my wrists were hooked onto a chain dangling from the ceiling.

Oh God. No. Don't do this. The sobbing began again as I kicked, and my body swayed back and forth, the chains jangling.

"Please. No!" I cried. Tears I thought had dried up now streamed steadily down my cheeks. The man chuckled then strode away, and I heard him talking with the other guy, but I couldn't understand them.

I was facing a brick fireplace with my feet barely able to touch the floor. Completely helpless.

Fear crept across my skin. What were they doing? Why were they doing this? Who were they?

"Give her water."

My head jerked up at the word water, and I tried to swing around, but the man grabbed my hair and jerked my head back then started pouring warm water down my throat. I didn't care if it was the filthiest water in the world, just the sweetness of something gliding down my throat was heaven.

It drizzled out the corners of my mouth, and I choked a few times as he continuously poured. I swallowed as fast as I could, afraid I wouldn't get any more.

I heard a door creak open then slam shut. Alfonzo shoved my head away from him so hard I swung back and forth on the chains.

Then—

"Are you screwing up our deal already, Raul? She is mine. That was non-negotiable. I believe I made myself perfectly clear."

I broke. Logan's voice swam into my trembling body and wrapped me in its warmth. I started sobbing, my head falling forward making my arms and shoulders scream in pain as I shook. Logan had come for me. He's here to take me away. To stop the pain.

"She's yours when I tell you she is. And lose the attitude or our deal is finished."

Silence. I could hear the wind whistling through the cracks in the window frames.

"Our deal is solid."

Logan? What were they talking about? What deal? A deal to get me out of here? I tried to turn around to see him, but I couldn't get enough of a foothold to swing myself around.

Laughter. Cold. Violent. Sinister. It was like the crackle of fireworks mixed with the screech of tires on wet pavement. "She likes to fight." His accented tone deepened, and all amusement left it. "You're lucky I'm allowing this. She'd make a hefty amount on the market. Would you prefer I test that theory?"

"Logan?" I called. "Logan. Please." Why wasn't he helping me?

"No. You have what you want, and I have what I want—her. The rest is left alone."

His voice. It was different. Colder. Logan always exuded coolness, but this change was more than that. Like an anger simmering beneath the surface. Why wasn't he running to me? Holding me in his arms? How did he find me? Why was he talking to the guy like he knew him? Did he not see me? Maybe he didn't recognize me?

"Logan! Please." I fought the manacles again, my wrists raw from the metal cutting into my skin.

"Never call him that!" the man shouted. "He is Master to you now."

A lash of burning ripped into my back, and I screamed. Intense, throbbing aftershocks tightened my flesh as my body tried to contain the pain.

Oh God. No. Please. No. "Logan!" I shouted.

"Do exactly as you're told, Emily." Logan's words were stiff and controlled. I wasn't even sure it was Logan. Was my mind playing tricks on me? I couldn't understand why he wasn't coming to help me.

I heard the slither of leather sliding across the floor and then the whoosh in the air.

I tensed. Neck tight, eyes closed.

The whip came down hard again and I jerked, arching my back as it struck. My arms took the weight of my body as I hung limp from the chains ... sobbing, chest heaving, tears running down my cheeks.

Silence.

I heaved in and out, my back raw and feeling like a blow torch had been brushed across it.

"You speak only when you're told to or you'll feel the cut of the whip. Understand?"

The whip came down hard on my back again, and I gasped, throwing my head back as my body swayed back and forth. "Yes. Yes, I understand."

The sound of the guy laughing made my stomach churn, and the water threatened to come back up. I started breathing heavily through my mouth, desperate to keep the precious water in my stomach.

I heard the glide of leather on the tiles. "Please, no more."

My plea was ignored as the whip crackled and slashed into the back of my legs. I shrieked and tried to get away, yanking on the chains and moving my body back and forth.

Again it came.

Then again.

And again.

I lost count of how many times he whipped me over and over again, my skin searing and throbbing from my shoulders down to my ankles. I swung back and forth on the chains limp and unable to fight anymore. My mind kept crying, but I was silent, afraid to scream, to cry, to do anything that might make them continue hitting me.

Then it stopped.

"We leave in two days. Take her to the transporter's location. He will crate her and meet—"

"No," Logan said. "That won't be necessary." Inside I was begging him to hold me, take me in his arms and tell me everything was going to be okay. That he was going to take me away from here.

"Do you think I trust you?" I heard the scrape of something heavy sliding over the floor.

"She dies in transport then you have nothing. And I have nothing. The girl stays with me."

Silence.

"Very well, but Dave and Jacob will accompany you. Logan ... no mistakes. *Compendia?*"

Suddenly I felt a body behind me, and I panicked as I smelled the gym-bag scent of Alfonzo. A hand slowly slid down my back over top the welts and then stopped on my stinging ass. He squeezed, and I winced as his fingers cut into the welts. I could feel his body against mine, his hard cock pressed into me.

I moaned and shook violently causing my body to sway on the chains. He laughed in my ear, his breath wafting across my cheek. His hand slid further down, hesitated, then cupped me hard between my legs.

I cried louder, pulling my bonds, blood dripping from my wrists. "Please don't touch me. Help me ..." I stopped myself from saying Logan's name, afraid they'd whip me again.

"He won't help you anymore. No one will," Alfonzo whispered in my ear. He pushed aside my panties and slipped a finger inside me. A part of me died that moment. It was like all the crying, the thirst, the pain was nothing compared to the violation of my body while Logan stood behind me and did nothing.

"No. Please no. Why are you doing this?"

How could Logan do this? How could he watch another man hurt me? I sobbed quietly while his thick finger pressed in and out, his heavy breathing next to my ear. I heard his clothing rustling as if ... I couldn't think. My mind was in a haze with disbelief smothering out any hope that Logan was going to stop this.

I heard sharp angered voices behind me. I couldn't make out what was being said, and really, I no longer cared. I was so hurt and humiliated, and all I wanted to do was curl up and die.

I felt cold. Alone. And unable to stop the predator from violating my body.

Alfonzo made a low groan, stiffened, and then his finger withdrew. He nipped the top of my ear so hard I cried out. "Going to be sweet fucking you for real while you beg for mercy."

I swallowed the cry in my throat and bit my tongue so hard I could taste iron in my mouth.

He reached up and undid the manacles, and I fell hard to my knees.

It took me a few seconds before I could move past the pain and raise my head. Slowly I turned and looked over my shoulder for Logan.

When I saw him my heart stopped for a few seconds then started beating erratically. It was him, but nothing in his eyes was the man I knew. He was cold and expressionless as he stared down at me. Not a glimmer of sympathy in his eyes. I recognized nothing of the man I had fallen in love with.

Hope died as the realization hit me. He was part of this. He did this to me. I vomited all the water before everything went black.

Chapter Two

Day 3

Devastation overpowered all my other emotions.

Hopelessness.

Agony of being torn from everything I thought was real.

Raw pain made me numb to everything.

I lay on the cement floor of the basement where they threw me and two bottles of water after facing Logan. He'd betrayed me. He'd looked at me as if I was nothing. Like a piece of mold as I lay degraded and beaten on the floor.

My mind fought what I'd witnessed, trying to make sense of something that didn't make sense. How did I miss it? How did I not see that coldness I saw in him now? Was it possible I was so taken by him that I'd blocked out what I didn't want to see?

No. Kat said she'd seen it. He was in love with me. But the man I saw here wasn't a man in love. That was a monster. He'd looked right through me, his eyes void of emotion. He ignored my pleading while another man stuck his finger up inside me. He watched as I was whipped over and over again. That wasn't human.

But Logan had a band. Georgie and Deck knew him. He sang in Matt's bar. It didn't make sense, and yet ... he stood and watched me being abused. He talked to those men like he knew who they were.

I don't know how long I cried for. I was bleeding and alone, so hurt and desolate that when the numbness from shock came over me I let it. But it didn't last.

Anger came, with the hatred for Logan. The shaking stopped, and I sat for hours staring at the small window, most of the time thinking of nothing except the burning hate for Logan—no, Sculpt. Logan no longer existed.

What seemed like days later, but may have only been several hours, the door opened and footsteps stopped at the top of the stairs. I got up and walked up the steps toward Alfonzo, each step agony matched with despair bleeding through my veins. I had nothing to fight with any longer. Logan betrayed me. Matt nor the police were coming for me—no one was.

"Stop."

I did.

"Put this on." He passed me a clean T-shirt and jeans then threw a pair of flip-flops at my feet.

I knew asking for privacy was pointless, and it really didn't matter. My body no longer belonged to me. It had been starved, beaten, and blinded with darkness. The welts on my back and legs still throbbed, and I could feel dried blood where they'd whipped me so hard it ripped open my skin.

I'd never experienced such excruciating pain before; the worst was getting kicked in the ribs by a horse. But this pain wasn't just physical; it was emotional. Being locked away for hours, waiting for the unknown and praying for someone to save me, while Logan's cold voice, haunted every waking moment.

I unzipped what was left of my dress and stepped out of it. I could feel his eyes roaming over my naked skin. It was disgusting, and I felt dirty, and I quickly pulled on the jeans then put the T-shirt over my head at the same time as slipping on the sandals that were a few sizes too big. I briefly wondered about the girl who had worn them last.

I was waiting for him to touch me. To throw me down on the floor and kick me or use me, and the slightest movement had me jumping and recoiling.

Without a word he nodded toward a door at the end of a narrow hallway.

When we reached it, he threw it open and shoved me outside, and I stumbled down two steps onto a walkway. As soon as the scent of fresh air wafted into me I stopped and breathed it in. After days of smelling urine, I felt like crying just being given this chance to breathe fresh air.

When I looked around I saw nothing except fields. No one to help. No one to hear my screams. Movement to my left caught my attention, and I saw them ... horses off in the distance. The thrill of freedom beckoned to me, and I knew nothing could stop me.

I ran.

I heard his scuffle of feet as he dove for me then cursed when I slipped through his grasp. He shouted behind me as I kicked off the flip-flops and ran as fast as I could. My legs wobbled, and I stumbled as I raced across the gravel driveway toward the cedar fence. My mind roared with panic, adrenaline keeping me from falling flat on my face.

He was right behind me, swearing and cursing. I could hear his footsteps and knew if he caught me it wouldn't be good. He was mean ... cruel. It was in his eyes; I knew he would hurt me if he got hold of me again, and that thought pushed me to run faster.

If I could make it to the horses and get on one, ride it to wherever the stable was ... Someone had to be there to help me. Anyone. No way could he catch me on a horse. I could make it. I knew I could.

I felt his heavy breathing on the back of my neck as I dove for the fence. My hand touched the cedar rail, and then I had the wind knocked out of me.

His body trapped me against the fence, hand wrapped in my hair and yanking backward. I screamed out in pain then shot my elbow back, but this time he was ready and ducked to the side.

He retaliated with hooking his arm around my throat so tight I couldn't breathe. "Not this time, bitch."

He started walking, dragging me toward the van. I fought, kicking and writhing against his hold, but his locked arm around my throat squeezed harder until I was struggling for each breath. I was about to pass out or die when suddenly he let me go, and I fell to the ground sucking in air.

He slid the side door open on its metal tracks and kicked me hard in the stomach. "Inside."

I wheezed as I crawled to my feet, struggling to move, but knowing if I didn't he'd kick me again. He shoved me hard in the small of my back, and I fell forward, abdomen pushing into the metal edge of the van.

As soon as I was all the way inside he slammed the door shut.

There were no windows in the van, and the back door was chained with a heavy padlock. I heard a key turn in the lock of the side door and then the handle being tested. I felt like an animal being shipped for transport. A sharp, gruff laugh emerged from my throat—I was an animal. Actually less than that. A carcass, a piece of dead meat being hung up, cut, tasted, and thrown about.

I bounced around in the back of the van for what I guessed was an hour until I heard the tires slow, and crunch along a gravel road. The van stopped, and the door slid open.

"Out."

I was huddled in the back corner of the van. Too scared to get out and yet wanting to, but knowing whatever awaited me couldn't be good either.

"If I have to come get you, bitch, you won't like it."

I knew he meant it. It was like he enjoyed seeing me in pain. I slowly crawled to the door, and Alfonzo grabbed my arm and yanked. I didn't have time to gain my feet, and I landed hard on my knees on loose gravel.

I looked up, flinging my hair out of my eyes and came face to face with ... Oh God, Logan. It took me a second to register his face as he stood looking down at me. Steady. Composed. Almost as if five days ago he hadn't made love to me. As if he didn't even know me.

All the contained anger shot from my feet up to my skull and exploded.

"You fucking bastard," I screamed and went flying for him. My fist managed to connect with his face before I was caught from behind and dragged back by the hair. I thrashed against Alfonzo's hold, losing my footing and falling on my ass all the while Logan merely stood and watched.

"You done?" he asked when I stopped fighting and lay on the ground heaving in air while Alfonzo kept hold of my hair.

"She's one feisty bitch. I'm going to fuck her raw when you're done with her."

Logan moved fast, knocking his hand off my hair and grabbing him by the shirt and slamming him against the van. "She's mine. You get that. You don't get to touch her—ever."

The guy's face went beet red, and his lips pursed together as he spit out, "She's not yours. Raul owns her, and I train all his girls before he sells them."

The aluminum crinkled as Logan slammed him into the van again. "She'll be sold when I'm ready to sell her. You touch her again like you did at the farmhouse ... I'll cut off your cock and shove it down your throat."

Alfonzo's eyes glared at me lying on the ground, but finally he put his hands up, and Logan let him go.

"Get up." Logan stood in front of me, his feet inches from my hands that pressed into the gravel. He stiffened, and his eyes narrowed. "Now."

"Fuck you," I said and threw a handful of gravel at his face.

He was on me before my next breath, taking my arm and without hesitation dragging me toward another car. I pushed backward with my feet, trying to gain my balance, but he was walking too fast, and I couldn't do anything except feel the stones digging into my hips as he pulled me across the driveway.

"Transport her with the rest of them," Alfonzo yelled. "Bitch needs a fucking lesson. She arrives after that, she won't be putting up much of a fight."

As soon as Logan let me go, I leapt to my feet and was about to run when his hand trapped me by the throat. "Don't do it, Emily. You run and I have to chase you, it won't be pretty."

I was wheezing past the pressure he had on my neck, my hands on top of his trying to peel back his fingers.

A wave of memory—Logan's hand on the back of my neck—came plowing into me, and my breath hitched. *No, don't let me remember. Don't. Please.* I swear I heard him whisper my name, but it had to be my imagination. My mind was trying to find some sort of hope to grasp onto when there was nothing, and I wondered if maybe I was going crazy.

"Tell Raul I'll contact him once we cross the border." Logan opened the passenger door to the Lexus and put his hand on my head like the police do when they're putting criminals in the back of a cruiser.

I got in and noticed two guys sitting in the back seat. I recognized them, but I didn't know from where until it suddenly hit me as Logan walked around the front of the car. The fight—the bodyguards. The night Kat and I went to Sculpt's fight and I asked him to teach me self-defense. These men had been in the back of the warehouse watching Logan.

But that was months ago.

Oh God. Had they been watching me for weeks? Had every day with Logan been a lie? Was he, what, *testing* me for this? I started hyperventilating as I thought of all the times I'd been with

Logan. How he cradled me in his arms as we sat watching the horses. How he was so protective of me. Why would he have protected me if he was going to let me be beaten?

Confusion weaved so much anxiety over me that I was having trouble breathing. Logan knew these guys. He'd known them months ago. The truth was ... Logan did this to me.

The door slammed as Logan got in. He started the car and sped off. I noticed him glance briefly in the rearview mirror at the two men and frown like he was pissed off. At them? I thought he frowned at least, but I was thirsty and delirious and couldn't be sure if what I was seeing was real or what I wanted to see.

"They were at your fight."

Logan stiffened, looked in the rearview mirror again, and his hands tightened on the steering wheel.

"Why? Why did you even bother being nice to me?"

"Emily. Quiet."

"Why didn't you just take me weeks ago? What was the point being nice to me at all? Why did you—"

"Emily." His sharp tone was enough to stop me. "We'll go through this once. Once, Emily." He stared straight ahead, his voice calm and laced with cold, like an ice pick banging out each word. "Never speak unless asked a question. Do exactly as you're told without hesitation. The outburst you had ... That is reason enough to have you killed, and that's if you're lucky. Worse is giving you for the night to a group of workers. Then you'll wish you were dead."

I was finding it difficult to swallow, my mind sick with memories of letting this guy kiss me, hold me. Oh God, he made love to me. I couldn't believe this was the Logan who loved ice cream, who tenderly kissed me, held me in his arms, sang to me. Lies. Acid-dunked lies.

His monotone voice sounded like this was a casual conversation. I opened my mouth to ask about his other victims when I saw his jaw tighten and remembered what he'd said. I gritted my teeth together instead and let the betrayal fester.

"You'll eat, drink, and even piss when I tell you." His words ground out as if he was having trouble speaking, and his face was hard, eyes watching the road. "One mistake, Emily—one. And the guy at the farmhouse—Raul—he will break you and sell you to the highest bidder. If you want to remain with me ..." He accentuated the word want, "you do exactly as I say. Any questions?"

"Yeah. How many women have you fucked over? Let me guess, since you took your sweet ass time making me fall for you first, I'm guessing four girls a year. Do your bandmates know what you do in your spare time? What about your mother? Does she approve of your extracurricular activities?" My head was yanked back and the edge of a blade held to my throat.

Logan took in a long drawn in breath. "You see Jacob back there? The one who can easily slit your throat? Well, he doesn't listen to me. He is Raul's right-hand man and does exactly as Raul wants. And if Raul has told him to keep an eye on you and kill you for being a bitch then that's what he'll do, and I can't stop him." He paused then said, "Or, rather, I won't."

I felt the coldness of the blade slice into my skin. A trickle of blood dripped down my neck then slid onto my T-shirt and absorbed into a big red blotch. The creak of leather sounded as Jacob released me and sat back.

I wanted to fight, scream and rake my nails down Logan's face until he bled like I was. I even considered jumping out of the car and taking my chances with my injuries, but instead I sat quietly and stared at the highway ahead. After ten minutes of silence Logan shoved a water bottle into my hand and two pills. "Swallow them."

I considered throwing them back at him for about one second, and I think he knew it, because his frown deepened. Then I thought of hiding them under my tongue, but whatever the pills were they weren't going to kill me; they could've easily done that by now.

I tossed the pills in my mouth then chugged every last drop of water. I was so damn thirsty that my skin felt like it was shriveling up like a dead animal left in the desert sun.

"Check her."

Before I knew what was happening Jacob grabbed my chin and pressed—hard. I had no choice but to open my mouth. His finger slid inside, and I gagged and coughed as he crudely searched my mouth to make sure I'd swallowed the pills. I tasted cigarettes and wished I kept some water to wash out my mouth after he finished.

"Clean."

Logan nodded. "We're crossing the border." He pulled out a passport from his back jean pocket, and I gasped when he flipped it open and I saw my picture. Then I saw with it the round circular plastic case—my birth control. He tossed it on my lap. God, he'd thought of everything. I did wonder why he cared if I was taking my pills or not. "You're going to feel sleepy. If we're lucky they won't question us, but if they decide they want to talk to you and your wakened— We're going to a wedding in Ohio. We're all friends, and the bride is your friend, Kat. We have clothes in the trunk to prove all of this, so don't even think of fuckin' with it."

Kat. Oh God, Kat. I closed my eyes and thought of the last time I'd seen her. We'd both been laughing. Happy. Another sob escaped my throat.

"Emily?" his voice was gruff and cut into me. "The story? Do you have it?"

I nodded.

"Words, Emily."

"What?"

"You will always answer me with words."

"Yes." Humiliation swam over me, it was like he was talking to a child, and I couldn't wrap my head around the fact that I'd had sex with this man. I'd been held in his arms, slept in them. I couldn't grasp the idea that Logan was acting like this. He was going to be a rock star. He had a band. He had friends. Why would he give up everything to kidnap me? Had all that been a lie too?

I lay my head back on the seat and closed my eyes as tears threatened to fall. No, I wouldn't give him the satisfaction. He deserved my hate, not my tears.

Whatever he drugged me with began to take effect, and I couldn't remain awake any longer. At one point I heard voices, and I opened my eyes briefly, but I was too tired, and I curled up against the window and went back to sleep.

I was kept drugged for three days. The car stopped briefly for food, gasoline, and bathroom breaks. Most of the time I slept, too groggy to fight Logan, and too weak to do anything but eat when given food and go to the bathroom with Jacob who stood outside the stall door. Logan had offered to take me the first time, but that was nixed when Jacob grabbed me. Ever since then Logan stayed with the car. Anywhere I went Jacob went. The other guy Dave, who looked Hispanic and spoke very little, kept to himself and never once touched me even when I stumbled getting out the car once and he was closest to assisting me.

The days were a foggy haze of terror. I felt like I was living in the bottom of a well, cold and alone, barely breathing, and when I did breathe it was stale air.

I heard Logan's window slide down and then his sterile voice. "We're here. Open the gate."

Chapter Three

Day 6

Wherever we were it was completely surrounded by tall brick walls with guards standing at the gates and several walking the perimeter with German shepherds. The property was massive with several buildings and one main building that looked like a mansion. Logan drove up the long, narrow driveway then stopped at the house and shut off the car.

I looked at Logan, my body beginning to shake as I realized wherever we were was not a place I wanted to be. His hands gripped the steering wheel so tight that his knuckles turned white, and I could hear the leather crack beneath the pressure. It scared me. No, it terrified me.

He got out of the car as did the two men in the back, and I sat with my knees to my chest watching as he spoke to them and nod toward the house. Both men disappeared inside, and Logan stared at me through the windshield. It was like he was unable to move, his body stiff and looking every bit the fierce fighter, not the gentle rock star who wrote me a song I never had the chance to hear.

He strode toward me, and I wanted to disappear into the leather seat. I couldn't control the trembling, and it made me angry that Logan would see it. I wanted to be tough, to have him feel nothing but anger from me, but the panic treading across my body was too overpowering.

The door flung open. "Out."

It took me several tries to unclip my seatbelt, because my hands were shaking so badly. When I finally did, he snagged my forearm and pulled me out. "Do exactly as I say." His voice was low as he spoke. "Don't look at anyone. Eyes down at all times, and do not speak unless asked a question."

"Where are we? Logan? Please why are you doing this to me?" I couldn't help it. The words tumbled from my mouth in quick succession. What little connection I felt he tried to make shattered the moment Logan grabbed me by both shoulders and shook me.

"Don't you get it yet, Emily? Raul owns you. He's ruthless, and he'll break you down, torture you, and when you beg him for mercy he'll torture you some more." His bruising fingers tightened, and I winced. "Do not fuck this up."

I broke. I couldn't help it, and I hated myself for falling so low as to let him or anyone else see me do it, but for that one second I let the fear take hold of me as I said, "I'm scared."

Logan stared at me with eyes that were cold, dark, and without a spark of ... anything. "You should be."

My breath hitched, and it was at that moment I knew I had to face my fear head-on and conquer it or I was going to die. Logan wasn't going to save me; only I could do that.

Walking into what looked like a huge dining hall, I kept my head down like Logan told me to, but my eyes drifted upward. It was an uncontrollable reaction. Survival maybe, I didn't know why, but I was facing the unknown, and I had to look at what the unknown was.

The room was filled with over a dozen men, most sitting at a long wooden table laden with food. I could smell the aroma of cheeses, wines, and the sweetness of an array of fruits. The sound of laughter echoed off the walls, along with the clinking of glasses and men talking and shouting.

But it was the subtle sounds of groaning and sobbing that caught my attention. My heart started pounding harder and faster. The noises were wrong. They reminded me of trapped animals in cages and their sobs of despair. I raised my head, eyes searching the room as the sounds pulled at me.

Lying shivering on the floor was a naked girl.

Then another tied to a chair.

Beneath the table.

Over in the corner of the room, a girl kneeling.

My eyes widened, and my breath caught in my throat as I stared horrified at the women ... They were young, some maybe younger than me.

My stomach rolled and lurched, and I staggered backward, fighting against Logan's grip as I heaved with revulsion at the scene before me.

I shook my head back and forth over and over. "No. No ..." I repeated, my hand over my mouth.

One girl knelt at a man's feet while he fed her pieces of meat like a dog. She had a metal collar on that had a chain attached to the man's belt. She was naked, and I could see red welts running the length of her spine.

Beneath the table, another girl was between an overweight man's legs. She was ... her mouth was on his cock as he groaned and pushed her face back and forth into him.

But it was the girl kneeling on all fours nearest me that was the one sobbing quietly. Her cheek was pressed into the floor with her butt in the air as a young man pumped into her from behind. He was also naked and wearing a collar, and he had scars running the length of his back.

"Emily."

Alfonzo was standing beside the girl laughing and drinking his wine as he watched with a sickening gleam in his eyes. Another man, tall and lean, who looked in his thirties stood beside Alfonzo watching as well, but he wasn't smiling. The girl. Oh God, the girl's eyes stared at ... nothing. Blank and empty, yet filled with tears. Her body rocked back and forth, her hair swinging with the motion. It was when Alfonzo raised a crop and hit the guy on the back and said, "Harder" that I lost it.

I was hyperventilating, and I couldn't hold it together any longer as I turned my head away and bent over coughing and choking. I couldn't look as a girl screamed, and I knew ... I knew it was that girl with the dead eyes.

"No. No." My mind was like a tornado filled with the sounds and images of what Logan had walked me into. Nightmares couldn't compare to this. What I thought couldn't exist in this world ... The realization that people could be so cruel. That this ... slaves ... girls ... It was hidden from the eyes of the world, but it was alive and real.

Logan hauled me up beside him. His voice low as his steal tone whispered in my ear. "Pull it together. I told you not to look. You have to learn to trust me."

He was a lie. I didn't trust a single word from his mouth, but I nodded anyway, because I couldn't think of what else to do as the horror kicked me in the gut. I heaved in breath after breath, my chest wheezing, limbs shaking as I stared at the stone tiles beneath my feet and tried to get the images out of my head. They wouldn't leave me. The sounds of girls whimpering and screaming, the look of the girl with her cheek pressed to the floor.

I squeezed my eyes shut, trying desperately to block out what I'd seen, but it wouldn't go away. How could Logan be standing there so immune to the horror? Was he even human? No, none of them were.

I heard slow, casual footsteps approach, and Logan's grip tightened on my arm, and my body went rigid.

"After days in your care, I thought she'd be better prepared for what awaited her." The voice was the same one as in the house where I was whipped. The scent of sweat and garlic wafted off him.

"Look at me," he ordered.

Oh God. I didn't want to, yet I was terrified of what would happen if I didn't. When I raised my head, I instantly recognized him. The man from Sculpt's fight with the two bodyguards Jacob and Dave. I could remember him intently watching Logan after he'd won the fight. That night seemed so long ago.

The man's finger came under my chin, and I balked at his touch.

His fist punched me in the stomach so fast and hard that I stumbled backward and would have fallen if Logan hadn't been holding my arm. I tried desperately to suck in the air that he'd knocked out of me.

"That was unnecessary, Raul," Logan said in a calm, contained voice.

"You've taught her nothing," he shouted. "Nothing!"

Logan's voice remained controlled as he answered, "She was drugged."

"I gave her to you in good faith, but if she doesn't conform then I will take her myself, and she'll be sold."

"You think I don't know what's expected of her? Don't think for one second I've forgotten, Raul. She'll behave." Logan pulled me tighter into his side, and I could feel every muscle flexed and rigid. "When is my first fight?"

"Two days." I heard Raul shift his feet until he was standing directly in front of me. "You remember what I told you, Sculpt?"

I didn't dare look up, but I felt Logan's hand on my arm tense. "I'm here to fight, Raul. I won't lose, so don't ever question me on it."

"And I don't like your attitude. I taught you better."

"You taught me nothing except to fight. I'm here, and I'll

41

fight, but I get what I want."

"Then train her and keep her on a short leash, or Alfonzo will take her and she goes on auction."

I was humiliated and devastated when I saw Logan shrug. "She's mine, because I want to fuck her. Once I'm tired of her, you can do whatever you want with her."

Oh God. No. No.

I was so angry and terrified and grasping at everything that didn't make sense that I just couldn't hold onto my sanity any longer. Hearing those words flow easily from the man I'd fallen in love with was like an anchor sitting in my stomach with oil being poured all over the once beautiful rabble of butterflies, darkening the love I once felt for this man.

I hated him. I hated him so much at that moment that I couldn't stop myself. I reeled back and slapped him hard across the face. Then I spit at him ... turned and spit at Raul. "Bastards. Disgusting, fucking parasites." My yelling got the attention of the entire room, and even though I knew what I'd done couldn't be good for me—it felt unbelievably amazing.

Then I was down on the floor with a knee shoved into my back and a hand pressing my face into the stone floor. I cried out as my arms were wrenched behind my back and something rough and stiff was wrapped around my wrists. Then I was hauled to my feet by Jacob.

I glared at Logan. "I *hate* you. I'll *kill* you." I was hit hard on the side of my head, and I felt blood dripping down my cheek. "You're a monster." Logan's face remained unaffected by my words as his cold stare went right through me.

"You know what to do," Raul said, his breath seeping into my nostrils.

Jacob nodded.

"No," Logan said, his voice a deep, dark rumble. "I'll deal with her."

"She insulted us and a room full of men. She'll be treated as any other. You're lucky I don't strip her naked and let every man in here do as he pleases for the insult."

I struggled against Jacob, but he was big, and to him I was like a pesky little Chihuahua.

"Emily, stop." Logan's order plowed through my panic and anger, and I stood still. I didn't know how I knew this, maybe instinct, or it was the way Logan's eyes stared at me unflinching, but I knew I had to stop fighting. "You can't fight here, Emily. Ever." He chin-lifted to Jacob, and suddenly I was being hauled away.

It was almost like being separated from my safety net— Logan. He wasn't much of one, and it had holes all through it, but I still had some sort of connection to him, and even if I no longer trusted him, I didn't want to be taken from him.

I looked back over my shoulder. Logan stood in the same place staring at me. He never moved, never looked away. Somewhere inside of me I was hoping he'd stop Jacob. That he'd run after me, shout, do something, but he just watched me.

I pleaded and hoped that he'd change back to the man who swept me into his heart. Then I screamed silently for him to fight for me as I disappeared from his view.

I was so terrified, that I sunk so low as to beg. "Please. I promise to be good. Take me back to Logan."

Jacob ignored me like he'd done for the past three days. Not one word did he direct toward me. Instead, if he wanted me to do something he spoke to Logan who then told me.

He pulled me down a long, wide hallway with oil paintings of naked figures on the peachy brown stucco walls. Some were of a woman, others two women, or a man and a woman. They were beautiful paintings, and I suspected they were worth a fortune. Wherever we were, the place reeked money.

Jacob slid a key into a lock then opened a door. The heavy wood creaked, and when I saw it led down a staircase and into darkness, I started shaking. "Please." I pulled back on his grip and shook my head back and forth. I'd do anything not to be left alone in the dark again. "No. I'll be good." I hated the words I was willing to say, but I couldn't stop them. I began hyperventilating as Jacob pulled me forward.

"No. No. Please."

Jacob ignored my begging as he shuffled me in through the door and then down the stairs. I started to cry as the familiar mustiness sunk into me. I couldn't be locked up again. The terror gripped me, and I thrashed against Jacob's hold. My body moved like a trapped piece of paper flinging in the wind. My insides were ripping apart, tearing, burning with fear.

Jacob calmly continued down the stairs then walked along a hallway, me writhing against his hold the entire time, sobbing, begging. He remained unaffected as he kicked open a door and shoved me inside.

I jerked as it slammed behind me and Jacob then turned a key in the lock.

I slowly backed away from him. He brushed past me, and I staggered to the side, but he never grabbed me. Instead, he walked over to a tap in the wall and grabbed a bucket; then water started pouring out into the pail.

I turned and staggered to the door and started yanking on it. It wouldn't budge. Then I pounded on it and yelled for help. I knew it was pointless, but I couldn't help doing it. I guess I had a smidgen of hope that Logan would hear my panic and he'd come.

I was wrong.

Logan never came.

Jacob forced me over to a dirty mattress on a rusted metal bedframe and pushed me down. I instantly thought he was going to force himself on me, but he didn't take off my clothes. He pinned me down with the weight of his knee on my stomach then calmly tied my wrists and ankles to the bedframe.

I yanked and pulled, trying to get free, yet knowing it was pointless. I watched Jacob as he dragged a collapsible plastic chair behind the front of the bed near my head then brought the bucket.

My eyes widened with terror, uncertainty. Jacob sat, reached in the bucket, and pulled out a soaking wet towel.

That's when I knew.

I knew exactly what he was going to do. I'd seen it in the movies. Heard that it was used to get people to talk. Torture. Unimaginable torture.

A wet towel thrown over the victim and water poured over their face.

Drowning over and over again.

"No!" I went crazy. Struggling against the ropes as Jacob placed the towel over my face. "No. No. No. No."

He held my head back then the water came and my words were drowned with garbled screams.

Chapter Four

Day 7

The door creaked open on its heavy hinges, and then slow footsteps. Panic and fear reared, and I tried to fade back into the mattress, cowering.

Jacob had blindfolded me after the waterboarding. The agony ... Panic setting off every nerve in my body as I struggled to breath but sucked in water instead. I tried to scream, to beg, to break free from the bonds that latched me to the bed, but there was no escape.

I was fighting for survival, yet losing with every water-drawn breath.

Jacob had done it time and again, pouring water over the towel on my face. I begged him to stop when he let me cough up water and breath for a few minutes. I sobbed, and I promised to do anything he wanted.

He ignored my pleas and did it again and I gagged, choked and struggled. Then when he was done, he took off the towel and replaced it with a blindfold.

The footsteps drew closer.

Was Jacob back? Was he going to torture me again? I wanted to fight, but I knew that it only made the torture worse. So I stayed quiet and still as the footsteps drew closer. Then I breathed in the familiar scent of what reminded me of a fresh cut grass—Logan.

Relief. Yes, I felt it. Maybe I shouldn't have, but I did.

But my tears were gone, I'm not sure where. He'd stolen them away. Him or Jacob? I wasn't really sure anymore, because Jacob had broken me, and Logan had wrecked me. Tainted thoughts of Logan filled me. A hate I had to keep hidden and controlled, because if he left me here any longer I was going to lose whatever grasp on reality I had left. Already I'll never be the same girl again; I'd at least like to be sane.

I felt the soft brush of his fingers on my arm and recoiled. His touch stopped, and I heard him shift as if he was hesitating. Then he walked away. I bit my lip to stop myself from begging him to come back, to release me, to take me out of here.

He strode back, and this time he untied the ropes that locked my wrists and ankles to the bed, and gently helped me sit up.

"Emily." His fingers traced down the side of my face then to the curve of my neck. "You can't fight here."

His familiar touch awakened my oil-drowned butterflies, and I felt sick that my body reacted to his touch that way. I bit down hard on the inside of my cheek until I tasted blood.

"Do you understand why?"

"Yes." I had no choice. Hours I sat, blindfolded, shivering, wet, cold and alone while I contemplated my life. Fighting them would only make it harder on me. They wouldn't kill me. No, instead they'd make me suffer each and every day until I gave them what they wanted. I saw the proof of that with those girls. There was no running and hiding from what Logan had brought me into. There was no fighting. All I had left was survival and hope.

"Good." He put his hand under my elbow, helped me stand then guided me out of the room. He didn't remove my blindfold, and I didn't ask him to.

We walked for a while, going through doors and turns until I felt the brilliant sun beat down on my bare skin. I inhaled the scent of meat cooking and smoke as if I was at a barbecue. It mixed with the smell of flowers and ... Logan.

I had the urge to tear the blindfold from my eyes. Without my sight for hours on end, all other senses was heightened. Anxiety crept up on me with every step. I had no idea where we were going, if I was going to be tortured again. God, he could be leading me to a pit of lions and I wouldn't know it. The fear escalated with each unknown step, and I started shaking so badly that I stumbled.

"Emily." His voice was steady and calm, and for some reason it settled me enough to keep walking.

I jerked as I heard a door shut behind us. Logan put his hands on either side of my head, and I wondered if he was going to snap my neck, but when his fingers fiddled with the knot in the bandanna I breathed a sigh of relief.

He stopped, then he hands fell away. "Emily ...You're safer if you cannot see."

I was trembling so bad that my teeth started chattering. I wasn't certain whether it was from the weakness in my limbs or the fear of what he was going to do to me.

I heard him walk across the room, stop, and come back toward me. His tone was ... deadly. I'd never heard anyone's voice vibrating with such controlled fury before.

I jumped when his hand touched my cheek. "You need to fear me, not hate me."

I did. I feared him. But I think I hated him more. No, I knew I hated him more. For what he'd done. For what he was doing. For the betrayal. Most of all, for tarnishing something so beautiful and making it ugly. I trusted him. I gave myself to him, and he took me, peeled back layers of my soul until he saw it all. Then he took me.

"Do you understand what must happen here?"

I nodded. I did. I understood what Logan wanted of me. He

wanted what that girl with the dead eyes had become. The girl being rocked back and forth as some guy pounded into her from behind. He wanted the girl beneath the table. He wanted complete and utter submission.

He wanted me to be his slave.

"Answer me."

I jerked at his abrupt tone. "Yes. Yes, I understand."

His finger caressed my lower lip. "Open." I didn't want to. God, my mind fought it, and yet I swallowed my pride and opened my mouth. His finger slipped inside, and I wanted to bite down hard, but I didn't. "Suck." I did that too. "Good girl," he soothed. His other hand came around my waist and brought me up against him.

I remained calm, using my breathing to release the panic that tip-toed across my body. Being blinded kept the fear alive inside me. This is what he wanted—fear.

"Leave us."

I gasped, not realizing we weren't alone. I heard footsteps walk past us, then the door opened and closed.

"Raul is testing you." He ran a finger across my collarbone and then lower to the top of my breast. "And me." A feathered touch swept across my nipple causing it to become erect as if I wanted his touch. Oh God, how was my body reacting to him like this? Why? How could I like what he was doing? Why was there a familiar twinge between my legs?

No. Stop.

I stiffened and tried to tune out his movements. Block him. Keep him out of me. "Please Sculpt, let me go." It was natural calling him Sculpt as if using his real name would somehow weaken me to his power even more.

"That's not possible."

The anger simmered at the edge of my sanity. "So, what do you get for bringing me here? Besides the satisfaction of seeing a woman beaten, tortured, and humiliated?" I braved asking the question, knowing he may not answer, but hoping he'd give me something.

His hand stilled on my neck. I thought for a second he was going to choke me, but he remained completely still and quiet. I was waiting to be hit or dragged back to the basement, and I was now worried that I'd spoken when I shouldn't have. I wanted to run and hide—cower. I was a mouse quivering and scared of every squeak I made or movement. I was so uncertain of everything that I sought the only reassurance I could get, and that assurance was from Logan.

"I get *you*."

I felt the twitch of his finger on my skin. Logan was steady as a rock; he didn't twitch. Never did he falter. There was something more to his answer. Raul may be giving me to Logan, but there was something else he wasn't telling me.

"Why? Why are you doing this? Was everything we had ..." I couldn't finish the sentence. I shouldn't have asked, and yet, I was losing control. I wanted answers. To know why he lured me into his trap.

Logan pulled me further into the room then turned me to face him, hands on both my arms. "Do you fear me, Emily? Because if you don't Raul will know. He excels at knowing fear. You give him something else, he'll know. Then we're dealing with more than you ever imagined."

"I hate you," I shouted the words, and his grip tightened.

"I know," his voice was steady and composed as if he was unaffected by my words. "But fear must override your hate. Remember what I taught you? You can't have that here."

What he taught me? The self-defence? What did ...?And then it hit me—he'd wanted my anger when he'd been teaching me to fight. After Logan reluctantly agreed to be my teacher, he took my fear and turned it into a controlled anger. He gave me confidence to fight back, and now ... now he wanted the fear back?

"You will fear me, Emily. And if you don't ... I will make

you." His words were abrupt and unruffled. It sent shivers down my spine.

Did I fear him? Yes. I was scared of who he'd become, of what he was, and of that cold, emotionless face I thought I once knew. I was scared of how my body still reacted to him. How it betrayed me. And yes, I was scared that he'd give me to Raul. Because Raul I feared the most, and I was uncertain if I could survive him.

"This is his business. Raul kidnaps girls, women. They are trained then auctioned off. They bring him lots of money. You would bring him lots of money."

"Kat and Matt—"

"You're twenty, old enough to disappear. Raul made you disappear. One more girl missing won't bring the law down to Mexico looking for you, especially with a mother who doesn't give a shit about her daughter."

That hurt, but was unfortunately true. My heart rate picked up, and I licked my dry, cracked lips. Kat and Matt wouldn't give up on me. They'd come for me; they had to.

He took my wrists and tied what felt like rope around them. I start to hyperventilate, afraid of what he'd do, scared of being so vulnerable. "I do."

"You do what, Emily?"

"I do fear you."

Silence as he continued to tighten the ropes. All I could hear was the coarse nylon as it moved back and forth from whatever he was doing to it after he tied it to my wrists. Suddenly, he let me go, and I heard his footsteps stride away like he was angry. Then a door slammed in the opposite direction of where we entered the room.

I fell to my knees, my wrists tied together, and my skin cold and clammy and ... dirty. I felt so dirty inside and out. I'd been in the same clothes for days, no shower, little food.

The door opened again.

Footsteps. He stopped in front of me. "There are rules you have to follow. Kneel when someone enters the room. Never speak unless spoken to. Keep your head down, and if you want to live then you will submit to me." He grabbed my wrists, pulled me to my feet, and raised my arms above my head. I felt something snag on the rope.

He let me go.

I yanked and realized he'd tied me to something above me. I tugged harder, but I couldn't get free. Panic crawled over my skin.

His knuckles brushed over my neck, and then I felt the tug on the neckline of my shirt. With one yank he tore my shirt from my body.

I begged Logan in my mind. Begged and screamed to let me go, but I never emitted a sound. I took several deep breaths, knowing to fight would only prolong whatever he was going to do to me.

His hands undid my jeans, and he dragged them off as well; then my panties followed. I hung naked, quivering, and blinded. The degradation was so powerful that I wanted to curl up in a tomb and die.

He cupped my chin. It was soft and kind as if he was trying to give me some kind of reassurance. "It's in you. I saw the strength," Logan whispered. He ran his finger down my cheek then across my lips. "You need to be the lion here, Eme."

I choked back the sob in my throat at the sound of his voice, the one I had known and loved. The coldness had dissipated, and my mind was screaming for him.

I heard the door creak open. "He is ready for you."

Logan's hand stiffened on me. "No screaming."

I jumped at the tone of his cold voice.

He let me go, and I heard him stride across the room then abruptly turn and come back again. "Follow the rules. If you don't ... you will be lost to this world, and I can't stop it."

Maybe I want to be lost.

Yes. No. God, I just wanted to go back. My mind was so screwed up that I couldn't think straight. I was clinging to a man that no longer existed ... No, that was wrong. The man I knew had been a lie.

His breath drifted across my face, and then his hand was in my hair, pulling my head back. "Emily," he breathed, saying my name like it meant something to him. "Don't fail me." His words were barely a whisper. If I could have seen him I'd have imagined those eyes, the ones that pulled me in day after day as he taught me how to fight, when he sang to me in the horse field, when he wiped ice cream off my chin. His sweet whispered words were in the voice I grew to love, the one that promised to protect me no matter what.

He promised never to hurt me. He promised.

"When I come back ... remember the rules."

I heard his steps fade away, then the door closed, and the lock turned.

Oh God, help me. Don't leave me like this. Come back.

Three hours later

The blindfold was wet from my silent tears. I lost all the feeling in my hands from the ropes tied tight around my wrists. I prayed. For salvation. For death. For Logan to come back. I had nothing left inside. Nothing. The emptiness was like a vacant shell, hollow, alone without a single thought except the instinct to survive.

My lips were so dry now that they'd split open in several places like tiny paper cuts. I was cold despite the warmth in the room as I stood naked for hours. I listened for doors opening and footsteps constantly. It became so surreal that every few seconds, I swore I heard footsteps, yet it was nothing.

My imagination ran away with me, and I couldn't get it back under control. Images of being left here for days on end. Starving and alone. I never thought being alone would be so hard to endure, but the silence was like a knife being dragged across my skin. The fear of not knowing. The waiting. Unsure for how long I'd be left here.

I stood hanging by my arms, my tiptoes barely holding me up. Agony ate its way through my muscles as I shook uncontrollably.

Then, finally ... footsteps.

Voices.

The door opened, and I gasped, choking back the sobs. My chest heaved with relief and yet ... uncertainty. I knew I wasn't supposed to cry, and if I did he may leave me here longer.

Voices closed in on me.

Logan's and someone else's. The footsteps drew closer, and I tensed, waiting for the pain or a caress. I didn't know which. I couldn't. My body was so distressed with the frantic worry that I was sweating. I took deep breaths like Logan had taught me in self-defence to control my fear.

But that was what he wanted—fear. Well, he had it. I was living in an ocean of it.

The familiar scent of Raul drifted into me, and my nerves sparked.

Please. No. Don't let him take me.

I'd do anything, absolutely anything so that Raul didn't take me.

"I will not tolerate her behavior in my house, Sculpt. Some of the men asked me why I hadn't killed her for the disrespect."

"I know how you operate, Raul," Logan replied.

Raul's hand traced up over my breast, rough calloused hands far different than Logan's. I bit my lower lip until I tasted blood in my mouth. "Trust is earned, Sculpt. You must earn that. As must she." His fingers gripped my chin. "She is very beautiful. When you tire of her, she'll make a good amount on auction."

"I suspect she will. But for now, she is mine. Aren't you, Emily?"

Never. Never again. "Yes." I knew my voice was trembling. *Logan, God, don't do this to me.* Even though I couldn't see, I felt Logan tense. It was like the air stopped for a brief second as the room went silent.

"If you lose the fight, she'll be sold."

"I won't lose."

Raul's finger slipped across my dry lips, and I knew what I was supposed to do. I didn't want to do it, and my stomach churned violently at the thought of what I had to do. But I did. I couldn't face that room downstairs again. Not now. I didn't know if I ever could again. I slipped my tongue out and licked it then drew it into my mouth.

Raul chuckled. "Better." He let me suckle on it for a few seconds then withdrew.

My heart was pounding so hard, I swore they could hear it. The tears sat in the rims of my eyes, teetering like a ball on a ledge. I clenched my fingers into fists, nails digging into my palm, trying desperately to focus on anything but what was happening.

I was glad I was blindfolded. It may have kept the fear alive of the unknown, but it also saved me from seeing Raul. Of looking into his narrowed eyes as I sucked his finger. I'd have never been able to force myself to do it if I'd been able to see his face. Had Logan known that? Was there a reason to him keeping me blindfolded? No. I had to stop fantasizing Logan was in any way helping me.

"You're a lot like me, Sculpt," Raul said. "Determined. Resilient. And I see that merciless confidence when you fight."

"I'm nothing like you, Raul," Logan replied. "I have what you don't, and that is patience."

Raul laughed. "Ahh, you know me well. Yes, that is true. I'm not a patient man." Footsteps shifted, and the hardwood floor creaked. "She makes one mistake, and she leaves. I won't have disobedience in my home—ever. You should know that, Sculpt."

The door opened and closed then I heard a key turn in the lock. Silence. They'd both left. The sobs choked me as I broke into a thousand fragments. Why did he hate me so much to do this to me? What had I done wrong? Why me?

The blindfold was soaked by my tears. The pain had gone ... No, it was there; my mind had faded it out in order to survive. What remained was weakness. That was how I felt. Too tired to fight. Afraid to fight.

And God yes ... I wanted to be loved by him again. For him to hold me in his arms and take this nightmare away.

Did I really think that? How could my mind even contemplate loving him after what he's put me through? But I did. I couldn't control it. He'd swept me up and taken possession of my heart, even though he was now ripping it to shreds.

But I wanted Logan to save me.

I wanted the man I fell in love with to carry me away from this place.

And I wanted him to carry me away ... and then ... then I wanted to kill him.

The door opened a while later. I was half-aware of Logan's hands on my wrists as he undid the ropes and the blindfold. I was too weak and tired to do anything except fall into his arms.

He picked me up and carried me to a bed and then pulled a white silk nightgown over my head. I thought I heard him whisper something to me as he laid me down, but the pain in my body overrode his useless words as my body screamed with agony.

He walked away then came back, and the mattress sagged as he sat beside me. He took my right hand first, gently washed it with warm water then applied cream to my burned-raw skin. He slowly massaged my cold, numb fingers then repeated the process with my other wrist and hand. I closed my eyes and let him do whatever he wanted. It felt good, and yet I wanted the pain as a reminder of what he'd done to me.

He placed the cream on the nightstand, and grabbed a bottle of water beside it and held it to my lips. I didn't hesitate as I greedily drank. When I'd drained half of it, he pulled it away, and put it back. I watched as he stood, peeled off his clothes until he stood naked. Was he going to sleep with me? Have sex with me? Was he going to make me? Did he think it was okay because I'd willingly had sex with him once?

He stared down at me. I stared back. Neither of us moved for what seemed like minutes but was probably only seconds.

He looked beautiful, and it pissed me off that he could look so beautiful when he was so ugly. He pulled back the sheet and then slipped in beside me. I turned around and tried to scoot away, but he expected it and was ready, arms locking around my middle and dragging back against him, so my back was tight to his chest. I tensed as the pain from the welts intensified. He didn't lighten his hold as he then hooked his leg over mine like an anchor, the weight pinning me in place.

It was weird, the touch of his warm skin and his arms around me ... it was comforting. As if I'd been starved that feeling of kindness, and that I'd take it from the man who had stolen it from me in the first place.

God, was I that weak to take any gentleness that was offered?

His lips pressed to my ear, and my breath caught in my throat. Why? Why was he doing this? I was so confused at who he was. Cold and unattached one moment and now ... now he was holding me in his arms as if he cared.

Logan's fingers splayed over my stomach just below my belly button. I wanted to cry. Not for the pain that he was putting me through but for this moment that made me love him again.

I needed him to be cruel. It was easier to be disgusted by him.

But this ...

I tried to push his arm off and move away, but he tightened his hold. "Stay still, Emily."

I stopped.

He won. He'd told me that once. He always won.

As I lay in bed staring at the wall, my wrists sore, muscles aching from shivering for so long. I felt myself slipping. Not my mind, but myself. It was as if my body was separated from my thoughts and emotions.

I realized it felt safer this way. My body was just an apparatus, something to be used. It had no real value any longer. I could let it go and drift away to safer pastures with my mind. Some place where no one could reach me.

Even Logan.

But I missed him. It was crazy, I knew, but somewhere a part of me still loved the man that I'd fallen for. The man who kissed me and made love to me as if he thought I was the most precious woman in the world.

But that tiny memory of the Logan I knew was slipping past my reach. He was fading, and I wanted to latch onto him before he slipped away from me forever. In the darkness, in the familiar arms of a man I once loved, I pretended. I pretended that he was the Logan I fell in love with and he was here to protect me from the daylight and the reality that came with morning.

I closed my eyes; the heat of his naked body up against mine and then ... then just as I was falling asleep I felt his fingers interlink with mine and his lips kiss the back of my shoulder.

Chapter Five

Day 8

I woke to find Logan still curled around me, his head nestled in my shoulder, lips on my skin. His heated breath was slow and even to match his heartbeat against my back. His arm lay heavy over my side, and our fingers weaved together like lovers after a night of passion.

I squeezed my eyes shut imagining nothing in the last week had been real and that I lay in Logan's arms after he made love to me. He'd wake up and kiss me, and I'd be lost within his touch.

I felt the ache between my legs as I let my imagination roam. His thigh resting over mine, hard and warm. Him on top, the feel of his weight making my desire flood every nerve in my body.

His hands caressing my skin, soft then possessive as if he couldn't get enough of me. I moaned as I imagined his fingers playing with my hair while his other hand squeezed our interlocked fingers. Then his lips kissed my shoulder, and I nearly leapt out of my skin when the desire shot right through me, and I realized it was no longer my imagination.

I scrambled out of his arms so fast that I fell off the bed. When

I came to my feet Logan was lying on his back an arm casually laid over his abdomen. He turned slightly to look at me, and I felt the coldness in his gaze trickle over me.

"Go shower, Emily." He nodded to the right where I saw a door.

I didn't think twice about following his orders as I ran to the refuge of the bathroom, but before I could shut the door he said, "Leave it open."

My hand dropped from the door handle even though all I wanted to do was slam it shut and lock it; of course there was no lock to keep him out. Regardless, a deadbolt wouldn't keep Logan out. I suspected nothing would.

In a way, that was partly why I fell for him. He was determined and focused. Unfathomable. He was confident with no fear. A steady resolve as if nothing could break him. It was a scary hot, and it made me feel protected. Now ... it scared me. Because now I didn't trust him.

I started to undo the buttons of my white nightgown he'd given me to wear, and when I looked in the mirror I gasped. He could see me. From the bed he watched me in the mirror undressing. His hands were locked behind his head, and his face was unreadable as he stared.

My fingers fumbled on the buttons, and it took me several tries to get the last one undone. I closed my eyes as I slid the silk material off my shoulders and let it drop to the floor. I wasn't going to look at him, I tried to stop myself, but I opened my eyes and froze.

Heat. Blazing desire in the dark depths of his eyes. He looked me up and down slowly, casually as if he had all the time in the world ... And he did. He controlled everything about me now. If he became bored or annoyed with me he could sell me without a moment's hesitation. That alone made me do anything he wanted.

I lowered my head so I couldn't see his expression, and then opened the frosted glass door to the shower and stepped inside.

Was he going to come in after me? Would he touch me? Hold me? Make love to me? What was I thinking? There would never be making love again, it would be fucking. The question was whether it would be willing or not.

I turned on the tap to straight cold wincing as the freezing water hit my skin. It jolted any desire I was foolishly feeling over Logan right down the drain.

I quickly washed my hair then picked up the washcloth to scrub the stench off my skin. I rubbed so hard that my skin turned bright red. I lightened the pressure on the back of my legs and avoided my back, where my skin was still raw. I needed to get the feeling of Alfonzo and Jacob and Raul off me. Logan? Why hadn't I even thought of Logan? Why wasn't I sick to my stomach at the thought of him holding me all night?

"Come out here."

The washcloth dropped from my hands as I looked and saw the outline of Logan leaning up against the counter, arms crossed.

I turned off the taps and came out. He looked me up and down and frowned then reached over and grabbed the towel hanging on the hook. He came toward me, then began drying my skin. There was nothing methodical about it either. It was slow and sensual; he held the towel in his palm, so his thumb could brush over my skin with each stroke. His hand slid over my abdomen then lower until his hand rested on my mound. He stopped and looked at me. "Open."

I swallowed. Then inched my legs apart closing my eyes. I had mixed emotions, because I felt embarrassed, and yet there was a flicker of desire. There was a fine line he was drawing here, and I just wasn't sure which way it would go.

He stepped closer. His thumb skimmed between my legs with the towel trailing. I held my breath. He never took his eyes off me as he discovered the smooth silky moisture of my craving. I stopped breathing, hating that he knew I was turned on.

His eyes narrowed, and his jaw clenched.

Then like it never happened, he quickly dried my inner thighs then threw the towel on the floor. "Leave off the nightgown. Go kneel by the bed."

I opened my mouth to ... What, tell him off? Tell him no? Refuse to do what he asked and risk being beaten or thrown in the basement with Jacob? Or worse sold?

I walked out of the bathroom and heard the water turn back on just as I knelt on the floor. I knew what this was about; I wasn't stupid. I figured it out the second I saw the girls in the dining room. He was training me.

I was Logan's sex slave, although sex had yet to come into play, but I had no doubt it would. He'd brought my birth control pills for Christ's sake. I was to do what he wanted without question—never disobey, never speak unless asked to, and submit to all men. I belonged to him, and it was not by free will.

Logan came out of the bathroom naked. "Eyes down."

I could hear him getting dressed, the cupboard door opening, rustling clothes, and then a click as the cupboard shut again. His footsteps drew close then stopped in front of me.

"Open your mouth."

I did, and he put a slice of apple in my mouth.

"Today you will come with me to my training. You must learn what to do when in public, Emily." His fingers held another slice of apple, and I opened my mouth, and he slid it inside. "Behave like this, and we won't have any issues."

My stomach churned at the thought of witnessing the last scene in the dining area. I was afraid I'd panic and run or fight. Logan tried to feed me another piece of apple, but I turned my head away.

"You have to eat."

I shook my head.

"Open."

"No. I can't. Please. I feel sick to my stomach. Logan plea—" I stopped suddenly knowing instantly that I'd used his real name when I was told not to. I still had the red marks on my skin from the whip and never wanted to feel the cruel slice of it again. I lowered my head. "I'm sorry. I forgot."

I started trembling.

When his hand came down on my shoulder I lost it and started crying. Was going to whip me? Or take me to Jacob? It was a mistake. I didn't mean to call him by name.

"Emily." I kept sobbing, my head in my hands rocking. "Look at me."

I did. I had to or suffer something worse than what I anticipated.

He cupped my chin and rubbed his thumb over top of the crevice just below my lower lip. "You cannot use my name here. Ever. I think you know that." I nodded. "If you need to call me something, it must be Master."

My breath hitched.

"Say it."

The word was trapped in my clogged throat; I was filled with denial of what I had to do. For some reason the idea of calling any man Master was ... It was humiliating, degrading. God, it made me feel like an object with no self-worth.

His hand tightened on my chin. "Emily."

It was just a word. It was just a word. "Master."

"Good girl." He didn't smile; actually he frowned, and then he got up abruptly and went into the bathroom and slammed the door.

I waited on my knees until he finally came back out a cold mask of determination on his face. I didn't like that face, it wasn't mad or calm or smiling; it was unreadable, and that was dangerous.

"A girl will bring you clothes. Wear them. I'll be back to get you in a half hour." He didn't even bother looking at me as he walked past, unlocked the door, and left.

When he came back I was dressed in a black dress that dipped so low in the front that it barely covered my nipples. It fit tight to my body, over my hips to my upper thigh. It wasn't sexy; it was trashy, and I felt that way. I would have rather worn the white nightgown than this dress.

Logan told me to stand then looked me up and down, and then, as if satisfied, nodded and reached out his hand. I walked toward him and took it.

"I wanted to keep you hidden from this, but that isn't going to happen. You need to learn to tune out what is happening around you. Just like I taught you to overcome your fear with anger, you need to overcome your emotions and bury them. Numb, Emily. That is what it will take to survive."

Why was he telling me this? So, I didn't freak out again? What did he care if I was tortured? He watched another man shove his fat finger up inside me, did nothing as I was whipped over and over again. Why does he care about me at all?

"Come." He pulled me after him, and we made our way through the massive house, girls passing us, heads lowered, never making eye contact. Several guards wandered the premises, and I noticed some of the doors had a guard standing outside of them.

Logan ignored everyone and walked with long strides through the complex down a path to another building that had two guards standing on the outside. When they saw Logan they opened the double doors and nodded to him.

I kept my head down, but I tried to see as much as I could as we passed what looked like a set of weights then several red punching bags where two men were currently working out.

Logan stopped. "Stay here."

I waited, hearing the constant sounds of smacks and grunts as men trained. In front of me was a platform where two guys were sparing. I couldn't get a good glimpse without raising my head, and in a room full of men I didn't want to take the chance of anyone seeing me. I was learning fast about what was expected of me, and the pain and humiliation was far less if I kept my mouth shut and my eyes down.

Was that weak? No, it was survival. There's a time and place where I'd fight, and I would. I didn't know if it was in me to ever give up. I'd never given up on my dream to ride horses. My mom was an alcoholic who insisted I was useless, ugly, and fat, so I did what I had to ... I worked after school since I was sixteen and saved every cent. Then at eighteen I moved in with Kat and her brother Matt. It was Matt who let me borrow his car so that every weekend I could go to the stable.

"Emily." Logan's voice slammed into me, and I looked up at him. He frowned, and I quickly lowered my head again. He chin-lifted to a spot over to the right of the ring. "Kneel over there. I'll come get you when I'm done."

He wanted me to kneel on the cement floor? To stay there and wait for him like a dog? Why didn't he stick a prong collar on me while he was at it? My thoughts must have been vivid in my expression, because he grabbed my arm and walked me over to where he wanted me to kneel and pushed me down.

I opened my mouth.

"No." His abrupt, cold warning was enough to have me looking at my hands in my lap. He nodded to the left, and my eyes looked in the direction, but I was careful to keep my head down. My chest tightened when I saw Jacob, Alfonzo, and Raul. They were near the door talking to a guy hitting a speed bag.

I stiffened when they began their approach, and my entire body was already running and hiding in one of the cupboards on the other side of the room. A foolish and completely useless thought, but when men you feared were coming toward you, well your mind came up with the most ridiculous ideas.

"Sculpt," Raul said. "Where's Dave?"

"On his way."

"Good." Raul's eyes shifted to me, and I quickly lowered my head even further. "I have a shipment coming in that needs to be checked out. After training, you and Alfonzo will go look after the contents."

I knew how angry Logan was by the slight twitch of his index finger on his left hand. He wasn't happy about Raul's request or, rather, his order. "Send someone else."

Raul slapped Logan on the back and chuckled. "If I wanted someone else to go, I'd have asked them."

"I fight. I'm not one of your men."

Raul shrugged then reached down and grabbed me by the hair and pulled me to my feet and shoved me at Alfonzo. "You're right. You're not one of my men, and my fighters don't get slaves as they are a distraction." Raul nodded to Alfonzo. "Get her out of here. Put her up on auction. Forty thousand."

My eyes widened with panic as Alfonzo leered down at me. His beady eyes laughed at the fear trembling through my body.

"I'll do it." Logan's tone was cold and calm, but loud enough for Raul to take notice and hold up his hand to Alfonzo. "Let her go." Logan glared at Alfonzo, and I thought he might smash his fist into his face. "Now."

"Let her go, Alfonzo." Raul's thin lips pressed together as he stared at me, and I had the impression that he wasn't pleased with the fact that Logan had spoken up for me.

Alfonzo shoved me forward, and I fell on my knees in front of Logan. I kept my head down, my tears of relief hidden behind my veil of hair.

The door opened with a loud bang; then running feet came toward us. "Sorry I'm late. Let's do this, Sculpt."

Logan didn't wait to be excused by Raul. I saw his feet turn, and heard him walk away, leaving me with Raul and the others.

"Don't think he'll protect you all the time." Raul leaned over as he spoke in his squeaky, accented voice. He reached out, and it took everything inside me to remain as still as possible. I clenched my teeth together so hard that my head vibrated. His fingers slid through my hair then to my shoulder and across the front of my neck then down ... His hand cupped my breast as he ran his thumb back and forth over my nipple.

I kept my eyes closed and repeated over and over in my head that nothing could touch me, nothing could touch me.

"If he loses his fight you're mine." Raul squeezed my nipple hard, and I winced. "You're like all the rest. Do not think you're anything special."

With that he stood and strode away with Jacob and Alfonzo. I collapsed forward, my hands covering my face as I sobbed, letting my hair fall forward so no one could see. Raul was terrifying. Calculated and cruel. He enjoyed watching others suffer. He had no morals or values and did what he wanted without thought to the ramifications for others. It was dangerous. He was dangerous.

"Emily. Look at me." Logan was standing in the ring, sweating and his chest heaving. Our eyes met, and I saw the fury burning within the depths of his dark eyes. I didn't know whether he was angry at me, because I'd been crying or was it from something else? He stared at me for a few moments and finally I settled down enough to stop trembling. Then Logan nodded, turned away, and began fighting Dave again.

I had no idea what Logan's stare was about, but I did feel more together ... Well, as together as I could be kneeling in a gym surrounded by men who could and would abuse me if given the chance.

I guessed it was about an hour when Logan finished his practice. I watched him speak quietly to Dave away from the other men in the gym, and he didn't look happy. I saw Dave glance over at me, then his mouth moved quickly and angrily as if he was just as pissed off as Logan.

When Logan turned toward me, I quickly lowered my head and kept my eyes down. I stayed that way until I saw the tips of his toes next to my knees.

"Dave will take you back."

My breath hitched, and I wanted to protest, but I didn't. I couldn't. The fear of the consequences was too great to ignore. "He won't hurt you, Emily."

"Yes ... Master." I wanted to die. Oh God, I wanted to curl up in a ball and die of mortification. Calling him Master was degrading, and it made me feel like less of a person, like my mother used to do. A useless object that took up space and ate her food.

Logan stroked his hand over my head once then turned and walked away.

I stood when Dave told me to, then walked a few feet behind him back to my room. I never looked at anyone, not even out of the corner of my eye. I had no idea what Dave would do to me, and that was scarier than knowing. I'd been too drugged to remember much of what he was like in the car on the way here, but what I did notice was that he failed to have the lust lingering in his eyes when he looked at me. Instead, I saw sympathy and pity. I hated the pity, but I'd take it over Alfonzo's lust-filled threats.

Dave stopped outside my room. "He'll protect you when he can. But he's faltering. Do exactly as you're told, and you will survive this, Emily." I was taken aback by his words. He opened the door, and I walked inside. He shut it behind me, and I heard the key turn and then his footsteps walk away.

I was asleep in bed when I heard the door open later that evening. I sat up, pulling the sheet with me, and about to go kneel on the floor when his voice stopped me.

"Stay in bed." His tone was tired and gentle, quiet.

He walked straight into the bathroom, shut the door, and I heard the taps turn then the water blast. I lay back down and tucked the sheet around me. It wasn't long before he came out, the light in the bathroom illuminating his naked body.

The tweak between my legs shattered any resolve I had to not be attracted to this man. My belly dropped as I watched him stride over to the side of the bed and then drag the covers back with the sheet tucked under me.

He slipped in bed then laid back, his elbow crooked above his head and his other arm resting on his abdomen. He looked ... God, he looked like Logan. The Logan I knew. The Logan I fell in love with. There was nothing cold about him tonight; actually he appeared vulnerable, and his eyes ... his eyes held a hint of sadness. Could this man even feel sadness? Could I be reading him wrong? I'd read him wrong before, and yet ... I wanted to hold him. I just wasn't sure why.

Was it because I felt alone and scared, and I wanted someone? Anyone? Even if it was the man who brought me here? Or was it to solidify my place with him? To show him affection so he wouldn't be inclined to sell me.

I slowly moved closer to him, my heart beating erratically with fear of rejection, and yes ... yes, anticipation of touching him. Not because I had to touch him, but because I wanted to. I glanced up at his face, and his eyes were closed, his breathing even.

I pictured us lying beside one another in the park after he'd played me his guitar and sang to me. That wasn't a lie was it? How could it have been? It felt real and sincere.

I held my breath as I slipped my hand on top of his lying on his stomach. His breathing remained the same, and his eyes remained closed. I moved closer, my body inches from his, soaking in his heat, then I lay my head on his chest.

"Mouse," he whispered, and then his arm wrapped around me and tucked me into his side.

I sighed, and a few minutes later I was asleep.

Chapter Six

Day 9

It was still dark when I woke. My head was nestled on Logan's chest, and his arm was around me, fingers slowly caressing up and down my back. I knew he was awake; I could hear his breathing, and it wasn't slow, long breaths, but ... awake breaths. I wasn't sure if I was allowed to speak, but there was something in Logan that changed when we lay together like this. So I took the chance, and I shifted my head up, my cheek sliding over the smooth, hard muscles of his chest.

He was watching me, and when I met his eyes my breath seized. I was caught in the trap of his desire that was swimming in the dark depths. Controlling my reaction was ... well, it was impossible. He still could turn me on with one look, and all the sweet flooded back to me like being hit by a tidal wave.

"Logan." I stiffened after I said it.

He sighed and then closed his eyes. When he opened them again, I saw what looked like haunted turmoil.

I wanted to kiss him, touch him, feel him. Crush him to me

and take away all the fear and just ... I just wanted to feel protected and loved by him again.

My lips were close to his chest, and I couldn't stop myself as I kissed him. It felt as if it was a goodbye to everything we'd lost and sadness filled me. Especially when I realized that he hadn't lost anything, he'd gained. A single tear escaped to land on his skin.

I started to pull away and he groaned then his arm tightened around me. When I looked at him again, there was no anger, no aloofness, just Logan. The Logan I knew and ... yes, loved.

"Eme," he whispered.

The scorching flame between my legs was lit with hope, desire, and need. I craved this man; I loved him, and I wanted him back, but I was scared too. I was afraid of what these feelings would do to me when he turned around and became the man I feared.

I fought the desire, and I failed. He hadn't moved toward me, and I was uncertain why, considering Logan was always the dominant one. I knew he'd never love me or care about me like I'd once thought he had, but I wanted comfort. I craved it, and if he gave it to me physically than I'd take it.

I trailed kisses up his chest to his neck, and his fingers curled in my hair. He closed his eyes and groaned. Slow and hesitant, I moved up and onto his body, instantly feeling the heat of his skin sink into me. I'd only done this once and had hoped he'd take the lead.

"Eme." He tone was gentle, and a heated rush of goose bumps sprinkled across my skin. "Jesus, what you do to me."

My mind was all fucked up as it fought against the comfort I needed. I'd been beaten, threatened and starved, witnessed horrific abuse and I lived each moment in terror. I yearned for some kind of comfort—even if it was from the monster who had lied to me about everything. I had tried so hard to stop feeling anything for this man who shattered my heart and now ... now I wanted him to make love to me. It was sick. I was sick.

I lowered my lips to his, and at first he didn't reciprocate as I kissed him, slipping my tongue inside his mouth, and then ... then he broke, and his hands grabbed me on either side of my head, and he kissed me back.

Logan. He was my Logan.

I moaned as he rolled me over without our lips disconnecting. I wrapped my legs around his waist, and he was on his knees between mine.

"Oh God," I whispered breathlessly.

He pulled back, and I grabbed for him, but he'd become the one in control again, and he kissed his way down my body until he was hovering over my pussy. I pulsated. I panted. I needed him, and yet he stopped. He wasn't moving.

"Please, Logan."

"Tell me. Tell me what you want."

"You."

"You have me. What else?"

His mouth was inches away from me, and if I arched upward I could ...

"Tell me," he ordered.

"Kiss me."

"Where?"

Oh God. Why was he making me do this? I was so frustrated that I threw my arms back and gripped the headboard. "My pussy. I want you to taste me, Logan."

He didn't hesitate any longer, and within minutes I was writhing and screaming with uncontainable desire. He did that to me. Everything in him right now was the man I knew and loved. There was no fighting that fact.

Logan drove me to begging, and then I crested and came hard, screaming his name. He slid up my body and kissed me again with fierce possession.

We lay silent, him spooning me, and his fingers drawing slow circles over my abdomen. It was sweet, and I loved the feel of his hardened fingertips which I suspected came from playing the guitar. I never thought for a second that I'd fall into this man's arms again, and I knew when the sun's rays shone in the morning I'd hate myself, but for right now I was going to take what he'd given me—comfort.

After a while, when I couldn't fall back asleep, I asked, "What about your band? You ... I thought you were going on tour." It was a long shot that he'd tell me anything, but I hoped we could talk like we used to. Maybe I could learn why he was doing this. What had changed so drastically?

He kept drawing on me while he spoke. "We'll get there."

"When you leave here?"

"Yeah, Emily."

Okay, so that meant he didn't plan on staying forever. Or keeping me? Oh God, would he leave me here? Was he going to sell me? My throat tightened as I said, "When?"

"We can't be having this conversation."

I had to talk to try to stop the panic from taking control. I had to pretend, at least in the dark, that we were somewhere else. That if he left, he'd take me with him. "How did the band get together?"

Logan chuckled, and the sound made me jump then stiffen, uncertain why he'd laugh. My panicked mind thought maybe I'd pushed him with the questions and he was laughing because now he was going to punish me. God, that sounded ridiculous. Logan wouldn't laugh if he was going to hurt me, he'd be angry.

I was losing it. I was fighting the fear of him leaving me here or selling me and everything he did I was second guessing, trying to decipher what it meant. But I couldn't, could I? Because I didn't know who Logan was.

"From the moment I met you, you wouldn't give up. Why was I expecting any different even here?"

I took a deep breath when his voice was calm and playful. We'd met the night of his fight, when I'd asked him to teach me self-defense, he'd laughed; then after making fun of me he told me a direct no. But I wasn't taking no for an answer, and Logan found that out pretty quick.

"I met Kite when I was sixteen." My muscles relaxed as he started talking. "My mother and I had just moved to Toronto, and Kite and I went to the same school. We became instant friends." I felt him shrug. "Think it was his calm, take-no-shit attitude. First time I saw him was in the lunch room where a couple of guys purposely bumped him then pushed his tray out of his hands, spilling his food onto the floor. Kite picked up his tray, threw his ruined lunch in the garbage then strolled over to the guys who were now sitting at the table laughing.

Kite never said a word as he grabbed one guy and had him on the ground crying within seconds. The other guy took off running. There wasn't a flicker of fear or unease in Kite.

We started hanging out after that. He'd just left a band he was playing with. I found out the two guys were his old bandmates. Kite played drums, and we soon discovered I could hold a tune." Logan kissed my neck just below my ear, and I shivered. "We hung out at the local coffee shop where I started writing my own music. Georgie bought the place a couple years later."

"I didn't realize you knew her."

"She introduced me to Crisis and Ream. They were friends with her brother."

"Brother? She never told me she had a brother."

His finger stopped tracing for a second and then started again. "Yeah. Georgie's brother was in the JTF2—Joint Task Force 2— with Deck. A counter terrorism unit. Deck came back from their last mission, Georgie's brother didn't."

"Oh. God." I hadn't known. Was that why Deck was so protective of Georgie?

"Go back to sleep, Eme."

"Logan?"

"Yes, Emily."

"When can we leave?" I held my breath. Afraid to ask the question, yet needing to know if he was taking me with him when he left. I hoped. No, I prayed he'd tell me not to worry. That he'd never leave me. That he'd never sell me. But the truth was—I didn't know.

I felt his muscles stiffen, and he drew in a deep breath. Our moment was over. It changed within seconds, and I wanted to cry and hit him then yell and scream. Instead I watched him as he threw back the covers, got out of bed—still with a raging hard on—then strode into the bathroom closing the door.

The tears slid down my cheeks and I buried my face in the pillow as the sobs took hold. Logan was going to sell me.

The day was lonely after Logan left. He'd showered, dressed, then walked out without a single word to me. I waited all day for him to come back, uncertainty playing with my mind as I paced the length of the room. I ignored the food the girl brought and saw her frown when she came back to get the tray and the food remained untouched. In the afternoon the same thing happened except this time the girl kept her eyes lowered.

By the end of the day, I was exhausted from worrying if whether or not Logan was trying to find a buyer for me today. I'd upset him, pushed him with my questions.

When the door finally opened it was dark outside. I knelt in the corner of the room and held my breath until I peeked up and saw that it was Logan and not Alfonzo coming to drag me away. I wanted to throw myself into his arms with relief. I wanted to cry and I wanted to kiss him and thank him.

God, I was crazy. There was something wrong with me. I was so screwed up with my feeling toward Logan. One moment afraid of him, the next wanting him, then terrified he was going to sell me then having hope he'd get me out of here.

What did comfort me was that, if given the chance, I'd leave. I'd leave Logan, and I'd get out. I'd never look back. I may want him sexually or want the comfort of someone I'd once loved, but that would end the second I escaped.

I even wondered if I would kill Logan to do it. These thoughts are what happen when left alone for ten hours with nothing to do. My mind went on an imagination highway contemplating scenarios that may never be true.

But when I saw Logan walk in tonight the pain in his expression was worse than yesterday, and I began to wonder if the fight Raul had talked about was beginning to weigh heavily on him. Did he think he might lose? I hadn't considered Logan losing. I'd been so worried about everything else that I assumed he'd win, but he might not. What would Raul do if he lost? I'd be sold, but what would he do to Logan? I suspected Raul didn't take failure too well from anyone. Was Logan concerned about what would happen to him? But if Logan was worried about losing that meant he wanted to keep me right?

"Come here."

I got up and walked toward him.

He raised my head with the tip of his finger under my chin. "You can't do that again."

A crackle of fear went through me. I hadn't done anything wrong. I'd been good.

His thumb stroked my lower lip back and forth, and I didn't even think he realized he was doing it because ... because he used to do that all the time to me. "Last night was wrong." His hand dropped, and he strode to the other side of the room and stared out the window. His hands gripped the iron bars as he stood silent and still.

I knew what I had to do and there was a struggle within me whether I was doing it because I was trying to help myself or because I wanted to comfort him. I quietly approached him, stopping a few inches behind, and took a deep breath then reached out and placed my hands on his waist. "Please." I didn't know what I was saying please for; maybe to get him to talk to me, to turn and look at me, to hold me, God, to tell me that we were leaving.

"Let go."

I was going to. I stiffened and was about to, but he'd said those exact words to me the night I'd met him, and I didn't listen then. Yeah, stupid maybe, because this Logan wasn't the same one. But maybe he was? He had friends, a band, there was a chance that the Logan I knew existed. Maybe I just had to find him and bring him back to me.

I stepped in closer, kissed his shoulder then trailed kisses down his spine.

"Emily. Don't."

But he let me. My hands started at his shoulders then ran down his arms until they rested on top of his hands that were gripping the bars so tight that his knuckles were white. I peeled each finger away from the bars, until he let go, his arms falling to his sides, my hands holding his.

"Are you scared of me?"

I was thrown off for a second by his question; it seemed odd to ask me that now. I answered him honestly. "Yes."

His head dropped forward with a half-nod.

"I want to ..." God, I wanted him so much it hurt. It was ripping me apart having him next to me night after night. No matter how wrong it may be, I still wanted him. Or maybe it was I wanted to believe so badly that he was still the man I loved that I would do anything. Was that weak? Was I falling prey to what he wanted? Right now I didn't care. Tonight I wasn't going to care about anything except Logan and me.

"Please, Logan."

He turned. And any reservations I may have had lingering

were swept aside the moment I looked in his eyes and recognized the warmth within them.

"Please. I need you."

His hand swept into my hair, fingers curling around the nape of my neck. "You've never needed me, Eme." He was wrong, but I didn't argue because right now I wanted him to kiss me, so I stood on my tip toes and kissed him first.

The moment the heat of our lips pressed together I heard him moan. He swooped me up in his arms and carried me to the bed then placed me on the rumpled sheets. He leaned over me, both arms on either side of my head.

"You want this?"

I nodded.

"Tell me, Emily."

"I want this. I want you."

He stared at me for several seconds, and I didn't realize I was holding my breath until he finally spoke again. "Then tonight, show me. Show me exactly what you want and take it."

I nodded again, although I was feeling uncertain and nervous. My experience was, well, zilch, but Kat and I had watched pornos numerous times, laughing at the ridiculous positions and moaning, but still we'd learned a lot.

Logan slid off his jeans and his T-shirt, but left on his boxers then climbed into bed and lay on his back beside me.

He really was going to make me be the one to pursue this? "Logan."

"You want this then it has to be you."

"Why? I like it when ..." How did I say that I was totally turned on when he was the aggressor?

Logan stroked the back of my head, and I looked up at him. "I'll give you that. But not tonight."

I felt the heat in my cheeks as I thought of what I was going to do to him, the sweet ache in my belly as I anticipated tasting him and watching his face while I did it.

I slipped over top of his thigh so that I lay between his legs; then I put my fingers on the material that kept his cock hidden from me. I watched his eyes as I slowly slid his boxers down. He lifted his butt a little, and then my eyes moved down his abdomen to his cock as it sprang free from its confines.

I hesitated, and my hand reached out to touch the tip, feeling the moisture. He sucked in air and I got braver as I slid his boxers off the rest of the way and then wrapped my hand around the base of his cock.

Instantly, it jerked, and Logan groaned.

God, I felt powerful. It was incredible that I could make him feel like that with just holding him.

"Emily." His hand caressed my cheek, and when I looked at him I saw his features ease. I smiled. It had been over a week since I'd smiled, and it felt as if I'd been set free for that single moment. This was always how I imagined it would be like between us always.

I lowered my eyes to his cock again, and then my mouth followed.

"Fuck," he muttered.

I licked the tip and tasted a sweet saltiness that lingered on my tongue. Slowly, I took him in further and further until I couldn't anymore. My hand caressed his balls the same time as I sucked, soft then harder and harder, moving up and down, his cock pulsating in my mouth with each stroke.

"Jesus, Eme." His fingers curled in my hair, and he urged me faster.

He was arching off the bed to meet me, and a few times he pushed too far, and I gagged, and he immediately pulled back.

I teased him with my tongue, my lips, and then I gripped the base of him tight until he was swearing and groaning. Suddenly I was being pulled up on top of him, my face inches away from his.

"Are you going to fuck me now? Because I'm not lasting much longer."

"Yes."

"Then put me inside you."

I felt his cock between my legs throbbing, and I lifted up, took hold of it then slid it up and down my entrance, my wetness clinging to the tip of it.

"Now."

I let his cock go, and his breath hitched as his eyes widened with surprise. Then he frowned, and he got that scary look. For a second I let the fear in, and then I licked my lips, sat up straight, and put my head back, closing my eyes.

"Play with your nipples."

My eyes flew open and a tweak hit my belly at his words. I slowly slid my hands up my body to my breasts. When I started playing with my nipples the desire in his eyes intensified.

"Oh fuck." His entire body stiffened beneath me, and I didn't have to look at him to know what I was doing to him. And damn, it felt good. I still liked when he took control, but being where we were, and after giving all my control over to him, and knowing what this place stood for ... Well, having him succumb to me made me feel strong again.

I pinched my nipples hard and then reached down, grabbing his hands and putting them over top of my breasts. "Touch me, Logan. I need you to touch me."

And he did. There were no more games as both of us lost ourselves to the desire. Panting with the need for possession. He sat up, taking me with him, then his head lowered and he suckled my nipples, rolling his tongue over the tender surface.

"Now, Emily."

I wanted to tell him to wait, but the truth was I couldn't. I put my hand between us, took his cock, and guided it inside me. I threw back my head, and he groaned as I pushed him deep, and he fell back against the mattress.

I started moving, and he reached between my legs and circled my clit sending my body into a whirlwind of aching yearning that was climbing higher and higher with each stroke.

"Logan." I placed my hands on his chest and pushed harder and faster, my limbs shaking and stiffening.

"Fuck. Now."

"Wait." I demanded, and his fingers lost rhythm on my clit for a second at my words.

He made a low growling sound in the back of his throat, and then his hips were pushing up, matching mine as he drove inside of me.

I yelled, "Now!"

Logan threw me over onto my back in one motion and then thrust into me several more times—hard. Relentless.

I came hard. Long. And I screamed as I did it.

He was completely still, the veins in his neck throbbing, his cock jerking inside me as he finished coming.

When our eyes met we both knew that tonight was something more than either of us had expected. It was cathartic and powerful. Logan had given me control in a place where I had none. He'd given me the option to say no. He'd given me my dignity back.

He leaned down, and then he was kissing me soft and gentle; it was beautiful, and it was a kiss that had me sighing as he roamed over my mouth lazily.

Logan slipped out of me then went to the washroom where I heard the tap running. When he came back to bed, he instantly pulled me into his side then kissed the top of my head.

He never said anything, and neither did I. We'd always been good with quiet moments, as if we both knew words would only ruin the beauty in the silence.

It was only when I was drifting off when I thought I heard him say, "Dream sweet, Emily."

Chapter Seven

Day 10

"You interrupted me." His voice was steady and clear. "You spoke without being asked." His voice rose. "And you fuckin' called me Logan." He was pacing back and forth across the room. *"Fuck."*

I'd been kneeling beside the table in the main dining room. Dave had been there as had Raul. They chatted about the upcoming fight while I knelt for an hour on cold stone tiles beside Logan's chair and was fed from his fingers.

I had to go pee, and I'd made the mistake of calling him Logan. I'd never seen him so angry. His entire body went from relaxed and casual to rigid and dangerous within seconds.

Raul and Dave were silent as Logan turned to look down at me like I was some dog that just bit his ankle. His eyes ... God, they'd been intense, and yes, I was scared because of what I'd done. But it was a mistake, Logan had to have seen that.

He'd shoved back his chair so violently that it fell over backward, then he grabbed me by the arm, and before I could even

82

gain my footing he was dragging me out of the dining room.

He didn't stop until we were back at his room, where we were now.

Before last night I'd been a dying flower. Pieces of me falling to the ground, shriveling up and disintegrating day after day. I was surviving, but barely. I'd been losing the part of myself that thrived in the sun, the lightness that came with living. But then last night, Logan awoke the woman I used to be and gave me what I had starving for.

I thought things may have changed between us.

I was wrong ... The coldness had descended over him locking out everything we'd shared.

It was devastating.

And it was cruel.

"Emily."

I jumped at his sharp tone. "Yes. Master." I avoided his eyes, lowering my head. There wasn't a fight left in me. He'd taken away that trickle of hope with how he reacted in the dining hall. Did he do this to me on purpose? Maybe that was why he held me in his arms, brought my body alive at night ... So he could break me down in the morning, destroy me over and over again. So I could hate myself more than him.

His footsteps approached, and I stiffened, uncertain what he'd do, yet hoping he'd never physically hurt me. He'd awaken my body to his touch, but never once had he harmed me. But he let others hurt me, hadn't he? He watched them. Did he get off on that? Had he enjoyed watching Alfonzo whip me?

It was his quiet sigh that caused me to swallow my fear. His finger touched beneath my chin, and he raised my head. He was inches away from me, and I tried to stop feeling. I tried so hard, but I failed.

"Emily."

My heart crashed, because the way he said my name made the fear heighten.

"Don't do it again." He watched me for several seconds, then turned and walked out, slamming the door behind him. I collapsed onto the bed and cried.

It was dark by the time he returned, and I was brushing my hair after my shower while I looked out the window seeing nothing but imagining everything. As the door shut and locked behind him I turned and knelt on the floor, the brush laying forgotten beside me.

The floorboards creaked as he walked toward me then stopped.

I held my breath.

He reached down and drew me up in front of him then lowered his head. My heart skipped a beat, the pit of my stomach dropped, and my breath seized all at the same time.

His lips descended, soft and tender, as he slid his tongue inside my mouth. His arms encased me in his embrace, the hold on my body fierce and unrelenting, unlike his kiss that was sweet, gentle.

I tilted my head back, and he deepened the kiss groaning.

He nipped my lower lip then picked me up in his arms with one swoop and carried me to the bed. Without letting me go, he lowered me onto it then followed, his weight lying on top of me.

"You're mine. You'll always be mine."

I was in a way. I belonged to him. I had sex with him. And at night I loved him, but with the rise of the morning sun came the hate for the man who was doing this to me.

"Do you want this?"

Was I weak because I craved his affection? Wanted to be stroked and caressed and loved by this man so badly that I felt dead inside without him? Did it make me pathetic?

"Emily."

I closed my eyes and whispered, "Yes."

He gently dragged my nightgown up and over my head; then his eyes roamed down my body, and it felt as if the tips of his fingers were trailing across my skin. I'd never thought myself pretty or attractive, merely plain and average. My mother called me "a waste of space." But when Logan looked at me, it made me feel beautiful, and I never wanted it to end.

"Hands above your head."

I listened, wrapping my hands around the edge of the headboard.

I knew this is what he liked—complete submission—and it was maddening, because it turned me on. I liked it. I didn't even try to understand it.

I heard the sound of his zipper and then the rustling of fabric as he took off his clothes.

"Legs," he ordered.

I opened my legs.

He pulled them further apart and settled between them. He groaned as his fingers caressed my breasts then my nipples, hard, and yet, Logan had this sweetness in him. It existed; I knew it did. It couldn't just be my imagination.

"Not tonight. Not any night. Never call me Logan again."

I wasn't stupid. I knew I'd made a mistake. I had hoped that maybe Logan was protecting me against Raul. He'd blindfolded me when Raul had come to the room that one time. Could Logan have suspected I'd crack and fight if I'd been able to see Raul's face? Maybe that was why he dragged me out of the dining hall so fast. Or maybe I was just being absurd wanting Logan to care about me.

Then he kissed me, and the Lego blocks in my mind crumbled.

Logan's kiss grew stronger as I submitted to him. I didn't fight. No, I wanted to feel alive again even if it was wrong. Was it strength to submit to him because I wanted to? I was fighting for salvation, and if Logan gave me that then I won.

His fingers entered me, and I moaned. "Emily. You're my everything."

He drove his fingers in and out, his teeth grazing across my neck then to my nipples. He suckled and played with them then bit down, and I cried out with pain, and my hands let go of the headboard.

"Don't move." His voice was demanding, and I knew not to disobey, but I also heard a hint of sweet in his voice.

I put my hands back.

Logan bit me again, and this time I let the feelings flow across my body without moving. It was pain, and then pleasure came right after. It fed me. It gave me what I needed, and I awakened to him.

He gripped my chin. "Look at me."

I did.

"Tell me."

"What?"

"Tell me you want me inside you."

That's what he wanted. My permission. My complete submission. And I gave it to him. "Yes."

"Tell me."

"I want you inside me Lo—" I stopped abruptly.

He waited.

"I want you inside me ... Master."

"Wider, baby." I cringed when he called me that. It tore me apart. It was *how* he said it, his tone tender, as if he cared about me. "I want you to look at me when I put my cock inside your tight pussy."

I parted my legs wider as I stared up at him; then he entered me, and I moaned as his cock filled me completely. It was like the world became a safe place the moment he was inside me. As if he was mine and I was his and nothing around us existed anymore.

I hooked my legs around his waist and arched my back wanting him deeper, closer, needing him encased into me as he pumped madly. Our bodies slapped together as if he was spanking me, the sound vibrating through the room. I kept my arms above my head, but it was hard not to run my hands the length of him.

Suddenly he grabbed me around the waist and flipped me over. "Cheek to the pillow. One hand on the headboard."

My breath hitched.

"Ass in the air. I'm going to fuck you from behind, Emily."

I raised my ass and felt his hands grab hold of my hips. Oh God, it felt sweet and hot, and I wanted him back inside me. I knew I was going to come fast with him taking me like this.

He didn't enter me right away, instead his finger slid down my ass crevice then, slowly, further down into my pussy then back up again as he dragged the wetness up to my ass.

I tensed as he circled the tight opening.

"Relax." His voice was soft and sweet. "You need to relax and push out."

It was embarrassing, and I wasn't sure if I wanted his finger in that forbidden place. But it was also making me hotter.

His finger pushed, and I tensed.

"No, Eme. Don't fight it. I promise it'll feel good, but it can't be if you won't relax."

I took several deep breaths, then moaned, as he pushed his finger inside my tight ass at the same time.

"Oh God." It felt full and weird and ... fuck, it felt illicit and amazing too. Then when he started pushing his finger in and out like he was fucking my ass while he continued to play with my clit, I nearly exploded.

"I'm going to fuck your ass one day. So tight and sweet, and you'll love having me balls-deep inside you." God, why was I so turned on by that? "Now, I'm going to fuck your pussy, and you're going to scream."

He placed himself at my entrance then pushed hard and deep. His hand was on the small of my back pressing me down while his other grabbed my hip, fingers digging into my flesh. His balls slapped against me as he thrust over and over again.

I was panting and arching my back while I pushed back against him.

"Come, Eme. Touch yourself."

I did, and I within seconds I was coming and crying out as he continued to slam into me. Both hands were now holding my hips as he yanked me back into him with a fierceness that sent my orgasm into a long, drawn-out high.

"Fuck." He suddenly stopped moving, the tips of his fingers digging into my skin as I felt his cock jerk inside me. "Jesus."

When he slipped out of me, the syrupy warmth of Logan came with him and ran down the insides of my thighs. I was about to lie down, spent, and fully sated when he stroked my head then down my back to my ass where he caressed my ass cheeks.

"Don't move."

The mattress dipped as he lay down beside me and stared at me with my ass in the air, arched and body heated. After several minutes, he hooked his arm around my waist and pulled me down beside him then kissed my temple. "Your pussy is made for my cock."

Yeah, it was. The problem was despite what we shared sexually, I knew I'd leave him without a second of hesitation if given the opportunity to escape. Maybe I had this secret hope that we'd leave together, but it was small, a fleck of dust in a tornado.

I was falling asleep, wrapped in his embrace when I definitely heard the words, "Dream sweet, Emily."

Chapter Eight

Day 11

It was morning, and Logan left me alone like he usually did when he went to train. I lay in bed, lost in my thoughts of last night when the door suddenly opened. I scrambled off the mattress and knelt on the floor my heat thumping erratically at his unexpected early appearance.

Logan shut the door.

The lock turned.

Then he came toward me. I stared at the floor, hands resting on my thighs, although resting was not a word I should associate to how I was feeling—more like reeling with uncertainty. Had I done something wrong? Why was he back earlier? My mind went over in reverse everything that happened last night. Had I called him Logan? Did I not do everything he asked?

"Up."

I stood.

"Shower. Now."

I walked to the washroom, and he snagged my hand before I

had the chance to pull off the nightgown. It was flimsy and see-through, but it was the only clothing I was allowed, so I wore it.

"Undress me."

I looked up at him, and I saw the darkness mixed with lust swirling in his eyes. Hesitantly, I put my hands on the edge of his T-shirt then pulled it up over his head.

"Drop it."

I let the shirt slip from my fingers.

He waited. I was staring at his muscles that were tight and flexed. Logan didn't have a six pack; he had an eight pack and each one was glistening.

"Emily." His low, warning tone had me reaching for his shorts. My fingers gripped the material at his hips. "Slowly."

I moved downward, taking his shorts with me, his cock springing free and my mouth inches away from it. I licked my lips. He watched.

"Eme."

My breath hitched, my eyes meeting his. There was no more anger just pure unadulterated lust, and his lust was for me which turned me on more. I figured I knew what he wanted and took his cock in my hand.

I heard him inhale sharply, and he twitched in my grasp.

I went to take him in my mouth when he clutched my shoulders and shook his head. "Not now. In the shower." He pulled me to my feet then turned on the taps and brought me in close. "Wear the nightgown."

I stepped under the spray, the white material sticking to my skin the moment it got wet. It felt odd, like I should be taking it off, but the moment I saw Logan's eyes, I knew it turned him on big time.

He stepped in the shower then pushed me up against the tiles, his hands grabbing my wrists and locking them in his one hand above my head. It was heated and rough and a hint of fear shot through me as I realized that he could do anything he wanted to me right now.

His mouth took mine with such force and possession that it felt like I was breathing under water. There was something more in his kiss today, as if he was starving for me. Crazed with his need and possession.

It left me weak and trembling.

His mouth broke away, and he bent down suckling my nipples through the material then biting—hard. I moaned, arching against the wall, my muscles stiffening from the pain and then relaxing into the sweetness afterward.

His body slammed into me; his hand in my soaking wet hair then roaming down the front of me as he continued to kiss me. "No other."

He let me go then pressed on my shoulders, and I went down until I was kneeling in front of him, the spray pounding into the back of my head, dripping down my face like rain on a window pane.

He gripped his cock in his hand. "Suck me."

As soon as I placed the tip into my mouth, his hands gripped my hair, and he groaned.

I slowly teased him with my mouth, suckling the tip, sliding down then back up again. I slipped my hand around the base and tightened at the same time as I took him to the back of my throat and sucked hard.

"Jesus. Fuck." His hips began to move, and I relaxed the back of my throat as I took him deeper.

I pulled firmly on him with my mouth, and he shoved his hips forward as he groaned. I gagged, but didn't stop. Neither did he as he pumped into my mouth until I felt him stiffen and stop—his cock at the back of my throat, a loud growl escaping him as he said my name.

Hot, thick liquid squirted down the back of my throat, and I swallowed as it kept coming and coming. His cum slipped from the sides of my mouth, and the water washed it away.

His cock twitched for several seconds then went still. I went to pull back, but Logan held me in place, my mouth wrapped around him, sunk deep.

"Stay."

My jaw was sore, but I did what he wanted, my tongue slowly stroking the hot, wet surface of his cock.

"Your mouth around me ... never been so sweet." His hands smoothed back my hair as he looked down at me, my mouth still around him as his cock slowly subsided. "Get me hard again, Eme, then I'll fuck your pussy against the wall."

I was so turned on; it would only take him entering me to get me off. Knowing Logan, he'd make it last until I was begging him for release.

I started suckling his cock, the softness soon becoming hard and swelling deep in my throat. He picked me up, placed me against the wall, and then ordered me to wrap my legs around his waist. I did.

He hesitated and my body was begging for him to enter me. I saw his expression harden and when he spoke it was without warmth. "Don't ever think you're safe with me. I fuck you because I need release, that's all you can be to me."

Then he pushed inside me.

Day 15

Logan's routine was the same each day. He left me in the morning and returned at night, and we had sex. Passionate sex that made me forget, at least for a while, where we were and who he'd become. But, since those words in the shower, it had changed. Now, I kept my hope guarded. We had sex because it was what he desired and what I needed to make certain I wasn't sold.

I never called him Logan, and he always had the control, but in a way I felt like I had it too. I saw how much he wanted me, and it gave me power. Or at least I imagined it did.

Despite that, I still felt fear rush through me every time the lock in the door turned. I was never certain if it was the girl bringing my meal or Alfonzo or Raul coming to take me away. The threat of being sold was a constant terror, and I was always on edge on whether Logan was tired of me or had changed his mind about keeping me.

Today Logan didn't go work-out, and instead had breakfast with me then took me in the shower and washed every inch of me. I noticed the bruises on his skin and each day he looked to be getting more of them. Was his training not going well? Was there the possibility that the fighters here were better than Logan? Or maybe ... maybe the bruises were from something else? Was it possible that Logan wanted to leave here?

We came out of the shower and he picked me up, sat me on the counter and fucked me long and slow. He kissed me everywhere as if memorizing each curve and angle. It was sweet, and that smidgeon of hope rose again. I tried to smother it, afraid he'd say something to hurt me again, but it was hard to keep my emotions from reacting to his sweetness.

I knew it was dangerous thinking Logan would get us both out of here, but when he was like this, I couldn't help it. The constant fear was exhausting and hope was all I had left. I think my mind gave me hope on purpose to keep me sane. If I lost hope then I'd lose myself.

He left me for several hours and returned at dusk with an outfit in hand. I knew what it was for. Tonight was his fight. He'd told me he was fighting against a guy who'd never been defeated. He also told me there was a big dinner party planned afterward. One that would be like the first time I'd entered Raul's compound.

He laid the outfit, or lack of, on the bed then held out his hand, a piece of jewellery hanging from his fingers. It was just like what I'd seen the other girls wear—a collar. "Come here, Emily."

I rose and walked toward him, my heart pounding as I stared at the silver necklace.

"Turn around." I did. "This will protect you from the other men. You belong to me. They will know that." He pushed my hair aside then reached around, and I felt the coldness of the collar as it settled on my skin. "There's things you won't want to see tonight." I put my hand up and touched the intricate silver links that weaved around my neck. It was beautiful and yet ... this place and the meaning the collar represented made it ugly. He turned me around and placed his hand under my chin. "You must submit completely to me. If you do anything ..." His hand dropped, and he strode away and began pacing back and forth across the room, his hands shoved inside his front pockets. It was rare Logan looked uneasy and perturbed. He was always steady and certain of himself.

He looked different tonight—nervous. Could he be worried that he'd be defeated? "You must do exactly as I tell you."

I nodded. "I know." Behaving was imperative as Logan had told me some of Raul's top buyers were going to be present. What I didn't know was who they were buying, and I was terrified it would be me.

He stopped pacing then stalked toward me and grabbed my arm. "Do you? Emily, you have no idea the fuckin' shit that goes on here." He let me go, and I staggered backward until the backs of my knees hit the bed. I sat. "I will do nothing—nothing, if you make a mistake. I will let you go."

A shiver ran through me at his words. "I know." And I did. What I didn't know was why he was telling me this. The emotionless cold had been wiped from his face. A part of the man I once knew and loved stood in front of me again. It made my insides coil and spring toward him then spring back as if afraid to feel that assurance.

Logan gave an abrupt nod. "One slip and you'll disappear."

"Are you ... are you selling me tonight?" Fear escalated through my body when he remained silent. God, what if he was getting rid of me?

He sat beside me and laid his hand on the edge of the bed over top of mine. I inhaled sharply and stiffened while looking at him.

"If I lose the fight ..." I knew what that meant, and my body started shaking. "I plan to win. But tonight will push your limits. Don't think for one second it won't."

The image of the girl flashed before my eyes, her being fucked from behind, Alfonzo laughing and watching. Would he make me do that? Would I be subjected to being fucked in front of a room full of strangers?

"Will you ... will you give me to others to ... fuck?"

Oh God, I couldn't do it. What if another man wanted to touch me? Was that allowed? Would Logan give me to him?

"Look at me."

I couldn't. Suddenly the images became a movie reel, and my mind started thinking up the worst possible scenarios ... I couldn't do this. I was going to be auctioned off and never be found again. The collar around my neck started to tighten, choking me, strangling every breath.

Logan placed his hands on either side of my head, the pressure harsh as he forced me to acknowledge him. "Pull yourself together. You have to do this. You have no choice."

I shook my head back and forth. I couldn't be sold. I could handle Logan; I could be here with him, but the fear of the auction sat like a churning rusted chain in my stomach. "I can't. I can't. I can't. Don't make me go. Don't make me." All his warnings, his rules went through the floor. "Don't make me. Please." Tears streamed down my face, and with the pads of his thumbs he wiped them away.

"Emily."

"Please. I'll stay here. Leave me here. I'll be good. I'll kneel. I'll do whatever you want. Tie me up, blindfold me. Just don't make me go."

His voice was controlled and firm as he said, "I can't. Raul wants you there, so if I lose ..."

He didn't finish the sentence. I cried for who I'd become, this weak woman. I detested myself for loving a man that was saving me from Raul by keeping me, and I detested myself for hating that same man who was destroying my dignity.

His fingers weaved into my hair. "There's no other way."

"Why? Why me? I loved you." My voice rose, "I loved you." I sobbed the words, my breaking point crushing the calm, protective wall I'd carefully built around myself.

Logan stormed to his feet, walked to the other side of the room, and punched his fist into the wall. Blood dripped down the back of his hand as he turned back. Then he came straight for me. Terror pushed me to react against what I knew could get me punished and I ran for the door.

My hands curled around the doorknob just as Logan grabbed me by the shoulders and spun me around. He pulled me in hard so I was crushed against his chest. His mouth slammed onto mine, a rumbled groan escaping him as he curled me into him. His kiss was possessive and unbreakable; he was taking what had become his and yet giving me back the part of him I'd once known.

His lips softened as I leaned into him.

Our ragged breathing was the only sound in the room as we stared at one another for minutes.

"Get dressed," Logan said then spun and strode from the room.

I stiffened. Then I brought in the coldness he'd shown me and became who he needed me to be, because I knew he was the only one who could save me from tonight.

Chapter Nine

3 hours later

I'd watched Logan's fight sitting between Jacob and Dave, Raul a few seats away from me. This wasn't the typical underground dirty warehouse location. No, Raul had an actual ring and seating. He obviously had been organizing these fights for a while.

Logan defeated his opponent, but it'd been brutal and tough, and I'd been in perpetual anxiety the entire time. I knew if he lost I'd be sold, but it was more than that. A small part of me worried about him. Maybe it was human nature. Maybe love couldn't be stopped, or maybe I was just thinking irrationally.

I wore his collar, and noticed Raul's nod of approval when he saw me with Logan. Or was it my state of dress he approved? Or rather lack of dress. I tried not to think about it, but it was hard considering there was nothing beneath it. It dipped so low in the front that my nipples were exposed. When I first put it on, I tore it off again then threw it across the room.

I even went and put on the nightgown and waited beside the

bed for Logan to come back and see me not wearing what he put out for me. Then panic set in as I realized that he'd be back any second and I wasn't dressed.

Tonight wasn't an option. I had to do this. So, I put on the dress, and my breasts spilled out of the tight material, and I waited for Logan while kneeling on the floor.

When he saw me, it wasn't like I'd expected. He was angry as his eyes took me in, and then that cold, expressionless face pulled down over him. He never spoke a word to me as he got changed then took me to his fight where I tried to ignore the stares of the men as they panted over my body like animals.

"Emily." Logan had changed from his fighting shorts into a pair of black slacks and a white button-down top. He looked different, contained, formal, and I didn't like it. He grabbed my hand then chin-lifted to Dave who'd stayed with me until Logan came back. "Three days."

Dave nodded.

"That last shipment ... two were dead."

"I heard," Dave said. I didn't even want to imagine what they were referring to, but I remembered when Logan told Alfonzo not to crate and ship me.

"Something goes wrong ..." Logan began.

"Yeah, man. I know."

Logan gave an abrupt nod then we left Dave as we made our way back to the main house where Raul was holding the celebration. Not once did he look at me, almost as if he couldn't— like he was disgusted. I was disgusted in myself, humiliated being emotionally degraded in front of the other men. I was an object to them. That had become my reality.

I wanted to scream and hit and freak out, but stupidity had no place in my life. I had to be harder than them, unaffected and colder. Like Logan.

All my self-control vanished the second the sounds hit me. The moans of pain, the groans of pleasure, the grunting, the crack of the whip, the laughter, and then the sobbing.

I hesitated at the doorway, and Logan's hand tightened on my arm. "Block it out," he whispered in a harsh growl. "Keep your eyes closed if you have to."

He yanked me forward, and I stumbled further into the room. My chest heaved in and out as I tried to control the panic. There was no escaping this, but I did squeeze my eyes closed until I heard Raul's voice.

"There he is." A chair scraped over the stone tiles. "Sculpt. My prized fighter." There was a loud applause. Logan stopped, and despite having my eyes closed I knew Raul was near me from the scent of garlic and cigarettes. "I made a lot of money tonight. That is reason enough for a celebration. You fight better than I expected."

"I won because my opponent can't control his temper, and I was fighting for something I wanted—a slave who is a damn good fuck. I now realize why they are in such high demand." His voice was strained, and I could feel the tension in his body.

"Ahh, yes. She is your first slave. You've done well with her. I wasn't certain you had it in you, Sculpt." I opened my eyes just as Raul put his finger under my chin and forced me to look at him. I swallowed. "She is very beautiful. When you tire of her, I will find a buyer for her who appreciates a woman with—spirit."

"That won't be for a while."

Raul laughed as he stared at my breasts. "No, I suspect not." He slapped Logan on the back. "Enjoy your evening. I look forward to many more of them as should you."

Logan nodded and then led me away to a table in the far corner of the room where four men were sitting. I cringed when I saw there were two girls kneeling beside their owners; both wore collars and were naked. The other man had a male slave standing behind his chair wearing a black leather collar with studs and then a leather bra type thing that had criss-crossed straps and metal rings. When we approached the male slave looked directly at me and smiled. There was nothing in his handsome young face that said he didn't want to be exactly where he was.

I tried not to look at anyone else, but it's like when people slow down as they pass an accident on the highway. They have to look, it's an irresistible reaction, and when I glanced at the girl Logan made me kneel next to, I knew exactly who she was. Well, not her name or anything, but it was the girl who made my dreams into nightmares.

She never moved an inch as I knelt beside her; Logan's hand was on top of my head as if he was making certain that I didn't get up and run for my life. Which did cross my mind for two seconds. But Logan was right; fear of the consequences was what would keep me alive here.

"Sculpt. Good fight." The deep voice was controlled and sent shivers down my spine, and they weren't good shivers. "Kai." I didn't look up, but I assumed they were shaking hands. "I have no interest in the fighting circuit, but I was rather impressed by your ability. And I lost a lot of money tonight."

Logan began stroking my hair. "Raul mentioned your name in passing. I'm curious, why is it that you've travelled all this way for a fight you're not interested in?"

I tensed when I saw the man's hand reach down to the girl beside me and grab her by the chin and raise her head. "Her. I was curious when Raul sent me the invitation to the fight. I declined, however. Raul must have known I would, and he is intelligent. He also knew if I refused to come many other of my acquaintances wouldn't either, so he offered me her. Alfonzo's latest."

I quickly put my head down and covered my mouth with my hand to stop from crying out. I couldn't even imagine what Alfonzo's training meant. I didn't want to, and I was horrified with what the girl must have been through. Without moving my head, I glanced at her dead eyes. Alfonzo must have dug his filthy paws into her soul and ripped it out leaving this girl with nothing but a shell willing to do anything asked of her.

Logan's leg nudged me, and I lowered my hand from my mouth. "He is giving her to you? Raul doesn't like to give anything away."

Kai chuckled. "No, but I required a new girl, and Raul knew that. When I saw her picture I had to have her." I slid closer to Logan as Kai grabbed her by the collar and jerked upward. The girl never made a sound, but I did catch a glistening tear in her eye as Kai pulled her up on his lap and started fondling her. "He knows my type and this one ..." I couldn't help but glance up at Kai, "is special."

Logan saw me looking and quickly changed the subject to the fight. It was a couple hours later, after he'd fed me like a dog and I listened to the sounds swarming me like insects crawling over my skin, that Kai took interest in me.

"She is stunning."

Logan had his hand on the nape of my neck, and I felt it stiffen. "Hmmm."

"Dinner appears to be over, and my understanding is Raul likes to play afterward. Care to indulge?"

Oh God. No. No, Logan. Please.

"Not really."

"Then why bother having her? My suggestion is tame, nothing to frighten your little slave. She does look like she wants to be swallowed up by the floor." Kai reached over and stroked the side of my face with his finger. "Look at me."

I did. My eyes meeting his flashing green intensity. He was handsome and dignified, like I'd imagine a business man with lots of wealth would look like. I guessed he was in his early thirties, and he had strong, defined features and really dark brows and tanned skin.

"I don't share," Logan said in what sounded like a growl.

"Neither do I," Kai said, and his hand dropped from me to stroke his girl's inner thigh. "But watching the women together. Two beauties ... now that I would enjoy."

"No." Logan's voice was stern.

"No, what gentleman?" Raul was standing behind Logan's chair, and I quickly lowered my head, my hair falling in front of my face.

Kai spoke, "I suggested a little play between the women. Sculpt has declined."

"I never said that."

My breath hitched. *Logan please don't make me.*

"I had something else in mind for tonight."

Kai shoved the girl off his lap, and she fell to the floor then quickly righted herself and knelt beside Kai. I reached out my hand to hers. It was instinctive and reactive, something I shouldn't have done, but seeing her treated so cruelly had sparked a fire in me. Dangerous.

The girl looked at me horrified, her face paling at the gesture. Then just as quick, she was holding onto Kai's leg softly stroking it like a dog licking its master.

"I'd be interested in hearing this," Raul said. "Kai, Sculpt has been hiding this gem away for over a week now. I was beginning to think that she'd escaped him." Kai laughed. "She was rather ... disobedient when she arrived. I was anticipating Alfonzo having to train her as he did your new slave. But," Raul gestured to me. "She has been reigned in. After being away from us for so long, I was thinking Sculpt had become soft."

"Then what do you have in mind for this part of the evening, Sculpt?" Kai asked.

Logan was silent, and I could feel his finger twitching. I held my breath, knowing that whatever he decided I wouldn't like.

I dug my nails into my thighs and tried to block out my whirling imagination. "Perhaps Kai can fuck her while she sucks you off."

"No," Logan said. "More of a show."

I couldn't control the sob that emerged from my throat, and Logan quickly reacted. He shoved the dishes off the table with one swoop of his arm, and then grabbed me by the arm threw me face down on the table, placing his hand on the small of my back.

"You want her fucked. And I want to fuck her." Logan yanked up my dress, and I could feel the warm air on my bare ass. My cheek pressed against the wood of the table, and when I opened my eyes I saw Kai watching me. Our eyes locked, and I saw the cool, unaffected expression to my terror.

My breath came in short, heaving gasps. I heard voices all around me and squeezed my eyes shut as the sounds grew louder and closer. They were going to watch Logan fuck me right here on the table.

"Legs," Logan growled.

I squeezed my eyes shut and did as he said. He nudged my legs further apart and then stepped between them, and I felt his cock and the material of his slacks against me. I started to struggle, and he pulled back and then spanked me on the ass so hard that I cried out.

"Stay still."

He spanked me again then he massaged my ass. He repeated it several times, spanking then massaging, and by then I was sobbing. It wasn't from being spanked, but from the humiliation. I felt the weight of him over me, and his mouth next to my ear.

"We have to do this, Eme. Don't think about anyone else. Focus on me. Nothing else." He kissed down my neck and then across my shoulder blades while his hand went underneath my dress, between my legs, and he began circling my clit.

At first I felt nothing, my body refusing to get turned on by this, by anything that was happening, but Logan was calm and gentle, and soon I felt the tingling, and Logan's hand pressing in my back eased.

"Why are you bothering to give her pleasure?" I heard Raul say.

"It's no fun fucking a dry slave," Logan replied. His clothes rubbed my back as he came over me again and whispered in my ear, "I'll be fast. Don't fight me, Eme. Okay? You get why we have to do this?"

I nodded.

I knew he was trying to protect me from something much worse than him publically fucking me. I wasn't wet, but mildly damp from his stimulation and when he pushed his cock inside me it didn't hurt.

My hips pushed into the edge of the table as he thrust into me again and again. I could hear the men talking around us merging with the sound of his pelvis smacking into my ass. Glasses clanged together and I heard men telling Logan harder. A girl sobbed and then the crack of a whip then more sobs. Raul laughed and then he was beside my head shoving his finger into my mouth.

"Suck it like it's my cock," Raul ordered.

Logan's hands dug into my hips as if in warning and I knew I had to. I willingly slid my tongue around Raul's finger, tasting the juices of meat from his meal. He shoved it back and forth into my mouth matching the rhythm of Logan as I suckled and teased his finger as if it was his cock.

Laughter surrounded me. Men yelling out suggestions that sent my stomach churning and I would've thrown up if Raul hadn't taken his finger out of my mouth at that moment.

I heard Logan grunt and tighten his hands on my hips as he jerked one last time into me.

He'd barely finished coming before I heard the sound of his zipper, then my dress was pulled down, and he was dragging me off the table.

"Now, I'm going to screw the shit out of her ass in privacy. Think I deserve that after winning that fight tonight, gentlemen." Logan took my hand, nodded to the men, and strode out of the dining hall, me in tow.

The ability to speak was torn from my mind as if Logan had ripped the vocal cords from my throat himself. Nothing could be said about what happened. I wasn't sure if he had the intention of fucking my ass, but as soon as we were out of sight of the others, it was like all the terror, anger, disgust, and horror rushed to my head.

I imagined grabbing the machine gun from the first passing guard and running back inside and killing every one of those men. Then I'd watch them writhe around on the floor, suffering a slow, painful death ... Because that's what each of them deserved—a slow, agonizing death. Nothing quick. Not jail—that was far too kind. Justice would be dropping them into a pit of rats, covered in blood, and having the rats gnaw at them over days ... no weeks.

Each and every molecule in my body had been slowly bottling up with rage and disgust through the dinner. I knew if I was shaken the wrong way, I'd explode into a frothy, screaming mess of a lunatic. I felt like I had to let go, scream, do anything to release all the emotions that were treading across my insides.

I'd survive it, but those girls ... I wasn't so sure how long they would. And Kai's newly acquired gift, God, her eyes would haunt my dreams for eternity. She'd been terrified when I tried to offer her comfort. Panic overrode any other emotion that may have once been part of that girl.

Tonight I had watched in horror the degradation of human beings.

Logan walked me back across the courtyard, his hand on the small of my back. "You did good, Emily." Logan's words hit me as if he'd taken a bat and slammed it across my face. Good? I did good?

His words were the wrong ones. They shook the rage-filled molecules, and they all popped at the same time.

"Good! Good! I did *good*?" I screamed and then threw myself at him and began punching. I didn't care where or how, just as long as my fists were hitting something. I heard his curse as my fist connected with his jaw.

"How could you? How could you? Why did you do that? And

those girls? You let them be abused. You let it happen while those pieces-of-shit men destroy them." I punched him again and again. "They're human beings, damn it." The images of the girl's dead eyes pressed into the forefront of my brain. "Kai is going to kill her. She's almost dead now. How can you let him do that?"

"Emily. Stop it." He tried to control me, but I was out of control, the images of what they suffered screaming through me. *"Mouse!"* Logan's use of my nickname was lost to my screams, drowned beneath the undeniable anger.

I was crying and screaming at the same time. My voice unrecognizable as I yelled at him. He hooked me around the waist, put has hand over my mouth and picked me up while I continued to scream muffled words. It was then I saw Alfonzo running toward us.

"Jesus, Emily. Damn it."

Alfonzo stopped. "Sculpt."

Logan let me go and placed his hand on my shoulder. "Knees. Now."

I knew what Alfonzo could do to me, so I did what I was told, but my body still shook with anger.

"Give her to me," Alfonzo said. "Raul is furious. We heard her screams inside."

I grabbed Logan's leg. "Please. No. Don't let him take me. I'll be good. I promise. Please."

I never in my life thought I'd beg like that, I don't think anyone ever thinks they will until they're faced with this. My mind was only built to take so much, and going through the torture again would kill me. I needed that piece of me that still wanted to live, to fight, to one day have my dream of freedom come true. Alfonzo was going to take that away. He was going to destroy that last fragment of hope, and I would become like those other girls. I'd die inside.

"No," Logan said to Alfonzo, and I choked back the sobs as overwhelming relief settled into me. "I'll take care of this."

The sound of long, casual strides came toward us. I kept my head bowed, but knew the moment he came near enough who it was by his distinct smell—Raul.

"Take her." Raul's instructions to Alfonzo were clear. There wasn't a single ounce of sympathy in his steel tone. "I knew it wouldn't last."

Alfonzo grabbed my arm and dragged me to my feet. I could've begged Raul, but it was too late. I knew that. I also knew I had nothing to lose because going to the room downstairs or being sold would be the end of who I was.

I stood immobile in front of Raul then slowly raised my head until I met his eyes.

They flickered with surprise for a second at my bold, direct gaze.

"Emily." Logan's warning was low and barely audible. "Alfonzo get her out of here."

Alfonzo tugged, and I whipped around, hitting my two forefingers into Alfonzo's trachea. He let me go, staggering backward, choking. Before Raul and Logan could stop me, I reeled around and slammed my elbow into Raul's face so hard I felt his cheekbone crack.

"Emily!" Logan shouted grabbing for me.

I knew I'd have no chance against him if he got a hold of me. He taught me everything I knew. It was Alfonzo who took me to the ground, his fury in every movement. His knee dug into the small of my back, and my arms were yanked behind me so hard I swear they both dislocated.

I felt something cold and hard press against my head. With my cheek shoved into the ground by Alfonzo's hand, I couldn't lift my head, but, from the corner of my eye, I saw Raul crouched down beside me, a gun pushed against my temple.

He cocked the hammer.

"Raul," Logan snapped.

"I knew you were too close to her." Raul pressed the gun

harder into my temple. "I should kill her right now." I could hear his heavy breathing and smelled the scent of his last cigarette. "It is a good thing you're beautiful. You're worth far more to me alive then the satisfaction of blowing your brains out. Perhaps Kai is interested. He did find you attractive."

"She's mine, Raul. I won the fight, or did you forget that?"

"And did you forget who you're talking too? Any of those men here tonight would be willing to buy her right now."

Silence.

"You know how I operate, and second chances don't exist in this world. She belongs to me now." Raul tapped his gun against my head. "Or would you rather I shoot her?"

I couldn't see what Logan did, but I heard the shuffle of feet, and I knew ... I knew Logan walked away.

Chapter Ten

1 hour later

I sat blindfolded in the torture room, tied to the metal bed. Every noise made me jump then my body quivered with fear as I waited for ... what, I didn't know. Was Raul selling me off right now? Were one of those men going to own me? Kai? Would Raul have Alfonzo "train" me first?

The waiting was driving me senseless.

Never knowing when anyone was coming. Afraid of the creak in the floorboards. Of a distant scream. Of how the air in the room shifted.

The sound of Logan's footsteps as he walked away echoed over and over in my mind. He'd left me. He gave me to Raul. He didn't argue. He acted as if I was nothing to him.

He told me he would, but I always had this crazy, far-off idea that he'd defend me. He may have brought me here and kept me in this place, but he'd also protected me against it too.

I was wrong.

He'd walked away.

He didn't care if I was sold or killed.

Logan walked away from me.

The door burst open, and I emitted a tiny scream, but I didn't cry. I wouldn't. No one deserved my tears in this place.

Hands grabbed my wrists, and I recognized them. Logan's. It wasn't Alfonzo or Jacob. Was he going to torture me? Was he the one taking me to a new owner? Could he be that cruel?

He took off the ropes on my wrists then tore off my blindfold and helped me stand.

Our eyes locked.

And somehow I knew. Whether I felt it or saw it in his expression, I didn't know, but the man standing in front of me was the man I used to love.

"One chance at this. One. We aren't ready, but there's no choice. He's selling you and ... Mouse, get changed. Now." It was then I noticed the clothes on the bed. Logan grabbed the front of the black lace dress and ripped it off me then threw it aside. I stood dumbstruck, staring until his voice cut through my shock. "Clothes. Now."

He picked up what looked like an oversized black T-shirt and a pair of jeans and tossed them at me, then walked back to the door. I kept looking at him as I changed, uncertain what was happening. There was a stern determination on his face, unrelenting and dangerous as he put his ear to the door.

I was doing up the zipper of the jeans when he strode towards me. "I needed you gone ten minutes ago—move it." He grabbed my arm just as the door burst open again. Logan shoved me so hard behind him that I fell to my butt.

"What the ... Sculpt?" Alfonzo's eyes went from me to Logan. "What are you doing here? She's sold, Sculpt. I'm taking her to her new owner."

"No." Logan's voice was steady and calm. "That is not going to happen."

I climbed to my feet.

Alfonzo's eyes kept darting between me and Logan. "Your father will crucify you, then her."

Father? What? My eyes widened, and I staggered backward until my back hit the damp cement wall. Raul?

Oh God. Logan was Raul's son? Logan was Raul's son.

"Maybe. But I get to live with the satisfaction of what I've wanted to do for weeks." Logan took two strides and swung hard and fast, his fist connecting with Alfonzo's jaw and sending him back into the wall. "You. Are. Scum. A parasite." Logan hit him again and blood splattered from his nose and upper lip.

Alfonzo grunted and tried swinging back, but he was no match for Logan, and as soon as he went for his gun, Logan kicked it from his hand, and it went sliding across the floor.

"You touched her. That was your mistake." Logan continued to punch Alfonzo again and again until Alfonzo was lying on the ground unmoving. I was staring, watching, confused and not knowing what the hell was going on except that Alfonzo looked dead and Logan was covered in his blood.

I glanced at the gun then back to Logan who stood over Alfonzo staring down at the motionless form. I didn't know what was going on, but I wasn't letting the chance escape me.

I dove for the gun.

My fingers curled around the butt, and I jumped to my feet just as I heard Logan's voice.

"Emily. Put the gun down."

I shook my head back and forth as the gun trembled in my hand while I pointed it at him. "No. I'm getting out of here. And you're not stopping me."

He took one step forward, and I steadied the gun with my other hand then cocked the hammer.

"You're right. You are getting out of here, but not on your own, and I think you know that. I'm going to help you."

I backed up as he came forward. "No. I don't believe you. Why would you do that? You brought me here. You've kept me here. He's your ... he's your father. That man is ..." I couldn't say it again; it made me sick to my stomach to think I'd willingly slept with that bastard's son.

"Put the gun down." He held out his hand. "I never lied to you."

I jerked the gun toward him as I spoke. "Bullshit. You lied to me every single day. Were the nights a lie too? Am I just like all those other girls? Maybe I'd be better off with a new owner, at least I know when he fucks me I will hate him. Not like you. You made me love you then you wrecked me with it. Then ... then you gave me back piece by piece every night only to take it away all over again in the morning."

"I've never lied to you. Ever." He nodded to the gun. "You shoot that thing in here—we're both dead. Every man in this place will be down here. I'm trying to help you, and this shit is about to blow up in our faces."

I didn't believe him. My trust had been destroyed, just like I was going to do to his heart when I shot him. "Stay back."

"I can't do that." He dove for me.

I tightened my finger on the trigger and closed my eyes.

Then I felt the jarring pain in my back when Logan threw his weight on top of me and we both crashed to the floor. He grabbed the gun out of my hands and slid it in the back of his jeans.

Without a word he pulled me to my feet, slid his cell from his pocket, and snagged my hand.

He pressed a number on his phone and put it to his ear. "Deck."

Deck? Georgie's Deck? What? No, it couldn't be.

"It's now," he said abruptly into the phone. "I don't care if your guys aren't ready. This happens. You sure your man has her safe? Good." He nodded then his back stiffened as he listened. "Not happening, Deck. I'm not taking that chance." Silence, except for the thumping of my heart and the blood rushing through my veins. Logan pulled me up the stairs. "Deck, I don't care. You hear me? Change in plans. She goes. I'll deal with Raul and the consequences." He propelled me down a hallway, then out a side door that led us outside. He stopped, placed his hand over the receiver and said, "Dave."

Dave appeared from behind the bushes. "We're taking a risk meeting." He nodded to the phone. "Taking a risk using that. It's for the end game."

"This is the end game. It needs to happen. Alfonzo is down."

"Shit. Sculpt that, wasn't—"

"We get her clear, and I'll look after the rest. You got the signal?"

Dave ran his hand through his hair. "Yeah, but Sculpt. Jesus. Not a good idea. Deck says—"

"Do I look like I care? Do it."

I was so confused having no idea what was happening except Dave was shocked, Logan was losing control, and Deck was yelling through the speaker. They were speaking to one another as if ... as if this was planned. Could it be true? Was Deck here? Could Logan be talking about getting me out of here? Why now? Why would he suddenly change his mind?

The flicker of hope was trying to emerge from beneath my fear. I was scared of what Logan was doing, of what would happen if he was caught, if we were caught. I was confused as to why Dave was helping and worried that this was some kind of setup.

"What?" Logan said into the phone.

I could hear Deck on the line, "Sculpt, you screw with this, you're fucked. I told you it will go down, but you need to wait. My men are on mission, I'm waiting on two more. We need them, Sculpt. We don't have enough men for a complete take down of this place. You fuck this now, he'll know something's up, and if he escapes neither of you will be safe for the rest of your goddamn lives."

"I'll deal with Raul. Get her out." Logan closed his eyes for a half a second then looked at me. The pain I saw there was so raw that my breath hitched, and I wanted to go to him to ease it. How could I feel this way? He didn't deserve anything from me.

"Raul will torture you until you piss and puke blood. Then he'll kill you," Deck shouted over the phone. "Just hold the fuck up. We know what we're doing."

"It's too late for that. Dave's bringing her out. Be ready." Logan dropped the phone from his ear. He must have pressed the End button, because Deck's shouts could no longer be heard. "You know what to do." He reached in his pocket and pulled out what looked like a passport. "This will get you home." He passed it to me.

My hand shook as I took it from him. Why was he doing this? It didn't make sense. He'd made her fear him and threatened to sell her. He'd told her he'd not protect her if she misbehaved.

"Man. Deck is right. A few more days—"

"She doesn't have a few more days, she has zero." He was talking about me as if ... as if he cared what happened to me. "Deck will meet you. Don't come back, Dave. Don't ever come here again. What happened to your sister ... fuck ... I'm sorry."

Dave stiffened and nodded as if no more needed to be said, and Logan put his hand on Dave's shoulder and squeezed.

Sister? What happened to Dave's sister? Could she have been a slave? Was she one of the girl's she'd seen? Had she been killed? Why did Logan care? How good of friends were they?

When Logan shifted, his eyes met mine.

The Logan I'd fallen in love with, not the cold man who held me captive, stood in front of me. I saw it in him, the way his eyes warmed, the way his fingers stroked the back of my hand.

And it terrified me. Because no matter how much I'd fought it, I still loved this man.

Dave tugged on my arm, and mine and Logan's hands separated. I stared, unable to move.

"Emily. Go."

Dave yanked, but I refused to budge. "*Chiquita*, we have to leave now."

Then the coldness descended over Logan's face. "Get out of here, Emily. This is who I am. Don't think any different just because I fucked you a few times."

I gasped. Dave swore beneath his breath.

"Get her out of my sight."

I glared at the man that just sucked the last bit of hope from my heart. "Why are you letting me go then? Just sell me, you bastard! Why take the risk?"

He shook his head. "I'm risking nothing. My father will be marginally upset, but I'm his prize fighter, and if I choose to let you go then that is my choice." His tone softened, the hardness in his eyes remained. "Go repair from this place, Emily."

"Sculpt." Dave sighed and lowered his head, clearly unhappy at what was going down.

My response was automatic, as if the words were sitting on the tip of my tongue waiting to be spoken. "Some things can't be repaired. You break them bad enough, they can't be fixed."

His body flinched. His jaw clenched, and I saw his index finger twitch against his thigh. He was angry, but I also recognized the pain in his expression. And I was glad he hurt.

I'd live. I'd survive.

I realized I didn't have it in me to forgive him or to forget. But I'd find a place in me that could—live.

Dave yanked hard on my hand and we ran. The last vision I saw of Logan was him turning his back on me.

Dave hauled ass through the compound, sticking to the shadows while dragging me behind him. I was too frazzled to do anything but follow him, and if it was true and I was getting out of here, then I'd do anything he asked of me.

He stopped behind one of the houses, his finger up to his mouth making certain I stayed quiet. I heard the steady patter of paws and feet and leaned up against the wall, holding my breath, praying they couldn't hear my heart thumping erratically.

When the guard and dog passed, Dave gestured to me to stay put while he crept low across the yard. I saw the flash of his knife reflect against the moonlight as he unsheathed it. In one swift movement the guard standing near the wall fell to the ground.

Dave gestured to me, and I went running to him.

Suddenly there were three loud gun shots and lots of shouts as guards started running toward the main house.

"Fool." Dave said staring off in the direction of the gunshots. "That's our signal."

He grabbed my hand again, and we ran the length of the wall. It felt like forever as I scrambled after him, trying to stop from ducking as more gun shots went off.

Dave stopped and dropped to his knees at a grate in the ground. He pulled several times before it gave way. "The ladder's slippery. Careful."

I slid through feet first and felt for the ladder rung then started climbing down. I stopped when I heard a clang of metal. "Dave?" I didn't trust the guy, and I had no idea why he was helping me escape, but right now he was all I had.

"Don't stop, *Chiquita.*" His voice carried down the damp sewer. "You need to hurry."

"Are you ... are you coming?"

"No, *Chiquita.* Go quickly."

Oh God, he wasn't coming. I was all alone in a sewer with no money and somewhere in Mexico. I froze on the ladder, fingers tight around the damp, thin metal. I didn't know what to do, where to go, or even how to get there. Maybe this sewer was a dead end? Had Dave even checked where this led? Was this a test? Was Sculpt testing to see if I'd leave if given the chance? Could all this be a cruel sick game to torment me?

"Emily?"

My body instinctively plastered against the ladder. The voice came from below me ... It was vaguely familiar, but I was so scared I didn't trust anything my mind was thinking right now.

"Emily? Hell."

Deck?

The rush of emotion hit me so hard I slipped down two rungs, and the sound echoed like a drum through the tunnel.

"Emily?" Deck called.

"Y-yes. Yes, it's me."

"Climb down, beautiful."

I was sobbing hysterically by the time I felt hands on my hips, and then I was being lifted and placed on my feet. I turned in Deck's arms and collapsed into them, my cheek pressed against his chest, and my arms holding him tight around the waist. I barely knew the guy, but he was the best sight I'd seen in fifteen days.

The relief was overwhelming, like I'd been pulled from being buried alive without hope, without breath ... alone with no one to trust—until now.

Deck stroked the back of my hair. "We have to move hard, Emily. You good to run?"

I nodded, sniffling.

"Matt's here. We're taking you home."

"Oh God," I cried. Matt. He'd come. Him and Deck. They hadn't forgotten me.

I heard several more gun shots and jumped. I thought about Logan; I couldn't help it. He had something to do with me getting out of here. Even though I'd never forgive him for what he'd done. He'd destroyed any innocence and tarnished it with mistrust and fear. He'd put me in a world that would live in my nightmares forever.

I didn't know why Dave didn't come with me. Logan had sounded like Dave was supposed to, but he'd opted to go back. For

Logan? Did Logan need help? No, Logan was Raul's son.

Deck squeezed my hand. "You're safe now, Emily."

Safe? I'd never be safe again. I knew I'd never be the same girl who walked into an illegal fighting ring and asked Sculpt to teach her how to fight. I didn't know who I'd become or how I'd do it or where I'd even go from here.

What I did know was that I'd never forget.

Chapter Eleven

2 years later

Gravel crunched beneath tires as the distinct roar of a motorcycle come barreling up the driveway toward me.

It was rare anyone came to the farm except Deck who drove his sweet black Audi with the tinted windows. It crept up the driveway so silently that I rarely noticed it. Actually, the car reminded me of Deck, mysterious, dangerous with a quiet calmness that awakened every nerve in the body. Deck had taken it upon himself to check up on me every so often ever since he and Matt had brought me back from Mexico. Georgie said it was his way, and I was "in the fold" now. Well, the fold could be a pain in the butt, and Georgie completely agreed as she'd been on Deck's radar since he was honorably discharged from the JTF2. He'd started his own company called Unyielding Riot. I recently found out that Riot was Georgie's brother's call name in the JTF2.

Deck had been a huge help when I came back. He assisted with the police and FBI investigation and was with me when I had to tell them the story. Although, certain details were left out—like Sculpt's identity. I never mentioned him; Deck's doing and I guess mine too. Sculpt had gotten me out of there.

Deck being an ex JTF2 often worked with law enforcement on cases and therefore had some 'friends' which helped when I wanted nothing more than to stop talking about it. He kept the pressure off of me and dealt with most of the questions and answers. At the time, I couldn't even recall most of what was said I was so numb to everything.

Stroking Havoc's sleek, white neck, I felt the veins popping out under her skin. A quiver raced through her body, and she trembled. Clucking, I moved Havoc into a walk. Horses were prey animals, and when scared—they ran.

The bike's roar closed in on us.

Havoc's ears pricked forward and her muscles coiled like a spring.

I sunk deeper into the saddle, yet made certain I stayed relaxed. Clamping down tight on a fearful horse was like a mountain lion leaping on their back.

"Good girl, Havoc." I urged her around so that we were facing the offending noise that still wasn't slowing. The bike paused at the fork in the driveway, one way went to the main house, the other to the barn. It revved then came straight for the barn.

"Damn it."

Havoc sucked in air to make a loud snorting sound.

I took my feet out of the stirrups to hop off, and at the same time the offending bike backfired.

Havoc exploded.

"Shit." I looped my fingers in her mane as Havoc went up on her hind legs, pawing the air. My lower back hit hard against the back of the leather saddle as she came down on all fours. She took off in a mad gallop around the ring, her hind legs kicking out to the side and throwing my body off balance.

Havoc came to an abrupt halt, her nostrils flaring and sides heaving.

Then it happened.

The bike skidded to a stop in front of the barn, dust and gravel pebbles flew into the air hitting the aluminum barn wall and making a loud crackling sound like fireworks going off. Havoc's ears went straight back, her spine arched, and both hind legs went straight up into the air as she squealed.

I careened over her head and landed smack on my ass. "Ughhh."

I fell backward and lay in the dirt while I listened to Havoc bolt around the riding ring kicking up dust.

Undoing my chin strap, I flicked off my helmet and stared up at the ominous clouds. "What the hell."

The gate clanged.

Footsteps.

I lay still contemplating what sort of pain I was going to cause the culprit. I'd spent months gaining Havoc's trust and this would set me back weeks, if not months. The six other traumatized and abused rescue horses that had come with Havoc from the slaughter house had already been rehomed. I'd helped them gain their pride and confidence back, but Havoc was taking much longer. She was an alpha mare and pushing her would only make her rebel—the last reaction I wanted.

I figured another couple years of helping clients with "problem" horses—more like problem clients who didn't understand their horses—and with the reselling of the abused horses to good homes I'd be able to buy my own farm. I loved living here with Kat, but I wanted my own place. I think in a way I needed it. I'd been latching onto Matt and Kat for too long, and I wanted a career and to be able to support myself.

The footsteps stopped beside me.

My eyes hit boots. Black leather with ankle mouldings—motorcycle boots that were hidden partially by faded jeans on a pair of long, lean legs.

My eyes went up and up then—

My world stopped.

Oh God, I'd worked so hard at burying the emotions, the pain, the hurt, and most of all the fear, and suddenly it was all back. Months of therapy obliterated.

I couldn't breathe.

Trapped within tightened lungs, suffocating with the shattering, mind-blowing knowledge of who was right next to me. It was like I had never left.

Logan.

Oh. My. God.

No. It couldn't be.

But it was.

Logan.

Then he crouched, inches away from me.

My heart rate tripled its speed, and the saliva in my mouth vanished as my past slapped me in the face. Emotions swarmed, attacking me from all directions.

I wanted to run and hide, maybe even cower. This was the man who caused me to hide a knife beneath my mattress for the last two years.

He looked different yet the same somehow. Harder—scarier, definitely. He had a scar running the length of his chin, the place where I used to run my finger across to trace his dimple.

"Mouse."

I stiffened. No one had called me that since him. Hearing his voice ... him calling me that again—

"Emily." His voice was barely a whisper, as if he had trouble saying my name.

Logan was still breathtaking, but now even more so, and it unsettled me that I thought that. His hair was a little longer, falling just below his ears in relaxed, soft waves, still messy and multilayered. The scruff on his face was new, and—This man had torn my heart out. God, he made me his sex slave.

Suddenly I was wishing Havoc would trample him, so I could run away.

Logan stood and reached out his hand. My eyes hit his right arm that was now covered in tattoos from his elbow up to beneath his T-shirt. He'd only had his left arm inked before.

Shuffling back on my ass, I scrambled to my feet. In my awkward rush I fell backward and tripped over my riding helmet.

He reached again for me.

"No. Don't." I held out my hands while I managed to gain my balance. Logan touching me again ... no. I couldn't yet register that he was here, in front of me, after two years. Three things crossed my mind. Run like hell. Beat on him, or leap into his arms and kiss him.

I did none of the above.

Logan ignored me and took my arm and pulled me back toward him before I had the chance to escape. I landed with my palms resting on his chest and my gaze hitting his neck. His corded muscles contracted, and his Adam's apple moved up then down as he swallowed.

Logan. I was in his arms. The guy who wrapped me up in his heart then destroyed it.

The guy I tried to forget. No, damn it, I did forget him. I lived every single day for two years without him. I lived. I suffered, and I breathed. Then I fought my way back and won.

Ironic that he was the one who ended up giving me the tools to repair from the very fear he had instilled in me.

His hand reached up to cup my cheek, and I turned my head away. Despite my lies to myself, I never forgot him.

"Mouse."

A sob wrenched from my throat as he called me by my nickname.

I tried to wiggle out of his grasp, but his fingers dug into my arms. He wasn't letting go, and despite Logan being leaner than when I knew him, he was strong as hell. My mind was reeling with fear, anger and despair. I had to get my shit together. I needed to. I didn't get this far only to get torn apart again.

Pushing up against the wall of his chest I prepared myself for meeting his eyes and grit my teeth. "Don't call me that."

"Emily." His voice was soft and gentle.

My instinct was to hurt him anyway I could. To push him to the ground and have Havoc stomp all over him with her hooves.

Maybe love couldn't be forgotten. But maybe, just maybe it could be smothered by hate.

He ignored my steady push on his chest and stroked my hair like he used to do when I lay in his arms. "You hurt?"

"Like you give a shit." I saw him flinch and was glad.

"Eme. Please."

My stomach bottomed out. Jesus, it was that voice. That tone. It was like a punch to the gut. "Let me go, Logan." I shouldn't have said his real name; I knew it. Damn it, I remembered. Not the bad, but the warm protective man that sang to me. Who picked me up every morning to take me to work. Riding on his motorcycle, my arms around him, feeling so in love—

I pushed on his chest again and the instant he let me go, I immediately took three steps back.

Distance. I may be a little older and have developed backbone but the moment I laid eyes on him again, that began to break away, and I *felt* him.

"No. You have no right to be here."

His eyes narrowed when I took another step back. "We need to talk."

I heard Havoc begin to paw the ground; it was a loud pounding that matched my beating heart. The swarm of heat that shifted across my body was intoxicating. Logan had made me feel real before he betrayed me, and yes, after it was a different kind of real. A raw and eye-opening real of what a man could do to you.

There was nothing to say. I had no words for him, so instead of standing in front of him looking like a mute, I swung around and headed for Havoc.

I heard the footsteps in the dirt behind me just as I reached the white Andalusian. He tagged my hand and pulled me to a stop. "Let me explain, Eme."

A tremor of fear shifted through me at his tone and the reaction made me angry. "You don't get to do that. You let me go, remember. I'm free now and I don't need anything from you. I'm not your fucking sex slave to cram your cock into every night."

"Jesus," he growled. "Not once did I take you without your consent. And you know it."

"That's because if I didn't, the consequences were worse." Okay, I was lying, because I was mad and hurt and yes, I was a little scared too. I had no clue why Sculpt was here, and the thought of going back ... no, I'd never go back.

His voice was quiet, "I never beat you, Emily. I tried to protect you."

"Is that how you live with yourself? No, you just took away my choices. You watched while *other* people beat me. You bled my self-esteem. Damn it, you tore my fucking heart out."

"I got you out when I could."

"Yeah, in pieces."

Logan never moved a muscle. Blazing, heated anger shot from his dark, chocolate eyes. "Emily." Logan paused, as he waited for me to look at him. "I've lived two years without you. I'm not doing it any longer. We *are* going to talk."

"What?" My heart was pounding so fast I felt I would soon go into cardiac arrest.

"The compound is destroyed."

My breath hitched as I immediately thought of all those girls. "The girls?"

"Most got out."

"Most?" What did that mean?

"Raul is dead."

"So you came to find me to tell me that? That your ruthless, piece-of-shit fucking father is dead? I don't care. I've moved on."

"Have you?"

I paused, and it was a mistake, because he noticed. "You need to leave."

He moved in, and I saw the intent on his face, the way his brows lowered, how his eyes turned dark. I knew what he was going to do, but before I could turn he grabbed me by the shoulders. "I let you go once, because I had to. Now I don't."

I started trembling with anger and fear stirred in my belly. There was an uncertainty if he was going to grab me and carry me away and I'd never be found again.

My trust in Logan had snapped, and it couldn't be reconnected. "Yeah well, tell that to the police when I call them and have you arrested. They know what happened to me." But they didn't know Logan was involved. Maybe that was a mistake. I reached into my back pocket then realized I didn't have my phone.

"Mouse." Logan's hand went to the nape of my neck, and his fingers caressed my skin causing disturbing goose bumps to rise. No. I didn't want my body to react to him. "You need to understand what went down and to hear it from me."

That pissed me off. He wanted me to understand? No. Nothing could ever make me understand. "I live every single day with what you did to me."

So much pain had risen to the surface, because he dared to come here. It hurt. He hurt. The memories hurt. I knew escape was my only answer before I fell back into a place I swore I wouldn't go again.

"Christ." Logan ran his hand through his bedroom hair, and the locks fell easily back in place. "I did it to protect you."

"So I needed to be whipped for protection? And tortured? Oh and let's not forget that time in the courtyard when I had a gun pressed to my temple *by your father* and you walked away. And the humiliation of being publically ... fucked."

Logan stepped closer, and I felt his breath on my skin, his

smell wafting into me just as I remembered it. "I never took you against your will. Ever."

He was right, he never did. Even when he fucked me in the dining hall he'd asked me. We did it to appease Raul and from making the situation any worse.

I felt like stomping like a fifteen-year-old when I was twenty-two. Instead I casually took the few steps to reach Havoc and picked up her lead. I started to walk Havoc from the ring when Logan called out. "Emily." I kept walking. "I'm sorry it had to happen that way."

My hand on the latch of the gate dropped. "You don't get to say that." I turned, fury encompassing me like I was lit on fire. I dropped the lead and strode over to him glaring, unflinching as he stared right back at me. "You don't get to say you're sorry, Sculpt."

He remained stoic and solid, and I was furious that he could be so calm and put together while I was falling apart inside.

"Emily." His arms came around me in one heated embrace, and the loss I felt the last two years, the devastation, the loneliness, it was smothered by the weight of him. The tightening in my chest hurt so bad I wondered if my ribs were poking into my lungs. Breathing became unbearable as the distinct memories of this man hit like a tidal wave. My fingers curled into his T-shirt, and I felt the hardness of his chest, the way it contoured over taut skin, remembered how his tattoos rippled when he moved. I remembered, and it pissed me off that it was so clear.

"Let me repair this."

His whispered words hit me, and I swallowed the sob threatening to escape and embarrass me. I was stronger now. I'd survived him and his father. And I'd survive this too.

I pulled back, instantly feeling the crushing despair descend on me. Why? Why did he come back? "You made me fear you. You made me fear myself. You locked me inside myself so deep that it took me months to break free again. Repair? You think you can repair that?" I huffed. "I think you should be looking at yourself and repairing your fucked up head before you offer to repair someone else."

I turned and walked away, staring straight ahead, ignoring the heat I felt blazing into my back. And I knew what it was from—Logan.

Chapter Twelve

I put Havoc in her field and was walking back to the house when it started to rain. I heard the motorcycle start up minutes later, and a wave of relief swept over me. I didn't know where he was going, and I didn't care as long as it wasn't here.

The reality was I had no idea who Logan was—the man I fell in love with or the son of a sadistic, ruthless Raul. Was he taking over his father's business now that he was dead? Maybe he was here to take me back?

Somewhere inside me, I knew that wasn't true. I'd escaped because of him. He'd managed to get Deck to Mexico to get me out. I'm not sure how or why, but that was how it went down.

When I'd left Logan that night all I knew was that Deck's men stayed behind. I never asked what happened, and Deck never told me. I had assumed the FBI had gone after Raul when I told them what happened. But why had it taken two years? And why wasn't Logan arrested if he was with his father?

I leaned over the fence and watched as Havoc galloped across the field toward her herd. The rain teemed down on me, and I closed my eyes, tilted my face to the sky, and let it trickle down my cheeks.

It felt cool after the blazing heat of the day. Within seconds my T-shirt was soaked and my breeches stuck to my thighs like Velcro.

I shook out my wet hair and ran my fingers through it. An image of Logan caressing my head, stroking my hair—

I slammed my palms into the fence and curled them. No. Stop.

I leaned my forehead against the cedar rail while the rain pounded hard onto my back and shoulders.

I'd liked it, his touch. How he was with me. I felt empty without him. Damn it, what was wrong with me?

My therapist had said the thoughts of what happened would fade, that with hard work and reconstructions, I'd stop hearing the girls screams and having nightmares. But she didn't know everything; she had no idea that I loved the man that brought me into that world. To her he was a stranger who kidnapped me and took me to Mexico to be a sex slave.

Sliding down to the ground, I sat with my knees tucked up under my chin and my arms wrapped around them.

For two years I'd been able to keep Logan locked up inside of me. My therapist and I worked through what I'd witnessed and suffered, and the nightmares did fade. When she began pushing to know more about what I endured from the hands of the "stranger", that was when I quit therapy. I refused to speak to Kat and Matt about what happened. Kat begged and pleaded with me to talk, but I couldn't. She knew about Logan and how I felt about him and I wanted to forget, not relive the humiliation.

But eventually they both stopped asking, and I slipped into my void of living. Georgie came by a few times a week, and she was her usual self, no-holds-barred Georgie. She told me about her brother Riot, and we talked about the loss and how Deck had been overprotective of her ever since.

My tears flowed like the rain, slipping down my cheeks as I

rocked back and forth, the needles pounding into me. I cried. I don't know why really. I just did. And it hurt. Seeing Logan tore me open, and I was bleeding, and the thing was I didn't know how to stop it.

"Mouse."

I jerked, raising my head. He stood in front of me, soaking wet, water dripping down his face like teardrops.

I stopped rocking. He looked like the man I loved standing there, with his hands tucked in his front jean pockets, a little uncomfortable, maybe unsure of himself. No, Logan was never uncertain.

He stepped closer.

"Emily." His voice. It was strained and harsh like it was when we ... we were together. He crouched in front of me, the rain having soaked his T-shirt, revealing the dark ink on his skin.

Logan had never left me. He'd always been in me, yet I'd denied it. Fought it because it was wrong. It was abnormal. I had to be crazy to still love this man, and yet ... some fragment of my soul did. I don't think it would ever be cut out. But I'd keep trying.

He reached for me.

"Stay away." I punched him in the chest then in the shoulder, my fists like drum sticks hitting him over and over again. "Why are you doing this to me? Just leave."

He held me by the shoulders, eyes never leaving my face, his expression calm as he let me assault him until I was exhausted. I closed my eyes and fell backward until I was sitting in the wet grass, chest heaving and fists throbbing.

"You done?"

My eyes flew open, and I raised my hand and slapped him across the face. The resounding sound echoed, and the palm of my hand stung like I'd slapped a marble countertop as hard as I could. I didn't care. I wanted it to hurt. I needed the pain.

I made a strange moan in the back of my throat and went to slap him again, but this time he caught my wrist.

"Once I'll take. Not twice."

When I relaxed my arm, Logan let me go. He took off his jacket and tried to wrap it around me, but I pushed him away. His frown lowered and eyes darkened as he relented and threw it over the fence instead. And it was him yielding, because Logan did what he wanted, and if he chose to wrap a friggin' jacket around me he would.

I stared as the familiar crevices of his chest molded through his tight, wet T-shirt. *Get a grip. He let me be tortured. He humiliated me.*

I bit the inside of my cheeks until it was so painful that I remembered what I'd suffered with Logan was a billion times more. "You left. I heard the motorcycle—"

"I put it in the garage, out of the rain."

"Well, I don't want it in my garage."

He ignored me. "We need to talk about this." He reached for my hand; his eyes were downcast and glassy, yet hard.

Emotions I'd hidden away torpedoed to the surface. *No. I don't want this.*

I shot for the house, but Logan was a fighter, quick and agile. He ran after me then snagged my hand, swung me back around, and trapped me against a tree trunk.

"You're ... scared and angry, and you're entitled." He stared at me, and I remained frozen, droplets of rain sliding down my cheeks. "Eme, I'm not here to take you away. I'm here to tell you what happened."

"I was there, remember, I know exactly what went down."

"No Eme, you don't." His eyes narrowed when I went to argue. I kept quiet. With Logan you learned when to pick your battles; this one wasn't one of them. "Believing the shit you are right now is eating away at you." How did he know that? "The truth, Mouse. You have to hear the truth. I couldn't let Deck tell you anything until Raul was dead, it was too risky ... And I wanted to tell you myself."

I did realize that he helped me get out. It just wasn't enough to erase everything else.

His arms caged me in as he leaned forward, his chest inches from mine, water droplets glistening on his tanned skin. He leaned closer, and I turned my head to the side. A spark ignited as his breath hit my skin just below my ear. A deep throbbing within me weakened my resolve to beat him with my fists.

"You are not shutting me out like you've done everyone else for the last two years." How did he know that too? His lips were so close to my skin that if I took a deep breath they'd touch. Tears teetered-tottered on the edge of my lids.

"Don't." It was me begging, because I couldn't tell him no any other way.

He tucked my wet hair behind my ear. "Eme, look at me."

I sucked in air as his hand cupped my chin and brought my head forward to face him. I kept my eyes downcast, afraid to look at him and get lost within the chocolate depths. "Sculpt, you have to let me go."

"Never ask me to do that."

I stiffened and tightened my jaw as I ground out. "Nothing you say will make a difference. Not anymore."

"I'm asking here."

Logan never asked. If I gave him this would he leave me alone? "Say what you need to then I want you out of my life."

He drew back, but still I could feel his breath on my face. "Raul—"

I stiffened and blurted out, "The man who had me waterboarded? Who dehumanizes girls? Who held a gun to my head? Are you referring to your fucking father?"

He grabbed me by the shoulders. "Yes, Emily. Yes. He was my father, but I didn't choose him just like you didn't choose your mother." Okay, point, my mother was unkind and selfish who cared for nothing except her next drink. She didn't even know what had happened to me, not that she'd care. "Do you think I didn't want to shoot every single disgusting lowlife in there? Do you think I didn't want to shove that fuckin' gun down my father's throat and pull the goddamn trigger?" I looked at my feet feeling vulnerable ... fine, I was feeling very vulnerable. Logan was always in control, and right now with his brows lowered, his jaw tight and his voice raised, Logan was losing that control.

"Emily. Please. Look at me." I did. "Everything that happened gutted me. I trained every morning to try and control the fury that was raging through me. So I didn't get you killed by screwing everything up. Damn it, Eme. I need you to look at me while I tell you this." I hadn't realized I was staring down again. Really, I was trying not to listen. I didn't want to hear what he was telling me. I'd managed just fine believing what I did, and I couldn't handle changing it. "I've lived two years knowing you hate me." He shoved away from the tree, from me, and ran his hands through his soaking wet hair. "Tell me. What else was I supposed to do? I did everything I could to save you."

I lay my head back against the trunk of the tree and closed my eyes feeling sick to my stomach. I was confused and uncertain. His eyes were filled with this destructive blaze of anger that was ... could it be pain? Was it real pain? Or was it a front? More lies.

I shook my head back and forth. No. No. Logan had watched. He'd done nothing. He'd driven me across the country to his father's compound of hell. Why hadn't he killed Jacob instead of driving me three days to Mexico? Dave had been his friend, he could've helped him. Why hadn't he just taken me someplace else to escape? He was a fighter; he could've fought.

No. Logan was just as guilty as his father.

He walked back toward me and leaned forward, hands braced against the tree on either side of me. He put his finger under my chin and kept it there. "Baby."

I wanted to run and hide. Forget he was ever here.

"My mother was Raul's slave for seventeen years." Oh God. My knees weakened at his words. I hadn't even thought of Logan's mother. "She became pregnant with me within a year of her capture. Raul wasn't happy about it until I was born a boy. Then he made plans for me."

"The fighting," I murmured.

He nodded. "My mother tried to protect me from that shit you saw, Eme. But in a place like that, it wasn't easy. I met Dave, and we both trained since we were five years old for the ring. That's all we did. I can't remember much else besides hanging out with Dave and fighting. We did go to school, but no one would talk to us. I imagine that was because of Raul. No one wanted to mess with anything of his.

"Raul had me in my first fight at twelve. I was gangly and hadn't bulked out, but I was agile and determined." He paused, and I felt his breath on my skin as he breathed in and out. "I was never part of what you saw in the dining room, Mouse. Never. Raul didn't care that I wasn't, because he was focused on me fighting, and he didn't want girls clouding my focus.

"My mother, she kept me real. She taught me what she remembered of her life, values, morals, what was wrong about my father and the life I grew up in."

"How old was she?"

"When she was taken?"

I nodded.

"Eighteen."

I lowered my head, and the rain hit the tip of my nose. God, that must have been terrifying and horrible, and she was there for so long, and here I was moaning about fifteen days.

"My mother had been planning to get us out for years. Finally an opportunity came, and she took it. We escaped."

I asked the question that I was afraid to ask. "Did you want to leave?"

He closed his eyes for a minute. "It's all I knew. Despite the stories my mother told me, that place was where I spent sixteen years of my life." The back of his hand stroked my cheek, and I wanted to lean into it, instead I pulled away. "Still, I hated that place. Every second of it. I fought to stay away from everything else, but I saw what went on there. The girls, the hurt, violence, the drugs.

"My mother and I needed money after we escaped, so I continued the fighting, but I never liked it. I did what had to be done, Emily. That was one thing I learned to survive my father, determination and the will to do what you have to. Giving up doesn't exist for me.

"That's how he found me. He tracked fighting circuits, sending his men to look for me. Took him eight years, but word reached him about an undefeated Sculpt, and he showed up at one of my fights."

"The night I asked you to help me."

He nodded.

"Is that why you moved up your tour date?"

"Yes. I had to leave. I had to get out of the fighting world, but it was too late. I thought once I refused to fight for him, he'd leave it alone, and he did for a month or so. I should've known better. Raul gets what he wants. And he wanted me fighting for him." He looked up and met my eyes. "I would've done it for however long he wanted me to if he'd promised to leave you alone."

My breath hitched. He couldn't do this to me. He couldn't make it better. I wasn't sure I could handle the truth.

He lowered his head while he ran his hand through his hair. "But you don't know him. He doesn't work that way. I knew that. Anyone who knows him does. He finds your weakness and destroys you with it."

"And I was your weakness."

"You and my mother. Raul had men on her, if I didn't show up with you in Mexico, she was to be killed and not just a gunshot to the head. Raul's kills are long, slow, and agonizing." That was why he never attempted to take off with me when we drove to Mexico. "Before I saw you, after you were taken by Alfonzo ... I contacted Deck. He was out of the country, but he dropped everything to come back. He told me what I had to do and what needed to go down. Deck managed to get my mother out from under Raul's men within four days."

I hadn't realized I was holding my breath until I let it go when he said that. He continued, "That's when I had to be really careful with how I treated you. Raul knew my mother was gone from his clutches and all he had was you for leverage. He didn't trust me, and I had to convince him that I was there because I wanted to fight and ... and that you meant nothing to me except a slave I wanted to fuck. If he knew how much I cared ... it was the only way to save you. I needed to give Deck time."

"But why didn't you tell me? We were alone most of the time. You could have told me, Logan."

"Answer me this, Emily. If I'd told you all this, would you have feared me? Would you have trembled? Would you have had that look of fear in your eyes?"

I knew the answer. No. I would've feared the place and Raul and Alfonzo, but I'd always feel protected by Logan. But none of it really mattered, because I still felt like I'd been ripped apart and was trying to put my pieces back together. "I feel broken."

His hand slipped into my hair. "We'll fix this."

I turned my head to avoid his touch. "Sculpt." I saw him flinch when I avoided using his real name. "It's too late. We can't go back. I can't. I'm sorry ... God, what you grew up with, what happened to you and your mother ... it's horrible, unthinkable, but I ... Sculpt, I want to move on with my life, and you're a reminder of what I want to forget."

"Mouse—"

"Maybe it is what you had to do. But when I look at you now, I'm not sure who I see, the man I fell in love with or the cold, expressionless man that watched me suffer and made me fear him." I took a deep breath and said the words I needed to say to save my already damaged heart. "What I'm sure of ... is that I'm better without either one."

I turned, slipped under his arm, and ran through the raging rain. I heard him shouting my name and curse several times before I reached the house. I went into my room, shut the door and leaned up against it, my chest heaving in and out and my nerves shooting off like the Fourth of July.

After I caught my breath I took off my soaking wet breeches and shirt then dried myself off and slipped on jeans without even searching for underwear. I had no doubt Logan would come after me. My running would not deter him from finishing what he started. I grabbed my pink T-shirt from my bed and pulled it over my head just as the door swung open.

Logan stood in the doorway with his hands braced on either side. He looked determined and impenetrable. Water droplets fell off the tips of his hair, and his T-shirt was plastered to his broad, hard chest. There was no softness in his eyes; he was hard and determined with glistening moisture clinging to his skin.

He stole my breath away, and for a moment I couldn't move. It was his authority that made my body hyperaware. It was like this basic need in me begging to be fulfilled.

"Maybe I'm like him. Because I'd have killed, murdered ... I would've done it all if he'd sold you. I'd have done those things to get you back. Yes, I watched you being whipped, fondled, dragged away, knowing you were going to be tortured. And yes, my own father held a gun to your head and I had to walk away or risk him killing you, just to make a point." His hands tightened on the wood frame of the door. "And I'd do it again. Because there was no fuckin' way he was taking you from me. You get that, Emily? That's what this is about. I did what had to be done. You survived. And I'm telling you right now, growing up with him, knowing what that shit was like, you wouldn't have survived being sold, and I wasn't going to let that happen. So, I did what I had to do, and so did you."

I sat on the bed, folding my trembling hands in my lap.

A tear slipped from its captivity, and I was furious at it. He didn't deserve my tears. "I hate what you did to me."

"You hate what I pretended to be. You hate that I wasn't your knight in shining armor. You hate that I made you fear me. But don't run from the truth, Eme. You want to hide behind your Lego blocks and not take the chance at being vulnerable again. But the truth is you're more vulnerable now, because you are hiding."

"You made me this way. You made me vulnerable," I shouted.

"That's bullshit. You were strong as hell fighting Raul and Alfonzo. Shit, you held a gun to me." He walked toward me, and his hands ran up my arms then back down again. "Mouse, we can fix this."

"It's not just broken, Sculpt. It's shattered."

He remained quiet, eyes meeting mine.

He watched me, and I continued to brush away the stupid tears that refused to stop.

"This. Us. It hurts too much." My words barely slipped from my mouth before he was lifting me up and kissing me. A slow, long kiss moving across my mouth like we'd been melted together.

His hands came on either side of my head as his kiss grew harsher, his tongue slipping inside, his grip on me tightening. It was so fresh and raw, as if both of us had been starved for one another.

I tasted the salt of my tears on my tongue as his mouth took mine in a sweet urgency.

My body responded, remembering the taste of him, the feel of him against my skin, and it wanted more and that terrified me.

"No." I pushed on his chest, and he backed away.

"Emily."

A part of me, the side that was completely crazy for this guy, wanted to leap in his arms and devour him. But there was so much crippling anguish inside me. And I suspected him too. At his father, and himself. We were bound to destroy one another more than we were already. "This can't happen, Sculpt."

"Try, baby."

I shook my head back and forth. "I did. I hoped. I tried to believe you were the man I first met. But you snuffed that out every morning, and then when you let me go ..."

"I had to be cruel, Eme. I was losing control, and I knew you saw it. You were beginning to have faith in me again. I needed you to leave."

"Why? Why, damn it. Why didn't you just come with me then?"

"Fuck." He ran his hand through his hair and groaned. "Raul ... wanted me. He used you to make sure he had me. So, it was imperative I stayed, so he wouldn't come after you."

I choked on my sob. I didn't want to believe him, yet I saw the truth like a flashing beacon in front of me. It was so much easier to bury the past than to have it plastered in front of me. And the reality was ... when I looked at Logan it hurt, and I didn't want hurt anymore.

"I can't do this."

"Emily."

"No. Please. I can't."

His eyes darkened for several seconds, and I shifted under his intensity. A tremor of fear slithered through me, and I wrapped my arms around my chest like a shield.

He strode to the door and turned. I recognized the look, because I often had it in my eyes whenever I looked in the mirror—torment. "I won't walk away from us."

"Sculpt—"

"You need time—I get that. But I won't give up."

"You can't stay here. I live here and—"

"I own the fuckin' place, Emily. You've been living on my farm for two years."

Chapter Thirteen

Kat found me an hour later sitting on the floor, leaning against the foot of my bed. Shock had settled in, and I felt as if I was buried under a sea of water. Too cold to react, numb and staring but not seeing.

Logan owned the farm. I'd been living here for two years thinking ... But the puzzle fit; it made sense—Matt bringing me here instead of the house in the city where the three of us had lived.

It had been their parents' house before they died in a drinking and driving accident—their father was the driver and the drunk. He smashed into a cement bridge going ninety miles an hour.

Matt put the house on the market, a house I never thought he'd sell. Not only that, he also put his bar up for sale. It took several months, but the house and bar sold, and Matt bought instead a condo downtown and the farm, at least I thought he had. With the sale of his old bar, he purchased a new one and named it Avalanche.

Had Logan told them to move? Or had it been Deck? Why did

they listen? How did they occupy the farm so quickly? And how did Logan buy it when he was with me?

Kat stood in the doorway. There were tears in her eyes. Kat never cried, not since we met when we were ten. "Can I come in?" And she never asked to come into my bedroom. She bounced in whenever it suited her.

I nodded, and she walked over and sat beside me, leaning against the bed, legs out, ankles crossed. She bowed her head and her short blonde hair swayed forward to cover her brilliant sea-blue eyes. She was a classic beauty; smooth and flawless skin, thin brows, and sharp features.

"Sculpt's gone." Of course if the farm belonged to Logan, Kat had known, and yet she'd never said a word. "When you disappeared that night ... God, Eme, it was like Armageddon." I could see her hands shaking. Kat was always steady and sure of herself, full of life, no regrets. Not now. Now she looked worried. "When you didn't come back from the bathroom that night, I got Matt. And then he called the police who weren't much help considering you're over eighteen, had been gone fifteen minutes, and we were at a bar. Matt lost it. He went right up on stage in the middle of the band jamming and shut it down. Everything. Closed the bar. When Sculpt found out ... he lost it. When his phone rang, his face ... as he listened ... it went so pale.

I was terrified. Fuck, it scared the shit out of all of us. Sculpt talked to Kite, and then he threw his guitar over the edge of the stage, broke it in half. He was ... Jesus, he was angry ... and scared, Emily. It was just a hint of it, but I swear he was scared. I didn't think a man like him ... I'd never thought I'd see something so raw and exposed in him." I pulled my knees up to my chest and lay my cheek on them. Tears began to leak from my eyes as I fought the feelings I was having at picturing Logan like that.

"He knew. He knew what happened to you. We weren't to tell the police anything otherwise your life ... He said if we did we'd never see you again. So we didn't. He promised to bring you back.

And then there was a mad rush to get hold of Georgie. She was the only one who had Deck's emergency number. Sculpt left that night. I hadn't seen him ... until today."

"Why'd Matt sell the bar, Kat? And the house? It was your parents' house. Why are you ... Why are we living on a farm that belongs to Sculpt?"

Kat reached over and took my hand. "I'd do anything for you ... you know that, right? Matt would too. You're our family, Emily." She squeezed my hand. "Kite told us about Sculpt's dad. The sex trafficking."

Tears fell faster as I thought of the girls I'd left behind, the girl with Kai who was so destroyed I didn't think she'd ever come back from the abuse she'd suffered. I'd tried to forget them when ... when maybe they weren't to be forgotten.

"Kite told us that if Sculpt ... no, *when* Sculpt got you out, you couldn't go home. That you needed to start a new life somewhere else in case ... in case the plan failed, and Sculpt's father tried to come back for you." She shuffled closer so our shoulders touched. "Everything Matt and I own is now under my grandmother's name, so Raul couldn't link it to you. Or at least not as easily."

"And the farm?"

"Sculpt bought it under a numbered company he has with Kite. I don't know when that was set up or why, but Sculpt emptied out his account the day he left, gave everything to Kite and told him to buy a farm in the company's name that had room for horses and immediate occupancy. He gave up the tour money. All of it, to buy the farm."

Oh, God. Logan. No. His dream. For ... for my dream.

Kat paused, and I raised my head to look at her. There were tears streaming down her face, her black mascara leaking lines onto her cheeks. "I wanted to tell you. But when Matt brought you back, you were so angry and hurt, and then you were ... you were a zombie, Emily. Matt and I tried to talk to you, but it was like talking to a stone wall. You wanted to forget. So, after a while we let you."

I lived in a dark hole for months, and it wasn't the therapy that brought me back, it was the horses. Kat made me come to the barn and help her offload six horses from the trailer. Horses that were so skinny their heads sunk in and their spines stuck out. Their coats so dull that you couldn't even tell what their real colors were. But the worst ... the worst was the look in their eyes. I knew that look so well. I'd seen it in Kai's girl. Their eyes were dead. Glassed-over and dead. Their spirit ... It was gone—broken.

That was the day I began to fight to put myself back together. The horses and I rebuilt our trust and refilled the light in our eyes. The horses started to gallop in the fields, and I began to laugh. It was also when I decided that I'd stop living and hiding under Matt and Kat and earn enough to buy my own place and build a cliental helping others with their horses.

"Kite asked us never to tell you Sculpt and him owned the farm. He said you'd leave and you needed to stay." Yeah, I probably would have. "I'm sorry. I don't know if we were wrong to not tell you, but when those horses came ... Emily, you came alive, and Matt and I knew it was the right thing. You belonged here. And damn it, I did too. Never thought I'd like shoveling shit, but the horses are amazing, and ever since I started painting them, the demand for my work has tripled. Who would've thought we'd both be living our dreams doing what we love."

I smiled. In the short time they'd been here, Kat was learning to ride and was often out fixing fences and repairing the tractor. She was also selling her art work in three galleries in the city.

I hadn't been the only one who suffered. Matt and Kat had too. I'd put them through months of not speaking, the unwillingness to continue therapy even though I probably needed it. They stood by me and were there for me, never once telling me to stop hiding, to stop hating Logan, to stop feeling sorry for myself. No, they'd just accepted who I'd become and embraced it.

"Was it Sculpt's idea to bring in the abused horses?" Of

course it had to have been. I'd told him my dream of having my own horse farm and helping abused horses, and now I was living it. I felt sick to my stomach at how much I'd loathed him, and he'd ... he'd given me my dream and taken away his. I made good money helping people with their horses. He'd given me that.

"I'm guessing, but I don't know for sure. None of us heard from Sculpt for months after you came back. Not even Kite. Deck went back down to Mexico, and this time he was gone a while. Don't know what happened, but when Deck came back Sculpt wasn't with him." Kat laid her hand on top of mine. "I'm sorry, Emily. God, I wish I could take away what happened to both of you."

"Do you know what happened there?" I could feel my chest tightening and the panic begin to creep into my veins at the thought of telling Kat.

She shook her head. "No. Not really. I just know when Matt brought you home you were so broken and hurt. I could see the anger behind your pain. I love you. Matt and I would do anything for you." Her voice quieted. "Sculpt ... I know you hate him, but now that you know the truth maybe—"

"Kat. God, he ... he did everything to get me out, but I can't. I just can't."

She lowered her head and nodded.

"I can't forget. I get it. He did it to protect me. He got me out. And I guess ... He was a victim too. But the memories when I see him ... They're too much of who he became."

"If you ever want to ... Shit, Emily, I know you don't want to go back to a therapist, but if you need to talk, I'm a good listener."

I smiled. "Kat, you're a horrible listener—you're way too impatient."

She laughed. "True."

"Kat, you and Matt mean the world to me. You're my family. After what happened ... you gave me time to heal. Yeah, I hate finding out Sculpt owns the farm. It makes me feel ..." Guilty, maybe. He'd given up his tour money so that I'd have a place to live and be safe from his father. "Kat, you and Matt gave up everything for me."

"God, I hate to say this but, so did Sculpt."

My breath hitched. I looked at her, and my insides twisted as if she'd just punched me in the stomach. She was right. He had. But she had no idea that Logan watched me being dragged away to be tortured. The worst was when Raul held the gun to my head and I heard his feet shift, and then ... he left me there.

In my head I knew the truth of why he had to do it that way, but I couldn't let him in again. The trust. The laughter. All that had been good between us, it was tainted.

A second chance ... there wasn't one for us.

Kat stood and placed her hands on her hips staring down at me. "I need a drink. You need a drink. Lots of drinks. And I'm sure Georgie needs lots of drinks, so we're going to Avalanche tonight."

I really didn't feel like dancing or socializing, but staying here wondering if Logan was coming back was the last thing I wanted to do. I needed to numb out the plague that was running through my head.

Kat went into action as she pulled open the closet doors and started tossing clothes out onto the bed. "Go put your makeup on. I'm picking you out something to wear. We're looking extra hot tonight."

What I wanted was a bottle of wine and to plop down in front of the TV. I walked into the bathroom and stared at myself for a long time in the mirror, unable to see who was looking back at me—the girl broken and lost to a man she fell in love with or a woman who learned to survive with a broken heart. Maybe I was a little of both.

Chapter Fourteen

Brett was serving like a champion, pouring three drinks at once while taking cash and using his hip to close the cash register. I waited patiently to catch his attention. I was in no hurry, Kat and I had been dancing for an hour already, and I needed a break and another shot. We'd chugged back three tequilas when we arrived, and I was due for another.

A hand slammed down in front of me. "Emily, been a while. Where've you been, hot stuff?"

For all the commotion, Brett looked damn calm. His blue eyes flickered with amusement as he poured a Stella from the bar tap and slid it down the bar, all the while his attention never wavered from me.

"Still recovering from our last night out." Kat and I were here a couple weeks ago, and the tequila shots didn't sit so well the next day, especially when having to ride Havoc and working with four rescue horses. We made it a habit to come to the bar twice a month and stay at the condo, so we could see Matt. Matt was so busy with Avalanche that we rarely saw him now. We'd also go see Georgie who recently wasn't making it out to the farm as often to see us.

"So, you saying no more tequila tonight, sweetie?"

I titled my head and raised my brows. Brett laughed and poured me a shot. He was nearly always serving at Avalanche. Kat swore Brett only worked there to pick up chicks, as during the day he was a real estate tycoon. It was hard to imagine the blond with the unruly curls and dashing blue eyes wearing a business suit.

I put down a twenty. "Nice try, Emily."

"It's a tip." Matt insisted we get our drinks for free, but I still tried to pay whenever I was here. The bar was kind of like therapy for me, being around men, dancing and losing myself to the music. The first dozen times we'd come here it had been disastrous. The second I felt a man near me I felt the fear, the terror that I'd be kidnapped and then forced into that world again. I'd have given up if Kat hadn't continued to push me to come back again and again. We'd dance and she'd keep close to me and talk to me or sing and make me laugh. Slowly over time the terror lessoned until I began looking forward to going out and dancing again.

"Don't need the money. Where's Kat?"

I gestured to the dance floor, and Brett glanced over then rolled his eyes and shook his head which unleashed a curl that dangled in front of his face. I followed his gaze and saw Kat rubbing erotically against some guy, his hands up under her shirt.

"She's going to land herself in deep one of these times. And I'm betting it'll be tonight."

"Why's that?" I asked. Kat was always a flirt, but there was something in the way she treated men that I thought was different in the last couple years. It wasn't like she enjoyed their attention, although she certainly looked like she did. It was more ... like she needed it and yet hated it at the same time.

Brett shrugged while pouring a rum and Coke. He plopped a lime in it then slid it to a young guy a few seats away from me. "Just a feelin' is all."

I noticed he was still watching Kat. "Why don't you date

her?"

Brett threw his head back and laughed. "Not touching that sweet ass. Number one, don't want or need a relationship. Number two, overprotective brother, and number three, she belongs to Ream. And he's back. I'd like to keep my teeth." What? Ream? The guy from Logan's old band? I'd never met him, but had heard his name when I researched Logan on the Internet back when we met and Logan had mentioned Ream was a friend of Deck's.

Brett leaned forward, propping his elbows on the bar. "Better keep a close eye on your girl tonight. She stirs up too much trouble with Ream here ... He won't like it. Don't think she even knows he's back yet. The band has kept it hush- hush." The band used to have a large fan base in Toronto a few years ago, but I'd thought they'd stopped playing when Logan went to Mexico. Maybe they'd found a new lead singer. Brett took another order and moved down the bar.

Before I had a chance to ask, Kat bumped me with her hip and grabbed the guy's beer next to us and chugged half of it. She ran her finger down his shoulder as he stared at her open mouthed. "Thanks, babe." Her voice was sultry and sweet, and it was enough to have the guy drooling instead of complaining.

"Ream? You've been seeing Ream?"

Kat's face fell for a brief second before she covered it up with a half-smile. "We hooked up, Emily—briefly, really brief, like not-even-worth-mentioning brief. When you and Sculpt ... Well, when you were gone he was around. Helped out, you know with moving to the farm and shit. I was upset, and he listened. Then you came back; I w asn't f reaking a nymore, a nd w e h ooked u p then unhooked. End of story." She threw her arm over my shoulders. "Come on, let's dance. It's lonely out there."

"Kat? Why didn't you say anything?"

"It was nothing, Eme. Besides, you didn't want to talk about anything to do with Sculpt."

She was right. I would've freaked if she'd mentioned Logan or anything to do with Logan. "Did you sleep with him?"

I knew immediately she had, because she completely ignored me and started jumping up and down dancing. Kat handled problems like a kid. You know when a parent is telling their kid to stop doing something or to put their toys away and the kid just sits their pretending not to hear them, but you know damn well he or she does? That was Kat.

"Come on, missy, we need to let loose tonight," Kat grabbed my hand and yanked me through the crowd to the dance floor.

I liked to dance, and I was good at it. I could close my eyes and let myself go. The music thrived in me, and my body moved easily to the beat. Kat was more of a wild dancer, jumping around, swinging her arms and singing out loud. And if that wasn't enough to draw attention the slinky, red dress certainly did.

My eyes closed as my body moved back and forth, hips swaying, hands sliding up and down my sides as I lost myself to Avicii's new song. Heat surged into my back and I was about to turn around when hands settled on my hips. It wasn't unusual to have a guy come up behind and start dancing with you, and if he could dance and didn't push the boundaries then I was okay with it—well that was a lie. I still felt uncomfortable, but the images of what happened at Raul's dining hall had faded and I no longer freaked out when a guy touched me from behind thinking he'd suddenly strip me down.

His thighs brushed against me as he moved closer, placing his hands on top of mine and sliding them up the curve of my hips to my ribs then back down again to my thighs. I bit the inside of my cheek to stop from pushing him away. I could do this. This was my therapy, my way to convince myself that I was getting over what happened. I used to dance with strange guys all the time, but that was before Mexico. Now the feeling of a strange man against me so intimately was constricting, suffocating.

The guy pressed closer, his chest against my back as we moved in perfect rhythm to the beat. I could smell the alcohol on him as he leaned in, his heated breath sweeping across my bare neck. My stomach churned, and I swallowed back the bile.

I needed this, damn it. Logan coming into my life again had put me back down into a feeling of uncertainty and confusion. I just wanted to feel confident and free of all the emotions that came with Logan.

His finger pushed aside my hair so that it lay over my shoulder, and then his hands went back to my hips. When his tongue touched the tip of my ear I jerked away, but his hands were ready, and he tugged back.

"Tease," he slurred and chuckled.

"Let me go." My heart rate tripled as I struggled to escape his arms. "Stop. No."

Suddenly, his hands were torn from me and I whirled around to see Logan shoving the guy backward.

"Hey. Fuck, man."

That was the last word my dance partner got out before Logan hauled off and punched the guy in the face.

He went flying through the crowd landing on his back on the tiled floor. Logan stalked toward him his face red, lips pressed together, eyes narrowed, and brows drawn over them. Oh God, Logan looked like he was going to kill him. And he could. Logan was a fighter; his hands were weapons and ...

"Sculpt, no," I shouted as he picked the guy up by the front of the shirt. I frantically shoved through the onlookers, forcing my way to him. My hands yanked at his arm. "Let him go. Sculpt." He'd kill him. I'd never seen this side of Logan. Even when he was in the ring, he'd been in complete control. This was out of control and so unlike him. "Logan, please."

The use of his real name seemed to work as Logan turned toward me. I gasped when I saw the steel, cold look in his eyes. He looked dominant, unyielding and furious.

He dropped my dance partner to the floor. Three security guys pushed forward and picked up my dance partner taking him away, but I kept my focus on Logan.

"What are you—"

Logan grabbed my hand and pulled me through the gawking crowd to the bar. He pushed up the bar flap, then slammed his palm into the swinging back door then dragged me halfway down the hall. He stopped, backed me into the wall, and then trapped me, his hands over my head, him towering over me.

"Logan—"

"No." He abruptly cut me off. I jumped, and he noticed. It was then I saw the fury slowly dissipate from his eyes. The lines around his mouth eased, and he drew in a deep breath. "Tell me you're not seeing that asshole."

"No. But he didn't deserve—"

"He had his tongue in your fuckin' ear."

"No, he didn't." Well, not technically anyway, but even if he did, the guy certainly didn't merit a fist to his face for it. "And even if he had, it has nothing to do with you."

"It fuckin' does, Eme. I didn't wait two years to get to you only to watch some dick with his hands and tongue all over you."

Oh. My. God. He'd lost it. Mr. Cool and Calm had literally blown a gasket. He was always in control of his emotions, even before Mexico. He'd hid them well, except maybe his desire. "Sculpt, I was dancing. With a guy. It wasn't a big deal." But it was. God, it was, because I hated a stranger's hands on me. "I can dance with whoever I want."

He grabbed me by the shoulders and leaned in, his eyes dark, pulse throbbing in his neck. "Not while I'm still breathing, you can't."

We stared at one another, emotions rocketing with anger, and yes, there was desire. We'd always had that between us, and even years later it pulsated.

"Why are you being like this?" I tried to keep my voice steady, but it quaked under his intensity, and Logan knew how to do intensity. "What right do you have to come here and start punching a guy I'm dancing with?"

He growled then backed away while running his hand through his hair before he came back and cupped my chin. "Mouse."

"And don't call me that."

A quiet calm came over him. I saw the change as if a shield lowered. I'd recognize that familiar coldness anywhere. "I will smash through them."

"Smash through what?"

"The Legos, Emily."

"And I told you it's not happening."

Kat came careening through the door. "Shit, there you are. Sculpt, what was that? Matt's furious. That guy you punched wants to press charges."

Logan pushed away from the wall and shrugged.

"Everyone saw what you did. Matt is trying to calm him down, luckily you didn't break anything. Otherwise the police would have to be called."

"Sculpt!" A guy yelled. I looked down the hall and saw three guys coming out of a back room. "We're up."

"Yeah. Coming." Logan chin-lifted to them and then turned back to me. His expression softened, and I felt myself melt just that tiny bit.

Logan being here was making my resolve to keep my emotions under control to fail miserably. His fingers slid across my collar bone back and forth, soft and slow.

"You still play?" I asked.

He moved in. My butterflies I hadn't felt in two years started to cheer when a slow smile formed lighting up his eyes. God, why did he have to smile? When he smiled like this I saw the man I fell in love. It plowed over me, and I felt everything he'd once meant to me.

The back of his hand brushed across my cheek. It was a fleeting moment, but still it sucked the breath right out of me. I put it off to the alcohol, but I knew Logan could make my body lose itself to him with a mere touch.

"We're called Tear Asunder now." He ran his finger over the cleft on my chin. "We're finally touring."

This time my breath did leave as I stared. His dream. All those days we'd spent sitting in the horse fields, him with his guitar, me watching the horses. "The band is still together?" With everything that had happened, he was still following his dream. Logan never let anything stop him; he was determined and relentless. It was one the reason I'd been attracted to him.

"Yeah, Eme. I needed to do something to keep from coming for you." He leaned in so close that his mouth touched my neck just below my ear. "God, you smell the same." He sighed. "Let me in."

Memories like ours lived with you forever, and I'd managed to numb them out. Now, with Logan back, they hit full force. "Sculpt, you gave me my dream. I ... I can't even find words to tell you what that did for me after ..." I closed my eyes and felt him stiffen. "But I can't." The words were soft, and I didn't even know if he heard me.

Kat cleared her throat, and it took him a second before he moved away and turned to Kat and said, "Matt reserved a table for you both near the stage." Then he looked at me again. "Stay and here me sing, Eme." He paused briefly as if waiting for a response from me, then turned and strode down the hall, and disappeared around the corner.

"Shit. What was that?" Kat said.

I needed escape. Fast. With tequila in my blood and my head filled with Ping-Pong balls smashing around, I was a mess. I had to get out of here. Away from him and what he could do to me.

"Kat. I have to go."

Kat took my hands in hers. "You're emotionally fucked up. I get it, and this is my fault. If I'd known they were here, I'd have never suggested we come. I didn't even know the whole band was in town. Come on. Let's go before they rock the stage."

Logan playing the guitar and singing was the last thing I wanted to see. I knew what he could do to me with his voice. He could wrap me up inside him with a pretty little bow and then with one pull unravel me into his arms. "You stay. Hang with Matt, calm him down. I'll grab a cab." Since we'd decided to stay at the condo tonight, which we usually did on our nights out, it was only a ten-minute cab ride.

"No way. I'm coming with you."

I squeezed her hands. "Kat. You're my bestie, I love you, but I need some time ... Sculpt ..." Fuck. How did I say that I just wanted to be alone?

"Let me call Deck. He can take you to the condo and hang with you for a while."

"Kat. No." Deck wasn't a babysitter. Jesus, the guy had been part of the most elite task force for counter terrorism.

Her eyes narrowed, and I tried my best to give her a half-smile. She nodded. "You want to be alone and don't want anyone pestering you." I nodded. God, she knew me too well. "Fine, but I don't like it. And text me as soon as you get home."

"Tell Georgie I'm sorry. I'll see her tomorrow for brunch."

"Georgie hasn't even left her place yet. She texted me ten minutes ago, said Deck stopped in to check in on her." Kat lowered her voice. "Her words, Emily, 'Deck needs a fucking army of red ants shoved up his ass.' Then she told me she had to go change her outfit. I swear Deck should just fuck her and get it out of both their systems."

I liked Deck, but I suspected he was the type who needed complete control and Georgie ... Georgie letting a guy like Deck tell her what to do ... well, that was an explosive overload.

We weaved our way through the crowd. I had just ducked under a guy's arm when I heard him speak into the microphone.

I sucked in air, closed my eyes, and stopped dead. I knew without looking it was his voice. It made my pulse leap and my stomach drop as if I was in a free fall. It felt like his words were drawing across my skin.

Logan.

I slowly turned and saw him on stage.

I was locked on him.

His presence was captivating. He dominated as if nothing could touch him up there. He was sexy with his half-smile and messy hair yet still dangerous and unapproachable.

God, he was confident, always had been, and now looking up at him on stage I realized that this was where he belonged. Not in the ring beating his opponent to a bloody pulp, but up there with a guitar slung over his shoulder.

I knew why this band without even singing a single note would hit the big time. Him. Logan. His magnificence on stage drew you to him. That ease in his stance, how he held the microphone as if he was holding a woman in his arms.

Jealousy bit a chunk out of me as I thought of Logan with another woman. It was a lead weight in my stomach, and I never wanted to picture him with his arm slung over a girl again.

As he spoke to the crowd, I was mesmerized ... lost to the sound of his voice that trickled down my spine and heated my entire body. If felt like he was next to me, his breath wafting over my ear, his hand pressed to the small of my back. Oh God, he was *in* me.

"Damn, he looks smoking. Matt told me they've been touring small-time gigs for almost a year and just got noticed by some manager who's taking them on," Kat said.

Yeah, they were going to be big. I'd known that since the day I first heard Logan sing. And listening to him sing tonight would undo me like it had before.

Did he think he was absolved because he let me go? Because he gave up his tour money? Because he did it to protect me? Because he was a victim of Raul too?

Yes. God, yes. He did deserve forgiveness, but I couldn't forget the image of him looking so cold and heartless at me. Was that inside him? Was there a part of him that could walk away if someone held a gun to my head?

I remembered him staring at me, expressionless, as I fell to my knees after being whipped. He watched it happen. He *let* it happen.

But Logan had saved me. Logically I knew that, but finding that trust again ... it was like reaching for an apple too high up in the tree.

Logan said something to the crowd, and then he laughed. It was the most magical sight. Logan rarely laughed, but when he did it was captivating. I couldn't look away from his bright smile, his sexy bedroom eyes. I swear I could hear the women in the bar moan, and I was among them.

I was about to uproot my feet and stop gawking at the man who made my body ignite when he found me.

He found me with his eyes and didn't let go. He was still talking to the crowd, but his eyes remained on me. His smile was gone, and even from a hundred feet away I noticed his hand tighten on the microphone.

Then he stopped talking and just stared.

My heart pounded at its cage. My blood pumped so quickly through my veins I thought I might combust. Logan was caressing me with his eyes and pulling at me to run to him.

And I did run—in the opposite direction—pushing my way through the crowd, ignoring Kat's shouts. I was out the door before Logan sang his first note.

Chapter Fifteen

I woke to Kat jumping onto the bed.

Kat landed on her stomach beside me, alcohol wafting off her skin. Her face was flushed, and she was smiling ear to ear. I groaned, flinging my arm over my eyes.

"What time is it?" I mumbled.

"Two. Nope, hmm, maybe fourishy. And you need to get up."

I pulled the duvet up over my shoulders and turned on my side. "Kat. Four in the morning? Not a chance. I have Georgie's brunch tomorrow morning then five horses to ride."

"It's tomorrow, and you *really* need to get up." She yanked on the covers.

"Kat, seriously. Whatever it is can wait til morning."

"Um, no. It can't."

I groaned and pried open my eyes. "Hope I'm waking up to some hot story about you and that guy Ream."

Kat barked out, "Bah. Fantasy fuck denied. Nope. Ream won't touch me with a thousand-foot pole. Actually, when he saw me tonight, he looked ill, then he walked away. So, I partied with

Crisis. Jesus, that guy is crude, but hilarious. Man-whore and totally fuckable." She put her finger to her lips. "Why did I come in ...? Oh yeah, your man is here."

I bolted up. "What?" Holy shit. Oh my God. At the condo? "What? You mean here? In the condo here? Or downstairs and wants buzzed up?"

Obviously drunk and unconcerned over my panic, Kat shrugged. "In the kitchen here."

"What?" I repeated then pressed my head into the pillow mumbling every swear word I could think of.

Kat fluffed her pillow and plopped her head down, closing her eyes. "I think he's hurt you didn't stay for the show. I saw him looking for you while he sang. He looked sad. Shit, I'm drunk." She moaned and curled onto her side. "I tried to stop him from coming here, but ... I'm drunk, and well ... even when I punched him and told him you wanted nothing to do with him ... he kept coming. Did you know that he has abs like a damn brick house? Shit. Yeah, of course you do. I think I broke my hand punching him." She lifted it up then let it flop back down on the bed.

"You didn't break your hand."

Kat mumbled something unintelligible. I think it was some sort of apology.

I heard a cupboard closing and then the fridge opening and closing. Then the sound of something being poured into a glass. He was here. Logan was in the kitchen. I shoved the covers aside, shaking my head at the passed-out Kat sprawled face first on my bed, her hands and legs spread-eagle.

Logan looked up the moment I appeared. It was an open-concept condo, and the only walls that existed surrounded the bathrooms and three bedrooms.

Time was in slow motion. His eyes started at my face, dipping down my body to my bare feet then back up again to meet my eyes. He leaned back against the counter and took a sip of his orange juice. A wave of desire hit me as I remembered him leaning against his truck eating ice cream and looking so ... so sexy. Like nothing in the world could touch him. I didn't know why, but his confidence was a huge turn on for me.

Suddenly I felt naked in my pink flowered boxer shorts and white camisole. His eyes taking me in, it felt like his fingertips were reading brail across my flesh.

But anger could undo my embarrassment, and it did as I stopped a few inches away and glared. "Not cool, you being here."

"Not cool, you taking off alone at midnight, drunk."

"I wasn't drunk exa—"

"You drink four tequila shots?"

How did he know that? "Well, yeah, but—"

"Then you were drunk. You should've had Kat or Matt bring you back here, Eme." He set his orange juice on the counter, and the sound made my pulse jump. His eyes remained on me, never once wavering. It's what he did well. He could make someone quiver in fear without even opening his mouth.

He nodded toward the bedroom. "Kat?"

I huffed. "What do you think? Passed out. It's four in the morning, and she's drunk as a beaver."

"Beaver." He frowned as he thought about it. "Your dad used to say that about your mom."

He remembered. I'd told him that one afternoon while we sat and had ice cream on the way back from the horses. My dad said beaver, because my mom used to move shit around in the house whenever she got drunk. I told Logan how my father tried to help my mom get sober, but then he got lung cancer and within six months he was gone. I'd been ten years old, and he died around the same time Kat and Matt lost their parents. I think that's why we all connected so well. We needed one another. "Yeah."

"Why'd you run, Mouse?"

"I have horses to ride tomorrow ... today and—"

"Stop biting the inside of your cheeks and tell me the truth. Why'd you run?"

Fuck. I so wasn't ready for this conversation. He didn't deserve to know that his voice lit me up like a firecracker, that staring up at him on stage undid me, and I couldn't control the want inside me.

Then Logan did something I hadn't been prepared for. He snagged my hand, jerked me up against him, and caressed my hair. "I like the bed look. And the pink boxers ..." He trapped my hand behind my back. "Liking those too."

Anger, where are you? This guy hurt me. He shredded every single part of my dignity and stomped on it. But Logan's words were erotic. Sensual. Just like when he was up on stage. It reminded me of how he was before. He wove through me, made my body sing. Logan was in my kitchen drinking my orange juice at four in the morning, and for a second I wanted him here.

"Sculpt. Let me go." That was all I could come up with; chicken.

"You left a bar alone looking beautiful and drunk. Don't do it again."

"Sculpt—"

He interrupted, his voice hard and unrelenting "No, Emily. Matt should know better. You don't take drinks from guys, never leave a drink unattended, go to the bathroom in pairs, and never fuckin' go home alone drunk. Jesus."

Was he serious? He pops back into my life after two years, stirs up the past, blows up everything I thought about him, and then makes demands of me?

"I see the Legos building. Stop thinking, and promise me you'll be more careful."

Okay, it was a little stupid. Drunk and cabbing it home alone was not smart, and despite wanting to tell him off, I nodded. Because fighting him on this was just making it harder on myself when all I could think about was him kissing me.

Shit, I seriously needed a loony bin.

"I wanted you to hear us play, baby."

"I don't want to hear you play." There was no chance I was going to torture myself listening to him sing. "You have to leave."

"Eme." His free hand came up and traced the curve of my neck. I swallowed. He watched. "Give us a chance."

"Log ... Sculpt, please ... don't." I pushed his hand off my neck then stepped back so I could take one breath without having to breathe in his delicious scent. He wasn't going to leave, and I needed him to—fast.

Silence.

I could hear the slow drip of the tap in the kitchen sink. *Drip. Drip. Drip.* It was driving me mad, and I was quickly becoming unravelled as he just stood there not saying anything.

Damn it. I strode over to the kitchen sink and pushed the tap all the way down.

Silence.

My hands gripped the edge of the counter as I kept my back to him, and if my fingernails could penetrate marble they'd be indented into the stone.

He moved behind me, his hands running down my naked arms until they were resting on top of mine. His hard chest leaned into me so I was pressed into the counter, no escape. No place to run.

"Mouse," he whispered in my ear, his breath like a warm breeze caressing my skin. "Don't let him win." His fingers forced mine apart so our hands could interlock. It was intimate, way too intimate.

"You wrecked me." I barely recognized my ragged whisper as my voice. "I was scared of you. I ... I still am."

"I know. Jesus, I know." His thighs were hard against mine; his groin pressed into my ass. "I will always do everything I can to protect you from others hurting you. I don't want you to be scared of me. I would do anything for you. You know that, right?"

A small part of me wanted to believe him, but mostly I didn't. "I was weak, and I hate myself for it."

He swore beneath his breath then pushed off the counter, and I instantly felt the coldness seep into my veins. "You're the strongest woman I know. But baby, you need to forgive yourself. Your body knew what your heart and mind didn't."

"What? That it was okay to be fucked by you? To forgive myself for enjoying it?"

"Yes."

"I gave in to you. I begged. I knelt on the floor and called you Master."

His eyes closed briefly and he took a deep breath. The outer corners of his lips pulled down and the darkness in his eyes, it was gone. Instead, I saw vulnerability. "Yes," he said quietly then ran his hand through his hair. "You submitted to me, in order to survive. If you hadn't, you would've died or, worse, been sold. That is strength, Emily. I ... I did everything I could to protect you. But bad shit happens. Sometimes, it can't be stopped. I couldn't stop it, baby." He shifted his weight and the floorboards creaked. "Jesus, I've missed you."

I swallowed, feeling the tears well up in my eyes. How could four little words make me want to run into his arms? No. I was stronger now. "Well, I can't say the same."

He sighed, and I saw the tightening of his face as if he winced at my words. "Eme, I'm leaving tomorrow."

His words felt like a slap in the face. Jesus. What the hell was wrong with me? I wanted him gone. I needed him gone. Why was every part of me screaming like a five-year-old not getting her way?

I shouldn't have looked at him, but I did anyway and turned around. "That's good." As soon as I said it, I wanted to take it back. It wasn't good; well, it was, but it wasn't. God ... I was more screwed up than I thought.

That cold expression I knew intimately was back. It was so controlled that for a second I felt that familiar fear. I mean, I didn't really know him did I? Tonight was a good example when he beat up that guy for dancing with me. I never thought he'd lose control like that.

He narrowed his eyes. His hands clenched; his body grew tight. And he still looked hot. My body should be sick with disgust. I should be screaming my head off to get him away from me; instead I wanted to scream at him to touch me.

"What we had, we can't get back, Sculpt."

"We can, 'cause it never fuckin' left."

I didn't say anything. My chest rose and fell unevenly, heavily, and I knew my nipples had to be showing through my snug camisole, although he wasn't looking there. No, his gaze never left my face—again. It was unnerving. Unsettling.

"Jesus, Eme. I don't know what to do. Tell me what to do and I'll do it."

I lowered my head. There was nothing he could do. I didn't have it in me to go through this with him again. To take a chance and then be wrecked apart. "Do nothing, Sculpt. That's what you should do."

He swung away then strode to the door and flung it open.

He was pissed, and yeah, I saw how much I hurt him. Logan may be hard and confident, but tonight I saw more of him. I saw him hurting. But I didn't trust him any longer.

He turned back around just as I was being stupid enough to admire his ass in his faded blue jeans. He caught me staring, and I felt my cheeks turn beet red, and I quickly looked at my feet.

I heard his boots on the hardwood floor come closer, and I gasped as he grabbed my chin. "Look at me." His thumb rhythmically stroked across the cleft in my chin. "Just... please give us a chance."

I lowered my eyes from his, and his hand fell away from my chin.

He moved in closer and his voice lowered to barely a whisper. "Eme. I'm sorry." Logan let me go, turned and walked out the door.

I collapsed onto the kitchen floor and began breathing again.

Logan just ran me over, backed up, and did it again.

Chapter Sixteen

I tried to extinguish Logan from my mind, but it didn't help that every time I heard a motorcycle my breath hitched, my heart started pounding, and the butterflies in my stomach erupted. I slammed the balcony door shut and locked out the sounds of the city streets, motorcycles included.

Then I kept hearing his voice saying 'I'm sorry' or 'I've missed you'. It was chewing me up inside, knowing I was doing the right thing, yet seeing the hurt I caused—no it was him that hurt me.

"You going to Georgie's for brunch?" Kat nabbed her coffee off the counter and took a sip.

"Yeah. Deck texted, said he'd pick us up since he's passing right by the condo." Since we'd moved to the farm, we made it a habit to visit Georgie whenever we stayed at the condo. Despite my head feeling like it had a set of drums vibrating in it, I knew I couldn't bail on Georgie since I missed seeing her last night. Matt hadn't come back to the condo, so we suspected he crashed at the bar like he often did.

"Can't go. Hank sent me a text this morning. The tractor needs medical attention, and he thinks he knows the problem and is planning on fixing it. I have to get there before he gets to the tractor. He'll have metal parts thrown all over the garage, and we'll be out of a tractor for weeks."

I smiled. Hank was an angel with the horses. But he had no skills when it came to fixing things. He was retired and kind of came with the farm. He had a little cottage at the back of the property and was super sweet. "Okay, so I'll see you at the farm later."

"Yeah. Let me know if anything juicy goes down. Deck looked pretty pissed off last night. I swear his eyes never left Georgie once and his scowl ... That guy *is* the definition of danger. I'm thinking Georgie's outfit had something to do with it."

Deck was cagey about what Unyielding Riot actually did, but considering he got me out of Raul's compound and often worked with the authorities it had to be dangerous. I was uncertain whether he kept a close eye on Georgie because he had the hots for her or because her brother never came back from their last mission and he felt obligated to watch out for her. There was also the possibility that Deck's work had potential repercussions.

"Why? What was she wearing?" Georgie dressed a little ... different, with no fear of what others might say.

"I'll put it to you this way. I bet Deck told her to change and she did ... into something even more revealing." Kat laughed. "Even Matt's mouth dropped open when he saw her. And about Sculpt—"

I stopped her. "Sculpt's gone, Kat."

"No listen, I wanted to apologize for letting him in last night."

"You were drunk. And you hurt your hand trying to stop him."

"Yeah. But still." Kat sighed. "I have a feeling he'll be back. Just saying ... Sculpt doesn't seem the type to give up easily, if at all."

I heard the buzzer and walked over to the door and pressed the

Talk button. "Yes?"

"A gentleman is here to see you."

"Okay. Thanks, Eddie. Let him up."

"Going to shower. Say hi to Deck for me." Kat headed down the hallway. "Oh and just so you know, Hank and I are putting the horses in the lower field today if you're going to ride later." Kat stopped. "Emily ... maybe it's time to, you know ... find someone. Let a guy back in. If not Sculpt then someone else." She disappeared into the washroom, and before I could even begin to contemplate her words, a knock sounded.

I turned the lock and opened the door.

Logan.

My stomach dropped hard and fast with a mixture of emotional uncertainty. Jesus, I was so screwed up whenever I saw him that my emotions didn't know how to react. Butterflies released in every direction, some looking for escape, others fluttering with joy.

He looked Häagen-Dazs delicious in his worn out blue jeans and a gray T-shirt that set off his dark eyes. And they *were* dark.

What was he doing here again?

"You going to let me in?"

He was frowning and looked like he hadn't slept, and yet still he looked irresistible. Even with that scar on his chin. I wondered where he got it from. Fighting in Mexico after I left?

"Mouse?"

Right. Let the guy in. I was so speechless that I couldn't even think straight. I stepped out of the way, and Logan strode past me. He went directly to the island and leaned against it crossing his arms. I stood frozen in the wide-open doorway.

"You going to shut that?"

I swung the door shut and leaned back against it mirroring him. He was watching me, eyes unwavering, intense, and yes, I recognized the hint of desire in his expression.

Finally I untangled my tongue, and I only did manage it,

because he was on one side of the room and I was at the farthest point away. "What are you doing here? Again."

"Come here, Emily."

I nearly did. It was automatic to do as he asked when he said an order like that. I had to stop myself and it felt like I was going against something inside me. No, I wasn't his slave anymore. Besides, stepping closer to Logan had an effect on me that I needed to stay clear of. That undeniable ache between my legs was dangerous, and distance was safety. Falling for Logan again was by far the worst sort of punishment I could put myself through. I had plans, and Logan was not part of them.

"Last night ... " He paused, and for a second I thought I saw that flash of vulnerability in his eyes again. Surprising since Logan had the confidence of a bull. All he had to do was walk in a room and all eyes would deviate to him as if he was someone important. "What I should've said was that I love you." My breath escaped, and I stared, mouth agape. And nothing deterred him it seemed. "I've never said that to anyone except my mother. Because I never loved anyone else—until you."

Oh God. He couldn't do this. I was prepared to handle him being angry and cold—not tell me he loves me and that he's never said that to anyone except his mother. A mother who risked everything in order to get her son out of a horrible immoral place.

"Eme. I wish—"

I shook my head back and forth. "Sculpt—"

"Let me say this."

My emotions were coiled tight, tied up with thoughts of Logan and when we first met. Thoughts of how when he looked at me— he really looked and saw *me*. His presence reminded me of how he said he'd hire a plane with a banner saying how beautiful I was to fly by my window. He'd said I needed to be told often after all that shit my mother put in my head. Had that been real? Had any of it? I was constantly fighting the memories of the two months we'd spent together to be overshadowed by the fifteen days of hell. Even with Logan telling me the truth, I was having trouble trusting that our time together had been real.

"Emily." His tone was hard and inflexible, and for a second I felt that flicker of tremor skip across my insides, but then just as quick as it came, it was gone again. "I wish more than anything I could've been here for you over the last two years. Helped you. Told you the truth. Jesus, sometimes I wish I never agreed to teach you self-defence. But then ... then I'd have never fallen in love with you.

"Baby, you're the one who gave me the strength to survive Raul. It has always been you. It will always be you. Emily ...you're my trophy. And I lost you." He closed his eyes and took a deep breath. "I can't lose you again. I have to do whatever it takes to win you back."

"And you never lose." I whispered more to myself then him.

He remained quiet.

I straightened my back and raised my chin, fighting against the urge to back down after hearing the most touching words I think I ever heard coming from Logan. My insides were churning and I was having trouble controlling my tears.

But I'd fought hard for two years to regain my confidence and like one of my rescue horses, I finally had some dignity again and I couldn't. I just couldn't let him in.

A knock on the door had me jumping away from it, and I looked from the door back to Logan. Eddie the doorman must have recognized Deck and sent him up. I was thankful and yet in some masochistic way disappointed at our interruption.

Logan watched me, and I nervously licked my lips under his gaze. His eyes followed the subtle action, and I quickly slammed my mouth shut then rubbed my arms as the shivers coursed through me.

Logan managed to erase every thought except for him and pulled me into a place I had no intention to ever go again. I was going to have my own farm, my business, and help save the horses that needed me. I'd never submit to another man again and be that weak.

Another knock.

"Do you want me to get that?"

"Um, no." I reached for the door handle, then stopped. "Sculpt?"

"Yeah, baby."

God, when he called me that I felt like I could just erase everything that happened and start over.

Another knock. Louder.

I looked at the door then back to Logan. "I'm not something to win."

Logan frowned. "No. No, you're not. But you're something to treasure."

"Logan—" I stopped as soon as his name passed my lips.

He began his approach, slow and steady. I thought he was going to touch me, pull me into his arms, even kiss me. Instead he reached by me, his arm brushing my lower back.

"And a trophy ... I will always treasure." Logan pulled the door open.

Deck stood in his faded jeans and black T-shirt as he looked from me to Logan then held out his hand, and Logan shook it. "Logan." I jerked. Deck called him by his real name. "Band sounded great last night. All good?"

"Could be better."

Deck's eyes swung to me. He was scowling, not that scowling was unusual, but it was directed at me, and I wasn't sure why. "You tell her?"

Tell me what?

"Don't go there, Deck." Logan's voice was low, and he ground out the words.

Go where? It was like suddenly I wasn't in the room and the two most assertive and self-assured men in the city were having a private conversation despite the fact that I was standing right there.

Deck gave a curt nod to Logan. "You coming with us?"

I stiffened and looked at Logan. "To Georgie's? Why would you come to Georgie's?"

Deck and Logan exchanged a look then Deck said, "Georgie invited the band over for brunch last night, Emily."

"Oh." I didn't like that. It meant Logan integrating into my life.

Logan put his hand on the small of my back. It was barely a touch, a light dusting of his hand, but it was possessive and ... it felt protective.

"I need to meet up with Matt then I'll be by. But you know what Georgie said last night?"

Deck nodded.

Logan's fingers squeezed my waist. "I want to see you before I leave, Mouse."

"What for?"

Deck's brows rose, and I noticed the slightest twitch at the corner of his mouth.

Logan's hand found mine and he interlinked our fingers and squeezed. "See you in a bit, Eme." And then he was gone.

A whirlwind had just swept through me. I was so confused and uncertain at how to feel about Logan right now that I felt sick to my stomach. It was too much. The same friends, him owning the farm. It was like I was being thrown at him from every direction, and Logan was right there waiting with open arms.

Chapter Seventeen

It took ten minutes to reach Georgie's, and Deck was silent the entire way. He wasn't a talker by any means, and I normally wouldn't have noticed if he didn't speak. Except Deck's expression was foreboding. Scowl in place, brows lowered, stiff shoulders, and lips tight. Something had pissed him off, but I had no idea what. I mean, he acted like he and Logan were cool with one another. Actually, it seemed like I was the one Deck wasn't cool with, and being on Deck's uncool side ... yeah, that made me edgy.

He pulled up to Georgie's semi-detached house in King Liberty Village, and we were walking through the alley between the houses to the backyard when Deck snagged my hand and brought me to an abrupt stop.

He was frowning in a way that caused shivers of insecurity to waltz across my skin. "You into him?"

"What?" Oh. My. God.

"You heard me." Sometimes his no-bullshit attitude was really annoying.

"Fine, I heard you. I just don't know what to say."

"Easy—yes or no?"

"Why, Deck? What does it matter? Especially to you."

"Beautiful, get your head out of your butt. No guy goes through what he went through if he isn't into her. Logan is into you. I know you're having trouble dealing with the shit that went down, but if you knew—"

"Deck—"

"I'm not done yet."

I bit my lower lip.

His tone softened. "What I just saw between you and Logan looks like something. Logan got you out of that shit, and he went through hell. You ask him what happened after you left."

"I know what happened. He fought for his father and—"

He cut me off. "No. You think you know. Ask him. You owe him."

"I owe him?" I couldn't believe he said that. Deck was as upfront as they came. He gave it to you straight. But in this case he was wrong. I owed Sculpt nothing, and yet, Deck was avoiding telling me something.

"He didn't have to come after you, Emily. Did you ever think about that? We could've got his mother out from under Raul and disappeared. Logan never had to see his father again or go back there. Yes, I would've come for you, but by then you would've disappeared. Logan made certain that didn't happen by acting fast and doing what he did." He put his finger under my chin so he could see my face. "He hated his father. He asked me when he was eighteen, way before any of this shit went down, to try and find a way to get to Raul. But I couldn't locate him. The guy relocated after Logan and his mother escaped." I closed my eyes against the tears. "Beautiful, he risked his life for you. And if you think for one second his life was not at risk even more than yours, then you're mistaken."

I nearly jumped out of my skin when the back gate clanged

open interrupting us. Deck's hand dropped, and he put his hand on the small of my back.

"No screwing chicks in the alleyway, Deck. Fuck, thought you were over that teenage shit." I turned around, and the guy's eyes rose with recognition. "Oh shit, you're Emily. Finally I get to meet the hottie Sculpt's been pining over." I couldn't imagine Logan pinning for anything. "I'm Crisis."

Oh, the band's guitarist. His blond curls blew in the cool summer breeze while his eyes danced with mischief. His blue eyes drooped in the outer corners, and his soft features made him look cute. He also had a killer smile.

"Deck giving you trouble? 'Cause I'm capable of kicking his ass."

"I doubt it," I whispered, but he heard me. Crisis looked lean and agile, but Deck was taller and had more bulk.

Crisis put his hand to his chest and staggered backward. "Ohhh, wounded."

Deck shook his head back and forth then urged me ahead of him into the backyard. My head was still spinning, and I couldn't get a handle on what Deck had told me. What was Logan hiding? Obviously, Deck thought it was important enough to push the issue.

The small backyard had a patio table and chairs with a gaudy orange, yellow and purple umbrella, a BBQ and a rock garden along the edge of the back fence. Georgie called it her postage stamp backyard, but for the city it was a good size.

When Georgie saw me, she squealed and ran over and hugged me. "Hey, Eme." She lowered her voice. "Oh my God, you should've seen Ream and Kat last night. Talk about a chemistry experiment gone wrong."

I raised my brows. Wow. Kat hadn't mentioned anything.

"Come meet Raven." Georgie pulled me to a girl sitting at the table with an untouched orange juice in front of her. From behind she looked frail, thin shoulders slouched forward as if she was trying to hide, and her hair hung in waves down her back. "Raven, this is Emily."

Raven lifted her head and our gazes locked.

I gasped. It was her. Kai's girl. That vacant look was something I'd never forget. I stood staring, and then I stared some more until Georgie nudged me, and I held out my hand.

"Hi, ah, Raven. Nice to meet you." I wasn't certain what to say really. I was so shocked the girl was here that I fumbled over my words.

The girl shook my hand, if you could call it a shake. It was more like she touched my hand. By the way her eyes widened, I knew she recognized me too.

I glanced over at Deck. He gave a subtle nod, and that's when I knew. He had gotten her out. Had Logan asked him to? When had it gone down? It had been two years since I'd seen her.

The screen door slammed, and Raven jumped. By the way she looked and reacted, my guess was she hadn't been rescued for very long. It was also bizarre she was here instead of with her family and friends.

Georgie's mom Karen came out and smiled when she saw me. I met Karen when I started working at Georgie's coffee shop a couple months before I met Logan. "Sweetie. Come give me a hug. We never see you anymore since you moved out to the farm." She squished me to her bosom then kissed my forehead. She lowered her voice and whispered in my ear. "You look better, sweetie. But still tired. You getting enough sleep? Do you need anything?"

Georgie's mom was the closest I had to a mother, and I suspected Georgie had told her about my mom being a bitch and thankfully out of my life.

"Deck," she yelled, "get Emily a drink." She lowered her voice. "Men these days, all macho and no gallantry. What happened to the James Stewarts of the world." Karen was into classic movies.

I wasn't going to tell her that Deck was better than James. All sweet was out; hot and scary with a teaspoon of sweet was in. Deck had that. Damn, Logan had that.

Deck poured me a glass of orange juice, passed it to me then slid into the seat across from Raven. She looked ready to bolt at the sight of him, although I noticed her eyes never directly looked at him. Instead, she kept her head down and her hands on the edge of the chair as if ready to push off and run at any second.

Deck sighed then glanced over Raven's head to Georgie. Georgie put her hand on Raven's forearm and crouched down quietly talking to her.

"Hey, Emily. I'm Ream." Oh wow. No wonder Kat didn't want to come today. Ream was here, and he was super-hot. He sat beside Deck, legs outstretched, hand casually turning his—beer.

I remembered Logan telling me that Ream and Crisis had been friends with Deck and Georgie before they even hooked up with Logan and Kite.

Ream looked at Deck. "Sculpt coming by?"

He nodded.

Deck glanced at me, eyes narrowed and his face pensive. Damn, the guy could send a girl to her knees with that look— except Georgie. I took a sip of my juice. When I glanced back at Deck he was still watching me.

I shifted uncomfortably in my chair.

Raven shifted uncomfortably in her chair.

Karen broke the silence. "Deck, you ask my daughter out yet?" That unhinged the stare, and he looked at Karen and there was a hint of a smile on her face.

Crisis opened the barbecue lid and checked the bacon. "So what the shit, Emily? Where were you last night?"

"Cussing in front of the girls. No gallantry. If Georgie's father were here right now, he'd cuff you to the bumper of his car and drag you ten miles."

"Fuck, I love your mom, Georgie," Crisis said.

Deck may have smirked, but it was more of a grunt.

Karen left before brunch was served, claiming she had to get home and feed the dog. Anyone who knew Karen, knew she was going home to her husband Frank who was usually gardening on a Sunday and she liked to be with him. When I met them, I instantly saw the love they had for one another. And now that I knew they'd lost their son ... it was nice they had one another to depend on after something so tragic.

We ate bacon, scrambled eggs and hash browns. Well. most of us ate; Raven picked at hers. I knew the shit that had gone down with her was really bad. Alfonzo was immoral, corrupt and cruel, and she'd been trained by him to be a sex slave.

Crisis did most of the talking, and the conversation was kept light, away from me, and nothing was mentioned about Logan, although I was constantly on edge waiting for him to come by. Wondering if he still was. Hoping he was, and yet praying he wasn't. Then wondering why it was taking him so long to get here. It was perpetual anxiety.

The gate clanged.

I didn't have to turn to know who was behind me as goose bumps sped across my skin. My belly dropped as I slowly turned and locked eyes with him. God, he was magnetic. There wasn't a flicker of uncertainty in him, and it was unnerving and ... attractive. Yes, Logan was attractive as hell standing there watching me as if he was going to eat me alive with his desire.

"Hey, man. What's up?" Crisis said, then looked at me and hit his head with the palm of his hand. "Of course."

Logan was moving. I heard mumblings from Ream telling Crisis he was an ass.

I stood, so did Georgie and Ream.

There was determination in his stride as if nothing could stop him from reaching me, and it sent my pulse racing.

Logan stopped in front of me. Paused for a second. Then hooked his arm around my waist and dragged me up against his chest. His warm body sunk into me, and I could feel his chest rising and falling as he kept me locked to him.

"Mouse." His whispered word dripped like honey across my mind, and I had a hard time not melting into him and ignoring the warning beacons. "We need some privacy. You good with that, Eme?"

Was I? Georgie took my hand and squeezed. "I specifically recall not inviting you, Logan. I told you last night, Emily was coming and it wasn't a good idea."

"Georgie," Deck said. "Leave it."

Georgie ignored Deck and looked at me. "You okay with this?"

I hesitated then nodded.

"We'll be back in ten." Logan tagged my hand and pulled me outside the gate and down the alley to the front of the house where he put me up against the wall and leaned into me. I wondered if he did it on purpose as the memory of him kissing me outside the Brazen Head restaurant hit me full force. I'd loved him then. I trusted him.

Logan slid his finger across my temple, down the side of my face to the curve of my neck where he stopped. "I wish we had more time together, Eme. I tried to get here earlier, but Matt had a lot to say."

I could imagine after the fight Logan started last night.

I stood against the wall; his fingers splayed on my neck, and with every word he spoke a breath of him swept into my ear. I ached. I wanted him, and yet, me giving him myself was all that I'd left behind. I couldn't do it. I wouldn't be that girl again.

"Give me your cell number, Mouse."

"No."

His body stiffened, and the rhythmic motion of his thumb stopped. I felt every muscle flex, and there was a coldness that invaded my body as my words hit him.

"Emily."

"It's not a good idea."

"Sure it is." His warm breath caressed across my cheek as he leaned into me. "Jesus. Why won't you look at me?"

I did and regretted it because my belly dropped. "Is your mother okay, Sculpt?"

He seemed to relax at the mention of her. "She's good."

I sighed and nodded. I couldn't imagine what his mother must have gone through living with Raul then being pregnant with Logan and raising a child in that place. Deck was right, that place was Logan and his mother's nightmare. And he'd willingly walked back into it.

He moved in closer. "Deck and his men took the place down a few months after you left, Eme. Raul escaped and went underground. Deck found him recently."

"A few months? What took so long, Sculpt? Why did you stay there?"

"You saw the place. It was well guarded. After you got out, Raul knew something was up and doubled his security. Took Deck some time to get organized and enough men to take out the compound."

"Where were you? After I got out, what happened, Sculpt? Did you stay to fight for Raul?"

It was rare Logan avoided my eyes, but he did, and I knew instantly he wasn't going to tell me. Another reason why I couldn't trust him.

"Raul is dead. We leave the rest out of our lives." He tilted my head up so I was looking directly at him. "Emily, you mean more to me than anything. I love you. I want to be with you ... Help you get through this. Baby, I missed you so much."

I pushed on his chest, but he didn't to budge, so instead I pounded my fists into him. "No. You can't do that. You can't tell me you love me and you missed me and think it'll make it all better. That I'll forgive you."

He remained stiff and unmovable. "I don't need your forgiveness. I did it so you'd stay alive, and if that meant I had to watch you suffer or make you fear me then that's what would happen." His hand went to the back of my head, and his fingers weaved into my hair. "You know why? Because I knew one day I'd get you out and it would all be worth it."

"You brought me into that. *You.* It's your fault." But I knew it wasn't his fault. Raul was the only one responsible; Logan just happened to be his son.

"Mouse." His hand tightened in my hair and he put his hand under my chin, to urge me to look up at him.

Oh God, he'd see the watery depths, and I didn't want him to.

"Yeah it's my fault he got to you. He saw me with you and knew you were my weakness. I have to live with that. But the rest ... I'd do it again. It'd kill me, but without hesitation I would. Because you're standing here in front of me." His voice lowered. "Every single time I've touched you it was real."

"I loved you. You used that against me," I whispered in a ragged voice.

"No. I used it to save you." His voice was quiet and steady.

The profound effect Logan had on me was undeniable. It was how he held me, how he looked at me, how he pushed me to my limits. My body and mind were starving for Logan, and I didn't want to admit it. Damn it, I wanted to submit to him. I wanted to surrender to him and I was fighting it with everything I had.

He pulled me into his arms wrapping me in his protective embrace, his hand stroking my back. I felt his breath in my hair then his fingers at the back of my neck, stroking, comforting.

He kissed the top of my head. "Please don't ask me to let you go. I can't do it. I'm not strong enough to do it again."

I remained quiet, but my head was reeling. The Legos started falling apart.

"Tour ends in a couple weeks." He stroked the side of my face with the back of his knuckles. "Then I'm back. In the meantime, I want you to be careful. You need anything Deck will help you, okay?"

I pulled away. "Tell me what happened after I left Mexico."

His eyes hardened and lips pursed together. "Nothing."

"But Deck—"

His brows dropped over his eyes. "What did he tell you?"

"He just said to ask you."

He didn't say anything, and I knew he wasn't going to.

"The girl ... Kai's girl. Deck got her out."

He nodded. "I told him about her. After you escaped, Kai disappeared in all the commotion."

"The gun shots."

"Yes. A distraction. Kai's low-key, and no one knows much about him, but he vanished the moment things became unsettled. The girl was left behind, not sure if it was done on purpose or not. I told Deck about her, and he tracked her down a few months ago. She was up for auction. Kai was there. Deck got her out before he had a chance to buy her."

Oh God.

"She's staying with Georgie until she's ready to go home. As of right now, she refuses to talk about it or go back to her family. They don't even know she's alive."

Alfonzo destroyed that girl. I couldn't imagine what had happened to her for the last two years. Kai ... I really wasn't sure about him, but I did know he was dangerous, and if he knew who took her, there was no doubt that Kai would come after them.

"Give me your phone, Mouse."

"You and me. We aren't dating." I had no intentions of dating anyone again, but I'd talk to him. It would be my therapy.

"No, we're not. We're way past that. Phone."

I hesitated. Logan frowned. Then I pulled my phone from my purse, typed in the security password then handed it to him. He looked at the screen then began pressing numbers into my phone then passed it back. He didn't take his out. "You're going to remember my number from one glance?"

"Emily. I lost you for two years. I finally got your number. Do you think I'll ever forget it? I programed my cell into your phone."

"Sculpt—"

"Answer when I call."

"Sculpt, I'm different now."

He moved in close, arm snug around her waist. "Yeah. You're stronger, sexier, and have an attitude. Makes me want you more."

Logan wasn't defeated easily. Actually, I don't think he was ever defeated and as I stood in his arms I didn't want him to be. "Okay."

He backed away, took my hand and squeezed, and then brought me back to the gang who were talking quietly on the patio. Well, Deck was standing alone leaning up against the fence.

As soon as we appeared, he pushed away from the fence and strode over.

"The band's leaving this afternoon," Logan said to Deck and jerked his chin toward me.

"Yeah. On it. You tell her?" Deck asked.

"I'm standing right here. You're on what? And tell me what?"

Logan stared at Deck a second. "Nothing bad touches her. She doesn't need that shit on her, and I expect you to keep it that way."

"Sculpt, what are you talking—?"

"Eme, I'll call you later," Logan interrupted, obviously on purpose. "Guys, I'm picking up Kite, see you at the airport. Crisis, you miss the flight this time, we're going on without you."

"You can't do that."

Ream picked up his beer. "Sure we can. You fuck up half the time anyway."

"That's horse shit ..." Ream and Crisis argued back and forth.

"I'll walk with you." Deck gave one extended glance at Georgie who was sitting with Raven, then followed Logan out of the yard.

I was left standing, staring after them.

Chapter Eighteen

It was morning, and I needed coffee.

Kat was already awake, and the scent of coffee brewing had me inhaling deep. She sat on the bar stool with her sketch pad in front of her.

"Hey, Emily, you working with Havoc today? I can put her in the round pen after I feed."

I shook my head. "I'm going to play with her out in the field. Free-work with the other horses around. See if I can get her to join up with me while they're distracting her."

Silence.

"You want to take the horses out this afternoon?" Kat tapped her pencil on the edge of the counter.

"Yeah, sure." We often took the more inexperienced horses out for a trail ride in the afternoons when Kat wasn't busy painting or fixing things. She'd taken a mechanic's course last year and even tuned up Matt and Deck's cars.

"Okay." Silence lasted all of ten seconds. Kat couldn't keep anything in. "What's happened between you and Sculpt?"

"Nothing."

"Bullshit. You guys are like oil and water in a blender set on full blast."

Yeah, they were like that. Trying to mesh, but unable to. "We're broken, Kat. What happened ... it broke us." My stomach turned over. I'd been a mouse in a world of snakes. "He hurt me. Even though I know now that he ... He doesn't fit into my life anymore, Kat."

"Do you still love him?"

Oh God. I really couldn't answer that, because I knew a part of me always would. A part of me would always be that innocent girl who fell in love with the guy who sat in the horse fields playing his guitar. But I wasn't innocent anymore, and he wasn't the same guy.

She looked at me, and I looked away for fear that I'd start balling. "I love you. More than anything, and if you choose to keep kicking Sculpt to the curb, I'll support you. I just want you to think about it before you do."

I looked down at my coffee and slowly turned the mug in circles. I kept remembering him standing there and watching me being dragged away, the sound of Logan's feet in the gravel as he walked away when his father held a gun to my head. I felt so betrayed and ... God, where was my hero? I wanted Logan to be my hero, damn it. Why hadn't he fought for me? I wanted him to shout and scream and move heaven and earth ... I wanted him to kill his own father.

And yet, that wasn't fair. I knew it. He did fight for me, but it was in another way. He fought for me more than I ever could've imagined. Maybe it was partly guilt that kept me pushing him away, because I had no right to hate him, and I had. I'd said some horrible things to him, and now knowing the truth, the words had to have hurt him. Maybe in his own right, he'd suffered more than I had. He'd grown up in that place, and still, he managed to be strong and determined and fight for what he wanted in life.

Kat put her hand on top of mine. "I saw the way he looked at you at Avalanche." She leaned back on the stool. "He loves you. I don't think he's ever stopped." The corners of her lips lifted. "We only have one life and ... well you never know when it will end. So, I'm thinking you should just fuck him and see what happens."

I spit up my coffee, spraying it onto the countertop.

She laughed and shrugged. "Just kidding—kind of. Okay, not really. Emily, I'm here for you and will be behind you one hundred percent. I'm also your bestie and will tell you what I think whether you want to hear it or not. Doesn't mean I don't love you, just means I care. If I didn't care, I wouldn't say shit. Okay?"

My phone vibrated on the counter between us.

Kat peered at the screen. "Sculpt. Huh. He got your cell number?"

I titled my head and gave her a *so what* look. I picked it up, plugged in my password, and read the text.

You sleep okay Mouse? xxx

"What did he say?" Kat asked.

"He asked if I slept okay."

"Are you going to reply?"

Was I? It was no big deal really. Texting was impersonal. But somehow it felt real personal. Logan made it feel that way. Even via text I felt the protectiveness about him that I craved. Was I pathetic because I desired that? But when I went to type a message back, my hand was trembling.

Fine thanks. You?

As soon as I hit send I knew it was stupid, and I couldn't take it back. Of course he didn't sleep well. He had a flight yesterday to Chicago then had a gig and was probably up all night.

Slept on the plane. Call you later. Miss you Eme.

How could I not melt after reading that? I closed my eyes imagining his deep voice whispering those words in my ear, and shivers sprinkled like rain drops across my skin. God, he was hundreds of miles away, and I still felt him.

I texted back.

Okay.

No x's and o's. No emotions. Simple. Why did it feel anything but simple?

The day was therapeutic, and I nearly forgot all about Logan. Nearly. He only popped into my head, oh, about a thousand times. Havoc felt my tension on the trail ride, prancing, spooking at everything and anything.

The entire day was exhausting mentally, and when I finally crashed in bed it was with my phone sitting in my hand.

I jolted awake to my hand vibrating. Without opening my eyes, I answered my phone.

"Hello?"

"Mouse."

"Logan?" I sat upright, suddenly wide awake. Then I realized I just called him Logan, not Sculpt, and wanted to kick my own ass to the curb. "What time is it?" I fell back against the pillows, looked at my phone's time—one in the morning. I sighed putting the phone back to my ear. "I should hang up on you."

He chuckled and I knew I wouldn't, not after hearing that sexy graveled sound. Logan rarely laughed, but when he did it was like a hit of something sweet. And damn, I forgot how hot his voice was on the phone. I could picture him lying in bed, his sexy bedroom hair splayed on my pillow, eyes tired and lazy.

"Wanted to say goodnight, Eme."

Oh. "I could've used that hours ago."

"Eme?"

"Yeah?"

"Wish I could be there with you." He paused. "I loved that. Us. Together every night. Feeling you next to me. I hated waking every morning knowing what I had to do. Knowing you'd hate and fear me when all I wanted to do was protect you."

Oh God.

"I'd watch you sleep for hours. Your nose would twitch whenever I stroked your hair and you'd smile then moan and cuddle closer to me."

I did? Shit.

"I hate you being alone. I should be with you."

"Alone? Who said I'm alone." I needed to stop him from saying things like that to me because it lit me up inside and I liked it, but it also scared me because every step closer to Logan meant uncertainty.

Silence. I could hear what sounded like his jeans as he moved.

"Sculpt?" My heart started pounding—hard. Despite knowing we weren't together, I still was glad he called. It must be that middle-of-the-night stupidity taking over my mind.

His voice was low and angry. "Jesus, Eme. I'm telling you how I feel. Trying like hell here and you're slexing with—"

"Slexing?"

"Yeah. Sex then sleep. Slexing."

"Well I'm not slexing or having sex, I'm just sleeping. Well not anymore, but I was, and it was a good dream."

He swore beneath his breath then what sounded like a groan. "What was it about?"

"What?"

He sighed and over the phone it came out rough and sexy. "Dream, Mouse. What was it about? I want to know everything about you, Eme. Even your dreams."

Oh. Crap. I scrambled for something to say and came up

nothing. So, I wisely moved on. "Listen, Sculpt, I was thinking and—"

"Baby, stop with the Lego building." His voice was demanding and harsh, and the butterflies airlifted. Was it from being turned on, or was it from my hint of fear? Or both? Why did I like it when he sounded like that?

"Maybe us talking isn't such a good idea."

Silence.

"Did you take anything in that I said yesterday?"

"What?" I pictured him scowling and his hand clenching the phone.

"Emily?"

"Of course I listened to you."

"So you heard that part where I said I loved you?"

Yes. And how he missed me. And I wanted to let him in—but it made me feel exposed.

"I'm not chasing after just some chick I want to fuck. I'm chasing after a woman I love who isn't letting me in."

"God, Sculpt. I'm pretty certain you don't have to chase any woman."

I heard a loud bang. "I don't give a fuck about other women. Are listening to me?" I was, but I was ignoring the parts about how he was chasing after a woman he loves. "What do you want me to do? What do you need from me and you have it."

I threw off the covers and sat up.

"What happened after I left, Sculpt?"

"No, Eme. This isn't about that. You're trying to push me away, because you're scared of how you still react to me. You're changing this into something else."

"Sculpt—"

"Emily, fuck. Tell me. Just tell me what the hell is happening in that head of yours."

I was so pissed off from him pushing me that I couldn't stop the overflowing words. "Do you want to know what it felt like when I saw you again? The anguish. The pain. The feeling like I was free-falling off a waterfall in the scorching heat. Like I lost my breath. A stupid tingling in my skin that felt like I'd been set on fire. The deep ache that refuses to go away whenever I think about you. Oh, and the butterflies in my belly, they go into a freaking frenzy every single time I hear your damn voice, but I'm uncertain whether all that is because I'm turned on or because I'm scared. Or what I'm scared of. I feel it all hanging around my neck like a cowbell. It's a reminder of how much I loved you and feared you. And how stupid I was to want you at the same fuckin' time. I want that out of me. I never want to feel helpless again. I feel like I'm out of control and only you know how to stop it and I hate that." I took a deep breath.

Silence.

More silence.

Then ...

"I'll be there in a few hours." I could hear him moving around. Rustling. A zipper.

"What?" I threw my legs over the side of the bed and got up and began to pace. "No. Why would you do that? You were just here. Don't be ridiculous."

"Fuck. I shouldn't have left. I should be there with you."

"Logan. Seriously—no. Please. I don't want you catching a flight just to come here. You're with the band. Doing what you've always dreamed of. You'll ruin your chances if you leave. Logan, think about what you're saying." God, was Logan crazy? No, he just went after whatever he wanted.

Silence.

Then, "Call me Logan. No more Sculpt."

Mistake. Twice I'd done that.

"Eme?"

I closed my eyes. "Yes?"

"Did you hear me?"

"Yes."

190

"Say it." It's that voice, the one I yearn for. And that terrified me because I felt ... God, it made me feel whole again.

I sunk down on the bed, lowered my head into my hands. "Logan," I whispered. I imagined the corners of his lips were edging up, and damn if I didn't want to see it.

"Dream sweet, Emily." Then he hung up.

I fell backward onto my bed, phone held to my chest with both hands. *Dream sweet, Emily.*

Chapter Nineteen

I threw a flake of hay into Stanley's stall for his night feed. He was a big Clydesdale cross that had several open wounds on his back from an improperly fitted harness when he used to pull a wagon far too heavy for one horse. His owner sent him to slaughter two weeks ago where Hank had seen him and picked him up.

Stanley and a few other horses with injuries came in the barn at night until they healed. We didn't have wolves, but there were coyotes prowling at night.

"You already did that." Kat was sitting on the cement floor with her sketch pad on her bent knees.

I looked over the stall door and saw the two flakes of hay. Shit. I had. Stanley would have extra tonight, which I'm certain he wouldn't mind.

I was completely distracted wondering why Logan hadn't called or texted yet. He always called before ten. Well, every night for the past ten days. I was used to it. I expected it. Shit, I was mad because I noticed that he hadn't called. Kat noticed that I noticed. And I realized that listening to Logan before bed was becoming something I looked forward to every night.

Last night we'd been talking while I lay in bed, and he was telling me about the last venue they played at and how Ream was giving attitude to a chick who'd been following them. The chick wanted Ream; Ream had her once and now no longer wanted her.

Logan then proceeded to tell me that Crisis fucked anything that had tits and ass. Kite was more subdued about it, but he did it too, just quieter than Crisis. I also found out that they were all coming back to the farm after the tour. They had a celebration bash planned at the end of the month their manager was organizing.

"You talk to Sculpt yet?" Kat was sketching again, trying to act nonchalant.

"Nope."

"Huh."

I knew she was waiting for me to say more, but I had no intention of talking about it. Logan was with the band. Or with a chick. Shit. I rested my forehead on the wood beam. Damn it. Damn it. I knew this would happen. I was getting too close again. I was thinking about him constantly. Counting the days until he came home. Home? I sounded like a girlfriend waiting for her boyfriend to get back.

Oh God. This was my home, and shit ... this was Logan's too. I was working hard to gain my independence from Matt and Kat, and I was feeling like I was losing it to Logan. He was taking it away by making me need him. God, what was I saying? Logan wasn't making me do anything. It was me. It was my need to surrender to him. He fulfilled something inside me that I was trying desperately to block out and deny.

I felt a hand on my back. "Emily, it's cool. He's in a band, they're unreliable. Shit happens."

I was trying to convince myself that I didn't care whether he called or texted. I thought I could get past the intensity between us. I failed. And it had only strengthened with his calls. We talked about everything except Raul and what happened. Mostly the band, his love of motorcycles and my love of horses. It was like we used to talk. We skirted around his mother, but he did tell me her name, Isabella, and that she had long, dark-brown hair with a slight wave to it. Logan also said she had a smile that lit up her whole face like a child opening presents at Christmas. Then he ruined that image with the fact that he rarely saw her smile.

I had to stop thinking about him. "Let's go to Avalanche," I suggested.

"What? Now?"

"I'm declaring it a girls' night." I needed to go out and forget. Drink. Have fun. "No guy talk. Just the girls." I stroked Stanley's muzzle and he nudged my shoulder.

Kat was already on her phone. "Texting Georgie."

We were showered and dressed within the hour. I wore tight jeans with my red strappy heels and a white blouse that fit snug at the waist.

"Kat. Emily. Looking good," the bouncer Dan said as he held the door open for us. "You girls hear? Real good band playing tonight. Matt hired them a few weeks ago. Have that Hinder feel."

"Oh raspy voice. Like it. Wicked. Thanks, Dan." Kat kissed him on the cheek, and we strolled in, quickly finding Georgie at a table near the stage. She had Raven with her who looked completely out of her element, all curled into herself. Her shoulders were slouched, hands clasped together in her lap; her head was down and her face hidden by her long, stringy hair. I wanted to wrap her up in my arms and just cry for her, but I suspected that would be the last thing she'd want.

We drank, talked, laughed ... well, all except Raven. Although, at the beginning of the evening I did chat with her a few minutes. I was surprised when she initiated the chat, leaning forward in her chair and looking up at me. She had dark circles under her eyes as if her mascara, that she wasn't wearing, had smudged. She asked where I was living now. I smiled and went to put my hand over top of hers, but stopped mid-approach when she flinched back in her chair.

I told her about the farm and the horses then suggested she come by and I'd take her riding. I thought her eyes would light up at that—they didn't. Dead. Dull. It was really eerie how she had no emotion except fear. Every movement made her jump, and she looked nervous and uncomfortable. I understood why. I mean I didn't, but I probably did better than anyone here. It would take a long time before she trusted again. If ever.

Kat and I danced a few times while Georgie stayed with Raven. I was on my fifth cosmopolitan by the time the band came on, and I was feeling it. I mean really feeling it as I danced to the music, letting myself get lost in the beat.

The band rocked. The lead singer was a thirty something blond with piercing blue eyes and a deep voice that gripped the music like he was part of it. We danced, drank, and laughed until my sides were hurting.

The band finished, and we were on our last drink as Matt had cut us off—to which we all laughed hysterically. He rolled his eyes and walked off giving Brett the cut sign over the throat. Brett and I met eyes then we both laughed. I nearly toppled off my chair and suspected I would've if it hadn't been for the hand grabbing my arm and holding me upright.

I glanced up. "Hey, thanks." Then I smiled when I recognized him. "Oh, you're the singer." Shit, I was slurring, and he had two noses.

He chuckled. "Yeah, Princess." He nodded to Kat, Georgie, and Raven. I noticed the other three band members had already sat at the table. Raven was looking uneasy as one of the guys, I think the lead guitarist, started quietly talking to her.

Lead singer guy pulled up a chair beside me and sat on it backward, leaning his crossed arms on the back of it. "That last song was for you ..."

I held out my hand. "Emily."

He took my hand and kissed the back of it then smiled. My blurred vision took in the dimples on his cheeks. "Ethan."

"Yep, I know you." I found myself leaning too far forward in my seat. I remembered his face; Kat showed me his picture in the Toronto Now magazine a few months ago.

"Not yet, but you will." He took my hands, and his thumb stroked back and forth across the backs of them. "No boyfriend tonight?"

Nope. No Logan. He was extinguished from my mind. Numerous cosmos could do that to a girl. "Nope."

"Good to hear, Emily. You want to give me your number?"

Number? That was fast. "Um, well ..."

"It's just a number, Princess. Been watching you all night and know I'd like to talk to you some more, but looks like Matt is shutting down soon, so your number would be nice."

"What the hell ... Why not?" After all, I'd given it to Logan. Who cares if this guy had it too? I was on a roll. Didn't seem to matter much tonight. Actually nothing mattered except finishing off my drink. I gulped back more of it before reaching into my purse and pulling out my phone. I typed in the password, well it took me three tries, then passed it to Ethan. "Might as well give me yours so I know who's calling when you call."

"Hey, you know you have twenty missed calls? Popular girl." He was typing in both our phones then passed mine back.

Twenty missed calls? I squinted as I glanced at the number. Logan. Shit. My phone lit up again, and his number flashed. Fuck. I quickly clicked it to silent and put it in my purse.

Ethan's brows rose. "Not into talking, I take it."

"Nope. Not ... to him." I leaned closer and bit my lower lip. I felt daring, bolder now. I was pissed, both in the angered way and in the drunk way. What is he doing calling twenty times? I'd normally be in bed sleeping by now. Why the hell was he calling so late? Why hadn't he called me earlier?

Kat pushed back her chair and came to her feet, swaying a

little. She had her phone to her ear and was yelling at someone. When her eyes darted to me I knew who it was.

"God, Sculpt, she's fine. What's the big deal? And if she doesn't answer her phone, she doesn't have to. How the hell did you get my number anyway?" Silence. "Fuckin' Ream." Kat shook her head, pulled the phone away from her ear, and pressed End. "You get that, Emily?"

I nodded.

Kat glanced at Ethan then back to me. "Think we should go. Washroom first." Kat snagged Georgie's hand. None of them ever went to the washroom alone—ever.

"What was that about?" Ethan shifted his chair closer. He reached forward and ran his finger across my chin. A soft, feathery touch that should've sent goose bumps waltzing across my skin ... instead, the caress sent nothing.

Ethan was rock star hot—tattoos, lean, tall, sexy as hell on stage with his raspy voice and sweet roll of his hips. Exactly what I promised to stay away from, and yet, tonight I felt like taking chances. I needed to prove to myself that I had control.

I leaned closer into his touch as did he. His finger stopped caressing my chin, and he cupped the nape of my neck, pulling me closer. We were a breath away and I wanted him to kiss me. I wanted him to erase the stamp of Logan.

"You're sweet, Emily. Real sweet, I'm guessing. And I'd like you to come back to my place tonight." Ethan's hand tightened, and I suddenly felt a tremor run through me, and it wasn't a good tremor.

"Emily."

I jolted back as Matt came up beside me holding his phone. "It's Sculpt." Then he turned to Ethan. "Hands off, Ethan."

Tonight was Forget Logan night, and I was doing a fine good job of it. Cosmos and Ethan.

"He's worried about you. I told him you're good, but he wants to hear your voice. What do you want me to tell him?"

"Give me the phone." Logan had no right calling Kat and now Matt trying to get to me. God, what was his problem? Why was he being like this?

"I don't think—"

"Matt. It's fine."

Matt placed the phone in my hand, but kept hold. "You sure?"

"Let go, Matt." He hesitated a few seconds then released his phone.

Ethan still held me, his hand having slid down to my waist.

"You want this gig, take your hands off before I make you," Matt said, glaring at Ethan. "She's drunk, man."

I put the phone to my ear as Ethan put both hands up and sat back.

"Stop calling." It was said in a mumbled slur.

"You're drunk."

This is why I knew I shouldn't talk to him. It was like his voice curled me into him—tight. All this work trying to drink him out of my mind and he plowed back full force with a few words.

"Emily. It's two in the morning."

"I'm ... stamping you ... out."

"Excuse me?"

"The stamp. I have to get rid of it." I knew my words were mumbled with the cosmos at full effect.

"Is Kat with you?"

I looked around. "Nope. Just Ethan."

Silence.

"Ethan? From Strikeback?"

I turned to Ethan. "You from Shrrikeback?" My words came out very slurred, but it sounded like he understood me.

"Yeah, Princess. My band." He smiled and winked.

"He says yep."

"Did I just here him call you Princess?"

Ummm.

"Give him the phone. Now." Oh, he sounded angry. What I

needed was another drink. I passed Ethan Matt's phone. "He wants to talk to you." I stood then stumbled to where Brett was cleaning off the bar. It took me three tries to get onto the bar stool.

Brett nodded toward Ethan chuckling. "I can hear Sculpt shouting from here. He just told Ethan he's going to kick his ass when he gets back."

"Oh God, no. He ... he can't do that." I didn't want Logan fighting anyone. I knew he hated it and ... Logan had gone to Mexico to fight for his father—to save me.

I nearly fell onto my ass when I went scrambling back to Ethan and grabbed the phone from him. Logan was still shouting something about his woman.

"Logan. Logan ... Stop yelling."

He went quiet then, "Eme." He sighed. "I'm glad you're out with your girls. But ... you need to go home. I need you to be safe, baby." I heard him swear as something crashed. Someone yelled in the background, maybe Ream or Crisis.

"Logan?"

"If anything happened to you ... I just—damn it, I need you to be safe."

God, he sounded so worried. I didn't understand what the big deal was and right now my head was pounding and I couldn't think straight.

I sank into the chair, my head in my hands. "I can't erase you. I tried, but I can't."

"You can't erase what's engraved."

"Yeah," I mumbled.

"Give the phone to Matt, baby."

"Okay." I passed it to Matt, and he kissed my brow before striding away, phone to his ear.

Kat was walking toward me, her brows raised at something over my left shoulder. She looked surprised and a little worried. I spun around, well I stumbled around, and had to grab the chair for balance.

"Oh look, trouble just walked in and is sucking the fun right out from between my legs," Georgie said as she followed Kat's gaze.

Kat looked at me then back at Deck. "You think he'll have a cosmo with us?"

Georgie picked up the remainder of her cocktail and chugged back half of it. "Can you really see Deck sipping on a cosmo? Besides, you see that wrinkle between his brows? Yep ... right pissed, like turnip-up-the-butt kind of mad."

I was either too drunk or too emotional after Logan's words to say anything. I slipped down into the chair closest to me, my ass cheek half off cause I kind of missed. Deck was making his way toward us, and his scowl was the kind that would have most running. I'd have hid under the table if I thought it would do any good.

Not sure why Deck's eyes were on me, as if I'd just brought hell down on him. I picked up my cosmo and slurped the last of it, making a loud sucking noise. Matt suddenly was at my side, and he snatched the drink from my hand and slammed it down none to gently on the other side of the table.

"I'm not happy," Deck said. Was Deck ever happy? I mean, really, he rarely spoke, and when he did it was serious.

"I am. Fantastic night," Georgie said smirking. "Cosmo, Deck? Might make you smile."

His eyes darted to Georgie, and she cocked her hip and held up her nearly empty drink. He grabbed it, chugged the contents back then tossed it on the table. "You see me smiling, Georgie?"

"Nope," Kat said and laughed.

Deck wasn't laughing. He was pissed. I was thinking either Logan called him, or Matt. Not sure why; I mean, we were out having fun and were a little drunk, but girls did that, and it was fun, and we were allowed to have fun.

"You get why I'm here?"

Georgie, Kat and I looked at one another and giggled while we shook our heads. Georgie was the only one smashed or stupid or brave enough to answer.

"You're hoping I'm drunk enough to take me home and fuck me all night long in every orifice possible?" Georgie said.

"Jesus, Georgie." Matt groaned.

Deck's brow lowered, and his hands clenched. "I'm not doing this shit every fuckin' night, Georgie. You need to get your crap together."

What was he talking about?

"I don't need a babysitter."

"Seems like you do. And dragging Raven out with you? What the fuck were you thinking?"

"She asked to come," Georgie objected.

Deck scowled. "Yeah right. Get in the car. All of you," Deck ordered, and even though I could see Georgie wanting to protest, she didn't.

I knew she was going out a lot, but the conversation sounded like she was "going out" a little too often, and Deck didn't like it.

Georgie walked over to Raven who was still sitting with the guitarist from Strikeback and put out her hand. Raven ignored her hand, but rose and followed behind her as Georgie waved to Matt and the band as if she hadn't just been given shit by Deck.

I started walking to the door when Deck fell in beside me. He gave a chin-lift to Matt who was on the phone, my guess with Logan.

"You're drunk, and you may not remember what I'm telling you, beautiful, but you need to hear it anyway." Deck pulled me to a halt before we reached the car. "He should've fuckin' told you the other day what went down after you left that shit hole. He didn't—his choice. Not mine." Deck grabbed my arm to steady me as I swayed. "It was bad, Emily. Real bad. He gained my respect for life for what he did for you, walking back into that hellhole ... Hard to get my respect, easy to lose it."

Deck respected Logan.

"This isn't him asking me to look out for you. This is me looking out for you, because I care about you and so does Logan. He's worried about you and he has every right to be." What did that mean? Deck swore beneath his breath. "Emily ..." He stopped at the car where Georgie, Kat and Raven were already piled in the backseat. I thought he was going to say something else, but instead he helped me into the car then shut the door. I was left wondering what the hell he was talking about. What did he mean really bad? I had this sudden need to talk to Logan, hear his voice and make certain he was alright. I clutched my purse to my chest to keep from taking out my phone.

Then Deck took us to the condo where I proceeded to throw up in the toilet then pass out on the floor.

Chapter Twenty

Waking on the cold, hard tiled floor sometime the next day, I felt as if a skunk had sprayed in my mouth and I had iron pokers sticking in my head.

Groaning, I used the toilet to hoist myself up to the sink, tagged my toothbrush, piled on toothpaste, and stuck it in my mouth. I did that three times then tilted my head into the sink and drank the cool water relieving some of my dry mouth.

As I shut off the water, my purse vibrated beside the toilet on the floor. Falling back onto my ass, I propped up against the cupboard while shuffling through my purse for my phone. I glanced at the screen and groaned again.

"You're calling me this early on purpose, aren't you? Punishment for my sins."

Logan chuckled, and despite loving the sound of his sexy, deep chuckle that I rarely heard, I held the phone away from my ear.

"Ouch."

"That good?"

"Hmmm." Closing my eyes, I brought my knees up to hook my arm around them.

"I should be there."

I huffed. "Yeah, you'd be clanging frying pans together."

"No, I'd bring you breakfast in bed with Advil."

Shit. Damn it, why did he have to do sweet? It made all my reservations about him blowtorch into ash. And I had no return comment.

"That's after I talked to you about last night, Eme." He paused, and I could picture him running his hand through his hair; I wanted my hands running through it. Well, maybe not such a good idea right at this moment. I put my head down and rested it on my knees. "When we talk, it's good. Then last night we didn't. I got caught up with the new manager, and I couldn't call you. We did our gig, and I tried after the set, but you didn't pick up. I thought you might be asleep, so I called Matt after we were done to see how Strikeback was working out, and he told me you were there. Then he said you were slurring your words. Eight cosmos. Eight."

"Um yeah. I'm paying for it today, trust me."

"Emily. You had eight cosmos, and I wasn't there to take care of you. I called, and you never picked up and ... fuck, Eme, I was worried."

Well, to be fair, I hadn't heard my phone ringing, although even if I had I wouldn't have picked it up. Not last night on my mission of stamp removal. "Twenty times," I mumbled.

"Yeah. Twenty times." He sounded really mad, the kind of mad where he just had to look at you and there'd be no more arguing. Luckily, I couldn't see his face.

"Logan, I didn't hear the phone."

"Yeah." He sighed. "Mouse, you go out with the girls, I need you to make sure you can hear your phone. You were drunk and slurring your words. Ethan was thinking he was getting some, and I wasn't there and couldn't get there. Jesus ... There's some shit happening that—" He stopped abruptly. "You not answering your phone and then getting drunk at the bar ..." He groaned and it sounded like he hit something hard with his fist. "Fuck." He paused then in a soft voice he said, "I get nightmares, baby. Everything inside me wants to protect you and I feel like I keep failing."

I lifted my head and hit it on the cupboard door. Wow. Just wow. And also shit. I quietly said, "Matt was there. And Logan ... you can't fail at something that isn't your responsibility."

I was hung over, sitting with the phone to my ear listening to Logan's words, and feeling like crying. Him saying stuff like that made it difficult to keep my emotions hardened against him.

Logan had been worried. He had nightmares. He thought he was failing me.

I wasn't going to cry. God, it felt overwhelmingly good that he'd been worried, and it scared me. I didn't want any guy to ever control me again.

He wanted to make certain I was safe. He knew Ethan was a dog and freaked on him. "I gave him my number," I blurted out.

He made a sort of grunt. "All I had to do was get you drunk? Eme, really?"

"Well, in my defense I was pissed at you. So I gave it to him."

"You were pissed at me?"

"Yeah, Logan. I was mad."

"Why, baby?" His tone had softened, and I imagined him singing a slow love ballad in his graveled, sexy voice, microphone between his hands, eyes closed. Yeah, I knew he could sing a love song really well. And I didn't want to answer his question. "Why?"

I rubbed my hand down the side of my face. If I wasn't so hung over I'd have some kind of evasive technique. "You didn't call."

"Sweet Jesus."

"I was being stupid, and I wanted to try and forget you, and alcohol can do that if you drink enough, which I tried to do but—"

"Engraved Emily." I knew exactly what he meant. "I know you're scared about us, but when I get back we'll work it out. Baby, if you need a call from me then call. If I'm busy I'll tell you I'm busy, and I'll call you back. Don't go out pissed off at me and drink with the girls all night and give your number to some guy you don't know." I heard him cover the mouth piece and shout something to Crisis. "Eme, I have to go."

"Okay. Logan?"

"Yeah."

"I'm sorry. I mean for whatever happened to you after ... you know, after you," I took a deep breath, "got me out."

There was breathing on the other end, but he didn't respond.

"Deck said last night ... he respects you. He said it was bad after I left. It had to do with me leaving, didn't it?"

He still didn't answer.

"Tell me he didn't hurt you." I felt the tears well up, because I knew. Deck wouldn't push this if it wasn't something horrible, and knowing Raul and his cruel streak, I suspected he didn't take me leaving and Logan's involvement very well.

"I'll call you later before the gig. Coffee. Advil. Then a big breakfast. Okay?"

"You're not going to tell me, are you?"

"Eat something, Eme."

"Okay."

"If Ethan calls, you tell him you don't date dogs."

I smiled. Logan hung up.

I held the phone to my chest, trying to hold back tears. I realized that Logan not saying anything meant whatever went down had been bad. Raul was cruel, but would he have harmed his own son? I knew already—yes. Raul wouldn't let anyone get away with making him out to be a fool.

Chapter Twenty-One

Logan texted me numerous times over the next couple days. Little reminders that he was sweet and ... yes, he was reminding me of the Logan I once loved. He still laid it out raw and in my face that this—us—was going somewhere, but instead of getting angry at him for pushing for more than I wanted, I found myself smiling and rolling my eyes.

Logan would be back in four days, and despite our recent texting and conversations, I still had trouble trusting him. Once he got back, I knew things would have to change, and I did realize that I may have to move from the farm sooner than I had anticipated. Logan and I may be talking, but living together was not something I was even close to considering.

He'd called last night twice. It was noisy and difficult to talk when Crisis and Kite kept yelling at one another while playing what sounded like a video game in the background. So, he called me back later after the guys crashed. I lay in bed talking to him for an hour, mostly about stuff we liked, music, food, movies. It wasn't deep, but it was nice, and it was normal. Logan and I hadn't had much normal.

I picked up my phone which sadly, I hated to admit, went everywhere with me in case Logan texted—pathetic—and ran downstairs. Kat was already sitting on the couch, a bowl of popcorn on her lap and two glasses of red wine on the coffee table. We'd decided that an evening of *The Walking Dead* was in order.

I plopped down and grabbed my pillow and beer then set my phone on the table. Kat glanced at it, brows raised. Then she smiled and stuck her tongue out and wiggled it.

"Gross, Kat."

"You won't be saying that when he gets back and has his head between your thighs." She turned up the volume on the TV when I started stuttering my objection.

I reached over and picked up a kernel of popcorn and threw it at her.

It hit her right on the temple. I heard the sound of ripping guts in the background.

"It's not like that." I popped a few kernels in my mouth and took a sip of wine.

Kat picked up a piece of popcorn and threw it back at me. I turned my head at the last second, and it bounced off my ear. "Sculpt wants in your pants."

"Sculpt was in my pants, now he doesn't get that." I threw the rest of my handful of popcorn at her. It tangled in her hair, and she set her wine down then picked it out one at a time. "Talking to Sculpt is my therapy."

"Bah, it's more than that. You're constantly looking at your phone to see if he's texted, you're so falling for him—again."

"You're wrong. It's not like that."

Kat put her hands over her ears and started singing—loud. I threw a handful of popcorn at her laughing. "I've seen the way you look at him. You're drooling. Panting. Your wet panties will be off the moment he says, 'Come here Emily.'"

I tried to control the burst of laughter at Kat's Logan

impression and failed. "Kat," I yelled then grabbed for the bowl of popcorn. She squealed diving for it at the same time. We both had a hold of the bowl, and popcorn was everywhere. Kat tugged hard, and I let go at the same time. We both went flying backward and landed on floor opposite one another. Kat grabbed a handful of popcorn and shoved it all in her mouth then we were rolling on the floor laughing hysterically.

"What the shit?"

I had no clue whose voice that was, and I quickly scrambled to my feet, hearing the crunch of popcorn beneath me.

"Ream," Kat garbled on her overflowing mouth of popcorn.

Oh fuck. Standing in the doorway looking at us like we were crazy was Kat's Ream. Well, not her Ream per say, but Brett said he was, and by the way his eyes were traveling over her I was thinking he was right.

Kat was still on the floor, her hair covered in white kernels.

"Kat." Ream walked further into the room then dropped his bag on the floor. He wore a white T-shirt, and ink crawled down his arms and up his neck on the right side. He was leaner than Logan and about an inch shorter which meant he was still really tall. "Emily." He nodded to me.

Kat got up and looked from Ream to the bag. "What's this?"

"Crashing here."

Kat slowly brushed off the white kernels. "Really? Surprising, considering you can't stand to be in the same room as me."

"Fuck, Kitkat." Kitkat? He had a nickname for her? Holy shit, there was way more between them than Kat had told her about. "Don't start."

"Not starting anything, just pointing out the facts." Kat started picking up the kernels on the floor and tossing them in the bowl. She was acting nonchalant, but there was more to it than that. Kat was uncomfortable; she never fidgeted. Right now she was doing everything she could to not look at Ream.

"Jesus, Kat, that's not true."

"You expect to stay here?" Kat grabbed the bowl of popcorn, walked into the kitchen and placed it in the sink before turning around and looking at Ream. "You have the nerve to stay here? I can't believe you."

"Farm is Logan's. The band is back in T.O., so that means we're staying here."

"Yeah, I know. But I assumed you wouldn't. You know I live here Ream, and I don't want you anywhere near me," Kat burst out.

Ream's face hardened, and I dropped to my knees and quickly began picking up stray popcorn kernels Kat had missed. The history between these two was explosive and not in a good way.

"Kat." Ream ran his hand through his hair. "You have to get why I couldn't do it."

"You fucked off as soon as I had a little freak out over my shit. Not cool. You need a reward for shittiest move ever."

"Kat, you're not being fair." His voice was calm, but there was an edge to it. "That's some serious shit."

Her voice hardened. "Damn right it is. And I saw your face when I told you. Your feet were running before I finished speaking."

I had no idea what they were talking about, which was strange because I'd known Kat since we were kids. What serious shit did Ream now know that I didn't?

Ream's face dropped. "Fuck, Kitkat. That's bull. I needed time to take it in."

Kat threw up her arms. "You know what? I really don't give a crap anymore. Sleep wherever the hell you want." Kat stalked off into her bedroom and slammed the door.

I looked up at Ream and wished I hadn't. The guy looked pissed, eyes cold as if he was going to join *The Walking Dead* crew and rip zombie heads from their shoulders.

"Sculpt's back but dealing with some shit."

"Why is the band back early?"

"That's Sculpt's deal." Ream avoided my eyes as he threw his bag over his shoulder then glanced at Kat's closed bedroom door, shook his head, and walked up the stairs to the second floor.

I finished cleaning up, turned off the TV, and went and knocked on Kat's door. "It's me. You want to talk?"

I heard her walking across the hardwood floors then the door opened. She'd been crying. Her face was all blotchy, and there were tears rolling down her cheeks. Shit. What was going on between those two?

I took one step and pulled her into a hug. She wrapped her arms around me and then sobbed on my shoulder. Kat pulled back and wiped her tears away with her arm then sniffled. "Thanks, Eme. But I can't talk about it now. And I see your face ... Yeah, I should've told you a long time ago, but it's ... I don't ever want to be treated differently."

I had no idea what she was talking about. Why would I treat her differently?

But whatever it was Ream knew, it was serious, which meant I understood why it was hard to talk about. "You need me ... anytime, Kat. Okay?"

She smiled, but her lips were quivering, and I knew she was trying to hold back. I heard her door close behind me.

Chapter Twenty-Two

The bed dipped.

My eyes flew open, and I came face to face with Logan. He was sitting beside me, his back up against the headboard, his legs resting on the mattress, ankles crossed. His hair was wet, and a few drops had fallen and were making blotches on the shoulders of his white T-shirt. He looked absolutely delicious and sexy, and he was in my bed.

"Logan?"

"Eme." His voice was low and quiet, deeper when he spoke like that. Sexier. "Go back to sleep."

He was going to watch me sleep? I was uncertain whether I was comfortable with that or not. The intimacy of him sitting in bed, albeit fully clothed, was unsettling. Okay, really unsettling, because it reminded me of those nights in Mexico when he held me to him after we had sex, and I had loved those moments.

I frowned when I saw the cut above his right eye and knew instantly why he arrived back later than Ream. I was disappointed really. He didn't have to fight anymore, and he'd told me he hated it. So, why was he still doing it? "Did you win?"

His mouth twitched, and my belly did this flip and dive and left an insatiable ache. God, I wanted to grab him and taste his lips so badly that I nearly reached up and touched his face. Damn it, my sleepy-self needed some control.

"I never lose. You know that."

Figures. Actually, it was hard to imagine Logan lying on the ground after getting the shit kicked out of him. My heart picked up speed at the thought. I never wanted to see him like that. Was that what happened in Mexico after I left? Was Deck trying to tell me that Logan had lost a fight really badly? Maybe Raul had done something to him because he lost?

"I don't fight like that anymore. Haven't since the night you got out." Oh. So that blew that theory up. "The cut is from breaking up an altercation Crisis had at the last venue."

"Then why are you here so late?"

I expected hesitation or some sign that he'd avoid telling me or not tell me at all. Instead he surprised me when he said, "Had a meeting with Deck."

"Deck? What kind of meeting?" Why would he have a 'meeting' with Deck?

"Go to sleep, Mouse."

"Logan, maybe you should—"

He scowled, and I felt like smiling. He was good at looking mad, and yet for some reason I just felt like running my finger over his lowered brows. It was strange, because this is how I used to feel when we were together.

I wanted him to hold me while I slept. There was nothing sexual about it, just to feel protected and cared for. He'd always given me that. Even when he had no choice but to hurt me, he still protected me, I just hadn't known it.

"Close your eyes." Logan looked down at me and waited until I did as he asked. "Dream sweet, Emily."

When I woke, Logan was gone, but his imprint remained on me and the bed. I had no clue how long he stayed; all I knew was that I could still smell him. I rolled over and hugged the pillow where he'd been and breathed in deep. He was back. I pressed the pillow into my face and moaned.

After showering, taking extra care to shave and wash my hair, I dressed in my chocolate-brown breeches with a snug black T-shirt.

When I came out to the kitchen, Kat was standing at the counter looking rather disheveled. She was dressed in ripped jeans, a grubby top with paint splattered all over it, and her hair needed an appointment with a brush. I found it surprising to see her awake considering she usually fell out of bed five minutes before she went out to the horses. But from the looks of her, she had probably been painting all night.

She half-smiled, and I noticed the puffiness around her eyes. Whatever went down between her and Ream was bad. Kat was tough, and this was wrecking her.

"Hey," Kat mumbled then tagged her coffee and went and sat at the island.

I was in the middle of pouring myself one when I felt a presence behind me. I nearly dropped the coffee pot when his hands rested on my hips. My body reacted to him instantly, and I felt the goose bumps race along my skin like wildfire.

His breath wafted across my bare neck, and I closed my eyes as I tried to control the urge to swing around and launch myself into his arms.

"Morning," he whispered into my ear.

It was the most erotic words I'd ever heard. Low and graveled with a hint of sex as if we'd just made passionate love all night and he was kissing my neck as he said the words. I wanted him to kiss my neck, to feel his lips against my skin. Damn it, the touch of his breath was enough to cause an ache so intense between my legs, I thought I might have to go back to my room and bring out my bunny before I could function.

I found my voice, but it crackled. "Um, morning."

"Dream sweet?"

I wish he'd back away so I could think clearly. I couldn't even pick up my coffee without him seeing my hands tremble. I nodded.

"Good." His fingers squeezed my hips as he leaned closer, his mouth inches away from my ear. "You're sexy while you sleep."

Jesus.

When he moved away, I took several deep breaths before turning around. Coffee in hand, I immediately met Kat's eyes. Her brows rose, and she pretended to undo her pants. I shot her an evil glare and glanced at Logan who thankfully had his back to us while he browsed through the fridge.

My gaze froze on him. Logan wasn't wearing his shirt, and every muscle was visible, flexing with each movement he made while shifting things around in the fridge. He had a tattoo that went from the top of his right shoulder down the back of his shoulder blade midway to his waist then it swung around to I guessed, his chest. I never expected the stunning drawings of what appeared like a horse merged with a hawk surrounded by what I could see of it—a dragon's tail. I also got a good glimpse of the side tat that said, Tear Asunder in calligraphy writing.

Christ, I was drooling.

He straightened then turned with the milk jug in hand. My mouth dropped open as I stared at his chest. Memories of him hit me like a huge wave of heat. How I used to touch him, hold him, curl into him, and yes, even the memories I tried to forget but couldn't. Of us in the shower. Kneeling. Taking his cock into my mouth. When he'd tell me to undress. To lie down and give myself completely to him. It turned me on and I wanted it again—I wanted the dominant Logan without the fear that had come with it during those fifteen days. And he was making that happen.

He must have known I was gawking by the way his mouth twitched as he watched me watch him.

I quickly looked down at my feet and went and sat beside Kat who was eyeing us both. She unzipped her jeans and the sound echoed. I gasped. She laughed then hid it by clearing her throat. At least I'd made her smile.

Logan wasn't paying attention to us as he chugged back the contents of the milk then threw it in the recycling bin. When he looked over at me, I glanced away. I was confident over the phone that I could resist him but now—now I wasn't so sure.

"When are you leaving to see that horse?"

He remembered. I told him about a new client the other day. The potential to expand my cliental from this one client was enormous considering he was involved in the thoroughbred racing community. If I helped his horse then word would spread and I could gain more cliental which meant having my own farm sooner than I planned. "Umm well, I said I'd be there for ten. So shortly." Was my voice quaking? Did he notice?

"I'll take you."

"What?" Shit. Not a good idea. Spending even a few hours close to him wasn't a good idea. Kat was right, I was caving and it terrified me. "I don't think that would be a—"

"Eme. Lego. Stop." His short abrupt use of my nickname sent a jolt right through me. "We've been talking on the phone for weeks, now were going to talk in person." He leaned against the counter, palms on either side of him resting on the marble surface. With his stance like that, it made his tatted arm muscles bulge and his chest to ... "Emily?"

My gaze darted away from his arms and up to his face. His eyes danced with mischief and I suspected Logan knew exactly how to make himself look irresistible. He'd never done that during the weeks in Mexico. Never flirted, never looked at me with anything other than cold steel eyes.

"I don't like people around when I'm working so ..." Yeah, he so wasn't going to take no for an answer.

"You're not going alone. You don't know who this guy is and

it's not safe. I'm not taking any chances." Logan's tone had turned calm and assertive. He was going to push this.

"Then I'll take Kat."

She held up both hands. "Sorry, Eme. No go. I have the farrier coming this morning and twenty horses getting trimmed and a deadline for the gallery for two more paintings by the end of the week."

Shit. "Then I'll call Deck."

"Deck has better things to do," Logan said abruptly.

Yeah, like hunt down guys like Raul and save girls like Raven. "I've been seeing clients' horses for two years. I'm not changing now because you're suddenly back and being overprotective. The guy is well known in the racing world and—"

"You're not going alone."

"Ugh." I looked to Kat and she immediately jumped in. "Sculpt, you're being ridiculous. This is her business now. She helps horses and—"

"Stay out of it, Kat. This isn't overprotective, this is being cautious."

I put my coffee cup down a little too hard on the counter and dark liquid spilled over the sides. "Fine." Was I crazy? Yes. I had sucker written all over my forehead, but a part of me—okay a huge part of me—was excited about spending the day with Logan.

Ream strode into the kitchen looking just as bad as Kat. The tension went from about sixty to a thousand within seconds. Kat's back stiffened and she glared at Ream who was avoiding looking at her all together. He did say morning though then grabbed a mug and poured a coffee.

Ream chin-lifted to Logan. I noticed his quick glance at Kat. "Where are Crisis and Kite?"

"Went to Avalanche last night. This morning ... passed out with chicks I suspect."

Ream huffed. "Thinking I should've been with them."

The scrape of the stool moving across the hardwood floors

sounded then Kat took off to her bedroom. I noticed as soon as her back was turned, Ream's eyes never left her.

Chapter Twenty-Three

When Logan said he'd drive, I didn't expect it to be on his motorcycle, I mean, I should've, but I didn't think about it.

He stroked the handlebars, his long fingers a gentle caress like he was touching a woman's back. My lips parted as I watched.

Damn it, I was going to explode before I even got on the bloody bike.

"You've been on my bike before, why do you look like I'm asking you to kick a kitten?"

"I just ... it's been a while. I'm uncomfortable." What woman wouldn't want to ride on the back of a bike with someone like Logan. This situation is like a fantasy come true and another step toward what I was desperately trying to avoid.

"Uncomfortable? I assume it's having your pussy tight to my ass that has you—uncomfortable." His lips quirked upward, and it catapulted me back to when he'd been eyeing a bike at the corner store where we used to stop and get ice cream. His eyes had lit up like a kid on Christmas morning. He had a bike; I'd been on it, but it was nothing like the one we saw that day.

The owner came out of the store, and they chatted for a half hour about motors while I went and got us ice cream sandwiches then ate both of them while leaning up against his truck admiring his sweet ass.

"You remember that bike we—"

"Saw at the convenience store," I finished. "Yeah. You had a hard-on for it."

Logan choked back a laugh, and the sound sent a thrill of desire straight through me. "Eme. I had a hard-on for you. The bike was a bonus." He picked up a helmet then gently slid it down over my head. He tucked in strands of hair then did up the chin strap. He leaned back. "You still rock a helmet, baby."

I don't know what came over me, but I hit a pose, putting my finger to my mouth and cocking my hip with my other hand resting on it.

This time he laughed outright, flashing his white, perfectly aligned teeth. I turned into a splat of butter sizzling on high heat. The guy was brooding and demanding most of the time. When he laughed, it was like filling me up with a rainbow.

He turned serious. "You still don't get how hot you are, do you?"

No. I was fine with how I looked; I mean, I accepted what I was given.

"Your mother is a piece of work. She put you down to make herself feel better. You deserve better than a piss-drunk mother."

"She had issues. And Logan, I think your father takes the 'piece of work' award."

"Fuckin' right he does. When we're good, you're meeting my mom and finding out what a real one is like."

I was taken aback by Logan's casual mention of his mom and me meeting her. He was right, my mom was a bitch. She never gave a crap when I moved out and in with Kat and Matt. The only time I heard from her was if she broke up with a guy and needed money, which I rarely had. Since she knew nothing about the farm or where to find me, I hadn't spoken to her in years.

"Eme?" He stroked a line down my nose. "You have that look. What's happening in that non-stop thinking brain of yours?"

"Nothing."

He slipped his hand into mine, and our fingers linked. The scent of his soap drifted into me, and I inhaled deep, closing my eyes. I couldn't let go even if a train came between us. I wanted to cry for what I was slowly losing—myself. I was losing myself to him again, and no matter how much I wanted to keep him out, he was breaking his way back in. But he'd leave with the band again, and I'd leave his farm. Even though Logan had given me the ability to have my dream, it wasn't my farm. I'd lived off Matt, now Logan. I couldn't do it anymore. I wouldn't. And soon, I'd have enough money to get my own place.

"Emily?" I met his eyes. "Let go of what happened for today."

Did I have that in me? Could I let the old Logan I loved in for one day?

"Baby."

The bike. The horses. Logan looking at me like I was the only woman in the world. All reminders. Could I trust him? No, that wasn't the question anymore, I realized. It was could I trust myself with him?

I nodded, and the weight of the helmet slipped forward, and he grinned as he shifted it back. "Small head considering all the shit it carries around."

I smiled. He was right.

He put on his helmet, and I slapped my hand on the top where the painted skull was. Underneath were the words Tear Asunder. "What does it mean? I mean I know it means tear apart, but what does it mean to the band? Why the band name?"

"What was done to us. The band voted. And since the band was also torn apart for a while, as well as you and I, well, it fit."

He snapped the kickstand up then started the bike, revving the throttle. He nodded to me, and I slipped on behind him. I was in shock. It meant ... it meant Logan had seen what happened between them as being torn apart. Not him pushing me away. Or me escaping him. It was both of us—Torn apart. Forced. Ripped. Broken.

Did the band know the details of what happened? They had to know about Logan's father and my kidnapping, but how much more?

The moment I slid up against him, my inner thighs next to his outer, my pelvis tight to his ass, I felt the scorching heat sweep through my veins. "Logan?" I barely said his name; it was a hint of a whisper.

"We were torn apart, because Eme—I'd never have stayed away from you any other way."

I had nothing to fight with. Nothing. I felt like falling against him and sobbing for him, for us, and for what had been done to us both.

His hand rested on my thigh, and he squeezed. "Feet." I put my feet up. "Need you closer. Arms." I snuggled in, and then felt the rumble in his chest and what sounded like a groan. "Christ, how far is this place?"

"Logan?" I wanted to tell him ... to have him turn and look at me so I could tell him that I felt it too. We had been torn apart.

"Not now, baby." He shook his head once. "How far?"

I relented. "An hour." I wrapped my arms around his waist, my fingers interlocking. I felt the muscles of his abdomen against my forearms, rock hard and tense. He was breathing in and out rather quickly, and I bet if I reached down I'd feel the hardness a little lower. I bit my lip, swallowed, and then closed my eyes.

"Fuck." Logan shot off, careening down the driveway as if the bike was part of him, and they were part of the road.

It took me five minutes before I relaxed into him. Then I raised my head that had been pressed up against his back and it felt like old times.

It was exhilarating.

The vibration of power beneath me took hold and refused to let go. I felt part of him again.

This was something he loved, which made me love it too.

The ride went by too quickly. Logan stopped the bike outside the gates to a long driveway lined with willow trees. Paddocks with thoroughbreds grazing on the lush grass lined either side. The owner had called me about a racehorse that'd been in an accident. The trailer had flipped over on the Four Hundred highway, and the horse had been trapped for hours. It took the Jaws of Life to get the stallion out, and since then, the horse panicked whenever he felt pressure on him. According to the owner, the champion racehorse also couldn't go into a stall without a tranquilizer.

Logan rolled the bike up to the intercom and pressed the button. A male, with a heavily accented voice, asked if I was Emily. The gates opened as soon as I verified who I was.

I gestured to the long driveway. "Take it slow, rock star. Scare the horses, and I lose this job."

The twitch in the outer corner of his lips appeared. "I like you calling me rock star, Mouse." He turned back, revved the throttle then passed through the gates at a snail's pace.

It took all of five seconds after meeting the owner of the estate and the racehorse before I had to stop Logan from knocking the guy on his ass. Tattooed rock star ex-fighter and rich developer didn't mix; unfortunately developer guy Rob wanted his racehorse fixed, and supposedly, I was his last hope.

Blame it on the sweetness of my name—shit, I don't know— but Rob took me in with his eyes, and it was clear he planned to have me in his bed by noon. Logan was juicing up his male testosterone, ready to slam his fist through Rob's aristocratic face as soon as Rob's eyes went from my face down to my toes.

Rob wore a cocky expression and a half-smile as he took my hand and kissed it. "I wasn't expecting a beautiful woman. I'm a little caught off guard here, Emily. I'm suddenly wishing now that I was the stallion with the issue."

Uh oh.

Logan was standing behind me, but out of nowhere he was in front, the bulldog effect. I put my hand on his arm and squeezed. *Please don't ruin this for me.* Rob was willing to pay whatever it took, and the horse needed me.

Rob laughed; it was more of a fake crackle really. "Sculpt from Tear Asunder. Just saw your picture in the *Toronto Now* magazine. Didn't know you had a hand in horses. Not thoroughbreds, I imagine. I know everyone in the racing world. Shetlands, perhaps?"

I balked. I knew Logan wouldn't have any idea what a Shetland was, and I was thanking God for that. The miniature ponies were cute and fuzzy, not something Logan would find amusing coming from Rob.

"Emily and I bring in abused horses. We're not prejudice about the breed." Logan looped his arm around my shoulders and tugged me close. Logan obviously believed that possession was nine-tenths of the law.

Suddenly Logan had made us into a couple, and I was uncertain whether he was just saying that to give Rob that impression or if he really did consider us together.

Rob's brows rose. "Oh, I didn't realize. And the pretty blonde in the picture?"

Wow. Rob knew how to play hardball, and I tried to ignore the comment, but still a wave of jealousy sifted through me at the thought of any pretty blonde on his arm. Was she a groupie maybe? Kat said the band was pretty popular now, and there would be tons of girls wanting more than just a picture with Logan.

I cleared my throat trying to draw both of their attention away from one another. "So, where's the horse?"

Logan set his helmet down on the seat of his bike. It was a calculated move—slow, deliberate, and it freed up his hands. I'm sure Rob had no idea that Logan grew up fighting.

And I was going to lose a client which possibly meant a whole slew of new clients.

"I don't play games, *Richard*. Emily belongs with me. You want to fuck with that then we have a problem. Give me a problem, then it makes Emily have one. She wants to work for an ass like you, that's her business. You hitting on her, that's mine."

Yeah. I just lost a client.

My heart was racing probably just as fast as a thoroughbred's in a starting gate. Rob was watching us both, his face showing me nothing as to whether he was going to kick us off the property or not.

"Let's see that horse, shall we." Rob turned and walked towards the barn, and I breathed a heavy sigh of relief. Then I smacked Logan in the chest. I hurt my hand, but refused to admit to it.

Logan didn't react, but what he did do was cup my face, lean down and meet my eyes. "You, Emily. You're worth fighting for. I fought all my life, but never for anything worthwhile. Now ... Now I'm fighting for my heart. Bullshit ends here and now."

Any argument I had was burned with those words. But I couldn't help still imagining him with his arm around some blonde. I pulled from his grasp and stepped back. "And the blonde?"

His look of surprise changed to a smile. "Blonde was a fan, baby. Wanted an autograph for her little brother." He was quick as he snagged me around the waist and kissed me on the lips. "But I love you being jealous. It's hot."

"Hey, you coming? Horse is behind the stable," Rob called.

Logan dropped his hands from my waist and I turned and headed for the barn, hearing Logan's sexy chuckle behind me.

Logan

Logan watched Emily work with the chestnut stallion in the round pen. The dance she played with the horse was mesmerizing.

She became another person, calmness settling over her as if nothing the stallion did could unglue her. She was patient and relaxed with a steady, consistent confidence that the stallion tried to test time and again with his antics.

It was magical. Emily was magical.

This bullshit she kept putting up between them had to stop. The bike—Christ, the bike with her up against him—was hot and pure torture. He could feel her body quivering, the pulse of her heartbeat against his back. It took two years to get the shit out of his life that robbed both of them of a chance together. According to Deck last night—that shit still wasn't gone.

Rob had sent him into fight mode. He made it damn clear that Emily was his, and if developer slime ball didn't respect that, then he was hauling her ass out of there. Not a chance was she working for some guy who didn't respect her. Shit like that led to unwanted attention, and unwanted attention led to worse shit.

Rob came to stand beside him, arms hooking over the third rail of the fence. Logan didn't bother acknowledging him.

"She's good."

Logan remained silent.

"I was skeptical when I heard about 'the girl who speaks to horses.' Googled her, but didn't find much. Surprising considering how good she is."

Logan kept his eyes forward. Emily was in the middle of the ring, eyes downcast, her body language inviting the stallion in. The horse's eyes were calmer now. Then he lowered his head and walked slowly toward her. It was a beautiful sight. Ten minutes ago the whites of the stallion's eyes were blazing, his muscles contracting, fear emanating from his every pore.

The stallion nudged her in the back with his muzzle, and Emily slowly turned and began stroking his nose.

"Ten minutes," Rob said while shaking his head. "My guys have been trying to get near this horse for weeks."

Logan chin-lifted toward her. "She's always had a way with

horses."

"Sounds like you've known her a while?"

"Yeah, a while." Logan kept his eyes glued to Eme. God, it reminded him of when they'd sit and watch the herd of quarter horses all day and she'd explain what they were doing, how a horse was telling the other to screw off. He could never see it, but Eme ... It was like she saw into them.

"Where did you meet?"

He really didn't feel like explaining his past to some dick who hit on his girl, but he'd play semi-cordial for Emily's sake. "An underground fighting ring."

"Damn." Rob cleared his throat then continued, "She needs a website. Your girl is good. She'd do well in the racing community. High profile. Lots of money." Rob nodded toward Emily. "She's a natural. If word gets out, and I'll make sure it does, she'll be turning down clients she'll be so busy."

He liked Rob calling Emily "your girl." Maybe the guy wasn't so bad after all— Fuck no. He was a guy, and he'd been thinking of getting in Emily's pants. That thought doesn't disappear because the guy got shot down. He's still thinking what's beneath her tight ass, and it pissed Logan off.

"Emily doesn't have a website, might be because she doesn't want to be busy."

"Money talks. Never known anyone who'd turn it down. You ever turn down a gig if the money is good?"

No. But he would if need be.

"Better clear it with her before you go publicizing." And she wasn't traipsing off to every dick's farm alone, not fuckin' now. Jesus, he was on edge every second she was out of his sight. Shit had to go down soon or he'd have to tell her what was happening and he'd do everything he could to avoid that. Seeing that fear in her eyes again—no. Never. Again. Deck said they were close. That he was handling it.

Rob turned to him, brows raised, eyes questioning. "Pretty

hard to stay in the shadows when you're dating the lead singer of an up-and-coming band."

"Yeah well, Eme's tougher than she looks. She'll deal with whatever is thrown her way." And those words were truer than Rob would ever know. Eme had spirit, more than she gave herself credit for; he'd seen it in her the day they met.

Shit, Emily had come right up to him at in an abandoned warehouse where he'd just pulverized his opponent. He had a cut on his temple, blood running down his face, and no shirt.

She'd wrapped her small, delicate hand around his bicep, and he remembered wondering where the sexy blonde who had latched onto him had fucked off to. He'd just won a shitload of money and was running off adrenaline. Raul had been there that night. It was the first time Logan had seen him since he was sixteen; so he was revved up and fucked up.

Emily had been wearing short cut-off jeans, a cute little pink top with sparkles on the front, and her hair was a mess. Her long, brown strands reached past her shoulders and were having a hard time deciding which side to part on.

Did he fall in love right there? No. Not even close. She was timid and couldn't meet his eyes; there was no sexiness about her. Fuck, he could remember thinking that fucking her would be boring as hell. He told her he didn't do brunettes. Not a lie, he never did.

He would've walked away and never given her a second thought except when she said, "I need to learn how to fight."

He'd laughed, pretty damn hard, and he rarely laughed. She looked like a mouse—small, couldn't be more than five foot four, tiny little nose, petite waist, sweet hips. He remembered thinking for one second, despite her meekness, that those hips would be nice to grab as he pumped into her from behind. That thought pulverized when she told him why she wanted to learn how to fight, and then he felt like a goddamn schmuck for thinking that.

Then Kite came up, and that was it. Girl forgotten.

But she persisted, and that's when he knew there was something more to her than he first thought. When she grabbed his arm, fingers curling around his bicep, he'd looked down at her small hand against his skin and felt strange warmth shoot through him. He told her to let go, but the words didn't stick, because for some reason he didn't want her to let him go. At the time, he'd put it to the adrenalinestill rifting through him.

He watched as she shook her head to tell him she wasn't listening. Her hair fell in front of her eyes, and he had the urge to push it back. It was like a sucker punch to the solar plexus. He didn't like getting sucker punched—at all.

She looked down at her feet, shuffled a bit then met his gaze dead on. When she said, "I was attacked after work by a guy ..."

Rage rose up in him so fuckin' high that he was ready to get in the ring and beat the crap out of his next opponent. The words tearing out of his mouth felt like acid, and he could only hold his breath waiting for an answer, because if this chick was getting—Jesus, he couldn't even say the word and the thought made him sick to his stomach. It brought back memories of the screams, the girls beaten, the abuse, and his father. It may have hit him harder than usual because of seeing his father that night. But when he asked if she was sexually assaulted and she told him no, it was like a wave of cool relief blanketed him.

Thank fuck.

He had stared down at the delicate fingers over his bulging muscle. Imagining that hand curled into a fist ... No, he couldn't.

Then he was being an asshole, telling her how she could never fight, because really, picturing this girl having to fight anyone was pissing him off. He felt like wrapping her up in his arms and carrying her away from all the bad shit in the world.

Then what did he fuckin' do ...? He led her into the worst sludge of the world—his father.

He'd brought her gift-wrapped to *his father*. "Jesus."

"Logan?" Emily's hand rested on his arm, still small and

delicate, just like the first time he met her.

Looking at her now, he didn't know why he hadn't fallen in love with her the moment he laid eyes on her. She was perfect—the way her lashes dropped to cover half her eyes when she was thinking, how her breasts peaked perfectly beneath her shirt, and her thighs, damn her thighs were rock solid. He felt every bit of them on his bloody bike.

But it was way more than that. His girl had a strong empathy for horses, and the way she was around them, it was sexy as hell. God, she couldn't see how beautiful she was which drove him crazy, but when she was with those horses, her uncertainty or insecurity or mistrust vanished. Determined as hell, yet still sensual and ... feminine. Her determination was playing against him right now, but despite that he respected her more for it, Jesus, he'd dragged her into hell and hurt her.

She didn't see her strength, but he saw it from the beginning. God, he prayed every fuckin' day that Raul or Alfonzo or Jacob wouldn't break her. And he'd been so fuckin' proud of her when she stood up to his piece-of-crap father, and even though it was the worst play she could've done, a part of him wanted to pull her into his arms and cry— Because she wasn't broken. Emily never gave up.

Logan groaned, as he wrapped her into his arms and sighed when she came willingly. Jesus, he loved this woman. He'd thought of nothing except her for two years. She didn't know what went down after he let her go, and he'd never tell her; she didn't need that tainting her life. But it was her that gave him the strength to survive the hell Raul put him through. Deck ... He owed Deck his life for getting him out.

He squeezed her to him. "You looked hot, Mouse. Out there with that stallion ... I'm buying you more horses."

"I can buy my own horses, Logan."

He loved when she called him Logan. Eme and his mother were the only ones who called him that. Now he was called Logan by two remarkable women in his life that survived his father. And Deck. Deck survived his father too and risked his life. He got him out of there and witnessed the shape he was in. Deck wanted him to tell Eme what happened, but he couldn't. She had enough horror in her life; she didn't need to hear his horror. He'd shield her from that forever if he could.

"I know you can, it's not the same thing."

He caressed her cheek, and she leaned into his touch, her eyes closing as she sighed.

"Rescue horses."

"Hmmm?"

"You want to buy horses? Save the ones that need it."

That was his Emily. "Whatever you want." He kissed her forehead. "Trophy, Emily. You're a trophy."

Chapter Twenty-Four

When we pulled up to the house, Crisis and Kite were sitting on the porch drinking beers, and Ream was leaning against the railing.

I unsnapped my helmet and passed it to Logan who placed it on the handle bars beside his. I quickly ran my fingers through my hair while avoiding his eyes. "I'll, ah ... see you later. I better check on the horses."

I turned, my heart in my throat and the familiar ache pulsating. Being with Logan today had been ... it was like the sun burning through the fog of my mind. And there in the brightness stood Logan and he was protective and strong and willing to do anything to repair us. Did I trust him? I believed him, so why was I hesitating on trusting him?

Logan tagged my hand and reeled me back in.

"No more running." His thumb casually stroked the back of my hand, and it felt good. Really good.

"I'm not running—"

"You are." He tugged, and I was up against his chest, breath seized, and he was watching me with those sexy heart-stopping eyes. "Why, baby?" His hands squeezed mine, and I felt that familiar warmth of his protectiveness come over me. He knew when I needed soft, encouraging words, or rough, harsh commands. He liked control; I got that and he did it well, I wanted that escape he gave me when I didn't have to think and just felt. God, he knew me better than I knew myself. In Mexico there had been no trust; now our relationship had to have it more than anything.

"Logan. The trust between us, it's still—"

He stopped me, leaning in and kissing me on the lips. It was hard, and it was sweet. When he pulled back, the soft skin on our lips held briefly together like when you touch your tongue to a dry ice cube. "Trust is built. Ours just needs to be rebuilt and it takes time. But baby, we'll do it together."

And for the first time, I gave into him completely. I let go of my head shit and what happened and took in what he was giving me—him. And God, it felt like the elephant sitting on my chest finally got up and walked away.

All chatter stopped, and three sets of eyes landed on me and Logan as we walked up onto the porch.

"Sweetness, looking mighty fine on that bike." Crisis winked. "I'm thinkin' now I need to get myself one." His slight draw was sex on wheels with that voice and look. "Pussy tight against—"

Logan interrupted abruptly. "And you know Kite." I nodded to him, and he smiled. With those cheekbones and brilliant green eyes, he must have broken hearts in every bar they went. "Emily. Good to see you again."

Kite had ink all over his arms, and the left side of his neck was a hawk or eagle in flight. He had a shaved head and several piercings, one being on his left eye brow. He looked scary, but he'd been sweet when he'd protected me against Matt's wrath that night we snuck in to watch Logan's underground fight.

"Hey, Kite."

"And you know Ream."

"Um, yeah. We met briefly at Georgie's and again last night." Kat's sexy, hot monster that lacked a smile but oozed in sex appeal.

"Be right back." Logan went inside, and the screen door slammed shut behind him.

I sat on the wooden swing chair, and it creaked.

"Haven't seen Sculpt look so relaxed in months." Kite winked at me.

"He's been a fuckin' asshole," Crisis said.

"You've been the asshole. With that shit you pulled with that chick's boyfriend. Not doing us any favors," Ream said. "You know you can leave the band any time you want."

Whoa. I was uncertain what was going on, but Ream was glaring at Crisis, and Crisis was smirking.

The screen door creaked open, and Logan came out holding two cold beers. He passed me one then sat beside me, his thigh right up against mine. He put his arm around the back of the swing, his fingers weaving into my hair as he played with it.

"Sculpt says you've been doing well with the talking to horses thing," Kite said.

"Well, I wouldn't exactly call it talking to horses. But yes, I communicate to them in their language—body language you could say."

"Know any other body language talkers, Emily? This horse could use a real talking to." Crisis looked down at himself, and both Ream and Kite sprayed beer out their mouths.

Ream wiped his mouth with the back of his hand. "Don't pay attention to him, Emily. He's just pissed his little pony didn't get any last night."

Logan stiffened. "Jesus, guys. Enough."

"Ream, what the fuck's your issue? On your monthly again?" Crisis set his beer down hard on the table beside him. "You all pissy because Kat asked me to go riding tomorrow and not you?

Bet you're wondering what kind of riding we'll be doing."

Ream was clenching his fists, and Crisis was smiling as if he wanted to fight. Logan leaned into me, his arm around shoulders pulling me closer as he whispered, "Baby. Shit, I'm sorry."

Crisis took a long drag of beer. "Logan was brooding and quiet, Emily. I swear the only time he spoke was when we got up on stage. I don't know why the fuck it took him ten months to get back here. Jesus, if I was screwing something hot like you, I'd have been back to Toronto fucking pronto."

"Jesus, Crisis. Cool it." Logan glared at him and was shaking his head back and forth.

"Two years you mean," Eme corrected.

Crisis's brow rose and he raised his beer to Logan. "You're up, buddy."

"Logan?"

He swept my hair back with his fingers then trailed a caress down the side of my face. "Took a while to get back. Needed some time alone after that shit."

"What Deck was talking about?"

He paused and I thought he wasn't going to tell me then he said, "Yeah."

I didn't push it. It wasn't the time or place to talk about it, but I was glad that he didn't close me down this time.

"Sweet mother of God, look at her." Crisis stood, his eyes on Kat who was walking toward the house. She had on a pair of tight faded cut-off jeans, an even tighter turquoise tank top, and a pair of leather paddock boots. "I so need to get into her pants."

Ream caught what Crisis was looking at, and I saw the instant tension go from his jaw right down to his feet. His eyes narrowed, and his brows lowered. His hands clenched the railing, and if the wood had any give in it, the thing was breaking under the pressure.

Kat walked up the steps.

"Fuck, babe. Lookin' good. That sweet ass can sit in my saddle anytime," Crisis said.

Kat laughed, but she didn't object and sauntered close to Crisis and snagged his beer, chugging back half of it before setting it back down on the table. That was becoming a habit of hers. Her slow, long lick of her lips had Crisis groaning.

"Jesus, Kat. Put some fucking clothes on." Ream's voice was bitter and cruel "You gonna screw everyone in the band like some groupie?"

Holy wow. Ream was raging mad. Like bull fighting mad. I could see his temples throbbing, and his lips were pursed together—tight.

Kat didn't flinch, and I have to say I was proud of her. She smiled and put her arm around Crisis who instantly reciprocated by placing his hand in her back jean pocket and squeezing her ass.

"Least it's only four of you. Not like you ... fucking the hundreds of groupies who kiss your goddamn feet like they're made of ice cream."

"Oh they're not kissing my feet, Kitkat. The ice cream is up a bit further," Ream shot back.

"Yeah, cold and always melting."

Insulting a man's dick was the quickest way to him hating you, and it looked like that was what she was aiming for.

Crisis and Kite threw back their heads in hysterics.

"That's only when you're around," Ream said.

Kat came at him, her cool finally breaking. Crisis snagged her around the waist as she kicked and shouted to let her go. He whispered something in her ear, and she settled down, but Ream was striding toward her and Crisis, and he was ready to pop a blood vessel.

"Not tonight, Ream. Let it the fuck go." Kite slapped Ream on the back, his hand digging into his shoulder, halting him.

"I swear, Kitkat, I'm going to—"

"Take a walk," Logan suddenly thundered.

"You'll regret it man, leave it alone." Kite guided him down the porch steps, and I saw Ream plow his fist into the pillar at the bottom of the steps.

"What's with them?" I whispered to Logan.

"I don't know. But whatever it is, they need to work it out before they kill one another."

Watching Ream walk across the yard with Kite, I knew whatever made Ream and Kat lash out at one another was big. I tried to recall Kat acting weird back when I'd come back from Mexico but I had been so self-absorbed after what happened that I may have missed it.

"So, barbecue. Steaks or burgers?" Crisis had let Kat go, but his hand was still in her back pocket. Kat was zoned out, eyes focused on one thing—Ream.

"You good with steaks?" Logan asked me.

"Well, I'm not really hungry—"

"You're eating, and then you're in my bed," Logan said quietly.

My breath hitched. "Logan, I—"

He was keeping his voice low, so others wouldn't hear. "Eme, we've slept together before."

It was like a medicine ball was lodged in my throat. I tried again. "That was different."

"Did you want to sleep with me?"

"What?"

"Answer me, Eme."

"That isn't fair."

"I'm asking for the truth. Did you?"

"Well, I didn't really have—"

"Eme."

God. "Yes. But Logan, I need some time to digest this. It's too fast, and—"

He pulled me to my feet and dragged me into the house, down a hallway then opened the door to the office. He slammed it behind us. "You had time."

I backed away until I was up against a desk, my hands

gripping the edge.

"But mainly, you're lying." He approached.

I knew that look; it was unbending. Determined. And I wasn't afraid. Not for one second.

I took several deep breaths.

"I see it." His voice was graveled and low.

What did he see? I raised my chin and locked my jaw.

"You want me." He kept his distance a few feet away. "Stop denying it. I know who you are. I know what you need and what your body needs. There wasn't a single time you weren't turned on when we were together. Not once."

"You're wrong. Public sex wasn't my thing."

He took the final steps toward me. I couldn't control it. Unleashed need blanketed me. He must have seen it, saw me wavering on the edge, the hook that was holding me back from trusting him slowly ripping from my skin.

"Let me love you."

And then I did what I wanted to do since the day he walked back into my life. I crumpled into his arms, and Logan wrapped me in his warm protective embrace. "I loved you, Logan. You didn't care what they did to me, and it was devastating. I know now why and that you had to, but sometimes ... I never want to feel that helpless again."

Logan caressed my hair while his other hand linked with mine and gave a reassuring squeeze. "Whatever happens between us now, it's because we both want it. No one—no one will ever make you feel helpless again. Baby, I love you. I never stopped, and regardless of how destitute you felt, you weren't alone. You'll never be helpless. You're too strong." His fingers stroked the side of my face. "You know what the first thing my mother taught me in that place? To take emotion out of the equation. That's what always made me a good fighter. I never lost control." He sighed. "I've hid my emotions for a long time. I'm good at it.

"When I came back here for you, I needed you to see who I

am, and yeah, I've lost it a few times like with your dance partner at the bar. But Mouse, I'm letting you see all of me so you can learn to trust me again. I need you to trust me again."

I knew that whatever Logan said or did it was always about protecting me. He pushed his authority and liked control, but I trusted him. Sexually, I craved that escape he gave me. It set me free from decisions and as Logan would say, "Lego building".

I sniffled and few tears fell. "I'm sorry. For what you and your mother have been through."

He kissed the tears. "Baby."

I knew that whatever Logan said or did it was to protect me.

Nothing more was said as he held me close. It felt right in his arms. He had done everything for me. That emotionless cage he locked himself in to hide his feelings from his father was to save me. He'd suffered too. We both did. And maybe my body had known all along that the Logan I hated was also the Logan I loved. Maybe my body knew that the man I feared wasn't the real Logan.

"You good, Eme?"

I nodded into his chest, the feel of his muscles sliding across my cheek.

"You're sleeping with me from now on."

My fingers curled into his shirt. Then I nodded.

"You need something from me, tell me. We fight this shit together."

A knock sounded on the door and Crisis yelled, "Hey you guys done makin' out? Fuckin' starving here."

"Emily?"

"Okay." It was a whisper of one word, and with it every Lego previously built up in my head crumbled to the ground at Logan's feet.

I was letting him back in.

He caressed the side of my face, and I leaned into it, sighing. "Make a salad with Kat. We'll do the steaks and potatoes on the barbecue. Okay?"

I nodded.

He took my hand and walked us out of the office.

When the boys yelled that the steaks were ready, Kat and I brought the salad and wine outside to the table on the deck which overlooked the pool. There was never lack of conversation as the men shared stories of the bars they'd performed in and then the excitement over acquiring their new manager Daryl.

"How long are you guys staying?" I asked, uncertain what Logan's plans were.

"Not sure yet, sugar," Crisis replied. "But I'm liking staying here if it means I get to check out two hot chicks every morning." Crisis winked at me, but when he looked at Logan, he was backtracking. "From a distance. Like a mile. Maybe ten miles. Fuck, sorry sweet stuff, but not going to admire you at all. I'll just admire Kat."

Kite chuckled. "You can admire all the babes you want at the party."

"Fuck yeah. Sweet asses aplenty." Crisis wiggled his brows. "This horse needs some jumping."

"You're a pig," Kat said laughing.

Crisis leaned over and put his arm around her, pulling her close. "How high can you jump, sugar?"

"She doesn't jump. Kitkat plows right through." Ream shoved back his chair, picked up his plate, and went inside. There was a loud bang and then crash. Then the front door slammed.

"Shit, Kat. You ever goin' tell us what the fuck went down between you two?" Kite sat back and stretched out his legs, crossing his ankles.

"No." She pushed back her chair and crossed her legs. "And it doesn't matter, I'm never touching that again."

Crisis coughed bullshit under his breath, and Kat smacked his arm. He rubbed it and feigned a pout.

Logan stood up and brought me with him. He leaned over and

whispered. "Help me with the dishes?"

"Yeah, sure." I may have been missing from Logan's life for two years, but I knew exactly what he was doing. Time alone.

Three trips with dishes to the kitchen, and then I was rinsing off the plates in the sink when Logan came up behind me and swept my hair aside with the lightest touch of his finger.

"Eme. Why are you doing that? We have a dishwasher." He shut off the tap, took my hands and pulled me around to face him. Then he grabbed me by the hips and lifted me up onto the counter.

"Logan."

He put his arm around my waist, the other to the nape of my neck. "Fuck, I love it when you say my name. I need to taste you again, baby." He pulled me toward him. The heat of his mouth hit the spot just below my ear and goose bumps sparked across my skin. He trickled light kisses downward, his tongue playing, tasting.

"I like how you shake in my arms. It's like your body can't wait to be with mine." His arm around my waist tightened. "It's known. All this time, it's known you belong to me."

I closed my eyes, my head tilting back. Oh God. What he did to me ...

"Eme."

I don't know why, and I swear I wasn't alone in this, but when a guy tucks your hair behind your ear, it's ... well it's the most erotic, attractive and panty melting move, and Logan did it all the time, so I melted—big time. Liquid heat was running through me, and I let it in.

I met his eyes and explosive desire hit me—hard. Logan's head was tilted, eyes were burning with craving; his lips were slightly parted. Melted wasn't good enough; I was boiling over.

He whispered my name again then claimed my lips; I was his. Not that I'd ever been anyone else's. No, I've always been his.

His pressed into me, hard and warm, unrelenting as his mouth took mine in a slow need, an exploration of what we both craved.

241

My arms wrapped around his neck, fingers curling into his hair, gripping, holding, never letting go as I pulled and tilted his head so I could get deeper.

His groan vibrated in my mouth, and my body shivered.

His hands gripped my ass. "Legs, Eme."

I wrapped my legs around his waist and locked my ankles. I never wanted to let go. Of him. Of Logan.

He trailed kisses down my neck, and I tilted my head back, eyes closed, sighing as his tongue flicked across my heated skin. The wetness between my thighs soaked my panties, and that intense twinge heightened.

"Logan," I murmured.

He groaned against my throat, hand coming up between us to circle my nipple then lightly pinch.

I gasped.

"Christ, I missed you." He continued to circle my nipple, then squeezed. "We're not wasting any more time." His other hand kept me in place holding the back of my head as he met my eyes.

I flexed my thighs, and I knew he felt it by how his hand tightened on the strands of my hair. I pictured him above me, my thighs around him as he slide inside me, the fullness, him driving into me hard then slow. Then I imagined Logan looking down at me before he comes, before I let go to join him.

"Fuckin' hell, Sculpt." Kite sauntered into the kitchen and threw his beer into the empty case on the floor.

I tried to unhook my legs, but Logan wouldn't let me as he grabbed my thigh. He leaned into me and whispered, "Stay. Don't move until I tell you."

Kite opened the fridge and grabbed another beer. "Better get out there. Ream's back and looks like he's pounded back more than a few of something burning."

"Shit," Logan said. "Crisis?"

"Riling it up." Kite opened his beer, and a hiss sounded.

"Fuck." Logan let my legs go, put his hands on my hips and

helped me off the counter. "I have to deal with this, Mouse."

"Okay, I'll finish up here."

Logan snagged my hand. "No. You're not staying here cleaning up. I'll do it tomorrow."

We went outside to the pool, Kite followed. Crisis, Kat, and Ream were there and it was heated. Gray slate cobblestones gleamed under the lights that surrounded the pool. The water glistened, and the moonlight reflected off the smooth surface.

"Back the fuck off, Ream," Crisis shouted. "What's your problem?"

"You're my problem, asshole. Get your hands off her." Ream's eyes shot to Kat. "You gonna fuck him too? Going to screw every fuckin' guy that looks at you? Ever thought of asking for money? You'd be rich by now."

Kat's face paled, and I suspected if Crisis didn't have his arm around her waist, she would've collapsed. Her expression was so damaged—eyes wide with horror, mouth open with shock. "Are you offering to compensate me for services rendered?"

"Fuck," Logan muttered. "Stay here." He started to walk toward them.

Ream was in Crisis's face, slurring his words. "Fuckin' Crisis, Kat? Man whore? This isn't going down. No fuckin' goddamn way."

"Ream, you need to walk away man," Kite said approaching.

"Ream." Logan's voice was more of a warning sound, and I recognized it well.

"You don't own me, Ream. Remember. You think I'm a piece of shit, so it doesn't matter what you think of me." I was close enough to see Kat's tears teetering in the rims of her eyes.

Ream's face dropped, and he ran his hand twice over his shaved head. "Where'd you get that shit from? I never said that. I never fuckin' said that."

"You look at me like I'm garbage. I might as well play the part."

Logan's body was tight, ready. Like he looked before a fight—controlled and calm but deadly. He chin-lifted to Kite then they walked up behind Crisis and Kat.

"Jesus Christ, I don't think that. But you keep this up and I'm changing my mind. Fuckin' hell, Kat, why are you doing this? The men. Jesus."

Kat slipped from Crisis and backed up. "You wouldn't even talk to me afterward."

Ream ran his hand through his hair, and he staggered a step as he lost his balance. "Kitkat ... I couldn't ... I couldn't face—"

Kat erupted. "You couldn't face it? Are you serious? *I* fuckin' face it! I knew it. I fuckin' knew this would happen. I never told anyone for this very goddamn reason." She walked toward him, her hands balled into fists. "I still face it, Ream. *Me.*" Kat shoved him in the chest, and he staggered back a step. "You have no right telling me who I can be with. None." She slammed both palms into him again.

"Oh shit," Logan swore as Ream lost his balance and went back several feet then slipped over the edge into the pool.

Crisis roared with laughter.

It took several seconds before he came sputtering to the surface. Crisis was still laughing while Kat frowned, her gaze focused on Ream as he swam to the side and pulled himself out.

His jeans and T-shirt clung to his body like a second skin, and when I looked at Kat, she was staring at Ream like ... she was in love with him.

Crisis was bowled over, clutching his stomach laughing.

But it was the look in Ream's eyes that had me worried for Kat. Logan got that look, a twinkle in his eyes that I knew meant mischief. Ream shook his head and droplets of water dispersed like a dog shaking after his bath. He looked nonchalant, casual, and that was dangerous.

"Kat—" I was too late. The moment I said her name, Ream dove for her. His head was down as his arms wrapped around her waist and heaved her over his shoulder. She squelched and kicked and struggled.

"Ream! Let me—" He jumped. Kat's scream was cut off as they disappeared beneath the surface of the water.

Logan looked at Kite. "We need to step on this shit."

Kite smacked Crisis in the arm. "You're no fuckin' help, asshole."

"Me? He needs to wake the fuck up. I'm helping him." Crisis's held up his hands, feigning innocence although his lips were twitching. What a shit disturber.

I bit my lip. Logan scoffed.

Ream and Kat came up from the beneath the surface of the water and Ream had his arm hooked around her waist, helping her to the side of the pool.

Logan met my eyes and I recognized the spark, knew it, felt it, and I remembered. I remembered when I'd first fallen in love with Logan.

He approached, a slow, casual stride. I stepped back one foot after the other. His eyes slid down me then back up again. Then, God that smile.

"Logan." I held up my hand as I continued backward.

His brows rose to match his grin.

"Logan, no."

"Yes, Emily."

I turned and ran, but he was on me in two strides, looping his arm around my waist and carrying me kicking and screaming to the edge of the pool.

"Logan! Logan, don't you dare." I pounded my fists into his back. "No. Please."

"Are you staying in my bed?"

"No, don't. I mean yes."

"I'm not understanding your answer. Maybe a little cold water will help."

"Noooo."

He leapt high into the air. I screamed.

I felt the cold water descend over my body, then my head as we went under. Logan's hands were on me, holding me against him as we hit the bottom and he crouched and pushed off.

The moment I could suck in air, I struggled to dislodge his hands so I could swim to the edge of the pool. Logan was laughing so hard that he couldn't hold onto me as I kicked out and hit him in the stomach.

"Bastard," I yelled. I was trying my hardest to hold in my laughter and act all pissy, but when he caught me at the side of the pool and dragged me into him, I felt his lips on the back of my neck then the touch of his hands under my shirt, his skin against mine. He was caressing my abdomen then up across my ribs and ...

"Water clear it up for you any?" He nibbled the lobe of my ear. "I'm not asking for sex. But you're in my bed."

Resisting Logan was like stopping a freight train with my hands. "Okay."

I saw Ream reach for Kat as she climbed out of the pool, snagging her hand. She paused, turned her head and all I saw the unquestionable rawness of hostility.

Ream said quietly, "Why, Kat?"

Kat never said anything, merely pulling away and walked back up to the house. Then Crisis and Kite cannonballed into the water.

Chapter Twenty-Five

Despite the cold water from the pool, I was burning up. There was no denying my attraction to him had catapulted to another level. This wasn't just love, this was an overwhelming debilitating love that I couldn't even begin to decipher.

Soul gripping. Fuck, it was complete mind enfolding; not a single thought could be procured without him embraced within it.

Logan showed me to *his* bathroom upstairs on the third floor. Kat and I had stayed on the main floor since we'd moved onto the farm. It was odd seeing the second floor occupied by the band and third floor by Logan. The rooms had remained unused before the band came except for one on the second floor on the south side. Kat had been using it as an art room; now it was occupied by Crisis, when he stayed here.

The bathroom happened to have all my toiletries laid out; apparently Logan moved them from the downstairs bathroom. He took my hands, held them at my sides, and then bent his head and kissed me.

"When did you ...?"

"Texted Kite when you were working with the stallion." He caressed my cheek then nodded to the right. "Wear the shirt to bed, baby."

"What?"

He picked up a white button-down men's shirt. I went to object and tell him I had my own pajamas when he scowled. "Seeing you in my shirt is sweet. And I want sweet tonight."

Damn it. Stop. Why did he have to say shit like that? I mean what girl didn't want to hear a guy telling her he wanted her in his shirt. That he wanted sweet and she'd be sweet in his shirt.

My mouth opened then slammed shut as he went over, turning on the taps. Water blasted out of the showerhead. He adjusted the water temperature.

He stood up straight. "You need help taking off those wet clothes?"

I rolled my eyes heavenward. "Out."

Logan grinned holding up his hands. "Trying to be helpful."

I let my pursed lips slip, and I smiled. I couldn't help it, seeing Logan laugh and smile was contagious. "Out. Now."

Watching Logan casually stride from the bathroom, I admired his ass in wet jeans, the corded muscles on his back visible beneath his white T-shirt clinging to his body like a second skin.

I leaned over and felt the temperature of the water—perfect. Peeling off my clothes, I hung them on the towel rack then stepped under the warm spray.

I washed as fast as I could to avoid the image of Logan that was afflicting me as I ran my hands over my body. I was imagining my touches were his hands on every inch of me.

Everything he'd done, he'd done to save me. To save us.

I was letting him in, and he was letting me in. I was sleeping beside him tonight, and I felt all giddy inside and a little nervous, but it was a good nervous.

I closed my eyes, hands against the wall, the water pounding into my body like he had during my captivity two years ago. His hands had been on my hips, fingers digging into my flesh as he fucked me from behind that day in the shower. His lips nibbled at the crook of my neck as he slowed, sliding in and out. I moaned, then begged for him to go harder, faster as he pulled out, hands wrapping around my hair and yanking my head back so he could take my mouth with a cruel, deep kiss that had my body screaming for more.

He'd been right. He was engraved in me, and no amount of time or washing or running was going to get him out of me. I had to accept that. I did accept that.

I leaned back against the tiles as more memories flooded.

I never heard the door open, nor the dropping of clothes on the floor, still lost in my grip of desire.

Hands cupped my cheeks, and my eyes flew open.

Our eyes locked.

Held.

Desire spiraled around us tying us together. Logan tilted his head, the water pounding down on him as he leaned closer.

I closed my eyes and inhaled him.

He was part of me.

Logan had never left me. And I knew that even if I denied us, I'd never get him out of me. Love didn't work that way.

"You don't get to touch that yourself without me."

I moaned, and that was all it took before his lips crashed down onto mine. Our need was so intense every part of my body ached.

There was nothing sweet in his kiss. His force was bruising, relentless, and he stole my breath. My hands were all over him, gripping, fondling, pulling at his hair one minute then stroking his back the next.

"Emily," he murmured as his mouth scorched my skin and nibbled across the curve of my neck until he was suckling my shoulder. His hands ran down my sides to my thighs then back up again. I leaned my head back, his rough hands caressing my wet skin. I needed it stronger. I wanted more.

He stopped. "You still on the pill?"

"Yes."

"Thank fuck."

His hands leaving me drained my body of heat even though the water was still driving down on us. My eyes flew open.

"Logan?" I was breathing hard, and I reached for him unable to stop myself. I needed him, screw sensible. I didn't know how to be sensible around him. He knocked sensible right out of the universe.

"Don't move."

I gasped. It was that voice. That deep, resounding voice he used when I was forced to call him Master.

My body lurched with desire, and I stopped breathing as I stared at him watching me. This man controlled everything about me.

"Please," I begged.

"Part your legs."

I did.

"Wider."

I did, my chest rising and falling as my eyes never left his. He moved in, then his hand cupped me, and I moaned at the touch.

"Shh, Emily. No sounds."

"Logan." It was me still begging. His hand moved away, and I cried out grabbing for his hand to put it back. But he stopped me with one look, and my hands dropped to my sides, and I knew exactly what he was doing to me. He'd make me wait. He'd fill my body with such need that I'd do anything for him so he'd end my blissful torture.

"No touching." The orders were familiar, but this time I knew the intent of the man who said them. Logan loved me, and damn it, he knew this is what I needed. He'd known all along, and he was showing me that no matter what he'd done to me for those two weeks, I desired this. I wanted this and still did.

He never forced me. He gave me what I wanted, yet I tried to deny.

I nearly broke when his fingers glided down between my breasts to my bellybutton then lower until he was slipping back and forth through my folds. My eyes closed, legs shook, and I held my breath as he tortured me. The pads of his two fingers scissored on either side of my clit, just touching then backing off again. I was about to break when his fingers drove inside me, and my head fell back hard against the tiled wall. When I moaned, he withdrew, and I nearly screamed at him, but knew that I got nothing doing that, so I looked at him and swallowed, waiting.

"Good girl." He smiled, and his fingers circled my clit, slow and soft until I was panting, the urgency building in me so intense. I was desperate to come.

But Logan didn't let me as he pulled back and bent his head to suckle my nipples, first one and then the other. His hands gripped my hips while he relentlessly pulled on the sensitive nipple with his teeth until he saw my body tense and arch against him in pain. Then he let go and circled the sensitive nub with his tongue.

"Turn around."

The moment I had my cheek up against the tiles, he took my hands and placed them above my head spread eagle. His hands curled around my wrists and locked them there.

I pushed back into him and felt his cock twitch as it touched my ass. He groaned, and his mouth delved into the crook of my neck. "I need my cock inside you. I need to fuck you so hard I'm afraid I'll break you."

In response, I wiggled against him, and he let go of my wrist to slide down my chest to between my legs where he began his assault, bringing me so close yet stopping again and again until I almost cried.

"Logan. Now. Please. Please."

"Bend over." He took a step back so I could.

He groaned, and then his fingers wove into my hair and pulled back so he could reach my mouth. His kiss was fierce as he pushed inside me so deep it was almost painful. He filled me, the swell of him stretching my insides as he began to move in and out. His arm locked around my waist, my hands pressed up against the wall, his mouth at my ear, hearing his rough, harsh breathing as he went faster.

"Baby." He drove harder, and I pushed back against him. "I can't ... I can't stop."

"Don't stop. Don't ever stop."

He pushed again and again, pumping into me, water pounding onto our backs and shoulders. The water may be running cold by now, but I didn't care, because I couldn't feel it. All I could feel were Logan's teeth biting my shoulder and mine biting my lip.

When his hand came between my legs and touched my clit, I screamed and went over the edge, long jolts ricocheting through me as he relentlessly pounded until his entire body tightened, and he shoved hard one last time.

Twitches flickered through my body as he leaned into me, hands covering mine against the wet tiles. His fingers curled until our fingers were knit together then I felt the jerk of his cock before he pulled out.

"Jesus," Logan whispered close to my ear. He brought our arms down then locked his around me. He kissed the side of my neck. "I'd have never fucked you if you didn't want it. Never. When we were together ... Eme, that was just me and you. No one else. I was scared there too, and I needed you." He stepped out of the shower and snagged a towel. "Come here."

I turned off the taps and came to him. He dried my body, slow and gentle, taking his time. It was erotic the way his hands ran over my skin in a rhythmic stroke with the softness of the towel.

"You good?"

I nodded. I'd just been given an orgasm to kill all orgasms. Yeah, I was good.

He nodded once then grabbed a towel and walked out of the bathroom.

I stood staring at myself in the mirror, my skin pink from the water and Logan's hands. I could see his teeth marks in my left shoulder and another red mark further up, below my ear. I ran my finger across it then down to my shoulder where he left his mark on me, and then I closed my eyes and wrapped my arms around myself. I still felt him all over me, inside of me like he was swimming through my veins.

I loved him. This man that had broken me, and at the same time saved me. We were both broken in a way. I realized that he was more than me. We were unable to be repaired. But maybe that was why we were so good together.

Logan

Logan heard the door to the bathroom open and his cock sprang to attention before she even appeared. Fuck. It was like the flood gates of the Hoover Dam had been broken. He wanted to have her again so bad it was excruciating. Nothing, not even the months of torture he'd endured had hurt more than being denied Emily.

Logan lay on his back, one arm crooked above his head as he watched her walk out of the bathroom wearing his white button-down shirt that barely covered her ass. She looked like a timid angel; she was nervous, her steps hesitant and pausing near the bed. He made no secret of his appreciation and took in every inch of her. She flushed under his intense gaze; and it was sweet, and his cock was already swelling, needing her again.

He thought he'd lost this woman. He thought he'd die in that shitty cold cellar. Raul had done a number on him, gutted Dave right in front of him, and that was only the beginning. Being a fighter didn't help against chains that held his muscles stretched past there limit. He could remember hearing the click of the door, the inevitable slow stride of Raul as he walked through the darkness until father stood in front of his son. Then Raul asked the same question he asked every single day for months. "Where are they?"

And Logan gave his same answer. "Fuck you." He'd suffer a thousand years before he'd give up Emily or his mother's location. Deck had relocated his mother, and Emily was safe at the farm with Deck and his men making certain nothing touched her.

Yeah, he was screwed up after Deck got him out of there, took three months to physically recover and then another few to get his head on straight. He grew up with fucked up shit; he knew how to cope, block shit out. That didn't mean he didn't have trouble dealing; it meant he found an outlet—his music.

"Logan?" Her soft voice was a whisper of sweetness, and he shoved the memory into the locked, black box of his mind.

"Baby, come here." She almost looked fragile, the shielded look in her eyes was gone. He'd fucked it right out of her. It was about goddamn time too.

She knelt on the bed, and the shirt moved up to reveal her inner thigh. He groaned as his cock twitched again. This is what she did to him. He was putty in her hands, and the fucked up thing was she thought he was the one in control.

When she started to crawl up from the end of the bed toward him like a cat, he nearly blew his load. Every muscle tensed, and he was panting like a female dog in heat. She wasn't trying to be sexy; it was just the way she moved that sent his libido through the sky right into Pluto.

He couldn't take watching her anymore and grabbed her under the arms and pulled her up against him. "If you're not sore, I'm fucking you again."

Heat flashed in her eyes, and he wanted to bow to the Gods for giving him this woman. A water droplet slipped down a strand of her hair, and he caught it between his fingers before it dropped onto her shirt. He slipped his finger into his mouth and tasted the scent of her shampoo, coconut papaya with a hint of vanilla.

He rolled her over onto her back then came on top of her, grabbing her hands so they were above their heads. "Hold the rails."

His cock was at full attention and hardened further when he saw her submit to his command. She was so submissive, and she didn't even know it. Damn, she was made for him. Screw the shit that went down. Screw everything; this woman had him locked to her, and he'd suffer a million Rauls in order to be right where he was now.

"Logan."

And that right there, her soft begging of his name could undo any man. He grit his teeth to keep from plunging into her and not stopping until he came. Instead, he hardened his jaw and gave her what she wanted and needed.

"Use one hand. Play with your breasts." He waited, watching to see what she'd do, and slowly, she obeyed, caressing the swells, her fingers circling her nipples. "Pinch them." Her mouth fell open, hesitant at first, but she did it. And it was beautiful. Her back arched, and she gasped as her fingers tightened on the perky red peaks. Damn.

"Harder." He saw the reluctance again. She needed this just as much as he did. "Harder, Emily."

When her fingers squeezed her nipples this time, he saw her wince, and every one of her muscles lying beneath him tightened. Perfect. Fuckin' perfect. He pushed her hand aside then leaned down and grabbed her nipple between his teeth and pulled until he heard her suck in air. Then, he swirled his tongue soft and sweet around the nub, soothing the pain.

"Open your legs, baby." There was no hesitation at that, and he smiled as he reached between them and felt her soaking wet already—or still. Whichever, it didn't matter. Her pelvis tilted toward him, and he shook his head. "No. Wait." He wanted to laugh when he saw her frustration, the adorable flash of defiance in her eyes and then the deep breath and her resolve to obey.

He slipped his finger inside her and groaned. So tight. No wonder his cock wanted her so bad.

He curled his finger inside her while his thumb played with her clit, circling, stroking, changing between hard and soft pressure, never letting her body know what he was doing next. He watched her face, the play of emotions telling him when she was getting too close and he needed to back off.

"I can't take it. Stop torturing me."

She was a little pissed now, and he couldn't have that. She should know better. He stopped his thumb's movement but kept his finger inside her, completely still. He let her make the mistake and move up against him, trying to get what she desperately needed. Fuck, it was like being handed a slice of heaven. He almost caved seeing her body move up and down on his finger, and if he hadn't just had her in the shower he would've said fuck it and taken her.

"No moving."

Her eyes flew open, and she stopped moving. There was that look of panic on her face, not from whether he'd hurt her, well ... a little ... but how he was going to make her scream. "I think you know the rules?"

Frozen, she gave him those begging eyes, and he wanted to eat her out for a goddamn two-week feast. Instead, he decided to eat her out and have her squirming into his mouth for mercy. And he'd let her scream, he decided. Just hearing her voice was going to make him come. Christ, little did she know that this was more torture for him than her.

"You're going to need to beg." His mouth twitched when he saw her eyes close briefly and her head sink further back into the pillow. Yeah, better lay back and relax, because he was taking his sweet ass time.

He kissed his way down her body, tongue tasting every inch of her delectable velvet skin until he reached her naked mound. Fuck, he loved that she kept herself shaved.

Her head moved back and forth as he took her in his mouth and sucked. Jesus, she tasted like paradise wrapped up in a bow.

He groaned, the vibration making her shudder and her legs quiver. He pushed her legs up so her knees bent more.

"Wider." That's all he needed to say; she hadn't forgotten. She parted her legs to the limit, and he moved in to start his feast, tongue rolling over her clit then sliding down into the wetness and back up again. He used his fingers to part her and sunk in deep, pushing his tongue up into her.

"Oh God, Logan. Stop."

She wasn't in pain. He could hear the pleasure in her voice. And if it pleased her, he would never stop. He ignored her pleas and swirled his tongue around her clit, feeling her tremble and her back arch up pushing herself further into his mouth. She was close. Fuck. He wanted her to come so he could swallow every inch of her.

"Please, honey. Please let me come."

He couldn't let that happen, not yet. He slipped his fingers into her and pumped hard and fast, but purposely avoided touching where she was burning for him to finish her off. Not yet.

"Eme, legs." She was trying to close them, to find some sort of relief. "Open. Now." She instantly obeyed hoping he'd give her a reward sooner. Not happening. He lived to see her writhe beneath him.

He moved up her body and heard her groan of frustration, but he wouldn't let it deter him. She needed this just as much as he did. He stopped to circle his tongue around her nipples then continued upward until he was face-to-face to her half-lidded eyes.

"Let go, Emily." He wanted her hands on him, touching him, setting him in flames like a fuckin' city on fire. Her hands sunk into his hair, and he took her mouth, kissing her until she was gasping for breath. When he drew back, he saw the complete and utter submission, and if he wasn't lying on the bed, he'd be on his goddamn knees. She did that to him.

"I'm making you come in my mouth. Then I'm fucking you until you come again." He didn't expect a reply; she could barely breathe by the way her chest was heaving beneath him.

By the time he reached her pussy, her hands were gripping tightly in his hair and her body was wiggling. He thought she'd come before he even reached his destination.

"Tilt for me." When she pushed up with her pelvis and he stared down at that gleaming, naked pussy, he came a little bit, and it pissed him off. He was losing control, and fuck if that was happening. As his eyes roamed up her body to lock with hers; he knew that this woman could destroy him. He let go of his emotions to get her back; he never felt so vulnerable as he had in the last few weeks, but it was worth it.

He stared at her as she lay panting. "Logan?" It was a mix of begging and uncertainty.

"I love you, Emily. You don't get to take that from me. Ever. No one does." He saw her eyes light up with surprise, and then he went down on her and made her world spiral out of control, and fuck, did she scream.

When he entered her she was limp and pliable beneath him. "Legs." He helped her slip them around his hips, and then he had his way ... Well, he always had his way, but it was all about her. Always. It was knowing what she needed and when. With her pleasure, came his. He went slow and took his time, building her up again until she was quivering then calling out his name as her body tensed and shook.

God, it was the most beautiful sight. Emily wrapped around him trembling, her lips against his, the sweet scent of her skin so close he tasted it. And when he released into her groaning her name, his hands interlocked with hers above their heads.

When Logan rolled over, he took her with him so her one leg was over top of his and her head was on his chest. He stroked her hair and closed his eyes, squeezing her to him.

"I've always loved you, Logan," she whispered.

He smiled. "Eme, us ... We're only broken when we're apart."

Chapter Twenty-Six

I woke to my face snuggled into the crook of his neck, hand resting on his chest and my legs entwined with Logan's. The scent of him with each breath had my insides quaking and my stomach dropping. It felt warm and safe and protective.

Logan. It was hard to fathom that I was in his bed. My body sore but still wanting more of him. I inhaled deep, and my nipples brushed up against him. He was intoxicating, and I didn't want to get out of bed ever, but another need pushed me to get up.

I slowly tried to slip my legs out from under his and lift his arm that was slung over my waist. I'd made it a few inches before he moaned and, with one rough yank, pulled me closer.

"Not ready to get up," he mumbled. "Kiss me good morning, baby."

"What?"

"You heard me. Kiss me. And if it's good, I'll let you go."

"Don't be ridiculous," I stammered.

One of his eyes flicked open, and his brows rose. "I can lie in bed all day. How about you?"

"I have to pee, Logan."

"Better kiss me quick then."

"Fine." I really did need to pee and arguing over this was only going to make it harder on me. Besides, I wanted to kiss him. Tilting my head up so my lips were on par with his, I leaned forward and kissed him. The second moisture connected to moisture, I shivered.

"Mmmm." He rolled me over to my back and hovered above me.

I was breathing hard, my heart pounding and everything inside me pulsating as I met his eyes. He did that sexy half-grin, and his eyes were dancing.

"Are you good?"

I nodded. Too breathless for words. Afraid my voice would crack.

The weight of him felt so good, powerful and warm and ... and all Logan. He was my sweet. My popsicle and I was melting into him further and further. I still was uncertain for how long, but for now I was letting him in. I'd think about my plans to move out later; right now I felt as if I was finally healing, and I was grabbing hold while I could.

He groaned and backed off, swinging his legs over the side of the bed. "Go pee. I'll make coffee. Two creams, no sugar?"

"Yeah."

He nodded then left, and I got up and went to the bathroom.

I came downstairs wearing my black breeches and pink T-shirt. I had tied my hair back in a low ponytail, and after contemplating how much makeup to put on for a good ten minutes, not wanting appear like I tried too hard, because despite what I tried to convince myself, I did want to look good for Logan.

I ended up with mascara and light pink lip gloss.

I padded into the kitchen and didn't think he'd even heard me when he nodded toward the steaming coffee on the island. "Yours, Mouse."

Walking toward it, I couldn't help but eye his broad naked back as he flipped something in the frying pan. He reached up into the cupboard. There was a tat I'd noticed last night on the opposite side of his Tear Asunder tat. It was of a horse, rearing up, but it was broken like a heart cut in half. Jagged edges split it down the center. The edges matched perfectly or at least it appeared as they did. Between the two pieces of the horse was a guitar with its strings broken, and the intense, black lines looped around the horse's neck.

"You hear me?"

I jerked. "Sorry?"

He half-turned toward me. "Toast, baby. Push it down for me. Eggs are nearly done."

"Oh yeah. Sure." I walked over to the counter and pushed the lever down, and the bread disappeared.

"You want orange juice or is coffee good?"

"Just coffee."

He took the frying pan off the burner while I got the plates. He scooped a heaving amount onto both plates then set the pan in the sink and started the blender. He still did his protein shake.

I smiled as I went to the toaster just as the toast popped to a nice golden brown. Wasn't often a toaster did its job to perfection. I quickly pulled them out and placed two pieces each on our plates then buttered them.

He looked relaxed working in the kitchen. It was sexy and ... Well, it was hot having a guy standing over the stove making eggs. If he grew up in the compound with Raul, he couldn't have spent much time doing stuff like this. My guess, Raul had slaves to feed them.

I felt him come up next to me, and I looked up just as his hand settled on top of mine. "You're drowning the bread."

I looked down and laughed, noticing the gobs of butter on one piece of toast. "Oh." I began scrapping it off when he stilled my movements. He leaned his back against the counter then swung me around so that I was up against him, butter knife in one hand and my other grabbing hold of his bicep.

"You're cute when you're distracted. What's up?"

"Nothing."

He squeezed me. "Try again."

"You're comfortable here. The kitchen I mean."

"Yeah, lots of practice."

"Oh." Huh.

"Just ask."

I didn't want to hurt him bringing up his childhood. He'd always been closed off about his life. Would he not want to tell me? Would he let *me* in?

"Eme."

"Um, well you grew up with Raul. I just thought, that you ... I don't know, you wouldn't have learned to cook."

His hands rubbed slowly up and down my arms. "I didn't even see a kitchen there. Spent most my time training, but food was always available. I learned to cook after we escaped and came here. My mother was a ghost, barely spoke, just existed. It was like all the adrenaline and fight she had was to protect me and then to get us out; the trauma finally caught up to her, and she crashed. So, I looked after her. And I learned to cook." Logan stopped stroking my arms, and I looked up into his eyes. "I grew up in a shit place with shittier people who had no morals or values. My mom tried to shield me from that. She fought hard against it so I wouldn't get stained by it.

"By the time I was six I was seeing and understanding what she saw, the horror and disgust with who Raul was. She shielded that from me as best she could. I learned patience and persistence from her too, resilience that I was better than all of them. The fighting helped to release my anger at what they were doing to the women, and yes, there were children. All Raul cared about was making me the best fighter he could. So I was left untouched by most of it. But my mother ..." I rested my head on his shoulder and tightened my arms; tears streamed down my face as I listened. "My mother wasn't so lucky. She suffered. But she also knew how to keep Raul happy, so she did what she had to do. To survive. To protect me. She gave me that will to fight for whatever I wanted. To never give up. And to protect whatever I love with everything I have."

"Logan. I'm so sorry."

"We got out. And I learned how to cook. I'd say that's a damn good thing for you."

I half-smiled into his shirt, and I could feel his chuckle rumble in his chest. "Mouse, eggs are getting cold." He grabbed the plates, and we went to the stools and sat next to one another. "You're dressed to ride."

Despite knowing what I was wearing, I still looked down at myself. "Yeah. I'll take Havoc out."

"I want you with me today."

"Well, ah I ..."

His fork dropped on the plate and made a loud clang. "No running."

"I'm not." And for the first time, I meant it.

He grabbed my chin and made me look at him. "Say it."

"What?" I attempted to dislodge his hand, but he held tight.

"Tell me you're not running."

"I'm not running."

He let me go and nodded as if satisfied with my answer. "You're meeting my mom. Not today, but you are."

"What?" Oh God.

"Your mom is no longer part of our lives, and I know you

263

haven't seen her in years. Now you're getting my mom."

I stiffened. "How did you know that?" But I knew the answer. Deck. It had to be Deck. In the two years Logan had been vacant from my life, Deck must have kept him informed. That's why he checked up on me. Oh God, all this time, Logan had been watching out for me. It might explain the "buddy" thing, how close they appeared now. Deck and Logan had been talking for the last two years.

When I met his eyes, he knew I knew.

"Yeah, Eme. I kept tabs on you. Deck made certain you were good. I had to be sure you were looked after. Even if I couldn't be with you. Even if this shit took me from you, I'd always know you were looked after. Now, go get changed. Wear jeans and a sexy white blouse. I'm taking you on my bike, we're riding a while then we're getting ice cream."

It was then I let it go. All of the mistrust, the pain, the hurt. I let it all go, and I let Logan's security wrap around my heart. He was mine, and I was his, and I *wanted* him to protect me. And it wasn't because I was passive or weak or helpless. It was because he gave me everything I needed. A basic pure and raw need he fulfilled because he cared about me.

Logan must have sensed some of my epiphany, because he was there, reaching out his hand and taking me into his arms.

Logan was my avalanche.

He crashed into my life again and wiped everything bad between us away, until I was naked with nothing except acceptance for what happened to us. It wasn't me anymore; it was us.

We spent the day on his bike, eating ice cream, and talking, We laughed. We went to the city and saw Georgie at the coffee shop then had dinner at the Brazen Head where we first ate when we were a new couple over two years ago.

Logan even kissed me outside, up against the wall like he'd done back then. We made it back to the farm record time, though Logan took care to obey most traffic laws. He'd once told me he liked to drive fast, but when I was with him, his cargo was more precious than his pleasure. We didn't stop to chat to Kite and Ream sitting in the kitchen; instead, Logan dragged me upstairs and we made love — hot, hard, and fast. Then I fell asleep nested within his embrace.

I woke to Logan nuzzling my neck, his leg between mine as he slid his cheek across my back. His arm draped over my hip, fingers splaying on my stomach. I smiled as shivers trickled across my skin when his velvet tongue licked the sensitive part below my ear.

"Mouse?" The gravelly whispered words made my insides ache to be taken again. "I can feel your heart pounding."

Linking my fingers with his, I pulled him closer. We were still naked, and his cock jerked against my butt. "Put it inside me, honey."

He tensed.

I smiled.

Then he let my hand go, and his fingers traveled down my skin until he slid into the heat between my legs. "Shit, you're wet."

"I'm always wet for you."

"Yeah. I love that." He untangled our legs then in a slow languid motion, he pushed himself inside me.

I groaned and pushed back against him.

"Damn. You're tight."

It was a slow before-breakfast sex, not the hard desperate need of last night. Instead, he held me close, our bodies connected, awakening from sleep with a slow ride into stomach dropping ecstasy.

It was hot.

Logan kissed my neck, my back then held me up against him while murmuring sweet words of love in my ear. Each sensation

265

was engraved in my mind, just like he was. We were set in stone.

The morning was lazy as we made love twice more, each time more intense than the last. I was raw and sore, but as soon as he touched me, I was ready for him again. There was no pretention, no worries, and I did as he wanted and left the thinking out of the bedroom.

By eleven we ambled from our nest, and I went to shower while Logan went to make some calls. He was on the phone when I came downstairs, hair still wet. I could see Ream and Kite outside by the pool talking.

Logan nodded to a mug sitting on the island then he walked to the sliding door that led out to the pool. He stepped out, and I sat on one of the stools and watched as he paced back and forth, his brows lowered and the crease around his eyes accentuated.

There was no doubt he was angry about something. He took long strides; his muscles flexing beneath his T-shirt, hair falling haphazardly across his forehead. I wanted to encase him in my embrace and take away whatever was riling him up.

He kicked one of the patio chairs, and it toppled over. He looked up. Saw me. Stared for three seconds then turned away and began pacing again.

When he came back inside he tossed his phone on the counter and came right for me. He sat on the bar stool, grabbed either side of my stool, and pulled me in close so my legs were between his. Then he rested his hands on either side of my outer thighs.

"You and me, we need time together. I'm trying to get that time." He rubbed his hands up and down my thighs and a quiver shot through me. "But—"

"You're giving me a but?" I raised my brows and tilted my head.

He huffed. "Smart ass."

I grinned. The first time we talked about buts, he took my

virginity.

Logan leaned in close and cupped my chin. "*But* I love smart ass Emily. She's cute, and I want to spend the next sixty years listening to her."

"Hmm, okay." I leaned forward and went into him, my mouth coming down on his as I took what I'd gone without for far too long.

"I have to meet Deck this morning. We have that party in a week, and we need to run over a few things."

"The party. Right." Logan had mentioned something about a party a while ago.

"We've had one almost every year at Matt's bar since the band started, but this year we're having it here. Manager has organized a few producers to come hear us play."

Oh. This was big for the band. "That's great, Logan. Really great."

He nodded.

"Maybe I'll come with you and go hang with Georgie at the coffee shop while you talk to Deck."

His face grew dark, and his hand tightened. "No."

"Why not? I don't have any horses coming today or clients, and I can ride Havoc later when it's cooler. What else am I going to do without you here?"

"Lie by the pool. Go back to bed. Watch a movie. Just promise you won't leave the farm. And no trail rides. I want you close by."

"Logan?" Something wasn't right. Why didn't he want me going on a trail ride? Why close by? "What's happening?"

"Nothing, Eme. I just worry when I'm not with you."

I knew the second that he said the words that he was avoiding telling me something when his index finger tapped against my hip. "Don't you trust me?"

"Jesus, it's not that at all.

"Then tell me what's going on."

It felt like minutes before he spoke and I could see him contemplate ignoring me, by the way he avoided looking at me. Then he did and I wished he hadn't because I knew what he was going to tell me wasn't good. "Deck has been looking for Alfonzo. He was seen at the auction Raven was at. That's how we found out he's alive."

I felt sick to my stomach. I'd assumed Alfonzo had died, if not when Logan had beaten him to a bloody pulp then when the compound was taken down.

Logan cupped my cheek. "Alfonzo has no clue about the farm. Deck's men have made certain none of us have been followed here for weeks."

"You've know about this for weeks?" Of course he had. That explained why he'd warned me to be careful, why Deck came to get them at the bar. Why Logan came with me to Rob's farm to work with the racehorse. Or that could've been just as he said—to be with me.

"Weeks, yes. But Alfonzo wasn't a threat to you. He was in New York up until yesterday. But, Deck's man lost him." Logan kissed me and it was long and slow, lingering. "I tried to cancel the party, but it's not just me here. It's the guys. They need this. Deck's doing security and is confident that the farm is still safe. That might change though."

I nodded. I was scared and nervous, but for some reason not as much as I thought I would be. I was more focused on the fact that Logan had trusted me to be able to handle this. Because I knew Logan and the reason he hadn't told me up until now was because he didn't want me feeling scared, or nervous.

"I guess I can stay inside and play with my vibrator."

Logan's brows lowered, and his eyes got that dark intensity. He was so sexy when he heard something he didn't like. "That pussy doesn't get fucked, touched, or played with without me. You need it, I'm happy to give it to you. But you, lying in bed playing by yourself—no."

I wanted to laugh; instead, I hid my smile, because I thought laughing might be bad considering he looked genuinely angry. I liked that he wanted to be the one to look after my needs. It was hot, and I felt wanted, treasured. "Okay, honey."

"I love it when you call me that. Cute and sweet." He got up and walked over to the sink and started putting dishes into the dishwasher. "What are you going to do while I'm gone?"

"Guess I'll ride your horse then lounge by the pool."

He stopped what he was doing and was quiet for a second. "They've never been mine, Emily. Any horse here has always been yours. The bike is my horse. I'm not getting on anything that can kick, bite, and toss me on my ass."

"A bike can toss you on your ass."

"Yeah, but it's not coming back to bite me afterward."

"Logan, the horses aren't going to bite you."

"They can stand up on their hind legs and dump me on my ass then come down on my head with big feet that cost a fortune every few weeks to get manicures."

I laughed. "You mean rearing up, and horses don't like to step on people. Actually, they avoid it at all costs, and their feet are called hooves which need trimming every six weeks or you'll have crabby horses walking around on overgrown turned up toes. For your information, Sculpt." He growled low, and then set the fork he had in his hand on the counter and started stalking toward me. I moved to my feet, but not in time to avoid his dive for me. He snagged my arm and, in one swoop, lifted me up and over his shoulder.

"My real name. Always."

"What are you talking about?" I teased.

"My name, say it."

I knew what would happen and it made me giddy inside. It had been a long time since I felt this playful and relaxed. Fine, I could admit to being totally and irrefutably in love. "And what if I don't want to—Sculpt?"

He smacked my ass and started for the stairs. "I'll fuck you all day." My heart rate tripled.

"You can't. You're meeting Deck."

"Deck will understand."

He squeezed my butt. "Sculpt. Stop." But really, I didn't want him to stop anything as he took the stairs two at a time, kicked the bedroom door open then closed, and then threw me on the bed.

"Say my name."

"Sculpt."

He came down hard on top of me, already tearing off my shirt. I struggled at first, laughing until his hand brushed against my nipple, and I gasped.

"Logan," I said, knowing if I didn't he'd torture me for longer than I wanted or could take.

"Again."

"Logan."

"You won't do that again, will you?"

I hesitated.

"Tell me."

"No, Logan."

His mouth came down hard on mine, and then he fucked me.

Chapter Twenty-Seven

We had a week of lying by the pool and having sex and doing nothing but being together. He did spend some time with the band practicing, but the guys made themselves scarce whenever they could. I rarely saw Kat, and my guess was she was staying at the condo with Matt most nights. Whether it was to give Logan and me some time alone or to avoid Ream, I didn't know for sure, but I was guessing the latter.

Georgie popped by with Deck, and we hung by the pool while Deck and Logan went off to chat. Logan had been strung up as tight his guitar strings, but he played it off as nothing but the plans for the party. I knew it was Alfonzo that was getting to him, but when I asked about it he threw me over his shoulder then took the stairs two at a time and tossed me on the bed where he had me forgetting everything except him between my legs. Then we did some slexing, and ate our next meal in bed.

It was sweet, and he fed me grapes and wine. He commanded and I surrendered to him. I never thought I'd find submitting to a man again sensual after what I'd seen in Mexico, but it wasn't about that. It was about submitting to the love we shared. I realized giving up my control to Logan didn't make me weak. It was my escape. My need, and he was fulfilling that by giving me what I needed. It was about complete openness and trust.

And I did love him. I never stopped; it had just been smothered.

"Eme."

I looked up. Logan had stopped playing his guitar and was looking at me with eyes that were so exposed and revealing. I felt like I could see right into them, all his desires and strength, even a hint of uncertainty that lay beneath the depths.

We were sitting in the horse field like we used to do, and he was playing me the new song the band was debuting tonight at the party. It was mellow, raw, crass, and it brought tears to my eyes. His voice cut through the words as if he hurt to say them.

It was called "Torn from You," and it was about us.

He reached forward and wiped the stray tear from my cheek. I leaned into his hand and smiled, closing my eyes. I never thought we'd get back to this place. I think I was afraid to hope that we could.

"That song's going to make you famous. It's beautiful. I love you, Logan."

He put his guitar aside then grabbed me, flipped me onto my back and hovered above.

Slowly his weight lowered onto me, and I felt his cock press between my legs. It sent the raging through my body.

"Are you good with being fucked out in the middle of a horse field?"

I laughed, because it was out in a horse field where he had taken my virginity. "Yeah. I'm good with that. Now kiss me," I ordered.

He chuckled. "I'm rubbing off on you."

"Then stop messing around and put your cock inside me, rock star."

"Jesus, Eme." He groaned, and his mouth smashed onto mine. It was hard, and it was Logan taking what I was giving to him with every part of myself.

We were putting our clothes back on—well I was; he was doing up his jeans—when I heard the gate off in the distance clang.

I looked up. "Deck."

Logan turned then quickly stood in front of me while I finished clasping my bra and pulled on my shirt. When I was done, I came up beside him and took his hand; he squeezed.

"Emily. Logan." Deck chin-lifted. He looked pissed, but then again, Deck always was hard to read. His mood could easily be off because he had a shitty coffee this morning. "We need to talk." He directed the statement at Logan.

Logan stiffened, and I knew Deck didn't have a problem with shitty coffee. This was about Alfonzo.

"Eme." Logan leaned down and kissed me then let my hand go.

"Is it about him?" I asked Deck. "Did you find him?"

"I told her." Logan put his arm over my shoulders.

Deck nodded once. "He hasn't resurfaced yet. But we do know he hasn't crossed the border. We have that angle covered." Deck nodded to me. "You mind giving us a few minutes, Emily?"

There was no point in asking if I could stay. Both these guys were super protective and they'd want to keep as much of this from me as possible.

"Okay. I'll start getting ready for tonight." I started to walk away when Logan snagged my hand and brought me up against his chest. Deck stepped away from us and turned his back. Then Logan was whispering into my ear with that sexy voice that dialed up my desire once again.

"Take a shower. Then lie naked on our bed on your back. Arms above your head. Legs apart, knees bent."

My breath hitched, and I pulled back.

"I'm going to tie you up."

Again my breath hitched, but because I remembered the last time I was tied up and left alone for hours.

I was still shaking my head no when he tucked my hair behind my ear and kissed the tip of my nose. "You trust me?"

I did. Despite what happened, I knew everything he'd done was to protect me. "Yes," I whispered.

"This isn't about being helpless. Or me dictating or controlling. It's about you trusting me to give you what your body needs. It's knowing I'll always take care of you."

I nodded, still hesitant at the thought of ropes around me. It made me nervous and unsure of myself, and yet, I wanted to trust him.

"I'll be there in twenty."

I nodded, and then he let me go, and I was walking away, my heart slamming against my ribs. Fear or excitement tap danced through me. There was a fine line between the two.

By the time Logan came into the room, my limbs were trembling so badly the bed was shaking.

His eyes traveled down my naked body then back up. His expression to others would look cold, dark, maybe even stiff, but what I saw was deeper, and it was awe. It was what kept me on my back and not running for my life. He looked so floored at the sight before him, and all my confidence skyrocketed, because I could do this to him.

He kicked the door shut, and the loud noise made me jump, but I kept in the position he'd asked of me.

"Emily." His eyes were on my pussy that I swear was leaking wetness down the inside of my thighs having him stare at me like that. "Jesus." His eyes came to mine. "I don't deserve you."

"Logan." I wanted him to stop standing there and come to me, but he was taking his time, just admiring the sight, and it made me hotter, and I was shifting uneasily as my need heightened.

"Please."

Logan walked over to the dresser by the far wall, and opened the lower drawer. I heard him shuffling around and then he stood up straight with a black silk scarf in his hands. My chest started heaving.

The bed dipped.

He knelt near my head, the silk falling over his wrist as he reached for my hands. I jerked away, and he frowned. "You're safe, baby."

I nodded, but the thought of being tied up again and unable to get away sent my stomach churning.

He let the scarf fall to lie over my wrists then cupped my chin and turned my head to look at him instead of at the scarf. "You can always say no. One word and it stops. I think you need this. We need it. I want your trust, and to get that we have to work through what happened. Change what you're feeling to something beautiful."

"I have," I breathed, and it was a lie.

"No, baby. You haven't. I saw your face when I mentioned tying you up." Logan leaned forward and kissed me. "You're not ready, we'll wait."

He left the bed taking the scarf with him. The drawer opened, and the disappointment I felt was overwhelming. I did want this. I wanted him to have control. I needed to let go—completely. I wanted to wash away the bad memories with good ones, and Logan could do that.

"Okay."

Logan turned.

"Please. I want to. I trust you, Logan."

He walked back over to me and slid the silk over my wrists. I felt the desire swim through me to replace the fear. The smooth material caressed my skin like the tip of a feather as he glided it up each arm and then down again. It wasn't rough and chafing, but soft and cool to my heated flesh.

He slowly wrapped the silk around my wrists above my head, but he didn't tie them to the bed rungs like I thought he'd do. "You're not ready for that. Another time."

I was. I wanted whatever he wanted from me.

He stroked the side of my face. "I want you to submit and give all of yourself to me. Fear isn't part of that."

He slipped off the bed then began to undress, and I watched, aching to touch myself as each piece of clothing fell to the floor. Then he crawled up from the bottom of the bed, so his head was between my legs.

I was gripping the bed post so tight I heard it creak with my movements. I was arching toward him, wanting him to lick me, give me what I hungered for. What I needed.

"Stay still." He ordered, and at the sound of his deep, resonate voice a wave of desire shot through me. He leaned closer, and I could feel his breath on my pussy, scorching heat blazing so hot that I was ready to scream at him to just touch me. I knew my sweet torture would last longer though.

"You're swollen and glistening. God, Emily. You're mine. This pussy is mine. Nothing touches it but me."

"Honey. Please." My knees were trembling so badly that he had to steady them with his hands around my ankles.

Then he spread my lips apart, and his tongue touched me. I moaned, sinking further into the bed as he began suckling deep and hard, then soft and sweet. Dragging my wetness upward with his tongue, and then swirling over me, he had my entire body arching to meet him.

Unable to touch, my hands were tied together, and Logan had complete control over my body; it was a release of pure ecstasy. A giving of myself to him, trusting him to do what I needed, what my body desired.

I was near exploding as two fingers drove inside me at the same time as he sucked hard on my clit. I screamed, arching, and he put his other hand on my stomach to keep me in place. He pulled his head back.

I moaned. "Oh God, Logan. Please."

"Not yet. You will wait, Emily. Every time, unless I tell you otherwise." Then he turned around and lay on his side beside me, his cock inches from my mouth, so close I could've swept my tongue out and touched it. I wanted to, God, I wanted to taste it.

"You want this?" He gripped his cock in his hand.

I nodded.

"Good. Because I'm giving it to you." His knees came on either side of my head, and then he lowered until the tip of his cock was touching my lips. "Open. Take all of me. I'm coming inside your mouth, baby."

I opened, and his heated hardness came into my mouth, and I wrapped my lips around him tasting the sweet, salty pre-cum on the tip of my tongue.

He stiffened and groaned. "Oh fuck." He settled further on top of me, and then I felt his hands pushing my legs open.

I sucked while he moved up and down, fucking my mouth while he drove his fingers inside me and licked and sucked until I was screaming inside, wanting release. Yet every time I got close, he backed off.

His balls hit my face as he pumped hard into my mouth again and again, and I knew he was close when he began sucking on me ruthlessly.

"Now, baby."

I sucked his cock hard, taking him deep into my throat, my wrists straining against the silk scarf as my body arched then reached its peak at the same time as I felt him stiffen. His cock was deep in my mouth, and the spurt of his cum slipped down my throat. I swallowed and moaned and swallowed more as he came at the same time I did. It was beautiful and it was him giving me everything I wanted.

He pulled out then turned around and pulled me into his arms. "I love you, Eme." He stroked my back then over my ass then up again until his hands undid the scarf, and I was finally able to touch him.

And with my hands on his chest feeling his heartbeat, and my head nested in the crook of his arm I fell asleep.

Chapter Twenty-Eight

"Mouse."

I woke to Logan's sexy voice, but it wasn't beside me.

"The party has started. Let's go, baby."

"Shit. You let me sleep?"

"You needed it."

I stretched like a cat after a good nap and felt the sweet soreness in my jaw and smiled. Damn, I'd never done anything so erotic as last night. The thought of Logan sent a wave of heat through me. A heat that filled my heart and made it feel— complete. And when I looked up at Logan standing at the end of the bed dressed in dark jeans and a purple pinstriped button-down dress shirt, I totally fell in love all over again.

I could lie here for hours and admire him with his delicious bedroom hair and purple shirt that showed off his russet eyes.

He frowned. I licked my lips.

God, I loved him. He looked so confident and self-assured even though tonight the band had to impress some big names in the music industry. I was probably more nervous than he was.

I couldn't believe this man was mine. He never gave up on me. He never gave up on us.

"Do I get a kiss?"

"Right now, all I want to do is say fuck it and crawl back into bed with you. So coming any closer ... is a bad idea."

The sheet slipped to my waist as I sat up and I heard him groan.

"Fuck."

There was no question I wasn't getting a kiss, so I threw the covers aside and slipped to the edge of the bed.

His hands clenched into fists as his eyes travelled down my naked body then back up again. He shook his head back and forth and inhaled a deep breath. It felt amazing that I could do that to this man, make him want me. He'd always made me feel beautiful. He still did, and I loved him even more if that was possible.

He cleared his throat, but it was still a little unsteady as he said, "I bought you a dress. It's in the bathroom."

I sat up. "You bought me a dress?"

He gave a curt nod. "Shoes are there too."

"When did you do that?" We'd spent nearly every moment of the last week together.

"When I went to see Deck. Get dressed, Eme. Meet me downstairs. I want you to meet our new manager." He walked out of the room shutting the door a little too hard behind him, and I laughed. I also noticed how his jeans had become snug between his legs when I'd thrown back the covers.

When I walked downstairs, following the sound of voices out onto patio that now had a huge white canvas tent over it, I was feeling ... well beautiful. I couldn't remember the last time I truly felt attractive. I mean, I definitely didn't when I was a girl growing up with my mother's constant belligerence.

Logan was staring at me.

Our eyes locked. The guy he was chatting with stopped talking and turned to look at me too. Yeah, I felt beautiful. Logan had always made me feel that way. No matter what crap my mother spilled, it was all lies. The only way to make herself feel better was to put someone else down, and that someone happened to be her daughter.

My dress fit perfectly, a simple asymmetrical white chiffon skirt, plunging neckline top with a dipped back that contrasted with a subtle black lining. Logan had laid out a pair of stunning white and black strappy heels which, surprisingly, fit too. I wondered if Kat had anything to do with it.

Then there was the box he left wrapped with a yellow bow on top of my makeup bag. I gasped when I opened it, eyes filling with tears as I saw the pendant necklace laid in blue velvet. The tasteful diamonds hung on a solid, thin gold chain. When I put it on, the necklace fit snug to my neck, the pendant touching the center of my throat so that you could see my skin through the center of the diamonds. It was striking, and for a few minutes I admired it in the mirror as it nestled against my skin. I wasn't sure where he had the money for it, but it was from him, and he'd been thinking about me.

When I saw the note folded neatly below the box, I smiled.

It said,

"No panties tonight, Emily. I want to be on stage knowing you're naked beneath that dress. I love every part of you."

Now he was standing in front of me and I felt like we were the only two people in the room.

"Emily," Logan looped his arm around my waist as he leaned in and whispered in my ear "You make me breathless."

"Thank you for the necklace."

"Did you do as I requested?"

I wanted to laugh at him using the word "requested." Logan rarely requested; he spoke, and it was done, and that wasn't only with me. I nodded, and he swore and groaned then kissed me. "Good girl."

Then we were pulled apart by a voice. "Now I understand what kept you away from my office this week."

Logan squeezed me in tight. It was possessive and was saying something to the guy. "Emily, this is our new manager Daryl. Daryl, Emily."

I shook his hand and instantly felt the warmth emanating from him. He wore a suit and tie that fit his lean, tall form, and his hair was kept short and styled close. There was no rock star look in him. He was controlled, yet he had this casual air that made me feel relaxed.

We chatted for several minutes until the crowds started to arrive, and I was swept up into the fray as Logan introduced me to people I recognized from Avalanche, but mostly the guests were strangers. I caught a glimpse of Deck at one point, but he was in work mode, prowling the grounds and making certain the security was tight.

"Emily!" Georgie called as she pushed aside the throes of guests and came toward me.

She looked me up and down. "Damn, you look like you're ready to be fucked or were just fucked." She shrugged. "Whatever, it's smacking hot. Logan, what the hell? You tying this girl up all week or what? Haven't heard a peep from her."

I felt my cheeks heat up at the mention of being tied up, and typical Georgie didn't let it pass.

"Ha, well strap me down." She grabbed me by the shoulders and pulled me in to whisper, "Rock star fighter who likes a little extracurricular activity in bed? Damn, he is one hell of a cupcake. Wonder if he likes spanking?"

Matt and Kat arrived, Kat looking stunning with her little black dress and blonde hair falling down over her slim shoulders.

She was nearly as tall as Matt since she was wearing her spikey black heels, and she towered over me.

Logan leaned in and squeezed my ass. "Stay close to Matt. He knows what's going on. You're safer in a crowd, so don't leave the party. I mean it, Eme. Not for a second." I knew he was concerned about Alfonzo even though Deck and his men had the place covered. "You need to go the bathroom or freshen up, call Deck. He will have his phone on. No one else."

I nodded.

"I hate to be away from you even for a second."

I caressed his cheek and he took my hand and kissed my palm. "My heart is repaired, Logan. You did that."

"Baby." He pulled me into his arms, his hands on either side of my head as he kissed me. It was hard and intense and made me forget that we were surrounded by people. "You obliterated the bad in my life." He kissed my forehead then drew back. "I have some suits to impress. You good?"

"Yeah, honey."

He chin-lifted to Matt, and there was a look between them. And then Matt was beside me, his hand on the small of my back. Logan nodded then disappeared through the crowd. I saw him stop and talk to Ream who was with a cute little blonde, and then they were walking toward the stage.

It was another ten minutes before the band came on stage, and I was able to see Logan again. He was comfortable as he stood in front of the crowds, his confidence was natural, like being on stage was where he belonged.

And he did. There was no doubt that Tear Asunder was making it big, and Daryl obviously thought so, too.

Logan said a few words to the crowd and had them laughing and instantly falling under his spell. It was incredible that this man who oozed authority and power could have a group of posh executives melt at his feet. When Logan was on stage, it was like no one spoke unless he told them to.

He turned me on, but it was so much more powerful than that. It was like he was inside me, making my heart beat, my lungs breathe. He made me feel like whole again.

He did repair us.

Logan's eyes found mine. I waited breathless then he winked, and I felt like he'd just swept his hands over my heated skin.

"This is a new song we're playing tonight called 'Torn from You.'" He closed his eyes and nodded his head three times then Kite clicked his sticks together.

They brought it, real and raw with each cord, each note rushing a thrill through the crowd. Logan's voice was powerful, graveled and crass with the chorus, then seeking the soft deepness that sent shivers across my flesh during the verses.

"Fuck. They rock." Georgie was nodding her head to the beat, and as I looked across the crowd, everyone was riveted to Logan. "Thinking maybe I need to get some of that."

My mouth dropped open.

Georgie laughed. "Not your man, girl. Crisis. That tongue could do me wonders."

I rolled my eyes, and Matt grunted, obviously hating to hear anything about Crisis, tongue, and Georgie in the same sentence.

The rest of the night, I didn't see much of Logan, but who I did see a lot of was Deck. He was always within eye sight of me, and Matt never left my side.

It was one in the morning by the time everyone cleared out except the band, Georgie, Matt, and Kat. Deck appeared out of nowhere as we hung by the pool. He nodded to each of us then spoke quietly to Logan for a few minutes before he walked down the path toward the front of the house.

When Logan came back to me I looked up at him and he knew exactly what I wanted to know before I even had to ask. "No sign of him. Deck says it's highly unlikely Alfonzo can find out about the farm unless he's been following any of us, which I told you, Deck's men has made certain he hasn't. We're just taking precautions until he's located. There is no reason he'd even want to come after you, Eme. It would be stupid if he did. He knows Deck's after him."

Deck shouted, "Georgie. We're leaving."

Georgie came up beside me and threw her arm around my shoulders. She was slurring her words, and her weight was on me. "I'm staying here."

"Georgie. Get your ass over here." Deck's voice was harsh and a little annoyed. Okay super annoyed.

"Pooh. No fun. I'm not going with ... you." Georgie stumbled forward right into Crisis's chest. "Going to get fucked by Mr. Delicious here."

Crisis's eyes widened then he put his arm around Georgie. I wasn't certain if that was to keep her from falling or because he was going to screw with Deck and take Georgie to bed.

"Fuck." Logan swore under his breath as Deck came striding toward Georgie. "Let up, Crisis."

"Yep. Not fucking with that." Crisis whispered something into Georgie's ear, and her smile faded, and her lips pursed together in a drunken pout.

She must not have heard Deck's approach, but we all saw it, and suddenly, she was being picked up and carried over his shoulder like a sack of grain.

He never said a word as he left with a dangling Georgie that was laughing and cursing at the same time.

Logan watched them leave then without even looking at me he said, "Eme. Bed. Now."

Oh, caveman Logan. No more rock star with the sexy wink and to-die-for grin.

We said goodnight to everyone, and then as soon as we were out of sight, Logan was slamming me up against the wall and kissing me. "Fuck. I've wanted to kiss you all goddamn night."

His cock pressed into me as his hands weaved into my hair, and we devoured one another. It was wild and raw with nothing but raging need between us. I didn't think we'd make it to the bedroom, but we stumbled up the stairs, and I had him half naked by the time we got there and slammed the door.

Logan didn't wait to take my dress off. He yanked it up, and then had me against the door, lifting me up. "Legs," he demanded.

I wrapped my legs around him, hooking my ankles, and then he plunged inside me.

My head hit the wall hard with each thrust as he groaned and took me without mercy, and I wanted it.

"Harder, Logan."

His hips pushed back then shoved forward harder, and I felt him sink even further into me. "Oh, God. Yes. Logan."

He rested his head against my shoulder, teeth biting my flesh as he groaned and thrust. "Now, baby. Now."

I was there already. Each thrust putting me closer to the top until he shouted my name and I crashed and shouted with him.

"Fuck." He was sunk deep inside me, and I could feel his cock twitching. He raised his head from my shoulder and kissed me, hard and relentless.

He carried me to bed where he slowly undressed me, and then we made love until early morning. We fell asleep with tangled naked limbs.

Chapter Twenty-Nine

When I woke, Logan was gone, but there was a note on the pillow, and I smiled as I unfolded it.

"Love you baby. In the city at the studio with the guys. Don't leave the farm, Emily. Matt's staying with you for the day. Dinner tonight, my mom's coming over."

Oh, shit, I thought, then finished reading.

"Don't panic, Mouse. She'll love you. And I'm cooking. Call me when you're awake."

His mom was coming over, and that felt serious, because Logan hadn't shared his mom with anyone except maybe Kite. I realized that we were going to be together, but I still needed my own place. This was Logan's farm, and I know he'd say different, but it felt like his, not mine. It wasn't my home, and regardless of what was happening to us, I still needed that. The question was when and how was I going to bring that up to Logan.

I reached for my phone and already there were three messages: one from Georgie asking what the hell happened last night and how did she end up sleeping in her bra and panties on

Deck's bed, another from Kat about ten minutes ago asking for help rounding up the horses in the east field who broke through the fence—my guess it was Havoc reacting to all the noise last night, then a text from Logan saying good morning and to call him.

I quickly dressed, a little sore from last night's marathon. I texted Georgie back first as I went to wake up Matt.

Drunk. Deck took you home. And he didn't look happy.

Georgie immediately texted back.

Not drunk. Sloshed. LOL. Feel like Deck plowed my head into the side of his car. Did he?

I laughed. No doubt Deck felt like doing that.

Not that I know of. Text you later. Horses broke out last night, party must have scared them.

Georgie sent me a sad face.

Matt was passed out in the spare bedroom next to my old one. I nudged his shoulder. "Hey. Horses are out. I need to go help your sister round them up."

Matt groaned then rolled over and threw the covers back. He still was wearing what he had on last night. "Fuck. How'd they do that?"

"We had a party last night, Matt. The horses were probably scared of the noise. Come on. If they get on the road, someone could get hurt."

"Yeah. Yeah. I'm up." Matt ran his hand back and forth over his head and then down his face. "Give me a sec."

I quickly called Logan while Matt went the washroom, but it went straight to voice mail.

"Morning, honey. Have fun at the studio. Still thinking about last night and thinking I need some more of that tonight. *After* you mother leaves. And Logan, thank you. For wanting to share her with me."

As we walked out to the back field, I didn't see Kat or the horses. Shit, that meant they'd probably gone over to the neighbor's or on the road.

"So, you and Sculpt are good?" Matt said, his arm slung over my shoulder as we walked up the hill.

I smiled. "Yeah. We are. Really good, Matt."

He squeezed my shoulders. "He loves y—down." Matt suddenly shoved me away from him and I fell to the ground.

Bang.

"Matt!" I screamed as I watched him crumple to the grass. "Matt. No, Matt."

"Go near him and she dies." Alfonzo held a gun to Kat's head, and I could see blood dripping from her temple. She was gagged, and her hands were tied behind her back. Her eyes were wild with a mixture of fear and anger.

"Come here," Alfonzo bellowed.

I hesitated as I looked to Matt who was clutching his leg and trying to crawl to Kat.

Bang.

I screamed as Matt's body jerked and he fell forward onto his face. "No. Stop. Stop. I'll do whatever you want."

Alfonzo was burning with hatred, his eyes wild and unsteady as he leered at me. His clothes were dirty and his hair was greasy like he hadn't showered in weeks.

"Bitch, get on the ground."

I slowly sank to my knees sobbing.

Kat made a sound, and Alfonzo raised his gun and slammed the barrel into her head. She cried out and fell to her side, and he reared back and kicked her in the ribs.

"No!" I screamed and jumped up, running toward her. I fell on top of Kat to save her from the brunt of his abuse. He continued to boot me in the side until finally, he stopped, and picked me up by the hair and forced me to kneel in front of him.

Alfonzo raised the gun.

Click.

Bang.

I screamed at the same time the bullet went off, and I saw Kat's body jerk.

"Nooooo! Oh God. Oh God. No. Kat." I was screaming hysterically now, tears streaming down my cheeks as a pool of her blood started to seep into ground staining the green grass.

"Shut the fuck up, bitch." Alfonzo aimed the gun at me, and I waited for the pain as I crouched over Kat, refusing to leave her.

"They'll crucify you," I promised through sputtered breaths. "Deck and his men. Logan. They'll kill you." My voice grew steadier. If Kat was still alive then her only chance would be to get pressure on the wound and to a hospital.

Over Alfonzo's shoulder I saw the white mane--Havoc. She must have heard my screams and the gunshot. Eyes steady and watching. Nostrils flaring. It was the only thing I could think of—I whistled a long, high-pitched sound.

Havoc's ears perked, and she tossed her head then came galloping toward us. Alfonzo heard the hooves pounding into the hard ground and turned. I did two things—pressed Redial on my phone then dove for Alfonzo.

I landed hard on top of him, my hands going for the gun. Havoc's hooves kept coming toward us. Alfonzo elbowed me between the ribs and knocked the wind out of me. I fell backward, and he came on top, the gun shoved hard into my chest.

"I like fighters. The more you fight the better. I'm going to string you up and fuck you until you bleed. You're going to suck me, and then when I'm done I'm going to sell you."

I grit my teeth and refused to look away from him.

Havoc whinnied behind us, then reared up, legs flailing.

Alfonzo turned and pointed the gun at Havoc. I yelled just as the bullet went off.

I felt the vibration in the ground as Havoc fell.

"Havoc," I yelled.

Alfonzo jammed his gun so hard into my chest that my breath was cut off.

"Don't move." I could hear Havoc screeching and thrashing to get to her feet. "Raul should've killed Sculpt when he had the chance. Bastard was too greedy. Thought his son would join him and become his prize fighter. I knew. I warned Raul Sculpt was planning shit. But the bastard was too cocky. He thought no one would attempt to take him down."

"When Logan gets his hands on you—you'll wish you were dead."

He laughed. "He can try. But once we disappear in that world, no one will find us. Not even those elite commando guys. And your boyfriend? That bastard's blessed as fuck he's still alive. Your fighter boyfriend didn't look much like a fighter when his father tortured him for months after he let you go." I swallowed the bile in my throat. Oh, Logan. No.

"I bet he couldn't even walk when that Deck guy got him out. That bastard managed to shut us down. Found Raul too. But he hasn't found me and now I have you. Raul intended for Sculpt to die a long, slow death for his betrayal. Instead, I've made it my mission to let you take his place."

Alfonzo got up, and then pulled me to my feet. He put my hands up behind my head and tied them together.

I glanced over at Kat, trying to see if she was still alive, but I couldn't see anything. Matt moved his leg, then I saw him slowly reach in his pocket and take out his phone. He was halfway to reaching the phone to his ear when he dropped it and went still. "You can't leave them like that."

Havoc was lying on her side, her chest heaving in and out, but there was no longer any fight to get up. Deep red blood soaked into her white coat where the bullet had penetrated her neck.

He pulled me behind into the tree line. "Kat!" I screamed.

I tried to pull free of Alfonzo, but with my hands tied above and behind my head, I quickly lost my balance and fell hard to my knees.

"Get up." He kicked me in the side, and I tried to stand, but couldn't. He grabbed hold of my elbow and pulled me through the bush until we reached the road where a car was parked.

I knew the worst thing I could do was panic, Logan taught me that. He also said to never get into a car. They always had the advantage at a second location. I knew once I disappeared, I'd be lost. Logan had told me that. Alfonzo told me that.

He patted me down, found my cell, and cursed, throwing it into the long grass in the ditch. I prayed it had gotten through to Logan, but I didn't know, and all I could rely on right now was myself.

He opened the trunk and tugged me toward it.

No. This wasn't going to happen to me. I swung around just as he was about to push me inside, and my elbow hit him in the side of the face, then I ducked at the same time as he made a grab for me. I stumbled. Fell to my knees on the gravel and tried to get up.

His hands were around my waist, and I was picked up off the ground kicking and screaming as loud as I could.

"Logan! Kat's shot. Matt. Havoc's field. Alfonzo." I prayed my screaming reached the phone. That somehow, Logan's voicemail picked up what was happening.

The trunk slammed shut, and I was immersed in darkness.

Logan

"We hitting Avalanche later?" Crisis asked. "After smokin' hot Georgie last night, I need some pussy riding this horse fast. Damn, that woman rocks. I think I came a little bit when she said she wanted to fuck me."

"Touch that ass and your ass will be no longer. That's Deck's." Kite tossed his sticks in the air, caught them, then placed them in his back pocket.

Logan looked at his phone and grinned when he saw a missed call from Emily. His cock twitched when her sweet voice sounded on his voice mail.

"What the hell, Kat's Ream's, but he's not doing her, and Georgie's Deck's, and he's not doing her. I'd be doing them both and at the same fucking time."

"Jesus, Crisis." Kite said.

Logan glanced at Ream who was standing with his hand on the doorknob ready to leave the studio. The voicemail clicked to the next message, and while he waited for her voice again he said, "Having dinner with my mother tonight guys. Emily is—fuck." Logan raced toward the door, the phone pressed to his ear.

"Man. What?" Kite said.

"Sculpt? What the fuck?" Crisis said following.

Ream yanked opened the door. "Sculpt?"

"Call the police, and have an ambulance meet us at the farm."

Ream grabbed his arm just as Emily's screams went through the phone.

"Fuck," Logan shouted. No, fuckin' way. Alfonzo was not getting his woman. Logan had never felt this intensity of fear and rage cut through him. He needed to reel it back in before he lost it completely. He pressed the phone harder to his ear and listened closely. There was the sound of Emily screaming Kat's name. Then Alfonzo was talking about the torture. He heard a car door then Emily screaming for him. She yelled something indistinguishable and muffled then the word shot and then Havoc something. Logan heard the squealing tires and the line was silent.

The ambulance was waiting when he arrived. Deck was talking with two officers, but as soon as he saw him he jogged over.

"The police are searching the house, and my men are already headed for all known locations for transporting girls."

Logan felt sick to his stomach. "I was supposed to protect her. I promised her." The emotions running rampant through him were debilitating as thoughts of any harm coming to Emily. "Fuck." He smashed his fist into the hood of the car.

"There was no way Alfonzo could've known she was here. Someone had to have told him. Someone we trust."

"Jesus." Logan started toward the house, but Deck stopped him grabbing his arm. Logan shoved his hand away. "I have to find her."

"Yes, we do. But that's not going to happen if you're acting irrational. You know that better than anyone. I need to hear her message."

Trying to act calm and patient was killing him. All he wanted to do was find her. Hold her. Protect her. God, he didn't deserve her. Fuck. How did this happen?

Logan took out his phone and cursed when he saw his hand shaking. He went to his voice mail, then passed it to Deck.

Emily's voice could be heard over the phone and it felt like a knife was ripping through him. When he heard her scream the name Havoc this time he heard the word field too. He looked at Deck and they both went running for the horse's field.

It felt like his feet were in quicksand. The thumping of feet were behind him as they all went running. He went over the dip in the hill and stumbled when he saw first the horse's body lying in the grass, then Matt and Kat.

"I got Matt," Deck shouted.

"Jesus." Logan dropped down beside Kat's body, blood pooling beneath her.

Logan checked for a pulse. *Fuck, Kat.* He needed to keep it together. Calm and controlled.

"No." Ream's stunned voice was behind him.

Logan nodded to Kite who grabbed Ream's arm just as he fell

to his knees beside Kat.

His voice was a haunted whisper as he repeated Kat's name over and over again. One of the paramedics snapped a collar around her neck then they gently rolled her over onto the stretcher.

Matt was surrounded by three officers and a paramedic. Logan heard someone calling in another ambulance over the radio.

Deck had his phone to his ear and was calling out orders to whoever was on the other end.

Logan's mind was in a whirlwind, and he was trying desperately to keep control, but Emily's scream kept haunting him. He knew the sex trafficking ring; he knew how fast girls disappeared, and if Alfonzo still had connections, Emily could be out of Canada within hours never to be seen again.

Fuck, he knew it. Deck said Alfonzo had surfaced, but neither of them thought he'd link the farm to Emily. They'd taken precautions just in case, had security at the party, kept a man following them whenever any of them came to the farm to make certain they weren't tailed. But Alfonzo had somehow found her.

"Fuck!"

One paramedic applied pressure to the stomach wound while the other took one end of the stretcher and Crisis the other.

"Kitkat," Ream said. "Don't you dare die on me." Ream had tears in his eyes as he gripped her hand.

"Kat." Logan heard Matt shout and a paramedic urged him to stay still and don't talk. "Is she alive, damn it?"

Logan heard the paramedic trying to keep him calm and then Kite was talking to him, telling Matt Kat was fine. Logan wasn't sure if that was true or not, but Matt had to calm down or he'd do worse damage to himself.

An officer was beside Havoc applying pressure to the bullet wound, but the mare wasn't moving.

Logan looked at Deck and he shook his head. He knew what it meant—no sign of Emily.

His heart felt like a cement block had landed on it. He was

having trouble breathing; even the churning in his stomach had stopped as if it was building into a huge wave of unbearable pain.

Ream and Crisis helped the paramedics with the two stretchers back to the ambulance, and Ream jumped inside.

"I'm going to the hospital too," Crisis said.

"Not good, man. You and Ream all fucked up and in the same hospital. I'll go," Kite offered.

"No. It may not look like it, but Ream's my best friend. This is his chick, and she's my friend, I'm going."

Another ambulance pulled up and the paramedics rushed to load Matt into it. Crisis jumped in with Matt.

Deck was striding to the car as he listened to whoever was on the phone with him.

Logan started after him then jumped in the car. Kite got in the other side and nodded to him.

Kite was the guy that would stand behind you a hundred percent even when there was a chance you might not come back alive.

Deck threw the car in gear. "That was Georgie. Raven was the one who gave away Emily's location. She's helping Alfonzo."

Chapter Thirty

I was thrown onto the floor, and my nose hit hard and immediately started bleeding onto the carpet. Orange shag carpet. Not many people had orange shag carpet, except Georgie.

"Keep it on her," Alfonzo said. "She makes a move, shoot her in the leg."

I looked up and saw Raven pointing the gun at my head. Oh God, no. Why? Why would Raven help him? Why were they at Georgie's?

"Where's the other girl?"

He had to be talking about Georgie.

"She ... she heard me talking to you on the phone and ran. I ... I didn't see where she went, Master. I'm sorry. I'm sorry, Master."

"Fuck. Stupid girl. We have to get out of here." Alfonzo took out his phone and started to walk in the other room.

"Raven?"

Alfonzo came charging back, phone to his ear as his fist plowed into my stomach knocking the wind of me. "No fucking talking." I heard his phone ring, and then Alfonzo was walking into the other room talking quietly. He sounded frazzled as he paced back and forth.

"Raven. Please." I struggled to sit up then rubbed the blood from my eyes as best as I could with my shoulder. "Why?"

Raven was trembling and pale. The gun wavered, and her eyes were blank as she did as she was told. She looked terrified. I wondered if she was doing this out of fear of Alfonzo. A fear likely ingrained so deeply that she was like a robot, unable to act on her own free will any longer.

"Raven. Please. Deck will help you. Don't do this. You don't have to do this."

She was shaking so badly now that she had to clutch her arms close to her sides to keep from dropping the gun.

"Yes, damn it." Alfonzo was shouting in the other room. "You'll have her back." He kicked a chair in the kitchen, and it went flying into the fridge.

"Where's Georgie, Raven?"

Raven stared at me as if I hadn't spoken.

Alfonzo came striding from the kitchen, and Raven flinched so hard she dropped the gun.

"Useless slut." Alfonzo picked up the weapon, then grabbed her around the neck, hauling her against him. "Aren't you?"

"Y-yes, Master," Raven replied in a quivering whispered voice.

"Kai says to behave yourself, Raven. Keep doing exactly as I say, and he'll still buy you." He lowered his mouth and kissed her cruelly. "You've been good. Very good at getting the information for me."

She nodded. "Yes, Master."

Shit. That's why Raven came and talked to me at the bar. I thought it had been strange she'd taken initiative like that, but she has been feeding Alfonzo information. Had he put her on auction, set it up so Deck would get her out? Had Raven refused to go home because she knew she had to get information for Alfonzo as to where I was?

"You keep doing as I tell you, and I will sell you to him. You want to go to Kai? Or stay with me?"

Oh God, the thought of Raven under Alfonzo's hand for the last two years made me sick to my stomach. I really had no idea if Kai was any better, but I understood why Raven would do anything to get away from Alfonzo.

Raven didn't answer, and he raised his hand and slapped her across the face. She didn't even whimper, but she lowered her eyes from Alfonzo and said, "To him, Master."

I saw Raven's eyes close in defeat; Alfonzo would punish her for that, for answering a question he forced on her. A slave admitting she wanted someone other than her Master is against the rules.

I heard a sound above me—attic. Georgie? If she was hiding, there was the chance she had called Deck. God, please, let her have told someone where we are.

"Now, Emily."

I jerked at the sound of Georgie's muffled voice above me, but didn't hesitate as I pushed to my feet and ran bent over at Alfonzo, head-butting him in the back of the legs.

He went buckling forward, into the porch door, and the gun went flying. "Bitch!" he yelled. "I'm going to fucking torture you until—" Georgie landed on top of him as she came out of the scuttle hole in the ceiling.

They rolled out the screen door and down the steps of the porch. I could hear Alfonzo shouting as I used the wall to gain my feet again. I was about to follow when I saw Raven with the gun pointing at me.

"Raven. No. Put it down. I'll help you. You don't have to go to Kai."

She shook her head, tears streaming down her face.

Raven cocked the hammer and pointed the gun at my leg.

"Raven. No. You don't want to do this."

"I ... I ... have to." Her voice was a whisper of a shiver, and I could tell that she didn't want to do it, but she thought she had no choice—that whatever was driving her made her do this.

"He doesn't want you to hurt me, Raven. You have to protect me."

She was shaking so badly I thought she'd pass out, her face pale and her eyes wild as she kept flinching from the noises made by Georgie and Alfonzo fighting outside.

Then suddenly silence.

Raven's eyes darted to the screen door, and I leapt.

I tackled her, the gun sliding away across the orange carpet, and my body landing right on top of her. I almost wanted to say I was sorry, because it felt like her frail bones cracked under my weight and she didn't even struggle.

Suddenly I was dragged off her by the leg and picked up with a hand latched around my upper arm. I started struggling until I heard the voice. "Stop."

I did. I was shocked to see him. And terrified because this wasn't Alfonzo—instead a man who was more than likely deadlier.

Kai exuded power, even more, I expected, than Raul, and that made him extremely dangerous. "Raven," Kai said. Raven was on her feet and at his side. He didn't even look at her. "Where is the transporter?"

Alfonzo had brought Georgie back inside. He kicked her in the back of the legs, and she winced as she fell to her knees. He had ropes on her wrists behind her back. All I could think of was Deck and how he was going to have a fit if he saw Georgie like that.

Alfonzo picked up his gun. "I promised you Raven. You have her. That's our deal."

Kai's hand tightened on my neck. "Our deal has changed. What are you doing with that one?" Kai nodded to Georgie.

"She's coming with us. And that bitch" he nodded toward me, "escaped Raul. No one escapes Raul."

"Raul's dead."

Alfonzo kicked Georgie in the back, and she grunted and fell forward. "Once I'm done with their training, they'll go on auction and never been found again. That's if they live through it."

I knew Georgie couldn't keep her mouth shut no matter how much pain she was in. Her lips were pursed together and her brows were drawn down over her eyes. Suddenly, she slammed her head backward into Alfonzo's knee.

I heard the sound of her skull hitting his knee cap; then Alfonzo was yelling.

"No!" I shouted as Alfonzo raised his gun to Georgie.

"Killing her is a waste," Kai stated, his voice steady and cool. "Take me to the transporter. I need to see him."

Alfonzo had his gun to Georgie's head, his fingers weaved into her hair. "I can't do that. That wasn't the deal. Raven and the money. That's it."

"It's the deal now." Kai remained unflinching.

Alfonzo's face turned beet read. "I'm selling you the girl for half her price."

"I could have easily found Raven myself. I found you, didn't I? What I want is the transporter."

"No one gets to meet him. He doesn't meet with anyone. Ever."

Kai shrugged. "He will me. Call him."

Alfonzo blanched. "You just don't call him. It's been set up already—"

"Raul is dead. That means you and your transporter no longer have a main source. Call him. Now. Or I kill you and take all three girls myself."

"Fuck." Alfonzo was fumbling and upset. His fingers were jerking on the gun, and it was obvious he was scared of Kai and what he'd do if he didn't call this transporter guy. Alfonzo raised gun and hit Georgie on the head.

"Georgie." I tried to pull away from Kai, but his grip was unrelenting. "Please don't hurt her."

Kai's voice was low and almost inaudible as he said, "It's better this way."

Alfonzo tied a strip of cloth around Georgie's arm and I saw the syringe. I didn't know if it was street drugs or something else, but anything put into her system was not good. I struggled to get to her, my legs kicking out at Kai. "Please, don't. Georgie."

"Stop." Kai yanked on my arm to the side and I cried out in agony.

Georgie didn't move, but I could see her eyes flickering, looking dazed from the blow. Alfonzo slid the needle into her vein, and within seconds her body relaxed and her eyes closed.

I started crying, and my legs gave out, but I didn't fall. Kai held me against him, his arm now locked around my chest. Whether it was to keep me upright or to stop me from running to Georgie, I didn't know.

Alfonzo was on the phone mumbling something about Kai and a meeting. Then he hung up and nodded to Kai.

"Let's go," Kai ordered.

Alfonzo slung Georgie over his shoulder, and we walked out the back door.

Chapter Thirty-One

I lay on the cement floor beside Georgie. We were in some kind of warehouse that looked like it had once been a factory. I could smell the distinct odor of the Don River which was the acrid scent of garbage. I guessed since we hadn't driven very far that we were still downtown. Alfonzo had blindfolded me and tied my wrists together before he shoved me in the trunk, but I'd managed to slip off the blindfold about an hour ago.

Kai was standing with his arms crossed, leaning against a large piece of machinery looking completely relaxed. Raven knelt beside him, her hands in her lap and her head bowed.

Georgie was still drugged, and her eyes were glassed over and she was not responding to her name. Her breathing was slow, but steady, and I suspected whatever they'd given her wasn't harmful enough to kill her.

Alfonzo paced back and forth constantly looking to the door then his phone.

Finally the metal door slid on its tracks and opened.

It was dark, and I couldn't see the large shadow that came

toward us until the moonlight hit him just as he stopped in front of Kai.

Fear and recognition slammed into me.

Jacob.

He had waterboarded me again and again without mercy when I was held captive. He tortured me without pity, and he looked stone cold now.

"I don't like changing plans," Jacob said to Alfonzo. "It causes mistakes."

Kai kept his eyes on Jacob. "Raul's right hand man. I thought you were dead."

"So does everyone." Jacob nodded to Raven. "You've travelled a great distance for one girl, she doesn't look worth it."

"Where are the other girls?"

"Here. Awaiting shipment."

I was about ten feet away, and I noticed the tension in Kai go from zero to a hundred within seconds. Something wasn't right. "Georgie," I whispered. "Georgie." I nudged her with my shoulder, and she moaned. Kai, Jacob, and Alfonzo's attention were on one another. "Georgie."

It happened so fast, Jacob pulled a gun, turned, and shot Alfonzo in the head.

Alfonzo dropped to the ground.

Kai never moved a muscle, instead he looked even more casual as his hand went to Raven's head, and he stroked her hair as if to soothe her.

"I told him, I don't meet clients. He didn't listen."

"So that would make me a liability." Kai sounded as if he didn't care that Jacob had just killed Alfonzo and that he might be next.

I was holding my breath, waiting for the loud bang that would kill Kai. It didn't matter to me if he died; Jacob was just as dangerous as any of them, but every dead man is one less to defend again.

"Your offer piqued my interest." He thought about it for a second. "I require a base to bring the girls before auction. You can provide me with that."

Kai's hand stopped stroking Raven's hair. "Who has been providing since Raul's death?"

Jacob slipped his gun back into his belt. "No one. This is our first shipment in over a year. That guy Deck and his men have been all over us, and now, Alfonzo screwed up taking that one." He nodded to Georgie. "I don't make mistakes, Kai. I'm careful. Alfonzo wasn't."

"Oh, but you made a mistake, Jacob."

I could only see a side profile of Jacob, but his face suddenly flashed with a moment of surprise, and then he dove and rolled just as Kai threw a knife narrowly missing Jacob's throat.

"Raven. Go to the girls," Kai demanded, and then he was moving.

Jacob had disappeared behind a large piece of machinery.

I needed to get Georgie out of here.

Raven came and sat beside us, her features expressionless, but there was something in her eyes, a look of panic as she kept looking around the warehouse.

"Untie me, Raven."

She ignored me, and I used a stronger voice. "Raven. Untie me now."

That got her attention, but she still didn't make a move to help. Fuck. "Kai will be angry if you don't untie me and we get hurt. He'll be angry you've lessened our value."

I turned my back to her so she could untie the rope. I waited for what seemed like forever; then I heard a gunshot echo, and her hands were on my wrists. I was nearly hyperventilating, I was so anxious to get free. I wanted to scream at her to hurry up, but knew it wouldn't do any good.

Finally, the rope slipped from my sore, raw skin, and I went for Georgie who was moaning and—what the hell?—smiling.

Whatever they had given her, she was enjoying. I pulled her up under the armpits and started walking backwards dragging her toward the door.

I was halfway there when I saw him—Logan. I held in my sob, but kept pulling Georgie. He hid behind a conveyor belt, and he had a gun. I didn't even know Logan knew how to shoot. But he had grown up with Raul, of course he did. I wanted to run to him, throw my arms around him. Cry. Tell him I loved him. I couldn't do any of that as he shook his head, telling me no.

I glanced behind me and saw Jacob. He had Raven held in front of him and his gun pointed at me. I slowly lowered Georgie to the ground and turned to face him.

Kai appeared to the left of Jacob, he didn't hold a gun but a knife, and it was held down by his side.

"Let her go." Kai's tone was furious. His eyes never left Jacob for a second, even when Raven whimpered as Jacob's hold tightened.

"In seconds, I can shoot Sculpt's woman and snap your slave's neck."

"Then do it," Kai said.

I glanced over at Logan, but he was gone. I didn't look for him. He wouldn't leave me here. I knew he wouldn't. No matter what he'd done when his father held a gun to my head, I knew Logan wouldn't leave me. I trusted him.

Logan had always been my knight.

That's when I saw Deck to the right of Jacob crouched behind a pile of barrels. He was motioning to Kai. It happened all at once. A gun went off, and I was thrown on the floor beside Georgie, the wind knocked out of me as a large body landed on top.

I smelled him; I felt the familiar length of him, and when I caught my breath, I said his name, "Logan."

"Stay down." He was covering my head with his hands, and I could hear the shuffling of feet and voices then the sound of a gun going off again.

I jerked.

Logan suddenly was flipping me over and looking down at me, his hands on either side of my cheeks. "Eme. God, baby." Deck crouched beside Georgie, and Logan leaned down and kissed me—hard.

"You found us. How's Georgie?" I asked, clinging to Logan and watching Deck inspect Georgie.

"High. But fine." Deck held Georgie's arm outstretched while he ran his finger over what I guessed was the needle mark.

"Heroin," said Kai's voice, and I jerked at the sound.

He was standing a few feet away, his arm around Raven's waist, her head tucked into his chest.

Deck nodded. "Probably better. Georgie would've gotten herself killed with that mouth of hers." Deck stood. "Police will be here shortly. You better go."

What? Deck was letting Kai go?

"Logan?" I whispered.

Kai untangled Raven from him, and I saw her eyes widen as he pushed her toward us. "You need to stay with them, Raven. Deck will take you home."

Raven's face dropped, and paled. She fell to her knees in front of him and grabbed his jeans. "Please. Please take me with you."

Logan's arms tightened around me as I watched Kai and Raven, horrified that the girl had the chance to go home, and she was begging Kai to take her with him.

Kai remained motionless as he looked at her. He sighed, and then nodded to Deck who strode over and snagged Raven's arm, pulling her away. Tears streamed down Raven's face, but she didn't make a sound. She looked so devastated that I broke inside for her. This girl was so screwed up that she didn't want to go home. I felt the tears slip from my eyes, and Logan brushed them away.

Sirens could be heard in the distance.

Kai took one last look at Raven then disappeared into the

darkness of the warehouse.

"Logan? I don't understand."

Deck looked at me. "Kai was never here. Do understand, Emily. Never here." Then he was on the phone, Raven at his side and Georgie at his feet. The police burst in with Kite, and Deck talked to the guy in charge, telling him everything. Everything— except not a word was mentioned about Kai.

Three Weeks Later

"Eme, get down here."

I stared at my name on the document and couldn't believe he went and did this without even telling me. I hadn't talked to him about buying my own farm, and yet, he knew. Logan knew what I needed. There was a yellow sticky note on the front of the envelope. It read:

"You've worked hard to make the farm a place for horses to heal. And Eme ... for you to repair too. You've made it a success. The rent you paid Matt went toward the down payment I made on the farm. I know you'd never be happy to live on my farm, so now it's yours, and you earned it. You bought it. The farm has always been yours, baby. Now sign the bloody thing, stop arguing with me and promise to come on tour with me."

I wiped the tears away from my cheeks and laughed. Then I picked up the pen on the vanity and signed the document and put it back in the vanilla envelope.

I took one last look in the mirror, dabbed my lips again, and then took a deep breath and made my way downstairs. My stomach had been tied up in knots for days. Ever since Logan told me his mother was coming to the welcome home party for Kat. My chest was tight; I had a rabble of butterflies dancing in my stomach, and my mouth was dry.

But Kat was finally coming home. She'd been in critical care for days, having lost a large amount of blood. She had bullet fragments extracted from her abdomen and damage to her bowels. The worry was she could die of infection, so she remained for weeks on intravenous antibiotics, under strict hospital observation.

Matt had been in the hospital for five days with superficial wounds to both legs. According to the nurses, he had been a horrible patient, having tried to get out of bed right after surgery in order to get to Kat. They had to keep him sedated for forty-eight hours.

When he was able to go to Kat's room, Logan and I had been sitting with her. We headed to the door to give him time alone with her, but before the door shut I heard Matt choke on a sob then say to his sister, "You've beat all odds before, baby sis. You can do it again."

Logan and I stayed downtown at Matt's condo most nights for the first week she was in the hospital. Matt was a wreck and shut down the bar for a week; then had Brett run it ever since. Matt was never far from the hospital and Kat.

Ream lived at the hospital for four straight days, and then when the nurses finally allowed him in to visit Kat—he left without seeing her. No one had seen him since.

And Havoc. She was like me ... a fighter. She fought her way back first from severe abuse and now from being shot. She was recuperating, with attitude, in the stable.

I walked down the stairs to the kitchen. When I saw a woman standing beside Logan in the kitchen, I knew ... I knew instantly that she was warmth and kindness. A dark-haired angel with the softest blue eyes and smooth, white skin. She had a classic beauty about her, subtle and sincere. There wasn't a hint of my mother in her and a wave of relief swept over me.

She was talking to Logan, her voice calm and quiet as she placed her hand on his chest as if she was saying something meaningful. I noticed she didn't smile, but I imagined if she did, it would light up her entire face like her son's. But there was a hint in her eyes, that glow I knew must have taken a long time to get back after living with Raul.

Logan lifted his head and saw me standing at the doorway observing them. "Eme." He walked over and snagged my hand, pulling me up toward him then stealing a kiss. "You look gorgeous," he whispered. "You do as I say?"

I wrapped my hand around the back of his neck and pulled him back down to me. "Thank you, Logan. For everything." I kissed his cheek and he groaned then tightened his hold and kissed me on the lips.

I pulled back. "Your mom is right there."

"Hmm, and she'll see that I can't keep my hands off you."

"Logan!"

He chuckled.

I glanced over at his mother who was watching us. "Your mother's gorgeous," I whispered.

"And excited to meet you." His hand slid down my back to my ass, and he slapped it inconspicuously. "Smile, Mouse."

I took a deep inhale. "I want her to like me."

"She loves you already. Any mother that sees her son as happy as I am loves the woman that does that to him."

I squeezed his hand. "I love you, Logan."

That's all I needed, his brilliant grin lighting up his entire face. When I faced Isabella, she was smiling at us, and that's when I saw it. Her smile was exactly like his, majestic.

Logan introduced me to his mom, and she immediately pulled me into a hug. There were tears in her eyes when she pulled back. She knew what happened to Logan and I. Well, she didn't know everything that happened—especially what Logan suffered for months after he'd got me out. As far as his mother knew and anyone else, Logan had stayed and fought for Raul until he finally left to join his band.

"What the fuck? Where's the guest of honor?" Crisis strode into the house and placed a case of beer on the counter then he came over and kissed Isabella on each cheek. "Hey, you're mom."

She blushed, and it was so sweet, I wanted to hug her again. Logan was right; this was what a mother was supposed to be like, warm and kind. Isabella had given more than most women; she gave her son a chance at a better life.

Kite opened the sliding glass door, tongs in hand. "Burgers are on. Where's Kat?"

"Coming," I replied. Matt texted me ten minutes ago from the hospital. "They're about fifteen minutes away."

The screen door squeaked as it opened. "Hey cupcakes. Whoa, wow, that your mom, Sculpt?" Georgie went straight to Isabella and pulled her into a hug. "I'm Georgie." She pulled back and smiled. "You're a real looker. Hot. Damn. Sculpt, what happened to you?"

Logan rolled his eyes and whispered something to his mom who gave a half-smile to Georgie and then turned her attention to Deck who had come in after Georgie. I excused myself to pull Georgie aside.

"Raven?" I couldn't get the girl out of my head, and I couldn't imagine what she had to have gone through to get to the point she was at—unable to mentally make decisions on her own, to be so conditioned to do what her master wanted, that she'd even kill someone.

"Deck is being tightlipped, and Deck being tightlipped means nothing gets past his sweet, sexy, fuck-me lips." Georgie looked over at Deck who was talking quietly to Isabella and Logan. "He says she's safe, whatever that means. Deck leaves tonight to fuck knows where for an undisclosed amount of time." She lowered her voice like Deck's when she said the "undisclosed amount of time" part.

Georgie always became a little unsettled when Deck went off on a job; I suspected it was because of what happened to her brother, but it was more than that. I knew Georgie really cared about Deck, maybe more than she'd ever admit. "Deck likes you, Georgie."

Georgie laughed—hard. So hard she smacked her hand onto the kitchen counter and everyone paused to look at her. She leaned in, hand on my shoulder. "I annoy the hell out of him. Deck's incapable of liking much except his way. And if you don't like his way, then he'll shove it up your ass, down your throat, and then make sure you learn to like it. I don't like his way."

Georgie and I chatted a while then Logan came over to join us, sliding his arm around my waist and kissing the side of my neck. Crisis was his usual loud and obnoxious self while Kite ended up chatting with Isabelle for a long while.

A car horn honked.

I slipped from Logan's arms, and Georgie and I went running out through the patio door and around to the driveway where Matt and Kat were getting out of the car.

I reached Kat and threw my arms around her. I was careful not to squeeze too tight, but it was hard not to. "God, it's good to have you home."

Kat pulled back a bit, and despite her smile, I saw the haunted look in her eyes. I'd seen it in the hospital too, but she was so closed off, she wouldn't talk about anything. I knew the feeling firsthand so I kept quiet and didn't push her.

"Come here, lollipop. Give me a hug." Georgie hugged Kat, kissed her on both cheeks, and then looped her arm around both of us and started walking back to the house.

Matt was getting the bags out of the trunk, but I noticed that his eyes never left Kat. It would take him a long time to get over this. I suspected longer than when their parents died.

"Hey, be careful with her, Georgie," Matt shouted as Georgie started skipping and jarred us both.

Everyone cheered and gave Kat hugs and kisses. Crisis passed her a beer and kept beside Kat as if he was her private bulldog, although from what I didn't know.

"You good, Emily?"

It was Deck. Logan had his arm around my waist and his fingers were caressing my bare skin beneath my blouse at my belly. I nodded. "Yeah, Deck. Glad to have Kat home."

Deck glanced at Logan then back at me again. "You need anything. Call. That goes for you both."

"Yeah, need you to convince her to leave Kat and Matt and come on tour with the band in a few months. Can you help with that?"

Deck lowered his head as if to hide the twitch at the corner of his mouth I caught a glance of. It was hot. Deck was hot, and Georgie needed to wrap her head around the fact that Deck didn't watch over her because he had an obligation to her brother; he did it because he cared, and Deck caring was huge. I guaranteed he didn't care easily.

Dinner was a barbecue on the patio, and it was nice. Better than nice. Georgie's mom and dad showed up. Her dad was cool, but he didn't take attitude from anyone, meaning he was scary, and he was also hot.

"Ream, buddy!" Kite shouted. "Where the fuck have you been, man?"

I glanced at Kite, then to where he was looking at the patio door. Then I searched out Kat, who was looking right at Ream. She paled. Turned white actually, and I think it had to do with the girl holding onto Ream's arm.

Logan's hand reached under the table and took mine and squeezed. He knew. He'd seen Kat's reaction too.

Ream chin lifted. "This is Lana." He didn't bother introducing her to any of us. Instead he leaned into her and whispered something in her ear. The tall blonde giggled, gave him a kiss, and then walked back into the house.

"Not smart, buddy," Kite said then turned away and started talking to Georgie's mom.

Ream ignored the comment as he met Kat's eyes. "You feel okay?"

I was holding my breath. I knew Kat she could fly off the handle pretty easily, and it was a real dick move for Ream to bring some chick to Kat's welcome home party. But she did something I hadn't expected—Kat nodded then looked away. She looked defeated, and it broke my heart seeing her like that. Crisis put his arm around the back of her chair, and his hand came on her shoulder and stroked back and forth. He leaned in and whispered something to her.

Lana came out seconds later with two beers, passing one to Ream.

The tension finally faded as everyone chatted and drank and ate a ton. It was Georgie getting drunk and stumbling into the sliding glass doors after coming back from the washroom that finally broke up the party.

"Well, shit." She rubbed her head where she'd hit the glass pane. "That thing is so clean I didn't even see it."

"You didn't see it because your vision is blurred the fuck up," Crisis yelled. laughing.

Georgie laughed then staggered out onto the patio. I got up at the same time as Deck.

"Eme, let him deal," Logan said and dragged me back down, but this time he put me on his lap and wrapped his arms around my waist.

"But—"

"Eme."

"But—"

"Emily," Logan growled in my ear, and it did two things—got me wet and made me concede.

Deck strode over to Georgie. She backed away. He pursued, and his face looked pissed. I mean, I know I wouldn't have fucked around with that face, but Georgie was Georgie, and she was drunk.

"You going to spank me again?"

Again?

Logan chuckled. And I saw Georgie's mom and dad weren't moving to protect their daughter from Deck.

Deck did briefly look at Georgie's dad Frank, and I noticed him nod at Deck as if he was giving his okay. To what?

"Deck." Georgie smiled. "You going to take me home again and put me in your bed naked?"

I bit my lip. Crisis out-and-out laughed, and I saw Georgie's mom smile.

"No," Deck said. "Going to do something else entirely."

"Oh. Sounds delicious."

"You're not going to like it."

Georgie frowned. "Think I'll stay here then."

Deck wasn't doing anymore talking as he latched onto her hand. He nodded to Logan then dragged Georgie inside. I could hear her squeal then shout, and finally, she was screeching profanities.

A car door slammed and then another.

Soon Georgie and Deck were forgotten, and the party broke up an hour later.

"Mouse." Logan had dragged me upstairs the second his mother and Georgie's parents left. He locked the door then pulled me hard up against him. "My mother loves you."

I smiled. "She's an incredible woman, Logan. You're lucky to have her."

"Yeah. She's yours now too."

That made me feel warm inside, and I moved into him further.

His hand curled around the nape of my neck. "You're touring with me."

It wasn't a question; it was a statement. "Logan—"

"I'm not asking anymore. This is big and I want you with me."

The band was asked to open for Damaged and they'd be gone six months. "Don't you think that's kind of selfish? I do have a business to—"

"No. I told you. We'll try and work in you doing clinics at the stops we make. We need time together, baby."

"Logan." He was right. We did. It was Logan's turn to live his dream. He'd given me mine now it was my turn to be there for his.

"Emily."

He leaned in and kissed me, and I melted. I mean it was an amazing kiss, one that took away any argument I had left, and he damn well knew it. I'd tour with him. I wanted to see him play in front of huge crowds; I wanted to hear him sing every night. God, I just wanted to be with him.

He sank his hands into my hair. "You're my everything."

I stared up at him, my finger tracing across his lips. He caught it between his teeth then drew it into his mouth and sucked. My rabble of butterflies took flight in every direction, and my stomach dipped. I smiled up at the man who had been my knight in shining armor all along, I just hadn't seen it.

Together we were able to repair.

I kissed him then nibbled at the lobe of his ear as I whispered, "You fixed me."

The End

Acknowledgements

Where do I start? Everyone who helped with "Torn from You"—a huge thank you. I know it's never enough, but it comes from a very special place in my heart.

Thanks to my editor Kristin Anders for putting up with my gazillion emails and for bringing me back on track when I was off-roading somewhere in the back forty with my story. You kicked me in the butt (nicely) then told me what I needed to hear and I was able to bring my vision back into focus.

Robyn ... yes bestie, I'm talking about you. I'm sorry I missed so many dinners and our riding time with the horses. You understood and never gave me shit when you knew I had a deadline. I'm following my dream and you are so supportive of that. But we did manage two vacations and some great quotes.

Mom, ahh, I can't believe you read this. Ha. You're my Isabelle. Thank you for taking the time to proofread "Torn from You". Those pesky little errors are like fleas ... hard to find and eradicate, but you did it.

To Melissa, my beta reader, my proofer, my emotional support ... ahhhh I'm so lucky to have met you online through my rocky path to publishing. You're always positive and have great advice. I can't wait until you publish your novel—it's outstanding!

To Kari, an amazing beta reader, fantastic cover designer, and fellow animal lover. I'm so fortunate to have found you. Our visions mesh perfectly!

Kat, yep stole your name for this one. Beta reader with an attitude that sits me down and tells me straight up. Love it :)

Stacey from Hayson Publishing, what I put you through…ugh, damn those pesky fleas. But you were patient and understanding and so helpful. And damn you did a fantastic formatter job. Thank you!

Jonel, blogger extraordinaire who has supported me from the beginning. Hope you like this one too. Love chatting horses with you and one day we are so meeting at a horse competition. http://purejonel.blogspot.ca/

Debra from http://bookenthusiastpromotions.com/ You ROCK! When things changed, you were understanding and patient. Without you I'd still be lonely on FB. You spread the word and I've met amazing people because of you. You're the best tour host ever—thank you!

Michelle, Jessica, Sarah, my "TFY" book club Admins. I met you on this journey and am so thankful. You girls are incredible and know that I appreciate everything you've done for me. Hugs and kisses.

Lovely Ladies and Naughty Books…just met you, but what a wonderful group of ladies. Can't wait to spend more time with all of you.

Bloggers, fellow readers, book lovers. Thank you for your support and the fun chats, for telling your friends and helping me bring "Torn from You" into the spotlight. I'm living my dream because of you.

Song:

Goodbye (feat Islove) Glenn Morrison

About the Author

Nashoda Rose lives in Toronto with her assortment of pets. She writes contemporary romance with a splash of darkness, or maybe it's a tidal wave. Her novel "Torn from You" is the first in the Tear Asunder series. When she isn't writing, she can be found sitting in a field reading with her dog at her side while her horses graze nearby. She loves interacting with her readers on Facebook and chatting about her addiction—books.

Happy Reading,

Nash

What's Next?

Tear Asunder Series
With You (free)
Torn from You
Overwhelmed by You
Shattered by You
Kept from You (Kite's Story:2016)

Where to find me

https://www.facebook.com/pages/Nashoda-Rose/564276203633318

https://www.goodreads.com/author/show/7246093.Nashoda_Rose?from_search=true

http://nashodarose.com/

https://twitter.com/nashodarose

With You

(Tear Asunder .5)

Nashoda Rose

Sculpt is an illegal fighter.

He's also the lead singer of a local rock band.

No one knows his real name.

And from the moment I met him, he made me forget mine.

Author's Note: This novella is Sculpt and Emily's beginning and how they met. It is an extra and not required to be read before "Torn from You". Their story and what happens to them is the novel "Torn from You".

Warning: Huge cliff-hanger. Like huge! But the novel "Torn from You" has been released.

*Due to sexual content and strong language not recommended for readers under 18.

Novella: 20,000 words

Books by Nashoda Rose

Seven Sixes (2016)

Tear Asunder Series
With You (free)
Torn from You
Overwhelmed by You
Shattered by You
Kept from You (Kite's Story)Date:TBA

Unyielding Series
Perfect Chaos
Perfect Ruin (December 2015)
Perfect Rage (February 2016)

Scars of the Wraith Series
Stygian
Take

Made in the USA
Middletown, DE
20 November 2016